I SEE YOU

CLARE MACKINTOSH

BERKLEY   NEW YORK

BERKLEY
An imprint of Penguin Random House LLC
375 Hudson Street, New York, New York 10014

Berkley trade paperback ISBN: 9781101988305

The Library of Congress has catalogued the Berkley hardcover edition as follows:

Names: Mackintosh, Clare, author.
Title: I see you / Clare Mackintosh.
Description: First Edition. | New York : Berkley, 2017.
Identifiers: LCCN 2016032022 (print) | LCCN 2016037680 (ebook) |
ISBN 9781101988299 (hardback) | ISBN 9781101988312 (ebook)
Subjects: | BISAC: FICTION / Mystery & Detective / Police Procedural. |
FICTION / Contemporary Women. | GSAFD: Suspense fiction
Classification: LCC PR6113.A2649 I35 2017 (print) | LCC PR6113.A2649 (ebook)|
DDC 823/.92—c23
LC record available at https://lccn.loc.gov/2016032022

Sphere UK hardcover edition / July 2016
Berkley hardcover edition / February 2017
Berkley trade paperback edition / November 2017

Printed in the United States of America
1   3   5   7   9   10   8   6   4   2

Cover art: *Escalator* © Florence Caplain/Ninestock;
Female figure by Mouton Laurence/Getty Images
Book design by Kelly Lipovich

PRAISE FOR *I SEE YOU*

"A brilliant second novel by one of Britain's most exciting newcomers."
—Jeffrey Archer

"Accomplished, addictive, and thought-provoking."
—B. A. Paris, author of *Behind Closed Doors*

"Mind-bending . . . [This novel] makes you reevaluate every step you take, and you will see the world in a different light. And *that* is genius."
—Alexandra Burt, author of *The Good Daughter*

"Both a compelling portrayal of modern family life and a superbly twisty thriller that keeps you guessing until the very last page. An edge of the seat read!"　　—Kate Hamer, author of *The Girl in the Red Coat*

"Mackintosh scripts a hair-raising ride."
—*Publishers Weekly* (starred review)

"[A] well-crafted blend of calculated malevolence, cunning plot twists, and redemption that will appeal to fans of Sophie Hannah, Ruth Rendell, and Ruth Ware."　　　　　　　—*Booklist* (starred review)

PRAISE FOR *I LET YOU GO*

"Chilling, compelling, and compassionate, *I Let You Go* is a finely crafted novel with a killer twist."
—Paula Hawkins, #1 *New York Times* bestselling author of
The Girl on the Train

"Astonishingly good."
—Lee Child, #1 *New York Times* bestselling author of *Make Me*

"*I Let You Go* is a master class in plotting, with a killer twist. I could not put it down."
—Jojo Moyes, #1 *New York Times* bestselling author of *Me Before You*

"The big plot twist in Clare Mackintosh's first novel, *I Let You Go*, is genuinely shocking. The jolts that follow, right up until the last page, are pretty good, too . . . [A] cunning psychological thriller."
—Marilyn Stasio, *The New York Times Book Review*

"An intense psychological thriller . . . [that] revels in surprises and twists . . . Outstanding."　　　　　　　　—The Associated Press

BERKLEY TITLES BY CLARE MACKINTOSH

I Let You Go
I See You

For my parents, who taught me so much

ACKNOWLEDGMENTS

It is an accepted fact that second books can be tricky beasts, and this one would not have happened without the support, guidance, and practical help of many generous people. My sincere thanks to Guy Mayhew, David Shipperlee, Sam Blackburn, Gary Ferguson, Darren Woods, and Joanna Harvey for their help with researching this book. All errors are mine, and artistic license is liberally used. Special gratitude to Andrew Robinson, who gave up so much of his time to help that I put him in the book.

Thank you to Charlotte Beresford, Merilyn Davies, and Shane Kirk for plot discussions and beta reading, and to Sally Boorman, Rachel Lovelock, and Paul Powell for bidding generously in charity auctions for the right to name a character.

The life of a writer is frequently a solitary one. Mine is greatly enriched by the communities on Twitter, Instagram, and Facebook, the members of which are always ready with encouraging words, virtual glasses of champagne, and suggestions for guinea pig names. In both my online and my real life I continue to be astounded by the generosity of the crime scene, which could not be more supportive. Authors are a great bunch of people.

I am lucky to be represented by the best agent in the business, Sheila Crowley, and I am enormously proud to be a Curtis Brown author. Special thanks to Rebecca Ritchie and Abbie Greaves for their support.

I wouldn't be half the writer I am without the talent and insight of my editor, Lucy Malagoni, who is a joy to work with. The Little,

Brown team is exceptional, and my thanks goes to Kirsteen Astor, Rachel Wilkie, Emma Williams, Thalia Proctor, Anne O'Brien, Andy Hine, Kate Hibbert, and Helena Doree for their enthusiasm and dedication.

There should be some kind of award for the families of writers, who put up with the mood swings, the deadlines, the burned suppers, and the late school runs. In the absence of medals, my love and thanks go to Rob, Josh, Evie, and George, who light up my life and make my books possible.

Finally, thank you from the bottom of my heart to the booksellers, librarians, and readers who loved *I Let You Go* enough to make it a success. I am so very grateful, and I hope you enjoy *I See You* just as much.

I
SEE
YOU

You do the same thing every day.
  You know exactly where you're going. You're not alone.

CHAPTER
ONE

The man behind me is standing close enough to moisten the skin on my neck with his breath. I move my feet forward an inch and press myself into a gray overcoat that smells of wet dog. It feels as if it hasn't stopped raining since the start of November, and a light steam rises from the hot bodies jammed against one another. A briefcase jabs into my thigh. As the train judders around a corner I'm held upright by the weight of people surrounding me, one unwilling hand against the gray overcoat for temporary support. At Tower Hill the carriage spits out a dozen commuters and swallows two dozen more, all hell-bent on getting home for the weekend.

"Use the whole carriage!" comes the announcement. Nobody moves.

The gray overcoat has gone, and I've shuffled into its place, preferable because I can now reach the handrail, and because I no longer have a stranger's DNA on my neck. My handbag has swung around behind my body, and I tug it in front of me. Two Japanese tourists are wearing gigantic rucksacks on their chests, taking up the space of another two people. A woman across the carriage sees me looking at them; she catches my eye and grimaces in solidarity. I accept the eye contact fleetingly, then look down at my feet. The shoes around me vary: the men's are large and shiny, beneath pin-striped hems; the women's heeled and colorful, toes crammed into impossible points. Among the legs I see a pair of sleek stockings; opaque black nylon ending in stark white trainers. The owner is hidden, but I imagine her to be in her twenties, a pair of vertiginous office heels stashed in a capacious handbag, or in a drawer at work.

I've never worn heels during the day. I was barely out of my Clarks lace-ups when I fell pregnant with Justin, and there was no place for heels on a Tesco checkout, or coaxing a toddler up the main street. Now I'm old enough to know better. An hour on the train on the way into work; another hour on the way home. Tripping up broken escalators. Run over by strollers and bikes. And for what? For eight hours behind a desk. I'll save my heels for high days and holidays. I wear a self-imposed uniform of black trousers and an array of stretchy tops that don't need ironing and are just smart enough to pass as office wear; with a cardigan kept in my bottom drawer for busy days when the door's forever opening and the heat disappears with every prospective client.

The train stops and I push my way onto the platform. I take the Overground from here, and although it's often as busy, I prefer it. Being underground makes me feel uneasy; unable to breathe, even though I know it's all in my head. I dream of working somewhere close enough to walk to, but it's never going to happen: the only jobs worth taking are in zone one; the only affordable mortgages in zone four.

I have to wait for my train, and at the rack by the ticket machine, I pick up a copy of the *London Gazette*, its headlines appropriately grim for today's date: *Friday, 13 November*. The police have foiled another terrorism plot: the front three pages are rammed with images of explosives they've seized from a flat in North London. I flick through photos of bearded men, and move to find the crack in the tarmac beneath the platform sign, where the carriage door will open. My careful positioning means I can slide into my favorite spot before the carriage fills up: on the end of the row, where I can lean against the glass barrier. The rest of the carriage fills quickly, and I glance at the people still standing, guiltily relieved to see no one old, or obviously pregnant. Despite the flat shoes, my feet ache, thanks to standing by the filing cabinets for most of the day. I'm not supposed to do the filing. There's a girl who comes in to photocopy property details and keep the cabinets in order, but she's in Mallorca for a fortnight and from what I saw today she can't have done any filing for weeks. I found residential mixed up with commercial, and rentals muddled up with sales, and I made the mistake of saying so.

"You'd better sort it out, then, Zoe," Graham said. So instead of booking viewings I stood in the drafty corridor outside Graham's office, wishing I hadn't opened my mouth. Hallow & Reed isn't a bad place to work. I used to do the books one day a week, then the office manager went on maternity leave and Graham asked me to fill in. I was a bookkeeper, not a PA, but the money was decent and I'd lost a couple of clients, so I jumped at the chance. Three years later, I'm still there.

By the time we reach Canada Water the carriage has thinned out and the only people standing are there by choice. The man sitting next to me has his legs so wide apart I have to angle mine away, and when I look at the row of passengers opposite I see two other men doing the same. Is it a conscious thing? Or some innate need to make themselves bigger than everyone else? The woman immediately in front of me moves her shopping bag and I hear the unmistakable clink of a wine bottle. I hope Simon has thought to put one in the fridge; it's been a long week and right now all I want to do is curl up on the sofa and watch telly.

A few pages into the *London Gazette* some former *X Factor* finalist is complaining about the "pressures of fame," and there's a debate on privacy laws that covers the better part of a page. I'm reading without taking in the words: looking at the pictures and scanning the headlines so I don't feel completely out of the loop. I can't remember the last time I actually read a whole newspaper, or sat down to watch the news from start to finish.

It's always snatches of *Sky News* while I'm eating breakfast, or the headlines read over someone's shoulder on the way in to work.

The train stops between Sydenham and Crystal Palace. I hear a frustrated sigh from farther up the carriage but don't bother looking to see who it's from. It's already dark and when I glance at the windows all I see is my own face looking back at me; even paler than it is in real life, and distorted by rain. I take off my glasses and rub at the dents they leave on either side of my nose. We hear the crackle of an announcement, but it's so muffled and heavily accented there's no telling what it's about. It could have been anything from signal failure to a body on the line.

I hope it's not a body. I think of my glass of wine, and Simon rubbing my feet on the sofa, then feel guilty that my first thought is about my own comfort, not the desperation of some poor suicidal soul. I'm sure it's not a body. Bodies are for Monday mornings, not Friday evenings, when work is a blissful three days away.

There's a creaking noise and then silence. Whatever the delay is, it's going to be a while.

"That's not a good sign," the man next to me says.

"Hmm," I say noncommittally. I carry on turning the pages of my newspaper, but I'm not interested in sports and now it's mostly adverts and theater reviews. I won't be home till after seven at this rate; we'll have to have something easy for tea, rather than the baked chicken I'd planned. Simon cooks during the week, and I do Friday evening and the weekend. He'd do that, too, if I asked him, but I couldn't have that. I couldn't have him cooking for us—for my children—every night. Maybe I'll pick up a takeaway.

I skip over the business section and look at the crossword, but I don't have a pen with me. So I read the adverts, thinking I might see a job for Katie—or me, come to that, although I know I'll never leave Hallow & Reed. It pays well and I know what I'm doing now, and if it weren't for my boss it would be perfect. The customers are nice, for the most part. They're generally start-ups looking for office space, or businesses that have done well, ready for a bigger place. We don't do much residential, but the flats above the shops work for the first-time buyers and the downsizers. I meet a fair number of recently separateds. Sometimes, if I feel like it, I tell them I know what they're going through.

"Did it all turn out okay?" the women always ask.

"Best thing I ever did," I say confidently. It's what they want to hear.

I don't find any jobs for a nineteen-year-old wannabe actress, but I turn down the corner on a page with an advert for an office manager. It doesn't hurt to know what's out there. For a second I imagine walking into Graham Hallow's office and handing in my notice, telling him I won't put up with being spoken to like I'm dirt on the sole of his shoe. Then I look at the salary printed under the office manager position, and remember how long it's taken me to claw my way up to something I can actually live on. Better the devil you know, isn't that what they say?

The final pages of the *Gazette* are all compensation claims and finances. I studiously avoid the ads for loans—at those interest rates you'd have to be mad or desperate—and glance at the bottom of the page, where the chatlines are advertised.

> Married woman looking for discreet casual action. Txt
> ANGEL to 69998 for pics.

I wrinkle my nose more at the exorbitant price per text than at the services offered. Who am I to judge what other people do? I'm about to turn the page, resigned to reading about last night's football match, when I see the advert below "Angel's."

For a second I think my eyes must be tired; I blink hard but it doesn't change anything.

I'm so absorbed in what I'm looking at that I don't notice the train start up again. It sets off suddenly and I jerk to one side, putting my hand out automatically and making contact with my neighbor's thigh.

"Sorry!"

"It's fine—don't worry." He smiles and I make myself return it. But my heart is thumping and I stare at the advert. It bears the same warning about call charges as the other boxed adverts, and a 0809 number at the top of the ad. A web address reads: *www.FindTheOne.com*. But it's the photo I'm looking at. It's cropped close to the face, but you can clearly see blonde hair and a glimpse of a black strappy top. Older than the other women pimping their wares, but such a grainy photo it would be hard to give a precise age.

Except I know how old she is. I know she's forty.

Because the woman in the advert is me.

CHAPTER TWO

Kelly Swift stood in the middle of the Central line carriage, shifting to one side to keep her balance as the train took a bend. A couple of kids—no more than fourteen or fifteen years old—jostled onto the train at Bond Street, engaged in competitive swearing that jarred with their middle-class vowels. Too late for after-school clubs, and it was already dark outside; Kelly hoped they were on their way home, not heading out for the evening. Not at their age.

"Fucking mental!" The boy looked up, his swagger giving way to self-consciousness as he saw Kelly standing there. Kelly assumed the sort of expression she remembered her mother sporting on many an occasion, and the teenagers fell silent, blushing furiously and turning away to examine the inside of the closing doors. She probably was old enough to be their mother, she thought ruefully, counting backward from thirty and imagining herself with a fourteen-year-old. Several of her old school friends had children almost that age; Kelly's Facebook page regularly filled up with proud family photos, and she'd even had a couple of friend requests from the kids themselves. Now, there was a way to make you feel old.

Kelly caught the eye of a woman in a red coat on the opposite side of the carriage, who gave a nod of approval at the effect she'd had on the lads.

Kelly returned her look with a smile. "Good day?"

"Better now it's over," the woman said. "Roll on the weekend, eh?"

"I'm working. Not off till Tuesday." *And even then only one day off before another six on the trot*, she thought, inwardly groaning at the thought. The woman looked aghast. Kelly shrugged. "Someone's got to, right?"

"I guess so." As the train slowed down for Oxford Circus, the woman began moving toward the doors. "I hope it's a quiet one for you."

That's jinxed it, Kelly thought. She glanced at her watch. Nine stops to Stratford: ditch her stuff, then head back. Home by eight, maybe eight thirty. In again for seven A.M. She yawned hard, not bothering to cover her mouth, and wondered if there was any food at home. She shared a house near Elephant and Castle with three others, whose full names she knew only from the rent checks pinned neatly to the board in the hall, ready for collection each month. The sitting room had been converted to a bedroom by a landlord keen to maximize his income, leaving the small kitchen the one communal area. There was only room for two chairs, but her housemates' shift patterns and erratic hours meant Kelly could go days without seeing anyone at all. The woman in the biggest bedroom, Dawn, was a nurse. Younger than Kelly, but far more domesticated, Dawn occasionally left a portion for Kelly on the side by the microwave, with one of her bright pink Post-it notes telling Kelly to *help yourself!* Her stomach rumbled at the thought of food, and she glanced at her watch. The afternoon had been busier than she'd thought; she was going to have to put in some extra hours next week, or she'd never get through it all.

A handful of businessmen got on at Holborn and Kelly cast a practiced eye over them. At first glance they looked identical, with their short hair, dark suits, and briefcases. The devil was in the detail, Kelly thought. She searched out the faint pinstripe; the title of a book pushed carelessly into a bag; wire-framed glasses with a kink in one arm; a brown leather watch strap beneath a white cotton shirtsleeve. The idiosyncrasies and appearance tics that made them stand out in a lineup of near-identical men. Kelly watched them openly, dispassionately. She was just practicing, she told herself, not caring when one of them looked up and found her cool gaze on him. She thought he might look away, but instead he winked, his mouth moving into a confident smile. Kelly's eyes flicked to his left hand. Married. White, well-built, around six feet tall, with a shadow around his jaw that probably wasn't there a few hours ago. The yellow flash of a forgotten dry-cleaning tag on the inside of his overcoat. Standing so straight she'd put money on ex-military. Nondescript in appearance, but Kelly would know him if they met again.

Satisfied, she turned her attention to the latest influx of passengers, getting on at Bank and filtering through the carriage to find the remaining few seats. Almost everyone had a phone in their hand: playing games, listening to music, or simply clutching it as though it were grafted to their palm. At the other end of the carriage someone lifted their phone in front of them and Kelly instinctively turned away. Tourists, getting an iconic shot of the London Underground to show back home, but she found the idea of being background scenery in someone's holiday snaps too weird to contemplate.

Her shoulder ached where she'd slammed into a wall, taking the corner too tight as she ran down the escalators and onto the platform at Marble Arch. She'd been seconds too late, and it annoyed her that the blooming bruise on her upper arm was in vain. She'd be quicker next time.

The train pulled into Liverpool Street; a throng of people waiting on the platform, impatient for the doors to open.

Kelly's pulse quickened.

There, in the center of the crowd, half-hidden beneath oversized jeans, a hooded top, and a baseball cap, was Carl. Instantly recognizable and—desperate though Kelly was to get home—impossible to walk away from. It was clear from the way he melted into the crowd that Carl had seen Kelly a split second before she had seen him, and was equally unenthusiastic about the encounter. She was going to have to move fast.

Kelly jumped off the train just as the doors hissed behind her. She thought at first she'd lost him, but then she caught sight of a baseball cap ten or so yards ahead; not running, but weaving swiftly through the throng of passengers leaving the platform.

If Kelly had learned one thing over the past ten years on the Underground, it was that politeness got you nowhere.

"Mind your backs!" she yelled, breaking into a run and shoving her way between two elderly tourists dragging suitcases. "Coming through!" She might have lost him that morning, and copped a bruised shoulder as a result, but she wasn't about to let him get away again. She thought fleetingly of the supper she had hoped would be waiting for her at home, and calculated this was going to add at least two hours on to her day. But needs must. She could always grab a kebab on the way home.

Carl was legging it up the escalator. Rookie error, Kelly knew, taking the steps instead. Fewer tourists to negotiate and easier on the thighs than the jerky, uneven motion of a moving stairway. Even so, Kelly's muscles were burning as she drew parallel with Carl. He threw a quick look over his left shoulder as they reached the top, then swerved right. *For fuck's sake, Carl*, she thought. *I should be booking off now.*

With a final burst of speed she caught up with him as he was preparing to vault the ticket barrier, grabbing a handful of jacket with her left hand and twisting one arm up behind his back with her right. Carl made a halfhearted attempt to pull away, knocking her off balance and causing her hat to fall to the ground. Kelly was aware of someone picking it up and hoped they weren't going to run off with it. She was already in the doghouse with Stores for losing her baton in a scrap the other week—she could do without another telling-off.

"Warrants have got a Fail to Appear with your name on it, mate," Kelly said, her words punctuated with breaths that were hard to take within the confines of a stab vest. She reached for her belt and unclipped her cuffs, snapping them deftly onto Carl's wrists and checking for tightness. "You're nicked."

I see you. But you don't see me. You're engrossed in your book; a paperback cover with a girl in a red dress. I can't see the title but it doesn't matter; they're all the same. If it isn't boy meets girl, it's boy stalks girl. Boy kills girl.

The irony isn't lost on me.

At the next stop I use the incoming swell of commuters as an excuse to move closer to you. You hang from the strap in the center of the carriage, reading one-handed, turning the page with a well-practiced thumb. We're so close now that our coats are touching, and I can smell the vanilla base of your perfume; a scent that will have long since faded by the time you leave work. Some women disappear into the loos at lunchtime; touch up their makeup, add a spritz of fragrance. Not you. When I see you after work the dark-gray makeup on your lids will have drifted into tired shadows beneath your eyes; the tint on your lips transferred to countless cups of coffee.

You're pretty, though, even at the end of a long day. That counts for a lot. Not that it's always about beauty; sometimes it's exotic looks, or large breasts, or long legs. Sometimes it's class and elegance—all tailored navy trousers and tan heels—and sometimes it's brassy and cheap. Slutty, even. Variety is important. Even the finest steak becomes dull when you eat it all the time.

Your handbag is larger than average. You usually carry it over your shoulder, but when the train is busy—as it is at this stage of your commute—you put it on the floor, between your legs. It has slouched open, allowing me to see inside. A wallet—soft brown calf leather with a gilt clasp. A hairbrush, blonde hairs trailing from its bristles. A reusable shopping bag, neatly rolled into a ball. A pair of leather gloves. Two or three brown envelopes, torn open then pushed into the bag along with their contents. Post snatched from the doormat after breakfast, opened on the platform while you waited for your first train. I crane my neck to read what is printed on the uppermost envelope.

So now I know your name.

Not that it matters: you and I aren't going to have the sort of relationship that needs names.

I take out my phone and swipe up to reveal the camera. I turn toward you; use my thumb and forefinger to zoom in until only your face is in the frame. If anyone noticed me now, they'd just think I was uploading a record of my commute to Instagram, or Twitter. Hashtag selfie.

A silent click, and you're mine.

As the train takes a bend you let go of the ceiling strap and lean down for your handbag, still intent on your book. If I didn't know you better I'd think you'd caught me looking and were moving your belongings out of view, but it isn't that. The bend in the track simply means it's nearly your stop.

You're enjoying this book. Usually you'll stop reading much earlier than this; when you reach the end of a chapter, and you slip between the pages the postcard you use as a bookmark. Today you're still reading even as the train pulls into the station. Even as you shoulder your way through to the door, saying "Excuse me" and "Sorry" a dozen times. You're still reading even as you walk toward the exit, your eyes flicking upward to make sure you don't bump into anyone.

You're still reading.

And I'm still watching.

CHAPTER
THREE

Crystal Palace is where my train terminates. Had it not been, I might have stayed in my seat, staring at the advert in the hope of making sense of it. As it is, I'm the last to get off.

The rain has slowed to a drizzle, but I've barely left the Tube station before the newspaper in my hands is sodden, leaving traces of ink on my fingers. It's already dark, but the streetlights are on, and the neon signs above Anerley Road's myriad takeaways and mobile phone shops mean I can see clearly. Garish lights hang from each lamppost in preparation for this weekend's Z-list celebrity switch-on, but it's too mild—and too early—for me to start thinking about Christmas.

I stare at the advert as I walk home, oblivious to the rain plastering my fringe to my forehead. Perhaps it isn't me at all. Perhaps I have a doppelgänger. I'm hardly the obvious choice to advertise a premium-rate chatline: you'd think they'd go for someone younger, more attractive. Not a middle-aged woman with two grown children and a bit of a spare tire. I almost laugh out loud. I know it takes all sorts, but that's some niche market.

Between the Polish supermarket and the locksmith is Melissa's café. *One* of Melissa's cafés, I remind myself. The other is on a side street off Covent Garden, where her lunchtime regulars know to phone ahead with their sandwich orders to avoid queuing, and the tourists dither by the door, deciding if the panini will be worth the wait. You'd think Covent Garden would be a license to print money, but the high rates mean that in the five years it's been open it's struggled to turn a profit.

This one, on the other hand, with its tatty paintwork and unlikely neighbors, is a gold mine. It's been here for years, raking in the cash long before Melissa took it over and put her name above the door; one of those hidden secrets that appear occasionally in city guides. *The best breakfast in South London*, reads the photocopied article taped to the door.

I stay on the opposite side of the road for a while so I can watch without being seen. The insides of the windows are steamed up around the edges, like a soft-focus photo from the 1980s. In the center, behind the counter, a man is wiping the inside of the glass display. He wears an apron folded in half and tied—Parisian-waiter style—around his waist, instead of looped over his head, and with his black T-shirt and dark, just-got-out-of-bed hair he looks far too cool to be working in a café. Good-looking? I'm biased, I know, but I think so.

I cross the road, watching out for cycles as a bus driver waves me across in front of him. The bell above the café door jingles and Justin looks up.

"All right, Mum."

"Hi, love." I look around for Melissa. "You here on your own?"

"She's in Covent Garden. The manager there's gone off sick so she left me in charge." His tone is casual, so I try to mirror it in my response, but I feel a swell of pride. I've always known Justin was a good boy; he just needed someone to give him a break. "If you give me five minutes," he says, washing his cloth out in the stainless steel sink, "I'll come home with you."

"I was going to pick up a takeaway for tea. I suppose the fryer's off now?"

"I've only just turned it off. It won't take long to do some chips. And there are some sausages that'll be thrown out if they're not eaten today. Melissa won't mind if we take them home."

"I'll pay for them," I say, not wanting Justin to get carried away with his temporary position of responsibility.

"She won't mind."

"I'll pay," I say firmly, getting out my purse. I look up at the black-board and calculate the price for four sausages and chips. He's right that Melissa would have given them to us if she were here, but she isn't here, and in this family we pay our way.

The shops and businesses peter out as we walk farther from the station, giving way to terraced houses in rows of around a dozen. Several are boarded up with the gray metal shutters that mean a repossession, graffiti adding red and orange fireworks to their front doors. Our row is no different—the house three doors down has missing tiles and thick ply nailed across the windows—and you can spot the rented houses by the blocked gutters and stained brickwork. At the end of the row are two privately owned houses: Melissa and Neil's, in the coveted end-of-terrace spot, and mine, right next door.

Justin's fiddling in his rucksack for his keys, and I stand for a moment on the pavement by the railings that run around what might generously be called our front garden. Weeds poke up through the wet gravel; the only decoration a solar-powered lamp shaped like an old-fashioned lantern, which gives off a dull yellow glow. Melissa's garden is graveled, too, but there are no weeds to be seen, and on either side of her front door sit two perfectly manicured box trees, shaped into spirals. Beneath the living room window is a patch of brickwork a shade lighter than the rest, where Neil scrubbed off graffiti left by someone in South London still narrow-minded enough to object to a mixed-race marriage.

No one has bothered to pull the curtains in our own living room, and I can see Katie painting her nails at the dining table. I used to insist we all sit at the table for meals, used to love the opportunity to catch up on what they'd done at school. In the early days, when we first moved in, it was the one time of day when I felt we were doing all right without Matt. There we were, a little family unit of three, all sitting down to a meal together at six o'clock.

Through the window—coated with the ever-present layer of grime that comes from living on a busy road—I notice that Katie has cleared a space for her nail kit among the magazines, the pile of bills, and the washing basket, which has somehow chosen the table as its natural home. Occasionally I clear the mess so we can eat Sunday lunch together, but it isn't long before a creeping tide of paperwork and abandoned carrier bags pushes us onto our laps again, in front of the telly.

Justin opens the door and I remember what it was like when the kids were little and they'd run to greet me when I came home, as though I'd been away for months instead of stacking shelves at Tesco for eight hours. When they were older it would be next door I'd call on, thanking Melissa for the after-school care the kids claimed to be too old for but secretly loved.

"Hello?" I call. Simon comes out of the kitchen with a glass of wine. He hands it to me and kisses me on the lips, his arm sliding around my waist to pull me closer. I hand him the plastic bag from Melissa's café.

"Get a room, you two." Katie comes out of the living room, her fingers spread out and her hands in the air. "What's for tea?" Simon releases me and takes the bag into the kitchen.

"Sausage and chips."

She wrinkles her nose and I cut her off before she can start moaning about calories. "There's some lettuce in the fridge—you can have yours with salad."

"It won't get rid of your cankles," Justin says. Katie hits him on the arm as he ducks around her and runs up the stairs, two at a time.

"Grow up, you two." Katie is nineteen and an easy size eight, with not a hint of the puppy fat she still had a few years ago. And there is nothing wrong with her ankles. I move to give her a hug, then remember her nails and kiss her cheek instead. "I'm sorry, love, but I'm knackered. The odd takeaway won't do you any harm—everything in moderation, right?"

"How was your day, honey?" Simon asks. He follows me into the living room and I sink into the sofa, shutting my eyes for a brief moment and sighing as I feel myself relax.

"It was okay. Apart from Graham making me do the filing."

"That's not your job," Katie says.

"Neither is cleaning the loo, but guess what he had me doing yesterday?"

"Ugh. That bloke is such an arsehole."

"You shouldn't put up with it." Simon sits next to me. "You should complain."

"To who? He owns the place." Graham Hallow comes from the breed of men who inflate their egos by belittling the people around them. I know this, and so it doesn't bother me. For the most part.

To change the subject I pick up the *London Gazette* from where I dumped it on the coffee table. It's still damp and parts of the print are blurry, but I fold it in half so the chatline and escort ads are showing.

"Mum! What are you doing looking up escort services?" Katie says, laughing. She finishes applying a topcoat to her nails and carefully screws on the lid, returning to the table to push her hands under an ultraviolet lamp to seal the varnish.

"Maybe she's thinking of trading Simon in for a newer model," Justin says, walking into the living room. He's changed out of the black T-shirt and jeans he was wearing for work, into gray sweatpants and a sweatshirt. His feet are bare. In one hand he carries his phone; in the other a plate heaped with sausage and chips.

"That's not funny," Simon says. He takes the paper from me. "But seriously, why are you looking at chatlines?" His brow furrows and I see a shadow cross his face. I glare at Justin. Simon is fourteen years older than me, although sometimes I look in the mirror and think I'm catching up to him. There are lines around my eyes I never had in my thirties, and the skin on my neck is beginning to crepe. I've never had a problem with the age difference between us, but Simon mentions it often enough for me to know he worries about it. Justin knows that, and takes every opportunity to stick the knife in. Whether he's getting at Simon or at me, I can never be sure.

"Don't you think that looks like me?" I point to the bottom advert, beneath Angel's "mature" services. Justin leans over Simon's shoulder, and Katie removes her hands from the UV lamp so she can get a proper look. For a second we all stare at the advert in silence.

"No," Justin says, just as Katie says, "It does a bit."

"You wear glasses, Mum."

"Not always," I point out. "Sometimes I put my contacts in." Although I can't remember the last time I did. Wearing glasses has never bothered me, and I quite like my current pair, with their thick black frames that make me look far more studious than I ever was at school.

"Maybe it's someone playing a joke," Simon says. "FindTheOne .com—do you think someone's signed you up to a dating agency as a joke?"

"Who would do something like that?" I look at the kids, wondering if I'll catch a glance passing between them, but Katie looks as confused as I am, and Justin has gone back to his chips.

"Have you called the number?" Simon says.

"At £1.50 a minute? You must be joking."

"Is it you?" Katie says. Her eyes are mischievous. "You know, for a bit of pocket money? Go on, Mum, you can tell us."

The uneasy feeling I've had since I first saw the advert starts to subside, and I laugh. "I'm not sure who would pay £1.50 a minute for me, love. It really does look like me, though, doesn't it? It gave me quite a start."

Simon fishes his mobile out of his pocket and shrugs. "It'll be someone doing something for your birthday, I bet." He puts his phone on speaker and taps in the number. It feels ridiculous: all of us crowded around the *London Gazette*, calling a sex line.

"The number you have dialed has not been recognized." I realize I've been holding my breath.

"That's that, then," Simon says, handing me the newspaper.

"But what's my photo doing there?" I say. My birthday isn't for ages, and I can't think who would find it funny to sign me up for dating services. It crosses my mind that it's someone who doesn't like Simon; someone wanting to cause problems between us. Matt? I dismiss the thought as quickly as it arrives.

Instinctively I squeeze Simon's shoulder, even though he shows no sign of being bothered by the advert.

"Mum, it looks nothing like you. It's some old bird with bad roots," Justin says.

There's a compliment in there somewhere, I think.

"Jus is right, Mum." Katie looks at the advert again. "It does look like you, but lots of people look like someone else. There's a girl at work who's the spitting image of Adele."

"I guess so." I take one last look at the advert. The woman in the photograph isn't looking directly at the camera, and the resolution on the image is so poor I'm surprised it's being used as an advert at all. I hand it to Katie. "Stick it in the recycling for me, love, when you go and dish up for the rest of us."

"My nails!" she cries.

"My feet," I counter.

"I'll do it," Justin says. He dumps his own plate on the coffee table and stands up. Simon and I exchange surprised glances and Justin rolls his eyes. "What? You'd think I never helped out around here."

Simon gives a short laugh. "And your point is?"

"Oh, fuck off, Simon. Get your own tea, then."

"Stop it, the pair of you," I snap. "God, it's hard to know who's the child and who's the parent sometimes."

"But that's my point, he's not the . . ." Justin starts, but stops when he sees the look on my face.

We eat on our laps, watching TV and bickering about the remote, and I catch Simon's eye. He winks at me: a private moment amid the chaos of life with two grown-up kids.

When the plates are empty of all but a sheen of grease, Katie puts on her coat.

"You're not going out now?" I say. "It's gone nine o'clock."

She looks at me witheringly. "It's Friday night, Mum."

"Where are you going?"

"Town." She sees my face. "I'll share a cab with Sophia. It's no different from coming home after a late shift at work."

I want to say that it is. That the black skirt and white top Katie wears for waitressing is far less provocative than the skintight dress she is currently sporting. That wearing her hair scraped into a ponytail makes her look fresh-faced and innocent, while tonight's do is tousled and sexy. I want to say that she's wearing too much makeup; that her heels are too high and her nails too red.

I don't, of course. Because I was nineteen myself once, and because I've been a mum long enough to know when to keep my thoughts to myself.

"Have a good time." But I can't help myself. "Be careful. Stay together. Keep your hand over your drink."

Katie kisses me on the forehead, then turns to Simon. "Have a word, will you?" she says, jerking her head toward me. But she's smiling, and she gives me a wink before she sashays out of the door. "Be good, you two," she calls. "And if you can't be good—be careful!"

"I can't help it," I say when she's gone. "I worry about her."

"I know you do, but she's got her head screwed on, that one." Simon squeezes my knee. "Takes after her mother." He looks at Justin, who is sprawled on the sofa, his phone inches from his face. "Are you not going out?"

"Broke," Justin says, without taking his eyes off the tiny screen in front of him. I see the blue and white boxes of a conversation too small to read from where I'm sitting. A strip of red boxer shorts separates his joggers from his sweatshirt, the hood pulled up despite his being indoors.

"Doesn't Melissa pay you on Fridays?"

"She said she'll drop it round over the weekend."

Justin's been working in the café since the start of the summer, when I had almost given up hope of his getting another job. He had a couple of interviews—one for a record store, and another at Boots—but the second they found out he had a police record for shoplifting, that was it.

"You can understand it," Simon had said. "No employer wants to risk taking on someone who might have their hand in the till."

"He was fourteen!" I couldn't help but be defensive. "His parents had just divorced and he'd moved schools. He's hardly a career criminal."

"Even so."

I left it. I didn't want to argue with Simon. On paper Justin was unemployable, but if you knew him . . . I went cap in hand to Melissa. "Deliveries," I suggested. "Handing out flyers. Anything." Justin was never academic. He didn't take to reading like the other kids in preschool—didn't even know the alphabet until he was eight. As he got older it became hard even to get him to school in the first place; the underpass and the shopping mall held more appeal than a classroom. He left school with a GCSE in computer science, and a caution for shoplifting. By then the teachers had worked out he was dyslexic, but it was too late to be of any use.

Melissa looked at me thoughtfully. I wondered if I'd overstepped the boundaries of our friendship; put her in an awkward position.

"He can work in the café."

I couldn't find the words. *Thank you* seemed inadequate.

"Minimum wage," Melissa said briskly, "and on a trial period. Monday to Friday, on a mix of earlies and lates. Occasional cover at weekends."

"I owe you one," I said.

She waved away my gratitude. "What are friends for?"

"Maybe you could start paying your mum some rent, now you've got a job," Simon says. I look at him sharply. Simon never gets involved in parenting. It isn't a conversation we've ever needed to have; the kids were eighteen and fourteen when I met Simon. They were almost adults in their own right, even when they didn't behave like it. They didn't need a new dad, and thankfully Simon never tried to be one.

"You don't ask Katie for rent."

"She's younger than you. You're twenty-two, Justin, you're old enough to stand on your own two feet."

Justin swings his legs around and stands up in one fluid movement. "You've got a fucking nerve. How about you pay some rent, before you start telling me what to do?"

I hate this. Two people I love, at each other's throats.

"Justin, don't talk to Simon like that." Picking sides isn't a conscious decision, but as soon as I speak I see the look in Justin's eyes, like I've betrayed him. "He's only making a suggestion. I'm not asking for rent." I never would, and I don't care if people think I'm soft. I won't budge. I could charge Justin rock-bottom prices for bed and board, and he'd still have next to nothing left over. How can he have a life, let alone put something aside for the future? I was younger than Katie when I left home, with nothing but a suitcase of clothes, a growing belly, and my parents' disappointment ringing in my ears. I want more than that for my kids.

Simon isn't letting it lie. "Are you looking for work? The café's fine, but if you want to buy a car, get your own place, you'll need to earn more than Melissa can pay you."

I don't understand what's gotten into him. We're not rich, but we do all right. We don't need to take money from the kids.

"Dad said he'd lend me money for a car once I've passed my test."

I feel Simon bristle beside me, the way he always does when Matt is mentioned. There are times when this reaction is irritating, but more often than not it gives me a warm glow inside. I don't think it ever occurred to Matt that someone else might find me attractive; I like that Simon cares enough about me to be jealous.

"That's nice of Dad," I say quickly; loyalty toward Justin making me say something—anything—in support. "Maybe you could consider taking the taxi licensing exam one day."

"I'm not driving a cab for the rest of my life, Mum."

Justin and I used to be so close when he was younger, but he's never quite forgiven me for walking out on Matt. He would, I think, if he knew the whole picture, but I never wanted the kids to think badly of their dad; didn't want them as hurt as I was.

The woman Matt slept with was exactly halfway between Katie's age and mine. Funny the details you fixate on. I never saw her, but I used to torture myself imagining what she looked like; imagining my husband's hands running over her twenty-three-year-old stretch-mark-free body.

"Beggars can't be choosers," Simon says. "It's a good job."

I look at him in surprise. He's been quick to slag off Matt's lack of ambition in the past. A piece of me feels annoyed that what I distinctly remember him calling a "dead-end job" is apparently good enough for my son. Matt was at college, studying engineering. That all changed the day I realized my period was so late it could mean only one thing. Matt walked out of college and got a job that same day. It was just laboring, on a local building site, but it paid well enough. After we got married he did take the taxi licensing exam and as a wedding present his parents gave us the money for his first cab.

"The café's fine for now," I say. "The right thing will turn up, I'm sure."

Justin gives a noncommittal grunt and leaves the room. He goes upstairs and I hear the creak of his bed as he assumes his habitual position, lying down with his head propped just high enough to see the screen on his laptop.

"He'll still be living here when he's thirty at this rate."

"I want him to be happy, that's all."

"He is happy," Simon says. "Happy sponging off you."

I swallow what I want to say. It wouldn't be fair. I was the one who said I didn't want Simon paying rent. We even argued about it, but I won't let him. We split the food and the bills, and he's forever treating me to meals out and trips away—the kids, too. He's generous to a fault. We have a joint bank account and we've never once worried about who pays for what.

But the house is mine.

Money was tight when I married Matt. He worked nights, and I did eight till four at Tesco, and we managed like that till Justin started school. By the time Katie came along things were easier; Matt had more work than he could handle, and gradually we were able to afford a few extras. The odd meal out; even a summer holiday.

Then Matt and I broke up, and I was back to square one. Neither of us could afford to keep the house on our own, and it was years before I was able to save for the deposit on this place. I swore I'd never throw my lot in with a man again.

Mind you, I swore I'd never fall in love again, and look what happened to that.

Simon kisses me, one hand cupping my chin and then sliding around the back of my head. Even now, at the end of a long day, he smells clean: of shaving foam and aftershave. I feel the familiar heat run through my body as he wraps my hair around his hand and tugs it gently, pulling my chin up and exposing my neck to be kissed. "Early night?" he whispers.

"I'll be right up."

I pick up the plates along with the *London Gazette*, carry them into the kitchen, and load the dishwasher. I drop the newspaper into the recycling bin, where the woman in the advert stares up at me. I switch off the kitchen light and shake my head at my foolishness. Of course it isn't me. What would a photograph of me be doing in a newspaper?

CHAPTER FOUR

Kelly snapped the hairband off her wrist and onto her hand, then tied back her hair. It was slightly too short; the consequence of a regretted crop in August, when a fortnight-long heat wave had made it seem like a good idea to lose the heavy curtain of hair she'd had down to her waist since her student days. Two dark strands fell instantly forward again. In the end it had taken two hours to process Carl Bayliss, after discovering he was wanted on a couple of theft allegations as well as the Fail to Appear. Kelly yawned. She was almost beyond hunger now, although she had looked hopefully in the kitchen when she got in, just in case. Nothing. She should have stopped off for that kebab, after all. She made herself some toast and took it to her ground-floor bedroom. It was a large, square room with a high ceiling and walls painted white above the picture rail. Beneath it Kelly had painted the walls pale gray, covering the past-its-best carpet with two huge rugs she'd bought at an auction. The rest of the room—the bed, the desk, the red armchair she was currently sitting on—was pure IKEA, the modern lines contrasting with the sweep of the bay window into which her bed was pushed.

She flicked through the copy of *Metro* she'd picked up on her way home. Lots of Kelly's colleagues never looked at the local papers—*bad enough we have to see the scumbags at work; I don't want to bring them home with me*—but Kelly had an insatiable appetite for them. Breaking news bulletins scrolled constantly across the screen on her iPhone, and when she visited her parents, who had moved out of London to retire in Kent, she loved to scour the village newsletter with its appeals for committee members and complaints about litter and dog mess.

She found what she was looking for on page five, in a double-page spread headed:

UNDERGROUND CRIME SOARS

City Hall chiefs launch an investigation into crime on public transport, after record increases in reported sexual offenses, violent assaults, and thefts.

The article opened with a paragraph rammed with terrifying crime statistics—enough to stop you using the Tube altogether, Kelly thought—before leading into a series of case studies, designed to illustrate the types of crime most prevalent on London's busy transport network. Kelly glanced at the section on violent assaults, illustrated with a photograph of a young man with a distinctive pattern shaved into the side of his head. The teenager's right eye was almost invisible beneath a black-and-purple swelling that made him look deformed.

The attack on Kyle Matthews was violent and unprovoked, read the caption. That needed taking with a pinch of salt, Kelly thought. Granted, she didn't know Kyle, but she knew the symbol shaved into his head, and *unprovoked* wasn't a term usually associated with its wearers. Still, she supposed she should give him the benefit of the doubt.

The photo accompanying the section on sexual assaults was in shadow; the profile of a woman just visible. *Stock photo,* the label read. *Names have been changed.*

Unbidden, another newspaper article appeared in Kelly's head; a different city, a different woman, the same headline.

She swallowed hard; moved on to the final case study, smiling at the face pulled by the woman in the photograph.

"You're not going to make me do a *Daily Mail* sad face, are you?" Cathy Tanning had asked the photographer.

"Of course not," he'd said cheerily. "I'm going to make you do a *Metro* sad face, tinged with a spot of outrage. Pop your handbag on your lap and try to look as though you've come home to find your husband in bed with the window cleaner."

The British Transport Police press officer hadn't been able to attend, so Kelly had volunteered to stay with Cathy for the interview, to which the woman had been quick to agree.

"You've been great," she told Kelly. "It's the least I can do."

"Save the compliments for when we find the guy who stole your keys," Kelly had said, privately thinking the chances were slim. She'd been coming to the end of a three-month-long transfer to the Dip Squad when the job came in, and she'd taken to Cathy Tanning immediately.

"It's my fault," the woman had said, as soon as Kelly had introduced herself. "I work such long hours, and my journey home is so long, it's too tempting to go to sleep. It never occurred to me someone would take advantage of it."

Kelly thought Cathy Tanning had gotten away lightly. The offender had rifled through her bag while she leaned against the wall of the carriage, fast asleep, but he hadn't found her wallet, zipped into a separate compartment, or her phone, tucked into another. Instead he'd pulled out her keys.

"It's not your fault," Kelly had reassured her. "You have every right to grab forty winks on your way home." Kelly had filled out a crime report and seized the CCTV, and when she'd picked up the call from the press office later that day, Cathy had seemed like the obvious choice for an Underground-crime poster girl. Kelly scanned the copy for her own quote, noticing she'd been referred to as DC rather than PC. That would piss off a few people at work.

> *Cathy is just one of the hundreds of commuters and tourists who fall victim each year to thefts from bags and coat pockets. We would urge passengers to be extra vigilant and to report anything suspicious to a British Transport Police officer.*

Kelly carefully cut out the article for Cathy, and sent her a text message to thank her once again for helping out. Her job phone was switched off in her locker at work, but she'd written down her personal mobile number in case Cathy needed to get hold of her.

Kelly was still in half-blues—a civvy fleece pulled over a white shirt denuded of its tie and epaulets—and she bent down to unlace her boots. Some of her old school friends were going out for drinks and had invited Kelly to join them, but she was up at five in the morning and there was no fun like being sober on a Friday night. *Toast, Netflix, tea, and bed*, she thought. Rock and roll.

Her phone rang and she brightened when she saw her sister's name flash up on the screen.

"Hey, how are you? I haven't spoken to you in ages!"

"Sorry, you know what it's like. Listen, I've found the perfect thing for Mum's Christmas present, but it's a bit more than we'd usually spend—do you want to come in with us?"

"Sure. What is it?" Kelly kicked off one boot, then the other, only half listening to her twin sister's description of the vase she'd seen at a craft fair. They were halfway through November; it was weeks until Christmas. Kelly suspected she had been born without the shopping gene, always leaving things to the last minute and secretly enjoying the fevered atmosphere in the malls on Christmas Eve, filled with harassed men panic-buying overpriced perfume and lingerie.

"How are the boys?" she interrupted, when it was obvious Lexi was about to move on to suggest presents for the rest of the family.

"They're great. Well, a pain in the neck half the time, obviously, but great. Alfie's settled into school brilliantly, and Fergus seems to have a good time at nursery, judging by the state of his clothes at the end of the day."

Kelly laughed. "I miss them." Lexi and her husband, Stuart, were only in St. Albans, but Kelly didn't see them nearly as much as she'd like.

"So come over!"

"I will, I promise, as soon as I get some time off. I'll check my duties and text you some dates. Maybe Sunday lunch sometime?" Lexi's roasts were legendary. "I think I've got a few rest days together at the start of December, if you don't mind me crashing on your sofa?"

"Brilliant. The boys love it when you stay over. Although not the second—I've got a reunion to go to."

The almost imperceptible hesitation and Lexi's subsequent deliberately casual tone told Kelly precisely what the reunion was for, and where it would be held.

"A reunion at Durham?"

There was silence at the other end of the phone, and Kelly imagined her sister nodding, her jaw jutting forward the way it always did in anticipation of an argument.

"Freshers of 2005," Lexi said brightly. "I doubt I'll recognize half of them, although of course I'm still in touch with Abbie and Dan, and I see Moshy from time to time. I can't believe it's been ten years, it feels like ten minutes. Mind you—"

"Lexi!"

Her sister stopped talking, and Kelly tried to find the right words.

"Are you sure that's a good idea? Won't it"—she screwed up her eyes, wishing she was having this conversation in person—"bring everything up?" She sat forward, on the edge of the chair, and waited for her sister to speak. She touched the half heart at her throat, suspended on its silver thread, and wondered if Lexi still wore hers. They'd bought them that autumn, just before they went off to uni. Kelly down to Brighton, and Lexi to Durham. It was the first time they'd been apart for longer than a night or two since they'd been born.

When Lexi eventually answered, it was in the same measured tone she had always used with her sister. "There's nothing to bring up, Kelly. What happened happened. I can't change it, but it doesn't have to define me." Lexi had always been the calm one, the sensible one. The two sisters were theoretically identical, but no one had ever struggled to tell them apart. They had the same squared-off chin, the same narrow nose and dark brown eyes, but where Lexi's face was relaxed and easygoing, Kelly's was stressed and short-tempered. They had tried to switch places many times as children, but no one who knew them was ever fooled.

"Why shouldn't I celebrate the good times I had at uni?" Lexi was saying. "Why shouldn't I be able to walk around the campus like the rest of my friends, remembering the nights out we had, the lectures, the stupid jokes we played on each other?"

"But—"

"No, Kelly. If I had left after it happened—changed uni like you and Mum wanted me to do—he'd have won. And if I don't go to this reunion because I'm scared of the memories it might drag up, well, he'll be winning again."

Kelly realized she was shaking. She put her feet flat on the floor and leaned forward, pressing her forearm over her knees to keep them still. "I think you're mad. I wouldn't go anywhere near that place."

"Well, you're not me, are you?" Lexi exhaled sharply, doing nothing to mask her frustration. "Anyone would think it was you it happened to, not me."

Kelly said nothing. How could she explain to Lexi that was exactly how it had felt, without implying her trauma was somehow on a par with Lexi's own? She remembered the session delivered at police college by someone from Occupational Health. They had worked through a case study of a pileup on the M25; dozens injured, six killed. Who had post-traumatic stress disorder? The trainer wanted them to guess. The highways officers, who had been first to the scene? The traffic sergeant, who had to comfort the mother of two dead children? The truck driver, whose lapse of concentration had caused the devastation?

None of them.

It was the off-duty police officer whose daily run took him over the motorway bridge; who witnessed the whole thing happen and called it in, delivering essential information to control room but ultimately powerless to stop the tragedy unfolding beneath him. That's who developed PTSD. Who blamed himself for not doing more. That's who ended up retiring due to ill health; who became a recluse. The by-stander.

"Sorry," she said instead. She heard Lexi sigh.

"It's okay."

It wasn't, and they both knew it, but neither of them wanted to fall out. The next time they spoke, Lexi would talk about the plans for Christmas, and Kelly would say how great work was, and they would pretend everything was okay.

Just like they'd done for the past ten years.

"How's work?" Lexi asked, as though she could read Kelly's mind.

"Okay. Same old, you know." She tried to sound upbeat, but Lexi wasn't fooled.

"Oh, Kel, you need a new challenge. Have you thought any more about reapplying for a specialist unit? They can't hold it against you forever."

Kelly wasn't so sure. Her departure four years ago from British Transport Police's Sexual Offenses Unit had been rapid and uncomfortable. She had spent nine months off sick, returning to what had been presented to her as a clean slate but was really a punishment posting. Kelly had thrown herself into shift work, quickly becoming one of the most respected officers on the Neighborhood Policing Team; pretending to herself she was a uniform cop through and through, when every day she yearned to be dealing with serious investigations again.

"The attachment you've just done must have helped." Lexi was persistent. "Surely now the bosses can see you're no longer—"

She stopped abruptly, obviously unsure how to summarize the time Kelly had spent off work, unable to leave the flat without breaking into a sweat.

"I'm fine where I am," Kelly said shortly. "I need to go—there's someone at the door."

"Come and see us soon—promise?"

"I promise. Love you, sis."

"Love you, too."

Kelly ended the call and sighed. She had so enjoyed her three-month attachment on the Dip Squad, the unit dedicated to tackling the huge number of pickpockets operating on the London Underground. It wasn't the kudos of being in plainclothes—although after years in uniform it had been a welcome change—it was the feeling of actually making a real difference; of making a dent in a crime wave affecting so many people in the city. Since Kelly had joined the job, more and more specialist units had been created: all the serious crimes were now hived off to squads, leaving the Neighborhood Policing Teams with little more than bylaw breaches and antisocial behavior. Kelly had been back in uniform for a week, and apart from Carl Bayliss's, the only collars she'd fingered had belonged to kids with their trainers on the seats, and the usual Friday-night drunks barging through the barriers and turning the air blue. Was she ready to go back onto a specialist squad? Kelly thought she was, but when she had broached the idea with her inspector, his answer had been short and to the point.

"People have long memories in this job, Kelly. You're considered too much of a risk." He'd given her the Dip Squad attachment as a consolation prize; a step up from shift but with little risk of becoming emotionally involved. He had intended it to satisfy Kelly, but all it had done was remind her of what she was missing.

Lexi was right; she needed to move on.

CHAPTER FIVE

I t's unusual to see Katie much before midday; the tips at the restaurant are better in the evenings than at lunch, and she's never been one for early nights on her days off. Yesterday, though, she was upstairs before ten, and when I looked in on my way to bed (hard to break the habit of a lifetime) she was fast asleep. Now, while I'm lying in bed trying to summon up some enthusiasm for a wet Monday morning, I hear the whine of the electric shower, accompanied by the knocking sound I'd hoped I'd imagined over the weekend.

"It's broken."

Simon makes a sound that might be agreement, reaching an arm above the duvet to pull me closer to him. I wriggle away.

"We'll be late for work. I'm going to have to get someone out to look at that shower; it's definitely not right."

"It'll cost a fortune—you know what plumbers are like. They'll invoice us for a hundred quid before they've even stepped through the door."

"Well, I can't fix it myself, and . . ." I let my sentence trail off, shooting a knowing look at Simon.

"Oi, I'm not that bad!" He pokes me in the ribs and I squeal. Simon's atrocious DIY skills are matched only by my own. The house Matt and I bought together was a repossession—we'd never have afforded it, otherwise—and the plan was we'd both do it up. After the second time I drilled through a water pipe I agreed to step away from the power tools, and DIY became one of those "blue" jobs, like servicing the cab, or putting out the bins. I got used to doing most things in the years when it was just me and the kids, but the shelf in the bathroom has fallen down three times, and the flat-pack wardrobe in Katie's room is decidedly wonky. Discovering Simon is as inept as I am at DIY was secretly rather a blow.

"Is there any point fixing the shower?" Simon says. "The whole bathroom needs redoing."

"Well, that's not going to happen anytime soon," I say, thinking of the Christmas presents I'll soon be putting on a credit card. "We'll have to get the shower fixed and put up with the rest." I snuggle under the duvet and feel Simon's warm body spooning my own, one eye on the clock.

"It's a waste of money." Simon pushes the duvet off abruptly, kicking it out of reach and sending a blast of cold air across us both. I sit up and look at him.

"Since when did you worry about money?" I'm the one who keeps track of how much we're spending. It's in my blood. Simon, on the other hand, is casual with cash in the way people only are when they've never been without it.

"Sorry," he says, with an embarrassed shrug. "Wrong side of the bed. It just seems a shame to patch up something that needs a bigger job on it. How about I get a quote for a complete refit?"

I imagine the bathroom of my dreams; all chrome and white tiles, like the hotel Simon took me to in Paris for our first anniversary. "We can't afford it, Simon, not with Christmas coming up."

"I'll pay," he says. There's something in his eyes that makes me think he regrets his recklessness, but he doesn't take it back.

"You won't let me contribute to the mortgage, so let me buy you a new bathroom." I wonder if Justin's comments have hit home; I open my mouth to protest but he holds up a hand. "I insist. I'll look for a reputable building company. If such a thing exists! Right, come on, I'll be late—and so will you." He leaps up and I swing my legs to the side and push my feet into fleecy slippers. My dressing gown feels cold

against my naked skin and I shiver as I go downstairs and put the kettle on. Biscuit weaves in and out of my legs, tripping me up until I
scoop a cup of food into his bowl.

I hear the whine of the shower come to an end, the bathroom door
open. There are footsteps on the landing, and the murmur of voices as
Katie and Simon pass each other. The whine resumes. Katie's in a
hurry today. If she's getting ready for a night out she can be in the
bathroom for what seems like hours—not that Simon would ever
complain. He'd go without a shower rather than rush her.

"Teenagers," he said with a shrug, when I told her off for hogging
the bathroom. "It's not like I need long to wash my hair." He ran a hand
over his head, feeling the thinning patch of gray with a rueful smile.

"You're very understanding," I told him. After Matt's hotheadedness
it's such a relief to be living with someone so tolerant; I've never seen
Simon lose his temper, not even when the neighbors came around for
the umpteenth time to complain about the music Justin was playing at a
level far more reasonable than their own screaming kids. Simon doesn't
have it in him to be angry.

Melissa narrowed her eyes when I told her Simon had lived on his
own for ten years before we met.

"What's wrong with him?"

"Nothing! He just hasn't found the right person. But he's perfectly
house-trained. Cooks, cleans, even irons."

"You couldn't send him around to mine, when you're done with
him, could you? Neil can build a computer from scratch but the switch
for the vacuum cleaner seems to elude him."

I laughed. I had a feeling, even in those early days, that I wouldn't be
sending Simon anywhere. I remembered the shiver of excitement I'd
felt when he kissed me for the first time, and the thrill of the fast, clumsy
sex we'd had at the end of that first date; all the more exciting because it
was so out of character for me. That's what I liked most about Simon;
he made me feel like a different person. Not a mum, or Matt's girlfriend
or wife. Me. Zoe Walker. I went straight from my parents' house to

living with Matt, and when I found myself single at thirty I was so worried about making sure the kids were all right that finding out who *I* was just wasn't important. Meeting Simon changed that.

I make the tea and take a tray upstairs with four mugs, then knock on Justin's door and pick my way carefully through the detritus on the floor so I can put a steaming cup next to his bed.

"Justin, cup of tea for you."

He doesn't stir, and I pick up yesterday's offering, its contents cold and untouched. I look down at my son, three days' growth hiding a gentle face with its dimpled chin; his hair long across his face and one arm outstretched toward his headboard. "Love, it's almost seven o'clock." He grunts. Justin's laptop is open on the bedside table, an open window for some music forum. It's black with white writing, and would make my head hurt if I looked at it for too long. On the left I can see the photo Justin uses online: it's his face, but almost completely obscured by a hand thrust toward the camera. On his palm, in black letters, is written his username, Game8oy_94.

Twenty-two, going on twelve. Katie was always in such a hurry to grow up—couldn't wait to leave behind the Barbie dolls and the My Little Ponies—but men seem to stay boys for so much longer.

I think about what Simon said the other night and wonder if Justin really will still be living here when he's thirty. I used to think I never wanted my children to leave home. I liked living here, the three of us, meeting for supper but otherwise simply coexisting. Katie and I would go out together occasionally, and Justin would lurk in the kitchen while I cooked tea, stealing chips before they hit the plates and sharing intricacies of Grand Theft Auto I didn't understand. Like flatmates, I kidded myself. It was only when Simon moved in that I realized how much I'd missed sharing that part of my life with someone.

Justin pulls the duvet over his head.

"You'll be late for work," I tell him. As I will be, I think, if I don't get a move on.

"I don't feel well," comes the muffled reply. I yank the duvet, hard.

"Melissa's gone out on a limb for you, Justin. You are not calling in sick, do you hear me?" The urgency in my voice finally gets through to him. He knows he wouldn't have a job without Melissa—without my asking her, come to that.

"All right. Don't go on."

I leave him sitting on the edge of his bed in his boxers, rubbing his head till his hair stands on end.

A fug of steam billows from the open bathroom door. I knock on Katie's door and she calls for me to come in. She's sitting at the desk she uses as a dressing table, drawing dark brows onto an immaculately made-up face, her hair twisted into a towel.

"You legend. I'll drink it while I do my hair. Ready to go at half seven?"

"Do you want some toast?"

"It'll bloat me. I'll have something afterward." She blows me a kiss and takes her mug, the one with *Calm down and watch TOWIE* on it. Even in a toweling dressing gown she's gorgeous. Legs up to her armpits. Heaven knows where she got those from: certainly not from me, and although Matt's taller than me, he's stocky with it.

"Bought and paid for," he used to say, grinning and rubbing his beer belly. He couldn't be more different than Simon; tall and rangy, with long legs that look great in a suit and endearingly comical in shorts.

"I bet he's never got his hands dirty in his life," Matt said scornfully, after the first time they'd met—awkwardly, on the doorstep, when Matt was dropping Katie home.

"Maybe he's never needed to," I retorted, regretting it the second it left my lips. Matt's bright. Maybe not academic, like Simon, but not stupid. He would have stayed on at college if it hadn't been for me.

I take Simon his tea. He's already dressed; a pale blue shirt and darker blue suit trousers, the jacket still in the wardrobe. He'll leave off the tie, in a concession to the *Telegraph*'s relaxed dress code, but he's not a chinos kind of man. I check the time and lock myself in the bathroom, hoping the others have left me some hot water; cutting my shower short when I realize they haven't.

I'm drying myself when there's a knock on the door.

"Almost done!"

"It's only me. I'm off."

"Oh!" I open the door, towel wrapped around my damp body.

"I thought we were going in together."

Simon kisses me. "I said I'd be in a bit early today."

"We'll be ready in ten minutes."

"Sorry, I really do need to go. I'll give you a ring later."

He goes downstairs and I finish drying myself, cross with myself for being disappointed he doesn't want to walk to the station with me; a teenage girl denied her crush's football jumper.

Simon used to work shifts, covering earlies and lates in the newsroom, and doing his share of the weekend rota. A few months ago—at the start of August—they changed things at work, putting him on permanent days, Monday to Friday. I thought he'd be pleased, but instead of enjoying more evenings together, he comes home grouchy and depressed.

"I don't like change," he explained.

"So ask for your old shifts back."

"It doesn't work like that," he said, frustration making him short with me. "You don't understand." He was right; I didn't. Nor can I understand now why he won't wait ten minutes for Katie and me to be ready.

"Good luck!" he calls to Katie, as he heads downstairs. "Knock 'em dead!"

"Are you nervous?" I ask her, as we walk toward the station. She doesn't say anything, which is an answer in itself. Under one arm she's clutching her portfolio, inside of which are a dozen 7 × 5 photos that cost a small fortune. In each one Katie's wearing something different; a new expression on her face. In all of them she's beautiful. Simon paid for the photos as a surprise for her eighteenth birthday, and I don't think I've ever seen her so happy.

"I'm not sure I can take another no," she says quietly.

I sigh. "It's a tough business, Katie. You're going to get a lot of nos, I'm afraid."

"Thanks. Nice to know my own mother has faith in me." She tosses her hair as though she'd be flouncing off if we weren't both walking in the same direction.

"Don't be like that, Katie. You know what I mean." I say hello to the dreadlocked musician standing by the entrance to Crystal Palace station and reach into my coat pocket for one of the coins I keep there. Her name's Megan, and she's only a little older than Katie. I know this because I asked her one day, and she explained that her parents had thrown her out and that she spent her days sofa-surfing, and playing guitar, and queuing up at the Norwood and Brixton Foodbank.

"Cold today, isn't it?" I throw ten pence into her guitar case, where it bounces on top of a handful of others, and she breaks off from her song to thank me before seamlessly catching up with the lyrics on the next bar.

"Ten pee isn't going to get her far, Mum."

The strains of Megan's song die away as we walk into the station.

"Ten pence in the morning; ten on my way home. That's a pound a week." I shrug. "Fifty-odd quid a year."

"Well, if you put it like that, it's very generous." Katie's silent for a moment. "Why not just chuck in a quid every Friday, though? Or give her a bundle of notes at Christmas?"

We tap our Oysters and push through the barriers toward the Overground.

"Because it doesn't feel like I'm giving so much this way," I tell

Katie, even though that isn't the reason. It isn't the money that matters but the kindness. And this way I give a little kindness every day.

At Waterloo we fight our way onto the platform and join the thick procession making its way onto the Northern line.

"Honestly, Mum, I don't know how you do this every day."

"You get used to it," I say, although you don't so much get used to it as simply put up with it. Standing up on a cramped, malodorous train is part and parcel of working in London.

"I hate it. It's bad enough doing it on Wednesday and Saturday night, but to do it at rush hour? God, it would kill me."

Katie waitresses at a restaurant near Leicester Square. She could find somewhere closer to home, but she likes being in what she calls the "heart" of the city. What she means is that she thinks she's more likely to meet a film producer or an agent hanging out around Covent Garden and Soho than in Forest Hill. She's probably right, although in the eighteen months she's been there it hasn't happened yet.

Today Katie isn't going to the restaurant, though. Today she's going to an audition, where the next in a long line of theatrical agencies will see her and—she hopes—agree to take her on.

I wish I believed in her as much as she wants me to, but I'm a realist. She's beautiful, and talented, and she's a great actress, but she's a nineteen-year-old girl from Peckham Comprehensive, and the chances of her hitting the big time are about as much as me winning the lottery. And I don't even play it.

"Promise me that if this one doesn't work out, you'll at least consider the secretarial course I told you about."

Katie looks at me scornfully.

"As something to fall back on, that's all."

"Thanks for the vote of confidence, Mum."

Leicester Square station is heaving. We're separated briefly as we approach the ticket barrier and when I find her again I squeeze her hand.

"I'm just being practical, that's all."

She's cross with me and I don't blame her. Why did I have to pick that moment to bring up the secretarial course? I check my watch. "You're not due there for another forty-five minutes. Let me buy you a coffee."

"I'd rather be on my own."

I deserve that, I think, but she catches the hurt in my eyes.

"To go over my audition piece."

"Of course. Well, good luck, then. I mean it, Katie. I hope it goes brilliantly." I watch her walk away, wishing I could have just been happy for her; cheered her on, the way Simon did before he left for work.

"It wouldn't have hurt you to have been a bit more enthusiastic." Melissa slathers margarine onto slices of bread, stacking them in pairs, butter-side in, ready for the lunchtime rush. In the glass-fronted cabinet are tubs of tuna salad, smoked salmon, grated cheese. The Covent Garden café is called Melissa's Too. It's larger than the Anerley Road place, with high seats facing the window, and five or six tables with metal chairs that stack in the corner each night so the cleaner can mop the floor.

"Lie to her, you mean?" It's ten to nine and the café is empty, bar Nigel, whose long gray coat is streaked with grime, and who sends a waft of body odor into the air when he moves. He nurses a pot of tea perched on a high stool in the window till Melissa shoos him out at ten each morning, telling him he's bad for the lunch trade. Nigel used to sit on the pavement outside the café, a cap on the ground in front of him, until Melissa took pity on him. She charges him fifty pence, two pounds less than the blackboard price, and he certainly gets his money's worth.

"Just support her."

"I *am* supporting her! I took a couple of hours off work so I could travel in with her."

"Does she know that?"

I fall silent. I'd been planning to meet her afterward to see how the audition had gone, but Katie had made it quite clear she didn't want me hanging around.

"You should encourage her. When she becomes a Hollywood sensation you don't want her telling *Hello!* magazine her mum told her she was no good."

I laugh. "Not you, too. Simon's convinced she's going to make it."

"Well, then," Melissa says, as though that settles it. Her blue hairnet is coming loose, and I tug it forward for her so she doesn't have to wash her hands again. Melissa has long, thick, glossy dark hair, which she wears in a seemingly complicated knot I've seen her create in a matter of seconds. When she's working she'll tuck a pen into it, which gives a misleadingly bohemian impression of her. Like most days, she's wearing jeans and ankle boots, with a crisp white shirt, the sleeves rolled to the elbows to expose skin as pale as her husband's is dark.

"Thanks."

"But then he's also convinced he's going to be a bestselling author." I grin, but even though I'm joking I feel instantly disloyal.

"Doesn't that involve actually writing something?"

"He *is* writing," I say, redressing the balance by leaping to Simon's defense. "He's had masses of research to do first, and it's hard finding the time around a full-time job."

"What's it about?"

"Some sort of espionage thriller, I think. You know me; it's not really my sort of book. Give me a Maeve Binchy any day." I haven't read any of Simon's novel. He wants to wait until it's finished before I see it, and I'm fine with that, because the truth is, I'm nervous. I worry I won't know what to say about it; that I'm not qualified even to know if

I SEE YOU 45

it's good or not. I'm sure it'll be good. Simon writes beautifully. He's one of the most senior journalists at the *Telegraph*, and he's been working on his book ever since I met him.

The door opens and a man in a suit comes in. He greets Melissa by name and they chat about the weather as she makes his coffee, adding milk and sugar without needing to ask.

There's a copy of Friday's *Metro* in the rack on the wall, and I pull it out while Melissa rings up the sale. Whoever was reading it has left it folded on a page headed *Underground Crime Soars*, and even though there's no one near me I instinctively move my arm over my handbag, the strap worn across my chest in a habit years old. There's a photo of a lad around Justin's age, his face badly beaten, and a woman with a rucksack open on her lap, looking like she's about to cry. I scan the article but it's nothing new; advice about keeping your belongings close to you, traveling in pairs late at night. Nothing I haven't told Katie, time and time again.

"Justin said your manager went home sick," I say, when we're on our own again.

"She's off today, as well, hence . . ." She gestures to the blue hairnet. "I bet Richard Branson didn't have these problems when he was building his empire."

"I bet he did. I'm not sure you can call two cafés"—I catch Melissa's glower—"two *brilliant* cafés an empire, though."

Melissa looks shifty. "Three."

I raise an eyebrow and wait for more.

"Clerkenwell. Don't look at me like that. You have to speculate to accumulate."

"But—" I stop before I cross a line I can't return from. Taking on a third café when my second was foundering would terrify me, but I guess that's why Melissa's in business, and I'm not. When I moved in next door to Melissa and Neil, I was doing a bookkeeping course through an Adult Education program. I'd been rubbish at math at school, but Matt only had the kids on Wednesday evenings, which meant it was that or upholstery, and I couldn't see me making a living from re-covering chairs. Melissa was my first client.

"I've done the business accounts myself up till now," she'd said, when I told her I'd signed up for the course, "but I've taken on new premises in Covent Garden, and I could do with freeing up some time. It'll be payroll and receipts—nothing too complicated." I jumped at the chance. And although it was only a year before another client—Graham Hallow—offered me a permanent job, I've carried on doing the books for Melissa's and Melissa's Too.

"Melissa's Three?" I ask now. She laughs.

"And Four, and Five . . . the sky's the limit!"

I'm not due into work until lunchtime, but when I arrive at eleven Graham makes a show of looking at his watch.

"Good of you to come in today, Zoe." As always, he's wearing a three-piece suit, with an actual pocket watch tucked into his waistcoat. "Professionalism breeds confidence," he explained to me once, perhaps in an attempt to encourage me out of my M&S trousers and into something similarly old-fashioned.

I don't rise to it. My two hours' leave was authorized and signed off by Graham himself before I left on Friday. "Would you like me to make you a coffee?" I say, having learned a long time ago that the best way to extinguish Graham is by being unfailingly polite.

"That would be most welcome, thank you. Did you have a good weekend?"

"Not bad." I don't offer any detail, and he doesn't ask. I keep my personal life to myself nowadays. When Simon and I first got together, Graham dared to suggest it was inappropriate for me to date someone I'd met through work, even though it had been months since he'd come into the office, inquiring about commercial rental rates for a piece he was writing.

"But it wouldn't have been inappropriate for me to date my boss?" I responded, folding my arms and looking him straight in the eye. Because six weeks after I'd found out about Matt's affair, when I was a quivering mess and didn't know which way was up, Graham Hallow had asked me out, and I'd said no.

"I felt sorry for you," he said, when I challenged him all those years later. "I thought you needed cheering up."

"Right. Thanks."

"Maybe that's what this new bloke thinks, too."

I didn't take the bait. I knew Simon didn't feel sorry for me. He adored me. He bought me flowers, took me to nice restaurants, and kissed me in a way that made my knees buckle. We'd been seeing each other for only a few weeks, but I knew. I just knew. Maybe Graham had felt sorry for me, but he never quite forgave me for turning him down. No more letting me leave early if the kids were unwell, or cutting me some slack if the trains were late. From that moment he played by the book, and I needed the job too much to risk breaking the rules.

Graham drinks his coffee, then puts on his coat and disappears. There's nothing in the schedule, but he mutters something about seeing a man about a dog, and frankly I'm just glad to be on my own. The office is unusually quiet for a Monday, so I start a long overdue spring cleaning, feeding papers through the shredder and moving ancient spider plants to dust behind them.

My phone beeps, and I pick up a text from Matt.

KT okay?

He shortens everyone's name like that. Katie is *KT*, Justin *Jus*, and I'm only ever Zoe when we're arguing.

I suppose Simon would be *Si*, if they had that sort of relationship.

Haven't heard from her, I reply. Not sure if that's a good sign or not!

Did she feel confident?

I think for a second. Optimistic, I put.

How about you? x

I register the kiss and ignore it. I leave the conversation hanging, carrying on with my dusting, and a few minutes later he phones.

"You did it again, didn't you?"

"Did what?" I say, knowing full well what he means.

"You put a downer on her audition." His consonants are muffled and I know it's because he's put a cigarette between his lips. Sure enough, I hear the metallic snap of a lighter, and he takes a long drag. It's been almost twenty years since I smoked, but I feel a physical pull as he inhales.

"I didn't," I start, but Matt knows me too well. "I didn't mean to, anyway."

"What did you say?"

"I just mentioned that secretarial course I told you about."

"Zo . . ."

"What? You said yourself it would be perfect for her." I hear the sound of traffic in the background and know that Matt is parked at a taxi stand, leaning against the cab.

"You've got to go gentle with her. Push her too hard in one direction and she'll only run faster the other way."

"Acting isn't a proper job," I say, because disagreeing with Matt is a habit that's hard to break. "She needs something to fall back on."

"She'll find that out herself soon enough. And when she does, we'll be there."

I finish dusting the main room and move on to Graham's office. His desk is twice the size of mine but almost as neat. It's one of the few things we have in common. A calendar sits parallel to the edge of the desk, today's motivational quote urging me to do something today my future self will thank me for. On the opposite side of the desk are three in-trays, stacked on top of one another and labeled *Incoming*; *Pending*; *Post*. In front of them is a stack of newspapers. Today's *London Gazette* is on top.

Nothing unusual in that. You'd be hard-pressed to find an office in London without a copy of the *Gazette* knocking about. I pick up the first issue, telling myself I'm still tidying, and see the paper beneath it is the *London Gazette*, too. As is the one beneath that; and the one beneath that. A dozen or more copies, neatly stacked. I glance at the door then sit down in Graham's leather chair and pick up the next copy. I scan the first couple of pages, but I can't stop myself from turning to the classifieds.

And then I feel a tightening around my chest, and the palms of my hands grow damp. Because on the last page of the newspaper in my hand—a newspaper dated several days previously—is a woman I've seen before.

We are all creatures of habit.

Even you.

You reach for the same coat each day; leave home at the same time every morning. You have a favorite seat on the bus or the train; you know precisely which escalator moves the fastest, which ticket barrier to use, which kiosk has the shortest queue.

You know these things; and I know them, too.

I know you buy the same paper from the same shop, your milk at the same time each week. I know the way you walk the children to school; the shortcut you take on your way home from Zumba class. I know the street where you part ways with your friends after a Friday night in the pub, and I know that you walk the rest of the way home alone. I know the five-kilometer circuit you run on a Sunday morning, and the precise place you stop to stretch.

I know all these things, because it's never occurred to you that anyone is watching you.

Routine is comforting to you. It's familiar, reassuring. Routine makes you feel safe.

Routine will kill you.

CHAPTER SIX

Kelly was leaving the briefing room when her job phone rang. *Number withheld* meant it was almost certainly the control room, and she held the phone between her ear and her right shoulder as she zipped up her stab vest.

"Kelly Swift."

"Can you take a call from a Mrs. Zoe Walker?" came the voice. Kelly heard the buzz of voices in the background: a dozen other operators taking calls and resourcing jobs. "She wants to speak to you about a theft on the Circle line—something taken from a bag?"

"You'll need to put her through to Dip Squad. I finished my attachment there a few days ago; I'm back on the Neighborhood Policing Team now."

"I did try that, but no one's picking up. Your name's still attached to the crime report, so . . ." The operator trailed off, and Kelly sighed. The name Zoe Walker didn't ring a bell, but in her three months with the Dip Squad she had dealt with more victims of stolen wallets than she could possibly remember.

"Put her through."

"Thank you." The operator sounded relieved, and not for the first time Kelly was glad she was at the sharp end of policing, not stuck in a windowless room, fielding calls from irate members of the public. She heard a faint click.

"Hello? Hello?" Another voice came on the line, this one female and impatient.

"Hello, this is PC Swift. Can I help you?"

"Finally! Anyone would think I was trying to phone MI5."

"Not nearly that exciting, I'm afraid. I understand you wanted to talk to me about a theft on the Underground. What was it you had stolen?"

"Not me," the caller said, as though Kelly was failing to keep up. "Cathy Tanning."

Calls like this were a regular occurrence whenever a police officer was quoted in the paper. Contact from members of the public, often with no relation whatsoever to the article itself, as though possession of your name and shoulder number alone made you fair game.

"She had her keys taken from her bag when she fell asleep on her way home," Mrs. Walker went on. "Nothing else, only her keys."

It was the type of theft that had made the job unusual. On her way to take the initial report Kelly had been of two minds about whether it should have been reported as a theft at all, but Cathy had been insistent the keys hadn't been lost.

"I keep them in a separate compartment in my bag," she had told Kelly. "They couldn't have fallen out." The pocket was on the outside of a rucksack-style handbag; a zip and a leather buckle stopping them from falling out. Both had been undone.

CCTV footage had showed Cathy entering the Underground at Shepherd's Bush, the buckle on her rucksack pocket apparently securely fastened. By the time she left the station at Epping, the strap hung loose, the pocket gaping slightly open.

As jobs went, it was a straightforward one. Cathy was the perfect witness: she always took the same route home from work, even choosing the same carriage on the Circle line and sitting—when possible—in the same seat. If only everyone was so predictable, Kelly remembered thinking, it would make her job so much easier. She had picked up Cathy on the CCTV footage within minutes of looking for her, but it wasn't one of their core nominals moving in on her. The biggest offenders on the Underground right now were the Curtis kids, but they wanted wallets and iPhones, not keys.

Sure enough, when Kelly seized the footage from the train Cathy had been on at the time of the theft, she almost missed the culprit altogether.

Cathy had been asleep, leaning against the wall of the carriage with her legs crossed and her arms folded protectively around her bag. Kelly had been so busy scanning the carriage for lads in hoodies, for pairs of women with headscarves and babies in arms, that she had barely noticed the man standing close to Cathy's legs. He certainly didn't fit the profile of someone running with the usual pickpocketing crowd. Tall and well-dressed, with a gray scarf wound twice around his neck, then pulled up over his ears and the lower part of his face, as though he were still outdoors, battling the elements. He had his back to the camera; his face turned resolutely to the floor. In one swift movement he bent down, leaned toward Cathy Tanning, then stood up, his right hand disappearing into his pocket too fast for Kelly to see what was held in it.

Had he thought there might be a wallet in that outer pocket? Or a phone? A lucky dip, turning to disappointment, when he realized all he had was a bunch of keys? Taking them anyway, because returning them was a pointless risk, dumping them in a bin on his way home.

Kelly had spent her last day on the Dip Squad trying to track Cathy's thief through the Underground, obtaining a still of such low resolution there was no point even circulating it. He wasn't Caucasian, that's all she could be certain of, and around six feet tall. The CCTV cameras were color, and the quality was impressive—you could almost imagine you were watching news footage of commuters on the Underground—but that didn't guarantee a positive ID. The cameras needed to be pointing in the right direction; be positioned just right for a full-frontal image capture.

Too often—as in this case—the offense happened on the periphery of the camera range. Zooming in for a better view meant a gradual pixellation of the image, until the all-important details blurred into a homogenous figure you didn't stand a hope in hell of getting an ID on.

"Did you witness the theft?" Kelly asked, pulling her attention back to Zoe Walker. Surely she would have come forward sooner if she'd actually seen the offense take place. It occurred to her that perhaps Mrs. Walker had found the missing keys; that they could send them for forensics.

"I've got some information for you," Zoe Walker said. She spoke formally, in an abrupt tone that bordered on rudeness, but there was an uncertainty beneath it that suggested nerves.

Kelly spoke gently. "Go on."

The sergeant appeared, tapping his watch. Kelly pointed to her phone; mouthed *Give me a minute*.

"The victim. Cathy Tanning. Her photograph was in an advert in the classifieds section of the *London Gazette*, right before her keys were stolen."

Whatever Kelly had expected from Zoe Walker, it wasn't that.

She sat down. "What sort of advert?"

"I'm not really sure. It's on a page with other adverts, for things like chatlines and escorts. And on Friday I saw the same advert, except I think it had a photo of me."

"You think?" Kelly couldn't stop a note of skepticism creeping into her voice. She heard Zoe Walker hesitate.

"Well, it looked like me. Only without glasses. Although I do sometimes wear contacts—I use those daily disposable ones, you know?" She sighed. "You don't believe me, do you? You think I'm some crackpot."

It was so close to what Kelly had been thinking that she felt a stab of guilt. "Not at all. I'm just trying to establish the facts. Can you give me the dates of the adverts you saw?" She waited while Zoe Walker checked the calendar, then scribbled down the two dates she gave her;

Tuesday, 3 November for Cathy Tanning's photograph, and Friday, 13 November for Zoe's own.

"I'll look into it," she promised, although when she'd find the time, she wasn't sure. "Leave it with me."

"No." Paul Powell was unyielding. "You had your three months swanning about in plainclothes while the rest of us were picking up the work; now it's time to do some real policing."

Kelly bit her tongue, knowing Sergeant Powell wasn't worth making an enemy of. "I just want to talk to Cathy Tanning," she said, hating herself for the pleading tone in her voice, "then I promise I'll come straight back." There was nothing more frustrating than a loose end, and even though Zoe Walker had sounded flaky at best, something was nagging at Kelly. Could Cathy's photo have appeared in the classifieds? Was it possible she wasn't a random victim of crime but carefully targeted? *Advertised*, even? It was hard to believe.

"It's not your job anymore. If there's an inquiry to be done, send it to the Dip Squad. If you're short on work you only have to say the word . . ." Kelly held up her hands. She knew when to quit.

Cathy Tanning had a house in Epping, not far from the Tube station. She had sounded pleased to hear from Kelly, suggesting they meet at a wine bar on Sefton Street when Kelly finished work. Kelly had readily agreed, knowing that if she wanted to pursue a lead on a case she was no longer officially attached to, she was on her own.

"You haven't found them, then?" Cathy was thirty-seven; a GP at a practice near Shepherd's Bush, with a direct approach Kelly suspected would get a few of her patients' backs up. Kelly rather liked it.

"Sorry."

"It's fine. I didn't really expect you to. I'm intrigued, though—what's all this about an advert?"

The receptionist at the *Gazette* had been surprisingly helpful, e-mailing a color copy of each of the pages appearing in the classifieds section of the paper, on the two dates mentioned by Zoe Walker. Kelly had examined them on the Tube, quickly finding the photo Zoe had identified as being Cathy's. Only a few days earlier Kelly had watched the *Metro* photographer take a multitude of different shots, noticing the way Cathy's fringe flopped to the right-hand side, and the slight furrow between her brows. The photo in the *Gazette* certainly bore a striking resemblance to her.

Kelly put the cutout advert on the table in front of Cathy, watching the other woman carefully for a reaction. There was little information beneath the photograph, but the advert was surrounded by listings for escort services and chatlines, suggesting the ad offered similar services. Did GPs moonlight as chatline operators? As call girls?

The first thing Kelly had done on receiving copies of the adverts had been to type the web address—FindTheOne.com—into her browser. The URL had taken her to a blank page; a white box in the center suggesting some sort of password was required, but giving no further indication as to what it might be, or how one might obtain it.

The surprise on Cathy's face was genuine. A moment's silence, then a short burst of uneasy laughter. She picked up the advert and looked more closely. "They could have chosen a more flattering angle, don't you think?"

"It is you, then?"

"That's my winter coat."

The photo was closely cropped, the background dark with no discernible detail. Indoors, Kelly thought, although she couldn't say why she was so certain. Cathy was looking toward the camera but not straight at it; she was gazing into the distance as though her mind was on something else entirely. The shoulders of a dark brown coat could be seen; a fur-lined hood loose behind her head.

"Have you seen this picture before?"

Cathy shook her head. Despite her self-assurance, Kelly could tell she was rattled.

"And I'm guessing you didn't place this advert."

"Look, NHS conditions might be tough, but I'm not quite ready to switch careers yet."

"Are you registered on any dating sites?" Cathy gave her an amused look. "I'm sorry to ask, but I wondered if the photos had been harvested from a legitimate site."

"No dating sites," Cathy said. "I'm not long out of a serious relationship and, frankly, getting into another is the last thing on my mind." She put down the photocopy, took a swig of wine, then looked at Kelly. "Level with me: should I be worried?"

"I don't know," Kelly said honestly. "This advert appeared two days before your keys were stolen, and I only found out about it a few hours ago. The woman who found it—Zoe Walker—thinks she saw her own photo in the *London Gazette* on Friday."

"Has she had something stolen, too?"

"No. But, understandably, she's uneasy about her photo being in the paper."

"As indeed I am." Cathy paused, as if weighing whether to continue. "The thing is, Kelly, I've been considering giving you a ring for the last few days."

"Why haven't you?"

Cathy fixed her gaze on Kelly. "I'm a doctor. I deal in facts, not fantasy, as I imagine you do. I wanted to call you, but . . . I couldn't be sure."

"Sure of what?" Another pause.

"I think someone's been in my house while I've been at work."

Kelly said nothing, waiting for Cathy to say more.

"I can't be certain. It's more a . . . it's more of a feeling." Cathy rolled her eyes. "I know—it wouldn't stand up in court, right? That's precisely why I haven't reported it. But when I got in from work the other day I could have sworn I smelled aftershave in the hall, and when I went upstairs to get changed, the lid to the laundry basket was open."

"Could you have left it open?"

"It's possible, but it's unlikely. Closing it's one of those automatic actions, you know?" She paused. "I think some of my underwear is missing."

"You changed the locks, though, didn't you?" Kelly said. "You were waiting for the locksmith when you called the job in."

Cathy looked sheepish. "I changed the front-door lock. I didn't get the back door done. It would have been an extra hundred quid, and to be honest I didn't see the point. There was nothing on my keys that would have given away my address, and at the time it seemed like an unnecessary expense."

"And now . . . ?" Kelly let the question hang in the silence between them.

"Now I wish I'd changed both locks."

CHAPTER SEVEN

t's almost three P.M. before Graham comes back to the office.

"Working lunch," he offers in explanation, and I deduce from his relaxed demeanor that lunch was accompanied by at least a couple of pints.

"Is it okay if I nip out to the post office, now you're here?"

"Be quick about it—I've got a viewing in an hour." Everything has already been stamped and is neatly stacked in rubber-banded bundles on my desk. I tip them into a tote bag and put on my coat while Graham disappears into his office.

It's so cold outside I can see my breath, and I screw up my hands inside my pockets, rubbing my fingers against my palms. A dull vibration tells me I've got a text message, but my phone is in an inside pocket. It can wait.

In the queue at the post office I unzip my coat and find my phone. The text is from PC Kelly Swift.

Could you please send me a photo of yourself as soon as possible?

Does that mean she's spoken to Cathy Tanning? Does it mean she believes me? No sooner have I read the text than another appears on my screen.

Without glasses.

There are six people ahead of me in the queue, and as many again behind. *As soon as possible*, PC Swift said. I take off my glasses and find the camera on my phone. It takes me a moment to remember how to turn it around to face me, then I stretch my arm as far out as I dare without making it obvious that I'm taking a selfie. The upward-facing angle gives me three chins and bags under my eyes but I take the photo anyway, mortified when the camera gives me away with a loud click. How embarrassing. Who takes a selfie in a post office? I send it to PC Swift and immediately see the notification that says she's seen it. I imagine her marrying my photo up against the *London Gazette* advert, and wait for her to text to tell me I'm imagining the likeness, but my phone stays silent.

I message Katie instead, to see how her audition went. She will have been finished hours ago, and I know that she hasn't been in touch because of the way I spoke to her this morning. I push my phone into my pocket.

When I get to the office I find Graham leaning over my desk, rifling through the top drawer. He stands up sharply as I open the door, the ugly red flush on his neck prompted not by embarrassment but by annoyance at being caught out.

"Are you looking for something?" There's nothing but an assortment of envelopes, pens, and rubber bands in the top drawer, and I wonder if he's been through the others. The middle one houses old memo pads, neatly filed in date order in case I need to look up something. The bottom drawer is a dumping ground: a pair of trainers from when I thought I might try walking to the river before getting the train, tights, makeup, Tampax. I'd like to tell him to get his hands off my personal belongings, but I know what he'll say: it's his business, his desk, his drawers. If Graham Hallow were a landlord he'd be the type to walk in on inspection day without knocking.

"The keys to Tenement House. They're not in the cupboard."

I go across to the key cupboard, a metal box mounted on the wall in the corridor next to the filing cabinet. Tenement House is an office block within a larger complex called City Exchange; I check the "C" hook and find the keys instantly.

"I thought Ronan was handling the Exchange?" Ronan is the latest in a long line of junior negotiators. They're always male—Graham doesn't believe women can negotiate—and all so similar it's as though they simply slip in and out of the same suit, one appearing days after the last has left. They never stay long; the good ones move on as quickly as the bad ones.

Either Graham doesn't hear my question, or he chooses to ignore it, taking the keys from me and reminding me the new tenants for Churchill Place are coming in to sign the lease later. The bell on the door jangles as he leaves. He doesn't trust Ronan, that's the problem. He doesn't trust any of us, which means instead of being in the office, where he should be, he's out on the streets, checking up on everyone and getting in the way.

Cannon Street Tube station is full of suits. I weave through the crowded platform until I'm nearly at the tunnel; the first carriage always has fewer people than any other, and when we reach Whitechapel the doors will open directly in front of the exit.

On the train I pick up today's *Gazette*, abandoned on the grimy ledge behind my seat. I flick straight to the back pages, where the classifieds are, and find the advert with its invalid phone number: *0809 4 733 968*. Today's woman is dark-haired, the hint of a full bust visible at the bottom of the picture, and a broad smile showing even white teeth. Around her neck is a delicate chain with a small silver cross.

Does she know her photograph is in the classifieds?

I haven't heard from PC Swift, and I tell myself her silence is reassuring rather than unnerving. She would have called straightaway if there was something to worry about. Like a doctor, ringing with worrying test results. No news is good news, isn't that what they say? Simon was right; it wasn't my photo in the newspaper.

I change at Whitechapel to take the Overground to Crystal Palace. As I walk I hear footsteps behind me. Nothing unusual in that; there are footsteps everywhere on the Tube, the sound bouncing off the walls, amplifying and stretching until it sounds as though dozens of people are walking, running, stamping their feet.

But I can't shake the feeling that there's something different about these footsteps.

That they're coming after me.

When I was eighteen I was followed on my way home from the shops, not long after I fell pregnant with Justin. Impending mother-hood had made me hyperaware, and I saw danger at every corner. The cracked pavement that could trip me up; the cyclist who would surely knock me over. I felt so responsible for the life inside me that it seemed impossible I could even cross the road without putting him in danger.

I had gone out for milk, insisting to Matt's mum that I needed the exercise, wanting to do my small bit to thank her for taking me in. It was dark, and as I walked home again I became aware I was being followed. There was no sound, no sensation; just a certainty that some-one was behind me, and worse, that they were trying not to be heard.

I feel the same certainty now.

Back then I wasn't sure what was best to do. I crossed the road; the person following crossed, too. I could hear their footsteps then, gaining on me, no longer caring about being heard. I turned and saw a man—a boy—not much older than Matt. A hooded top; hands thrust deep into the front pocket. A scarf covering the bottom half of his face.

There was a shortcut to Matt's house; a narrow street that ran be-hind a row of houses. Little more than an alleyway. *It'll be quicker*, I decided, not thinking clearly, just wanting to be safely home.

As I turned the corner I broke into a run, and the boy behind me ran, too. I dropped my shopping bag, the plastic top bursting off the milk container, sending a giant white spray across the cobbles. Seconds later, I fell, too, stumbling to my knees and immediately putting a protective arm across my stomach.

It was over in a moment. He leaned over me, only his eyes exposed, and reached a hand out, searching roughly through my pockets. He pulled out my wallet and ran off, leaving me sitting on the ground.

The footsteps grow closer.

I pick up my pace. Stop myself from running, but walk as fast as I can manage, the unnatural gait throwing me off balance and making my bag swing from side to side.

There's a group of girls some distance in front of me and I try to catch up with them. *Safety in numbers*, I think. They're messing around; running, jumping, laughing, but they're not threatening. Not like the footsteps behind me, which are loud and heavy and coming closer.

"Hey!" I hear.

A male voice. Rough and harsh. I pull my bag in front of me, keep my arm over it so it can't be opened, then panic that if someone snatches it they'll drag me with it. I think of the advice I always give the kids: that it's better to be mugged than injured. *Give it up without a fight*, I always tell them. *Nothing's worth getting hurt over.*

The footsteps come faster. He's running.

I run, too, but panic makes me clumsy and I twist an ankle, almost falling. I hear the same voice, shouting again, and now the blood is pumping so loudly in my ears that I can't hear what he's saying. I can only hear the noise of him running, and of the breath I'm forcing out in loud, painful bursts.

My ankle hurts. I can't run, so I stop trying.

I give up. Turn around.

He's young; nineteen or twenty. White, with baggy jeans and trainers that pound on the concrete floor.

I'll give him my phone—that's what he'll be after. And cash. Do I have any cash?

I start to pull the strap of my handbag over my head but it catches on my hood. He's almost on me, now, grinning as though he enjoys my fear, enjoys the fact that I'm shaking so much I can't untangle myself from the leather strap of my bag. I squeeze my eyes tightly shut. *Just do it. Whatever you're planning, just do it.*

His trainers slam against the floor. Faster, louder, closer. Past me.

I open my eyes.

"Hey!" he calls again, as he runs. "Bitches!" The tunnel curves to the left, and he disappears, the echo of his trainers making it sound as though he is still running toward me. I'm still shaking, my body unable to process the fact that what I thought was a certainty didn't happen at all.

I hear shouting. I start walking, my ankle throbbing. Around the corner I see him again. He is with the group of girls; he has his arm around one and the others are grinning. They're all talking at once; excitable chatter that builds to a crescendo of hyena-like laughter.

I walk slowly. Because of my ankle, and because—even though I can see now that there's no threat—I don't want to pass this gang of kids, who have made me feel so foolish.

Not every footstep is following you, I tell myself. *Not everyone who runs is chasing you.*

When I get off the train at Crystal Palace Megan speaks to me, but I'm slow to respond. I'm relieved to be out in the open air, cross with myself for getting in a state over nothing. "I'm sorry," I say, "what was that?"

"I just said I hoped you'd had a good day." There are still fewer than a dozen coins in her open guitar case; she told me once how she scoops the pound coins and fifty-pence pieces out throughout the day.

"People stop giving if they think you're doing too well," she'd explained.

"It was okay, thank you," I tell her now. "See you in the morning."

"I'll be here!" she says, and I find her predictability comforting.

At the end of Anerley Road I walk past our open gate and through Melissa's painted railings. The door swings open, a response to the text I sent as I walked from the Tube station.

Time for a cuppa?

"Kettle's on," she says, as soon as she sees me.

At first glance Melissa and Neil's house is the same as mine; the small hall with the living room door to one side, and the bottom of the stairs facing the door. But the resemblance stops there. At the back of Melissa's house, where next door you'd find my poky kitchen, is a vast space extending into the side return and out into the garden. Two huge skylights allow the light to flood in, and bifold doors run the whole width of the house.

I follow her into the kitchen, where Neil is sitting at the breakfast bar, a laptop in front of him. Melissa's desk is by the window, and even though Neil has an office upstairs, if he isn't working away he's often in here with her.

"Hi, Neil."

"Hey, Zoe. How are things?"

"Not bad." I hesitate, not sure whether to share what's going on with the photos in the *Gazette*; not sure I can even define it. Perhaps talking about it might help. "Funny thing, though—I saw a photograph in the *London Gazette* that looked just like me." I give a little laugh, but Melissa stops making the tea and looks at me sharply. We spend too much time together for me to hide anything.

"Are you okay?"

"I'm fine. It was just a photo, that's all. An advert for a dating site or something. But it had my picture in it. At least, I thought it did." Now it's Neil who looks confused, and I don't blame him; I'm not making any sense. I think of the kid on the Tube, running to catch up with his friends, and I'm glad no one I know was there to see how I overreacted. I wonder if I'm having some kind of midlife crisis; having panic attacks over invisible danger.

"When was this?" Neil says.

"Friday evening." I glance around the kitchen, but of course there isn't a *Gazette* lying about. In my house the recycling box is permanently crammed with newspapers and cardboard packaging, but Melissa's bin is neatly tucked away and emptied regularly. "It was in the classifieds. Just a phone number, a website address, and the photograph."

"A photograph of you," Melissa says.

I hesitate. "Well, someone who looked like me. Simon said I must have a doppelgänger."

Neil laughs. "You'd recognize yourself, though, surely?"

I go to sit at the breakfast bar, next to him, and he closes the laptop, moving it so it isn't in the way. "You'd think so, wouldn't you? When I saw it on the Tube I was convinced it was me. But then by the time I got home, and I showed it to the others, I wasn't so sure. I mean, why would it be there?"

"Did you call the number?" Melissa says. She leans on the island opposite us, the kettle forgotten.

"It doesn't work. Nor does the website; the address is something like FindTheOne.com, but it just takes you to a blank screen with a white box in the middle."

"Want me to take a look at it?"

Neil does something in IT. I've never been sure exactly what, but he explained it once in such detail, I feel bad for not remembering.

"It's fine, honestly. You've got proper work to do."

"And lots of it," Melissa says ruefully. "He's in Cardiff tomorrow, then at the Houses of Parliament for the rest of the week. I'm lucky if I see him once a week at the moment."

"Parliament? Wow. What's it like?"

"Boring." Neil grins. "The bit I'll be in, anyway. I'm installing a new firewall, so I'm unlikely to be rubbing shoulders with the PM."

"Is your October paperwork ready?" I ask Melissa, suddenly remembering why I needed to pop in and see her. She nods.

"On the desk, just on top of that orange ring binder." Melissa's desk is white and glossy, like everything else in the kitchen. A huge iMac dominates the surface, and a floating shelf above holds all the files for the cafés. On the desk is a penholder that Katie made in woodwork at school.

"I can't believe you still have this."

"Of course I do! It was so sweet of her to make it."

"She got a B for it," I remember. When we first moved in next door to Melissa and Neil, money was horribly, frighteningly tight. There were more shifts on offer at Tesco, but with a school run at three P.M. it just wasn't possible. Until Melissa stepped in. At the time she had only the one café, and she closed after the lunchtime trade. She'd pick up the kids for me and bring them home with her, and they'd watch TV while she did the food order for the next day. Melissa would bake with Katie, and Neil showed Justin how to add RAM to a motherboard, and I was able to pay my mortgage.

I find the bundle of receipts on top of the orange file, beneath a folded Tube map and a notepad filled with bits of paper, Post-it notes, and Melissa's neat handwriting.

"More world-domination plans?" I joke, gesturing to the notepad. I catch a look passing between Neil and Melissa. "Oh. Sorry. Not funny?"

"It's the new café. Neil's not quite as keen on the idea as I am."

"I'm fine about the café," Neil says. "It's bankruptcy I'm less enthusiastic about."

Melissa rolls her eyes. "You're so risk averse."

"Listen, I might skip that tea, actually," I say, picking up Melissa's paperwork.

"Oh, stay!" Melissa says. "We're not going to have a domestic, I promise."

I laugh. "It's not that." Although it is a bit. "Simon's taking me out tonight."

"On a school night? What's the occasion?"

"No reason." I grin. "Just a spot of Monday-night romance."

"You two are like a couple of teenagers."

"They're still in the first flush of love," Neil says. "We were like that, once." He winks at Melissa.

"Were we?"

"Wait till the seven-year itch hits them, Mel. Then they'll be watching TV in bed and bickering about who left the top off the toothpaste."

"We do lots of that, too." I laugh. "See you soon."

The front door's unlocked when I get home, and Simon's jacket is thrown over the end of the banister. I climb the stairs to the loft conversion and knock on the door. "What are you doing home so early?"

"Hey, beautiful, I didn't hear you come in. Good day? I couldn't concentrate in the office, so I brought some work home." He stands up to kiss me, careful not to knock his head on the low beam. The conversion was carried out on the cheap by the previous owners. They worked around the original rafters, so even though it's a big room you can only stand up in the middle.

I look at the pile of papers nearest to me and see a typed list of names, each with what looks like a brief bio below it.

"Interviews for a feature I've got to do," he explains, seeing me looking. He picks up the papers and dumps them on the other side so I can perch on the edge of his desk. "It's a nightmare trying to get hold of them."

"I don't know how you find anything." My drawers at work might be a mess, but the top of my desk is almost empty. A photo of the kids and a plant sit next to my in-tray, and I make sure everything is tidied away before I go home. At the end of each day I write a list of every-thing I have to do the next day, even when some of them are the things I do on autopilot, as soon as I get into work. Open the post, listen to the answerphone messages, make the tea.

"Organized chaos." He sits down on the swivel chair in front of his desk and pats his knee for me to sit on his lap. I laugh and sit down, one arm around his neck to keep my balance. I kiss him, letting my body relax into his before I reluctantly pull away.

"I've booked a table at Bella Donna."

"Perfect."

I'm not a high-maintenance woman. I don't waste money on clothes and beauty products, and if the kids so much as remember my birthday, that's good enough for me. Matt wasn't one for hearts and flowers, even when we were young, and neither was I. Simon laughs at my cynical nature; says he's slowly bringing out my softer side. He spoils me, and I love it. After years of struggling to put food on the table, a meal out is still a luxury, but the real treat is time together. Just the two of us.

I have a shower and wash my hair, spraying perfume on my wrists and rubbing them together, letting the scent fill the air around me. I put on a dress I haven't worn for a while, and am relieved to see it still fits, and pull out a pair of black patent heels from the tangle of shoes at the bottom of my wardrobe. When Simon moved in I squashed up my clothes to make room for his, but even so he has to keep some of his belongings in the loft conversion. The house has three bedrooms, but they're all tiny: Justin's is a single, and Katie barely has room to move around her double bed.

Simon's waiting for me in the living room. He's put on a jacket and tie, and he looks the way he did when I first saw him come into Hallow & Reed. I remember him meeting my polite smile with something far warmer.

"I'm from the *Telegraph*," he told me. "We're running a piece about the rise in commercial rental prices: independents being priced off the main street, that sort of thing. It would be great if you could talk me through what's on your books at the moment." He met my eyes, and I hid the ensuing blush in the filing cabinet, taking longer than I needed to find a dozen or so particulars.

"This one might be interesting for you." I sat down at my desk, a piece of paper between us. "There used to be a gift shop there, but the rent went up and it's been empty for six months. The British Heart Foundation will be in there from next month."

"Could I speak to the landlord?"

"I can't give you his details, but if you give me your number I'll pass it on." I blushed again, even though the suggestion was perfectly legitimate. There was a crackle in the air between us I was sure I wasn't imagining.

Simon wrote down his number, his eyes creasing into a frown. I remember wondering if he normally wore glasses, and if he had left them off through vanity, or forgetfulness; not knowing then the frown was simply a side effect of concentration. His hair was gray, although not as thin as it is now, four years on. He was tall, with a lean frame that fit easily in the narrow chair by my desk, legs crossed casually at the ankle. Silver cuff links just showing below the sleeves of his navy suit.

"Thank you for your help."

He seemed in no hurry to leave, and already I didn't want him to.

"Not at all. It was a pleasure to meet you."

"So," he said, watching me intently. "You've got my number . . . may I have yours?"

We hail a taxi on Anerley Road, even though we're not going far, and I catch the fleeting look of relief in Simon's face as the cab pulls over and he sees the driver's face. Once, when Simon and I were first dating, we jumped in a black cab, our coats pulled above our heads against the rain. It was only when we looked up that we saw Matt's face in the rearview mirror. For a second I thought Simon was going to insist we get out, but he stared out the window instead. We sat in silence. Even Matt, who could talk the legs off the proverbial donkey, didn't try to make conversation.

The restaurant is one we've been to a few times, and the owner greets us by name when we arrive. He shows us to a booth by the window and hands us menus we both know by heart. Fat strands of tinsel have been draped over the picture frames and across the light fittings.

We order what we always have—pizza for Simon, seafood pasta for me—and it arrives too quickly for it to have been cooked from scratch.

"I looked at the adverts in the *Gazette* this morning. Graham had a pile in his office."

"They haven't promoted you to page three, have they?" He cuts into his pizza, and a thin trickle of oil oozes from the topping onto his plate.

I laugh. "I'm not sure I've got the necessary attributes for that. The thing is, I recognized the woman in one of the adverts."

"You recognized her? You mean it's someone you know?"

I shake my head. "I saw her photo in another newspaper—she was in an article about crime on the Underground. I told the police about it." I'm trying to keep it light, but my voice breaks. "I'm scared, Simon. What if that photo in Friday's paper really was me?"

"It wasn't, Zoe." There's concern in Simon's face, not because someone put a photo of me in the paper but because *I think* they did.

"I'm not imagining it."

"Are you stressed about work? Is it Graham?"

He thinks I'm going mad. I'm starting to think he's right.

"It really did look like me," I say quietly.

"I know."

He puts down his knife and fork. "Tell you what, let's say the photo was of you."

This is how Simon addresses problems, boiling them down to their very essence. A couple of years ago there was a burglary on our street. Katie became convinced they were going to break into our house next, and the thought stopped her sleeping. When she eventually dropped off she had nightmares, waking up screaming that there was someone in her room. I was at my wit's end. I'd tried everything; even sat with her till she fell asleep, like she was a baby again. Simon took a more practical approach. He took Katie to the hardware store, where they bought window locks, a burglar alarm, and an extra bolt for the garden gate. Together they fitted security measures to the entire house, even coating the drainpipes with anti-climb paint. The nightmares stopped instantly.

"Okay," I say, finding the game oddly cheering. "Let's say the photograph really was of me."

"Where did it come from?"

"I don't know. I've been asking myself the same question."

"You'd notice someone random taking a photo of you, surely?"

"Maybe someone took it with a long lens," I say, realizing as I do how ridiculous it sounds. What next? Paparazzi outside the house? Mopeds zooming past me, a photographer leaning to one side in an effort to get the perfect shot for a tabloid splash? Simon doesn't laugh, but when I acknowledge the absurdity of the suggestion with an embarrassed grin, he cracks a smile.

"Someone could have stolen it," he says, more seriously.

"Yes!" That seems more likely.

"Okay, so let's imagine someone's used your photo to advertise their company." Discussing the advert like this, in such a rational, dispassionate way, is gradually calming me down, which I know was Simon's intention all along. "That would be identity theft, right?"

I nod. Giving it a name—and one so familiar—instantly makes it feel less personal. There are hundreds—probably thousands—of identity fraud cases every day. At Hallow & Reed we have to be so careful, double-checking ID documents and only ever accepting originals or certified copies. It's frighteningly easy to take someone's photo and pass it off as your own.

Simon is still rationalizing what's happened.

"What you have to consider is this: Would it really hurt you? More than—say—if someone used your name to open a bank account, or if they cloned your card?"

"It's creepier."

Simon reaches across the table and puts both his hands over mine. "Remember when Katie had that problem at school, with that gang of girls?" I nod, the mere mention of it filling me with fresh rage. When she was fifteen, Katie was bullied by three girls in her year. They set up an Instagram account in her name; posted photos of Katie's head Photoshopped onto various images. Naked women, naked men, cartoon characters. Infantile, puerile stuff that blew over before the end of the term, but Katie was devastated.

"What did you tell her?"

Sticks and stones, I'd said to Katie. *Ignore them. They're not touching you.*

"The way I see it," Simon says, "is that there are two possibilities. Either the photo was simply of someone who looks like you—although not nearly as beautiful"—I grin, despite the cheesiness of the compliment—"or it's ID theft, which—although irritating—isn't doing you any harm."

I can't argue with his logic. Then I remember Cathy Tanning. I produce her as though I'm playing a joker. "The woman I saw in the newspaper article—she had her keys stolen on the Tube." Simon waits for an explanation, his face registering confusion.

"It happened after her photo appeared in the advert. Like the photo of me." I correct myself. "The photo that looked like me."

"Coincidence! How many people do we know who have had their pockets picked on the Tube? It's happened to me. It happens every day, Zoe."

"I suppose so." I know what Simon's thinking. He wants evidence. He's a journalist; he deals in facts, not supposition and paranoia.

"Do you think the paper would investigate it?"

"Which paper?" He sees my face. "My paper? The *Telegraph*? Oh, Zoe, I don't think so."

"Why not?"

"It's not really a story, Zoe. I mean, I know you're worried by it, and it's a curious thing to happen, but it's not newsworthy, if you know what I mean. ID theft's a bit old hat, to be honest."

"You could pitch it, though, couldn't you? Find out who's behind it?"

"No." His abruptness marks an end to the conversation, and I wish I'd never brought it up. I've blown this whole thing up to be more than it is, and driven myself insane in the process. I eat a piece of garlic bread and pour more wine to replace the glass I hadn't noticed myself finishing. I wonder if I should do something about my anxiety levels. Mindfulness. Yoga. I'm becoming neurotic, and the last thing I want is for it to affect things between Simon and me.

"Did Katie tell you about her audition?" Simon says, and I'm grateful both for the change in subject and for the softness in his voice that tells me he doesn't hold my paranoia against me.

"She's been ignoring my texts. I said something stupid this morning." Simon raises an eyebrow but I don't elaborate.

"When did you speak to her?" I ask, trying not to sound bitter. I've only got myself to blame for Katie's silence.

"She texted me." I've made him feel awkward now, and I rush to reassure him.

"It's great that she wanted to tell you. Honestly, I think it's lovely." I mean it. Before Simon moved in, when things were already serious between us, I used to try to engineer occasions when he and the children would be together. I'd remember something I'd left upstairs, or go to the loo when I didn't need to, in the hope I'd come back and find them chatting happily together. It hurts me that Katie didn't text me, but I'm glad that she wanted to tell Simon. "What's the job?"

"I don't know much. The agency hasn't offered her representation, but she made a useful contact and it sounds like there's a part in the offing."

"That's great!" I want to get out my phone and text Katie, to tell her how proud I am, but I make myself wait. I'd rather congratulate her in person. Instead I tell Simon about Melissa's new café, and Neil's contract at the Houses of Parliament. By the time dessert comes we've ordered another bottle of wine, and I've got the giggles over Simon's stories of his time as a junior reporter.

Simon pays the bill, leaving a generous tip. He goes to hail a cab, but I stop him.

"Let's walk."

"It'll be less than a tenner."

"I'd like to."

We start walking, my arm tucked into Simon's. I don't care about the cost of a taxi ride home; I just want the evening to go on for a little longer. At the crossing he kisses me, and it turns into a kiss that makes us ignore the beep of the green man and have to press the button all over again.

My hangover wakes me at six. I go downstairs in search of water and an aspirin, and switch on *Sky News*, filling a glass from the tap and drinking greedily from it. When I've drained the glass I fill it and drink again, holding the side of the sink because I feel as though I'm swaying. I rarely drink during the week, and I'm reminded this is the reason why.

Katie's handbag is on the table. She was already in bed when Simon and I got home last night, both of us giggling at the irony of trying not to wake the kids as we crept upstairs. There's a piece of paper next to the kettle, folded in two and with *Mum* written on the front. I open it, my headache making me squint.

My first acting job! Can't wait to tell you all about it. Love you xxx

I smile, despite my hangover. She's forgiven me, and I resolve to be extra enthusiastic when she tells me about the job. No mention of secretarial college, or training to fall back on. I wonder what the gig is, whether it's extra work, or a real part. Theater, I suppose, although I allow myself a fantasy in which Katie has landed a job in TV; a part in some long-running soap that will make her a household name.

The *Sky News* reporter, Rachel Lovelock, is reporting a murder: a female victim from Muswell Hill. *Perhaps Katie could be a presenter*, I think. She's certainly got the looks. She wouldn't want to read the news, but a music channel, perhaps, or one of those magazine-style programs, like *Loose Women* or *The One Show*. I pour another glass of water and lean against the worktop as I watch the telly.

The image changes to an outside broadcast; Rachel Lovelock is replaced by a woman in a thick coat, talking earnestly into a microphone. As she carries on talking, a picture of the murder victim appears on the screen. Her name was Tania Beckett, and she doesn't look much older than Katie, although according to the report she was twenty-five. Her boyfriend raised the alarm when she didn't come home after work, and she was found in the park late last night, a hundred yards from where they lived.

Perhaps it's my hangover, or the fact I'm still half asleep, but I look at the photo on screen for a full minute before recognition kicks in. I take in the dark hair, the smiling face, the full figure. I see the necklace, with its gleaming silver crucifix.

And then I realize.

It's the woman from yesterday's advert.

How fast can you run?

When you really have to?

In heels and a work skirt, with your bag banging against your side: how fast?

When you're late for your train and you have to get home, and you race down the platform with seconds to spare: how fast can you run?

What if it isn't a train you're running for, but your life?

If you're home from work late, and there's no one in sight. If you haven't charged your phone and no one knows where you are. If the footsteps behind you are getting closer, and you know, because you do it every day, that you're on your own; that between the platform and the exit you won't see another soul.

If there's breath on your neck, and the panic is rising, and it's dark, and cold, and wet.

If it's just the two of you.

Just you, and whoever's behind you. Whoever is chasing you.

How fast could you run then?

It doesn't matter how fast.

Because there's always someone who can run faster.

CHAPTER EIGHT

There was a hand over Kelly's mouth. She could feel it pressing down on her face, could taste the sweat on the fingers slipping between her lips. A heavy weight shifted on top of her and a knee forced her legs apart. She tried to scream but the sound stayed in her throat, filling her chest with panic. She tried to remember her police training—the self-defense moves they'd been taught—but her mind was blank and her body frozen.

The hand slid away, but the reprieve was momentary. It was replaced by a mouth, a tongue forcing its way inside her.

She heard his breath—heavy, excited—and a rhythmic knocking.

"Kelly."

The knocking intensified.

"Kelly. Are you okay?"

The bedroom door opened and the weight moved from her chest. Kelly took a great gulp of air.

"You were having another one."

Kelly fought to get her breath under control. It was dark in her room, the shadow in the open doorway backlit by the light in the hall. "What time is it?"

"Half past two."

"God, I'm sorry. Did I wake you?"

"I'm just in off lates. You okay now?"

"Yes. Thank you."

The door closed and Kelly lay in the dark, sweat running between her breasts. It had been ten years since she had sat holding Lexi's hand, listening to her tell the police officer what had happened, then—later—watched her sister through a television screen as her statement was videoed. Watched her twin sister cry as she recounted every little detail; every humiliating, painful detail.

"I don't want Mum and Dad hearing all this," Lexi had said. Kelly had asked her once, years later, if she ever had nightmares. She'd said it casually, as though she'd only just thought about it. As though Kelly didn't wake with the weight of a man on her chest; with his fingers inside her.

"Once," Lexi had said. "A few days after it happened. But never again."

Kelly's pillow was drenched in sweat. She threw it onto the floor and rested her head on the sheet beneath. She was off work today. She'd go and see Lexi, maybe have supper with the boys. But first, there was something she had to do.

The *London Gazette*'s offices were in Shepherd's Bush, in a huge but unprepossessing building housing several other newspapers. Kelly showed her warrant card to the receptionist, then waited on an upright armchair far less comfortable than it looked. She ignored the knot of anxiety in her stomach: so she was working on an investigation in her spare time—it wasn't an offense to do unpaid overtime.

Even in her head it didn't sound convincing. Cathy Tanning's bag dip was no longer hers to investigate, and Kelly should have reported this new development to the sergeant on the Dip Squad as soon as it came in.

And she would, as soon as she had something concrete to report. But the Dip Squad was as strapped for resources as any other department. With nothing concrete to go on, Cathy's case might not be looked at for days. Someone had to make her a priority.

Three months before Lexi was attacked, she had gone to the police for advice. Someone had left flowers outside her room in student halls; there were notes in her pigeonhole that made reference to what she'd been wearing the previous evening.

"Sounds as though you've got yourself an admirer," the desk officer had said. It was making her feel uncomfortable, Lexi had told him. She was too scared to have the curtains open in her room, in case someone was watching.

When her personal belongings went missing from her room, they sent someone out. Recorded a burglary. Could Lexi be certain she'd locked the door? There was no sign of forced entry. What made Lexi think it was the same person who left the notes, the flowers? There was no evidence to suggest they were connected.

A week later, when she walked home from a late lecture and heard footsteps too measured, too close to be accidental, she didn't report it. What would be the point?

When it happened again, the following week, she knew she would have to go to the police. When the hairs on her arms prickled, and her breath caught in her throat from the fear that grew in her chest, she knew she wasn't imagining it. She was being stalked.

But it was too late. He'd already caught up with her.

Kelly thought of all the crime prevention initiatives she'd seen rolled out over her nine years in the job. Poster campaigns, leaflet drops, attack alarms, education programs . . . Yet it was far simpler than that; they just had to listen to victims. Believe them.

"Detective Constable Swift?" A woman was walking toward her, her head tilted to one side. Kelly didn't correct her. She was in plainclothes; DC was a fair enough assumption. "I'm Tamir Barron, I head up the advertising team here. Would you like to come on up?"

The walls of the sixth floor were lined with advertisements from the past hundred years, framed in thick oak. Kelly spotted adverts for Pears soap, Brylcreem, and Sunny Delight as Tamir swept her along the carpeted corridor to her office.

"I've got the results of the inquiry you sent through," she said, as soon as they were seated, "although I still don't see the connection to— what was it you said you were investigating? A robbery?"

There had been no violence, which meant the theft of Cathy's keys was a theft, not a robbery, but Kelly decided to gloss over that fact, in case the severity of the crime was directly proportionate to Tamir's level of cooperation. Besides, if Cathy was right and the offender had followed her home, and had since been using her key to gain access to her house, there was something far more serious going on. A shudder ran through Kelly at the thought of someone creeping around Cathy's house. What had he been doing? Touching her makeup? Taking her underwear? Cathy had said she thought someone had been in her house when she was at work, but what if that wasn't the only time? Kelly imagined an intruder moving quietly around Cathy's kitchen in the dead of night; creeping upstairs to stand by her bed and watch her sleep.

"The victim was on the Circle line at the time," Kelly told Tamir. "The offender made off with her house keys, and we believe he has since used them to gain access to her property. The victim's photograph appeared in the classifieds section of your newspaper two days prior to the incident." She hoped Cathy had now changed the lock on her back door. Would that be enough to make her feel safe? Kelly wasn't so sure.

"I see. There's just a small issue." Tamir was still smiling, but her eyes flicked down at her desk and she shifted slightly in her chair. "There's a certain amount of protocol that needs to be followed in the case of chatlines: companies have to be licensed, and when they advertise they have to provide the advertiser—us, in this case—with their license number. To be perfectly frank we don't go after chatline advertisers. You'll have seen the section is quite small. They're what I'd call a necessary evil."

"Why necessary?" Kelly said.

Tamir looked at her as though the answer was obvious. "They pay well. Most of that sort of advertising—sex lines, escorts, dating agencies, and so on—is all online nowadays, but our print readership is still high, and advertising is what pays for it all. As you can imagine, the sex industry is open to all kinds of abuse, so our measures make sure any chatline operators are properly licensed and therefore regulated." She looked down at her desk again.

"But these protocols weren't followed in this case?"

"I'm afraid not. The client first approached us at the end of September, with adverts to run daily throughout October. Shortly before the end of the month they submitted a second batch of adverts for November. The account was handled by a new member of staff, a man called Ben Clarke, and he processed the order without a license number."

"That's not allowed?"

"Absolutely not."

"Can I speak to Ben?"

"I'll get his details from HR. He left a couple of weeks ago—I'm afraid we have a rather high turnover of staff here."

"How did the client pay?" Kelly said.

Tamir consulted the notes written on her pad. "By credit card. We can let you have those details, and the address of the client, too, of course, but I'll need a data protection waiver from your side."

"Of course." Damn. Tamir Barron had agreed to see Kelly so readily, she had been holding out hope that the other woman would simply hand over the file. A data protection waiver would need an inspector's signature, which Kelly wouldn't be able to get without coming clean about her extracurricular investigations. "In the meantime, perhaps you could let me have copies of the adverts; both those you've run, and those waiting to run?" She held Tamir's gaze as confidently as she could.

"A data protection waiver—" she started.

"Is necessary for personal details such as addresses and credit cards. I quite understand. But there are no personal details in those adverts, are there? And we are talking about a potential crime series." Kelly's heart banged in her chest so loudly she was surprised Tamir couldn't hear it. Did she need a data protection waiver for the adverts, too? She couldn't remember, and she mentally crossed her fingers that Tamir wouldn't know, either.

"A series? Have there been other robberies?"

"I can't tell you anything else, I'm afraid." *Data protection*, Kelly wanted to add.

There was a pause.

"I'll get copies made of the adverts and have them sent down to reception. You can wait for them there."

"Thank you."

"Needless to say we've spoken to all our staff about the importance of adhering to procedure."

"Thank you. You'll cancel the remaining adverts, I presume?"

"Cancel them?"

"The adverts that haven't run yet. You can't put them in the paper. They could be facilitating crimes against women."

"I sympathize, DC Swift, but with the greatest respect, it's your job to protect the public, not mine. Our job is to print newspapers."

"Could you stop for a few days, though? Not cancel the adverts altogether, but . . ." Kelly trailed off, aware she sounded unprofessional. She needed concrete proof the adverts related to criminal activity. The link between Cathy Tanning's keys and her advert was clear, but Zoe Walker hadn't been a victim of crime. It wasn't enough.

"I'm afraid not. The client has paid in advance; I'll need to get permission from my boss before I can cancel the contract. Unless of course you have a court order?"

The expression on Tamir's face was neutral, but her eyes were hard and Kelly decided not to push it. She mirrored the other woman's polite smile.

"I don't have a court order, no. Not yet."

No sooner had Kelly pressed the doorbell than she heard the excited shrieks of her nephews, running to greet her. Five-year-old Alfie wore a Spider-Man outfit, teamed with a plastic Viking helmet, while his three-year-old brother, Fergus, ran toward her on podgy bare legs, his T-shirt sporting the Minion figures he adored.

"What's this?" Kelly said, feigning amazement as she looked at Fergus's lower half. "Big-boy pants?" The boy grinned and lifted his T-shirt to better show off his briefs.

"Early days," Lexi said as she appeared behind the boys. She scooped up Fergus and kissed Kelly in one fluid movement.

"Watch where you step."

Lexi and her husband, Stuart, lived in St. Albans, in an area teeming with yummy mummies and their strollers. After leaving Durham, Lexi had done a PGCE course, finding a job teaching history at the local secondary school. She'd met Stuart—the deputy head—there, and they'd been together ever since.

"Where's Stu?"

"Parents' evening. I did my lot yesterday, thankfully. Right, you two: pajamas. Go."

"But we want to play with Auntie Kelly!" Alfie moaned. Kelly dropped to her knees and gave him a squeeze.

"Tell you what: you two go and do your pj's and teeth double-quick, and then we'll have tickle time. Deal?"

"Deal!"

The boys ran upstairs and Kelly grinned. "It's a doddle, this parenting lark."

"You wouldn't say that if you'd been here about half an hour ago.

Meltdown central. Now, the boys have eaten, so I thought we could put them to bed then eat in peace once they're asleep; I've done a mushroom risotto for us."

"Sounds perfect." Kelly's phone beeped and she frowned at the screen.

"Something wrong?"

"Sorry, it's work. I just need to reply to this." She tapped out a message then looked up to see Lexi's disapproving face.

"You're welded to that thing. That's the problem with smartphones—it's like carrying your entire office in your pocket. You can't ever switch off." Lexi refused to buy an iPhone, extolling instead the virtues of her brick-sized Nokia that went three days without a charge.

"It's not a nine-to-five job. Not like you lot, with your three P.M. finishes and all summer off." Lexi didn't bite. Kelly read the incoming text message and fired off another reply. She'd been first on scene at a nasty fight on Liverpool Street concourse, tasked with gathering witness details once the troublemakers had been nicked. An elderly woman had been caught up in the skirmish, and Kelly had subsequently been in touch with her daughter, who had wanted to update her mum on the case.

"What she really wants is for me to tell her they're locked up," Kelly said, once she'd explained the situation to Lexi. "Her daughter says she's too frightened to go out in case she sees them again."

"And are they locked up?"

Kelly shook her head. "They're kids with no form. They'll get community service or a rap on the knuckles at best. They're no danger to her, but she doesn't see it like that."

"But surely it's not your job to counsel her and her daughter? Aren't there victim-support people for this sort of thing?"

Kelly made herself take a deep breath. "I don't tell you how to do your job, Lex . . ." she started, and her sister held up both hands.

"Okay, okay. I'll keep out of it. But please, for once can you switch off your phone and be my sister, not a cop?" She looked at Kelly, her eyes beseeching, and Kelly felt a stab of guilt.

"Sure." She was about to put her phone away when the screen flashed with Cathy Tanning's number. She looked at Lexi. "Sorry, it's—"

"Work. I get it."

She didn't, though, Kelly thought, as she walked into the living room to take Cathy's call. She never did.

CHAPTER
NINE

Cannon Street police station is just moments from where I work; I must have walked past it a thousand times or more and never noticed it. Never needed it. My headache hasn't shifted, despite the painkillers I took this morning, and there's an ache in my limbs that has nothing to do with a hangover. I'm coming down with something, and immediately I feel worse, not better, as though the acknowledgment alone gives the virus permission to settle.

My palms are clammy around the door handle, and I feel the irrational clutch of panic that law-abiding people feel when a police car drives past. Justin hasn't put a foot wrong in years, but I remember that first phone call from the police with painful clarity.

I don't know when Justin started stealing, but I do know that day he got nicked wasn't his first time. You take something small, the first time, don't you? A packet of sweets; a CD. You don't take twenty-five packets of razor blades when you're too young to shave. You don't wear a coat with the lining carefully cut at the top, so contraband can be dropped neatly inside. Justin wouldn't say a word about the others. Admitted the theft but wouldn't say who he was doing it for, what he'd have done with the razors. He got off with a caution, which he shrugged off as though it was a telling-off at school.

Matt was furious. "You'll have that on your record forever!"

"Five years," I said, trying to remember what I'd been told in custody. "Then it'll be spent and he'll only have to declare it if asked directly by an employer." Melissa already knew, of course, just like she knew about the fights he used to get into, and the worry he caused me when I found a bag of grass in his room.

"He's a kid," I remember her saying, after pouring me a much-needed glass of wine. "He'll grow out of it." And he did. Or he got better at not getting caught. Either way, the police haven't knocked on our door since he turned nineteen. I think of him now, wearing one of Melissa's smart aprons, making sandwiches and chatting to customers, and the image makes me smile.

The duty officer is sitting behind a glass barrier, like the type you see in the post office. He speaks through a gap big enough to pass through paperwork, or small bits of lost property.

"Can I help you?" he says, in such a way that suggests helping me is the last thing he wants to do. My brain feels fuzzy behind my headache, and I grapple for the words.

"I have some information about a murder."

The duty officer looks mildly interested. "Go on."

I push a newspaper cutting beneath the glass barrier. There's a piece of hardened chewing gum squashed into the corner, where the counter meets the wall, and someone has colored it in with blue pen. "This is a report in today's *London Gazette* about a murder in Muswell Hill."

He scans the opening paragraph, his lips moving slightly around the unspoken words. A radio crackles on the desk beside him. The details in the *Gazette* are scant. Tania Beckett was a teaching assistant at a primary school on Holloway Road. She took the Northern line from Archway to Highgate at around three thirty P.M., then the 43 bus to Cranley Gardens. *I was going to meet her off the bus*, her boyfriend is quoted as saying, *but it was raining and she said to stay inside. I'd do anything to turn back the clock.* There's a photo of him with his arm around Tania, and I can't help but wonder if we're looking into the eyes of a killer. That's what they say, isn't it? Most murder victims know their attacker.

I slide the second cutting under the barrier. "And this is an advert from yesterday's *Gazette*." White spots dance in front of my eyes, and I blink rapidly to clear them. I bring my fingers to my forehead and feel them still burning as I take them away.

The desk officer looks from one piece of paper to the other. He has the poker face of someone who's seen it all before, and I wonder if he's going to tell me I'm imagining the resemblance; that the dark-haired girl with the crucifix around her neck isn't twenty-five-year-old Tania Beckett.

But he doesn't tell me that. Instead he picks up the phone and presses zero; pauses and holds my gaze while he waits for the operator to pick up. Then, without taking his eyes off me, he says, "Could you put me through to DI Rampello, please?"

I text Graham to say I've come down with something and won't be coming back to work. I sip tepid water and wait for someone to come and speak to me, resting my head against the cool wall.

"I'm sorry," the desk officer says after an hour. He introduces himself as Derek, but it feels too familiar to use. "I don't know what's keeping him."

Him is Detective Inspector Nick Rampello, coming to Cannon Street from what Derek referred to as *MIT*, before apologizing for his use of jargon. "The Murder Investigation Team. That's the unit tasked with looking into this young lady's death."

I can't stop shaking. I keep staring at the two pictures of Tania and wondering what happened between her appearing in the *Gazette* and lying strangled in the park in Muswell Hill.

Wondering if it's my turn next.

It was my photo in the *Gazette* last Friday. I knew it the second I saw it; I should never have let myself be convinced otherwise. If I'd have gone to the police straightaway, maybe it would have made a difference.

There has to be a connection. Tania Beckett was killed the day her advert appeared; Cathy Tanning had her keys stolen forty-eight hours after hers. It's been four days since I saw my own photo; how long before something happens to me?

A man comes in to present his driving documents.

"Such a waste of time," he says loudly, as the desk officer methodically fills out a form. "Yours and mine." He glances at me, as if in hope of finding a sympathizer, but I don't respond and neither does Derek. He looks at the man's driving license and notes down details with a slowness I suspect might be deliberate. I decide I rather like Derek. When he has finished, the man slots the license into his wallet.

"Thank you so much," he says, in a voice thick with sarcasm. "This is exactly how I like to spend my lunch break."

He's replaced by a woman with a screaming toddler looking for directions, then an elderly man who has lost his wallet. "I had it at Bank," he says, "when I came out of the Tube. But somewhere between there and the river it . . ." He looks around as though it might materialize in the police station. ". . . vanished." I shut my eyes and wish I were here on such a mundane mission; that I could walk out with nothing more than mild irritation on my mind.

Derek takes the man's details, along with a description of the wallet, and I force myself to take deep breaths. I wish DI Rampello would hurry up.

The wallet man leaves, and another hour goes by, and finally Derek picks up the phone. "Are you on your way? Only she's been waiting since lunchtime." He glances at me, his face inscrutable. "Right. Sure. I'll tell her."

"He's not coming, is he?" I feel too ill to be cross at the wasted time. What would I have done instead? I wouldn't have gotten any work done.

"It seems he's been waylaid by some urgent inquiries. As you can imagine, the incident room is very busy. He asked me to pass on his apologies and said he'll be in touch. I'll give him your number." He narrows his eyes at me. "You don't look well, love."

"I'll be okay," I say, but it's far from the truth. I tell myself I'm not scared, just ill, but my hands are trembling as I find my phone and scroll through the contacts.

"Are you anywhere near Cannon Street? I don't feel well. I think I need to be at home."

"Stay where you are, Zo," Matt says, without hesitation. "I'll come and get you."

He tells me he's just around the corner, but half an hour passes and it's obvious that wasn't the case; I think guiltily of the fares he's missing out on while he makes a mercy dash for me. The door to the police station swings open, and to my embarrassment I feel tears rolling down my cheeks as I see his familiar face.

"You here for your missus?" Derek says. I don't have the energy to correct him and Matt doesn't bother. "Double-strength cold medicine and a drop of whisky, that's what she needs. Hope you feel better soon, love."

Matt settles me in the cab, like I'm a paying customer, and turns the heating up full blast. I focus on my breathing, trying to stop the violent shaking that seizes my entire body.

"When did you start feeling like this?"

"This morning. I thought it was odd I had a hangover—I didn't drink that much last night—then my headache got worse and I started feeling shaky."

"Flu." He diagnoses me without hesitation. Like most cabbies, Matt is an expert in everything. He watches me in the rearview mirror, his eyes flicking between me and the road ahead. "What were you doing at the cop shop?"

"There was a murder last night. In a park close to Cranley Gardens."

"Crouch End?"

"Yes. She was strangled." I tell him about the *London Gazette* adverts; about my own photo, then seeing Tania Beckett.

"Are you sure it's the same woman?"

I nod, although he has his eyes trained on the road ahead. He sucks his teeth, then spins the steering wheel decisively to the left, cutting through one-way streets so narrow I could reach through my window and touch the brick walls as we pass.

"Where are we going?"

"Traffic's a nightmare. What did the police say?"

I look out at the street, trying to get my bearings, but I'm not sure where we are. Children are walking home from school; some on their own, others still clutching their mothers' hands.

"They called the detective inspector in charge of the case, but he didn't come."

"Figures."

"I'm scared, Matt."

He doesn't say anything. He never was any good at handling emotions.

"If it really was my photo in the paper, then something's going to happen to me. Something bad." My throat feels scratchy; a hard lump preventing me from swallowing.

"Do the police think there's a link between the adverts and this murder?"

Finally we emerge from the warren of tiny streets, and I see the South Circular. We're nearly home. My eyes are stinging so badly it hurts to keep them open. I blink rapidly in an attempt to find some moisture.

"The desk officer seemed to take me seriously," I say. I'm finding it hard to concentrate on what he's saying. "But I don't know if the detective inspector will. I haven't told him about my photo yet—I didn't have a chance."

"This is weird shit, Zo."

"You don't have to tell me that. I thought I was going nuts when I saw the picture. I think Simon still thinks I am."

Matt looks at me sharply. "He doesn't believe you?"

I could kick myself. As if Matt needs any more ammunition against Simon.

"He thinks there's a rational explanation."

"What do you think?"

I don't answer. *I think I'm going to be murdered.*

We pull up outside my house and I open my handbag.

"Let me give you some money."

"You're all right."

"You shouldn't be out of pocket, Matt, it isn't fair—"

"I don't want your money, Zo," he snaps. "Put it away." His tone softens. "Here, I'll help you inside."

"I can manage." But as I stand up my knees start to buckle and he catches me before I fall.

"Sure you can."

He takes my key and opens the front door, then hesitates.

"It's okay," I say. "Simon's at work." I'm too ill to feel disloyal. I hang my handbag and coat over the banister and let Matt help me up the stairs. He pauses at the top, unsure where my bedroom is, and I point to the door next to Katie's. "I'll be fine now," I tell him, but he takes no notice, opening the door and keeping hold of my arm as we shuffle into the bedroom together.

He pulls down the duvet on the left side of the bed. The side I used to sleep on when we were married. Now it's Simon's things on the table to the left: his book, a spare pair of reading glasses, a leather tray for his watch and pocket change. If Matt notices he doesn't say anything.

I crawl into bed, fully clothed.

Simon wakes me. It's dark outside and he turns on the bedside light. "You've been asleep since I got home. Are you ill?" He's whispering, one hand clamped around my mobile phone. "There's a police officer on the phone. What's going on? Has something happened?" I'm hot and sticky, and when I lift my head from the pillow it aches. I reach for the phone but Simon holds it away. "Why are the police calling you?"

"I'll explain later." My voice disappears halfway through the last word and I cough to wake it up. Simon hands me my mobile and sits on the bed. I'm still feverish, but I feel better for having slept.

"Hello," I say. "This is Zoe Walker."

"Mrs. Walker, this is DI Rampello from the North West Murder Investigation Team. I understand you wanted to speak to me." He sounds distracted. Bored or tired. Or both.

"Yes," I say. "I'm at home now, if you'd like to come around." Simon opens his hands and mouths *What's happened?*

I shake my head at him, irritated by the interruption. The reception at home is bad and I don't want to miss what DI Rampello is saying.

". . . probably all I need for now."

"Sorry, what did you say?"

"You didn't know Tania Beckett, I understand?"

"No, but—"

"So you don't know if she was working as an escort, or running a sex chatline?"

"No."

"Okay." He's brisk; speaking fast as though I'm just one in a long list of calls he has to make tonight. "So Tania's photo appeared in a chatline advert in the *London Gazette* yesterday, Monday, 16 November. Is that right?"

"Yes."

"And you contacted us when you recognized her photo on the news this morning?"

"Yes."

"That's really helpful, thank you for your time."

"But don't you want to speak to me? Take a statement?"

"If we need anything else, we'll be in touch." He puts the phone down while I'm still talking. Simon now looks more cross than confused.

"Will you please tell me what's happened?"

"It's the girl," I say. "The one who was murdered. The picture I showed you this morning."

I ran upstairs this morning as soon as the news report finished, shaking Simon awake, my words falling over themselves.

"What if it's all to do with the adverts, Si?" I said, my voice cracking. "What if someone's putting in photos of women they're going to murder, and I'm next?"

Simon pulled me into an awkward hug. "Sweetheart, don't you think you might be overplaying this a bit? I read somewhere a hundred people are murdered in London every year. Every year! That's—what?—about eight a month. I know it's awful, but this has nothing to do with a free rag."

"I'm going to go to the police station at lunchtime," I told him. I could see he still thought I was being melodramatic.

"Did the police take you seriously?" he says now, sitting on the end of the bed. He squashes my toes and I pull my feet out of the way.

I shrug. "The man on the desk today was nice. But he called the detective inspector dealing with the case and he didn't come, and now he says they've got all they need from me and they'll call me if they want to speak to me again." Tears push their way out from the corners of my eyes. "But they don't know about the other photos; about Cathy Tanning's, about mine!" I start to cry, unable to think straight with my head pounding.

"Shhh." Simon strokes my hair and turns my pillow to find a cool bit for me to rest my cheek against. "Do you want me to call them back?"

"I haven't even got their number. He said it was the North West Murder Investigation Team."

"I'll find it. Let me get you some painkillers and a glass of water, then I'll give them a ring." He moves toward the door and turns, as though he's only just noticed something. "Why are you on my side of the bed?"

I press my face against the pillow so I don't have to meet his gaze. "I must have moved around in my sleep," I mumble.

It's the only thing we ever properly argue about.

"Matt is Katie and Justin's dad," I used to say. "You can't expect me not to see him from time to time."

Simon reluctantly conceded the point. "There's no reason for him to come in the house, though, is there? To sit in our living room; drink coffee from our mugs?"

It was childish and irrational, but I didn't want to lose Simon, and at the time it felt like a compromise.

"Okay," I agreed. "He won't come in the house."

When I open my eyes again there's a glass of water on my bedside table, next to a little foil packet of pills. I take two and get out of bed. My top is creased and my trousers are twisted: I get undressed and find a pair of thick cotton pajamas, wrapping myself in a big cardigan.

It's nine o'clock, and downstairs I find the remnants of what looks like beef casserole. My legs still feel wobbly, and my long sleep has left me drowsy. I go into the living room and find Simon, Justin, and Katie watching TV. No one's talking, but it's a comfortable silence, and I stand for a moment, watching my family. Katie sees me first.

"Mum! Are you feeling better?" She moves to make room on the sofa between her and Simon, and I sit down, exhausted by the effort of coming downstairs.

"Not really. I'm totally wiped out." I haven't felt this ill in years. My bones ache and my skin hurts to touch. There's a stinging sensation at the back of my eyes that only goes away when I close my lids, and my throat is so sore it's a struggle to talk. "I think I've got flu. Proper flu."

"Poor baby." Simon puts his arm around me, and for once Katie

doesn't say anything about what she calls "public displays of affection."
Even Justin looks concerned.

"Do you want a drink of something?" he says. *I must look really ill,*
I think.

"Just some water. Thank you."

"No worries." He stands up, then reaches into his pocket and hands
me an envelope.

"What's this?" I open it and find a thick bundle of twenty-pound
notes.

"Rent."

"What? We've been through this. I don't want rent from you, love."

"Well, food, bills—whatever. It's yours."

I turn to Simon, remembering how insistent he's been lately that
Justin shouldn't have a free ride. He shakes his head, as if to say it's got
nothing to do with him.

"That's really good of you, though, Justin. Well done, mate." The
colloquialism sounds forced on Simon's lips and Justin looks at him
scornfully.

"I thought you were broke?" Katie says, peering at the notes to
see how much is there. I put it in my cardigan pocket, trying to ignore
the voice inside my head that wants me to ask where it's from.

"Melissa's put me in charge of the café so she can set up the new
one," Justin says, as though he's read my mind. "It's only temporary,
but it comes with a pay rise."

"That's wonderful!" Relief that my son is neither stealing nor dealing makes my response disproportionately enthusiastic. Justin shrugs
as though the news is of no importance and goes into the kitchen for
my water. "I always knew he just needed a break," I whisper to Simon.
"Someone who could see what a hardworking lad he is."

I suddenly remember Justin isn't the only one with job news.

I turn to Katie. "I'm so sorry I wasn't more supportive before your
audition, love. I feel dreadful about it."

"Oh God, don't worry about that now, Mum. You're not well."

"Simon said it went brilliantly."

Katie beams. "It was amazing. So, the agent didn't take me on, because she already had a few on her books with my *look* and *range*—whatever that means—but I got chatting to a guy who was waiting in reception. He's the director of a theater company putting on a production of *Twelfth Night*, and their Viola has just had a skiing accident. I mean, *how* perfect?"

I stare at her, not following. Justin returns with a glass of water. He hasn't let the tap run, and it's cloudy and tepid, but I sip it gratefully. Anything to ease my sore throat.

"Mum, *Twelfth Night* was the text we did for GCSE English. I know it inside out. And he said I was *made* for Viola. I literally auditioned then and there—it was the maddest thing—and I got the part! The rest of the cast have been rehearsing for weeks, but I've got to nail it in a fortnight."

My head is spinning. "But who is this guy? Do you know anything about him?"

"He's called Isaac. Turns out his sister went to school with Sophia, so he's not a complete stranger. He's done stuff at Edinburgh, and—here's the exciting bit—they're going to take *Twelfth Night* on tour! He's incredibly ambitious, and so talented."

I spot something else in Katie's face. Something other than her excitement over an acting job. "Good-looking?"

She blushes. "Very."

"Oh, Katie!"

"What? Mum, it's all kosher, I promise. I think you'd like him."

"Good. You can invite him over."

Katie snorts. "I only met him yesterday, Mum. I'm not asking him to meet the 'rents."

"Well, you're not going on tour till you do, so . . ." We glare at each other, until Simon intervenes.

"Shall we talk about this when you're feeling better?"

"I'm feeling better now," I say, but my stubbornness is undermined by a wave of dizziness that makes me close my eyes.

"Sure you are. Come on, you: bed."

I remember his promise. "Did you call the police?"

"Yes. I spoke to someone senior on the investigation team."

"Rampello?"

"I think so. I said how worried you were about the advert—the one that looked a bit like you—"

"It *was* me."

"—and the guy I spoke to said he could totally see why you were anxious, but at the moment they don't think Tania Beckett's murder is linked to any other crimes."

"There has to be a link," I persist. "It can't be coincidence."

"You don't even know her," Justin says. "Why are you getting so wound up?"

"Because she's been murdered, Justin!" He doesn't react, and I look at Katie in despair. "And because my photo—"

"It wasn't your photo, sweetheart," Simon interrupts.

"—because my photo was in exactly the same advert as hers. So I think I've got every right to get wound up, don't you?"

"Those sorts of ads don't normally come with premium-rate numbers unless they're dodgy," Simon says.

"What's that got to do with anything?"

"Was she an escort?" Katie asks.

"Occupational hazard," Justin says. He shrugs and assumes his previous position on the sofa, phone in hand.

"They said on the news she was a teaching assistant, not an escort." I think of the photo they used in the paper, of Tania with her boyfriend. I imagine the headline above a report into my own murder and wonder what photo they'd put alongside it; whether they'd ask Graham Hallow for a quote.

"The advert didn't say anything about escort services, did it, Mum?" Katie says.

"It had a web address." I press my palm against my forehead, trying to remember. "FindTheOne.com."

"Sounds more like a dating site. Maybe she was killed by someone she met online."

"I don't want you going out on your own anymore," I tell Katie.

She stares at me, aghast. "Because of one murder on the other side of London? Mum, don't be ridiculous. People are murdered all the time."

"Men, yes. Boys in gangs. Druggies and stupid risk-takers. But not young women on their way home from work. You go out with a group of friends, or you don't go out at all."

Katie looks at Simon, but for once he backs me up.

"We want you to be safe, that's all."

"It's not practical. What about work? I don't finish at the restaurant on a Saturday night till ten thirty and now that I'm in *Twelfth Night* I'll be rehearsing most evenings. There's no alternative but to come home on my own." I go to speak but Katie interrupts me, gently but insistently. "I'm a big girl, Mum. I'm careful. You don't need to worry about me."

But I am worried. I'm worried for Katie, as she travels blindly home from work each night, her head in the clouds, thinking about red-carpet stardom. I'm worried for all the Cathy Tannings and Tania Becketts, who had no idea what life had in store for them. And I'm worried for me. I don't know what those adverts mean, or why my photograph appears in one, but the danger is very real. I can't see it, but I can feel it. And it's getting closer.

You never know where you might meet The One. Perhaps they always have the window seat on the train on your way in. It's possible you see them in front of you in the queue to buy coffee. Maybe you simply cross the road behind them every day. If you're sure of yourself, you might strike up a conversation. The weather, to begin with, and the state of the trains; but then, as time goes by, you'll exchange more personal snippets. Your hellish weekend; their slave-driver boss; the boyfriend who doesn't understand them. You'll get to know each other, and then one of you will take it to the next level. Coffee? Dinner? The deal is done.

But what if The One sits in the next carriage to you? What if they bring their coffee in from home; if they cycle to work; if they take the stairs instead of the escalator? Imagine what you're missing, by not bumping into them.

A first date; a second date; more.

Maybe it's not about The One; maybe you want something shorter. Sweeter. Something that'll get your blood pumping and your pulse racing.

A fling.

A one-night stand. A pursuit.

That's where it started. FindTheOne.com. A way of making introductions between London's commuters. A helping hand to bring people together. You could call me a broker; a go-between; a matchmaker.

And the beautiful thing is that none of you even know you're on my books.

CHAPTER TEN

stay in bed for twenty-four hours, sleeping more often than I'm awake. On Wednesday afternoon I struggle to the doctor, only to be told what I already know: I have the flu and there's nothing to do but drink water and take over-the-counter meds and wait for it to pass. Simon is amazing. He cooks for the children and brings me food I don't eat, going out for ice cream when I decide it's the only thing I could possibly swallow. He would have been a good expectant father, I think, remembering my pregnancy with Justin, when I sent a grumbling Matt out in the snow to find nachos and wine gums.

I manage to call work and tell Graham I'm ill. He's surprisingly sympathetic, until I tell him I'll be off for the rest of the week.

"Can't you at least come in tomorrow? Jo's off and there'll be no one to man the phone."

"I will if I can," I say. When morning comes I send him a text message, Sorry, still ill, then turn off my phone. It's lunchtime before I can face any food; Melissa brings me chicken soup from the café, and once I start eating I discover I'm ravenous.

"This is delicious." We're sitting in my kitchen, at the tiny table only big enough for two. "Sorry about the mess." The dishwasher needs unloading, which means everyone has ignored it and piled their breakfast dishes in the sink instead. A ring of empty packaging around the bin suggests that it, too, is full. The fridge is covered with family photos, held in place by the kitsch magnets it has become traditional to buy on holiday, as part of an ongoing challenge to find the cheesiest souvenir.

Currently in first place is Katie's nodding donkey magnet from Benidorm, its sombrero swaying every time someone opens the fridge door.

"It's homely," Melissa says, laughing when she sees my skeptical look. "I mean it. It's warm and full of love and memories—just the way a family house should be." I search her face for regret but find nothing.

Melissa was forty when we met—still young enough to have a family—and I asked her once if she and Neil were planning to have children.

"He can't." She corrected herself instantly. "That's not fair. I meant *we* can't."

"That must be hard." I'd been a mother for so long I couldn't imagine a life without children.

"Not really. I've always known, you see—Neil had leukemia as a child and the chemo left him infertile—so it was never part of our life together. We've done other things; had other opportunities." Work, I supposed. The business, holidays, a beautiful house.

"Neil found it harder than I did," she said. "He used to get very angry—*Why me?* That sort of thing—but nowadays we barely even think about it."

"Whereas I'd love a house like yours," I say now, "all clear surfaces and not a dirty sock in sight!"

She smiles. "The grass is always greener, isn't that what they say? Before too long, Katie and Justin will have moved out and you'll be rattling around in an empty house, wishing they were here."

"Maybe. Oh, that reminds me; what on earth have you done to my son?"

Melissa looks instantly worried, and I feel bad for trying to make a joke. I explain: "He presented me with money for rent on Tuesday. Without being asked for it. I gather you've promoted him."

"Oh, I see! He deserves it—he's doing a great job, and I need a manager. It's worked out perfectly."

There's still something troubling her. I hold her gaze till she breaks away, looking out of the window to our scrubby garden. Finally, she speaks.

"The pay rise." She glances at me. "It's cash-in-hand." I raise an eyebrow. I'm her friend, but I'm also her bookkeeper. I suspect she wouldn't have told me had I not mentioned Justin's pay rise.

"When customers pay in cash, it doesn't always go through the books. I keep a rainy-day fund. It covers the odd household bill without my needing to take a dividend from the business."

"I see." I should probably be wrestling with my conscience around about now, but the way I see it, she's not hurting anyone. She's not some global retailer, avoiding corporation tax with offshore accounts. She's just a local businesswoman, trying to make a living like the rest of us.

"It's not purely selfish, you know." I can see from Melissa's expression that she's regretting telling me; that she's worried I'm judging her. "It means Justin doesn't lose out to the taxman, either; he can start to put something aside."

I'm touched that she's even considered it. "So do I also have you to thank for him passing some of his pay rise on in rent?"

"We might have had a word or two . . ." She assumes an innocent face that makes me laugh.

"Well, thank you. It's good to see him finally growing up a bit. You're not worried about someone ratting you out to HMRC?" I add, my bookkeeper hat temporarily in place. It isn't just Melissa who should be worried. If she were to be caught, I'd be hauled in, too.

"You're the only one who knows."

"Knows what?" I grin. "I'd better get dressed—I must reek." I'm still wearing the jogging bottoms and T-shirt I slept in last night, and I'm suddenly conscious of the stale smell of sickness.

"I'm meeting Katie's new boyfriend-slash-director later—he's picking her up for rehearsal."

"Boyfriend?"

"Well, she hasn't called him that, but I know my daughter. She only met him on Monday, but I swear I haven't had a conversation with her since then without her mentioning his name. Isaac this, Isaac that. She's got it bad." I hear the creak of the stairs and I stop talking abruptly, just before Katie appears in the kitchen.

"Wow, check you out!" Melissa says, jumping up to give her a hug. Katie is wearing gray skinny jeans that look sprayed on, and a gold sequined sweatshirt that rides up as she puts her arms around Melissa.

"Is that your famous chicken soup? Is there any left?"

"Loads. So, I've been hearing about Isaac . . ." She emphasizes the vowels in his name, and Katie looks at me suspiciously. I say nothing.

"He's a great director," Katie says primly. We wait, but she won't be drawn.

"And dare I ask about the money?" Melissa says, ever the business-woman. "I know acting isn't the most lucrative of professions, but will it at least cover your outgoings?"

Katie's pause tells me everything I need to know.

"Oh, Katie, I thought this was an actual *job*!"

"It is a job. We'll get paid after the run, once the ticket revenue's in and the bills have been paid."

"So it's a profit-share?" Melissa says.

"Exactly."

"And what if there's no profit?" I say.

Katie rounds on me. "There you go again! Why don't you just tell me I'm shit, Mum? That no one will come and see it, and we'll all lose our money—" She stops, but it's too late.

"Lose what money? A profit-share I can understand—to a point—but please tell me you haven't actually *given* money to some bloke you've only just met!"

Melissa cuts in. "I think that's my cue to get going. Well done on getting the part, Katie." She throws me a stern look that means *Go easy on her*, and leaves us.

"What money, Katie?" I insist.

She puts a bowl of soup in the microwave and presses the reheat button. "We split the costs of rehearsal space, that's all. It's a cooperative."

"It's a rip-off."

"You know nothing about how theater works, Mum!"

We're both shouting now, so intent on making our points that we don't hear the key in the front door that means Simon is home early, as he has been every day this week, since I fell ill.

"You're feeling better, then?" he says, when I notice him leaning in the doorway, a look of resigned amusement on his face.

"A bit," I say sheepishly. Katie puts her soup on a tray, to eat in her room. "What time is Isaac picking you up?"

"Five. I'm not inviting him in if you're going to have a go about the profit-share."

"I won't, I promise. I just want to meet him."

"I bought something for you," Simon says. He hands her a plastic carrier bag with something small and hard inside. Katie puts down her tray to open it. It's an attack alarm—the sort that lets off an air-raid-type siren when you pull out the pin.

"They were selling them at the corner shop. I don't know if they're any good, but I thought you could carry it when you're walking home from the Tube."

"Thank you," I say. I know he's bought it for my peace of mind, really, rather than for Katie's. To make me feel better about her being out so late. I try to redeem myself for my earlier outburst. "When do tickets for *Twelfth Night* go on sale, love? Because we'll be in the front row, won't we, Simon?"

"Absolutely."

He means it, and not only because it's Katie. Simon likes classical music, and theater, and obscure jazz concerts in tucked-away places. He was amazed I'd never seen *The Mousetrap*; took me to see it and kept turning to look at me, to check I was enjoying it. It was okay, I suppose, but I preferred *Mamma Mia!*

"I'm not sure. I'll find out. Thank you." This, she directs at Simon, in whom I think she sees something of a kindred spirit. Last night he was testing her on her lines, the two of them breaking off to debate the imagery apparent in the text.

"You see how she personifies *Disguise*, and calls it a *Wickedness*?" Simon was saying.

"Yes! And even at the end no one's identity is really clear."

I caught Justin's eye, a rare conspiratorial moment between the two of us.

On our first date Simon told me he wanted to be a writer.

"But that's what you already do, isn't it?" I was confused. He'd introduced himself as a journalist when we met.

He shook his head dismissively. "That's not proper writing; it's just content. I want to write books."

"So do it."

"I will one day," he told me, "when I have time."

For Christmas that year I bought him a Moleskine notebook: thick creamy pages, bound in soft brown leather. "For your book," I said shyly. We'd been together for only a few weeks, and I'd spent days agonizing over what I could get him. He looked at me like I'd given him the moon.

"It wasn't the notebook," he told me, more than a year later, when he had moved in and was halfway through the first draft of his book. "It was the fact you believed in me."

Katie's jumpy. She's still wearing the skinny-jeans-and-sequined-sweatshirt outfit—somehow managing to look both casual and glamorous at the same time—but she's added dark red lipstick and a sweep of thick black eyeliner, curving up toward the outside of her eyebrows like wings.

"Fifteen minutes," she hisses at me, when the doorbell rings, "then we're going." Justin's still at the café, and Simon and I are in the living room, which I've hastily tidied up.

I hear low voices in the hall and wonder what Katie's telling her new boyfriend-slash-director. *Sorry about my mum*, probably. They come into the living room and Simon stands up. I can see immediately what Katie finds attractive. Isaac is tall, with smooth olive skin and jet-black hair, worn longer on top than underneath. His eyes are the darkest of brown, and the V-neck T-shirt under his leather jacket hints at a well-defined chest. In short, Isaac is gorgeous.

He's also at least thirty.

I realize my mouth has fallen open and I turn it into a "Hello."

"It's good to meet you, Mrs. Walker. You've got a very talented daughter."

"Mum thinks I should be a secretary."

I glare at Katie. "I suggested you do a secretarial course. As something to fall back on."

"Wise advice," Isaac says.

"You think?" Katie says incredulously.

"It's a tough industry, and cuts to Arts funding means it's only going to get tougher."

"Well, maybe I'll give it some more thought."

I turn my snort of surprise into a cough. Katie gives me a sharp look.

Isaac shakes hands with Simon, who offers him a beer. He declines, on the basis that he's driving, and I think that he at least has that in his favor. He and Katie sit on the sofa, a respectable distance between them, and I look for signs that, in the brief time since they met, they've become more than just director and actor. But there are no accidental-on-purpose touches, and I wonder if Katie's hero-worship is just a one-way crush. I hope she's not going to get hurt.

"I knew Katie was perfect for Viola the moment I saw her at the agency," Isaac was saying. "I sent a quick snap to the guy who plays Sebastian, to see what he thought."

"You took a picture of me? You never said! That was sneaky."

"On my phone. Anyway, he texted straight back to say you looked perfect. I'd already heard you speak—you were talking to the girl next to you, do you remember?—and I just had an instinct you were the Shakespearian leading lady I'd been looking for."

"All's well that ends well," Simon says with a grin.

"Very good!" Isaac says. They all laugh. Katie looks at her watch.

"We'd better get going."

"I'll drop her off after rehearsal, Mrs. Walker. I understand you're a bit worried about her taking the Tube late at night."

"That's very kind of you."

"Not at all. London isn't always the safest place for a woman on her own."

I don't like him.

Matt used to laugh at the snap decisions I made about people, but first impressions count for a lot. I watch Isaac and Katie through the living room window, walking a hundred yards down the road to where Isaac's managed to find a parking space. He puts a hand on the small of her back as they reach the car, then leans in to open the passenger door for her. I can't put my finger on what I don't like, but my senses are screaming at me.

Just a few days ago I resolved to be more supportive of Katie's acting; if I say anything about Isaac she'll see it as one more attack on her career choice. I can't win. At least she won't be coming home on her own tonight. I heard a report of a sexual assault on the radio this morning, and I couldn't help but wonder if the victim's photo had appeared in the classifieds first. Simon usually brings a *Gazette* home from work, but this week he's returned empty-handed; I know it's because he wants me to forget about the adverts. But I won't. I can't.

On Friday Simon comes with me to work. "Just in case you're still a bit wobbly," he says when we wake up. He holds my hand all the way there. On the District line I see an abandoned copy of the *Gazette*, and I resolutely ignore it, leaning into Simon with my face pressed against his shirt. I let go of the strap I am holding and instead put my arms around his waist, letting him balance us both as the train slows for each stop. We don't talk, but I can hear his heartbeat against my face. Strong and steady.

Outside Hallow & Reed he kisses me.

"I've made you late for work," I say.

"I don't care."

"You won't get into trouble?"

"Let me worry about that. Are you okay if I leave you now? I can hang around, if you like." He gestures to the coffee shop across the road, and I smile at the idea of Simon waiting all day for me, like a celebrity bodyguard.

"I'll be fine. I'll speak to you later."

We kiss again, and he waits until I'm safely installed at my desk before waving and walking away, toward the Tube.

As soon as Graham goes out on a viewing I close down the online listing I was updating and bring up Google. I type in *London crime* and click the first link I see: a website called London 24, promising up-to-the-minute information on crimes in the capital.

TEENAGER SHOT IN WEST DULWICH

**MAN FOUND CLOSE TO DEATH WITH MYSTERY
BURNS IN FINSBURY PARK**

This is why I don't read the papers. Not usually. I know all this is going on, but I don't want to think about it. I don't want to think about Justin and Katie living somewhere a knifing hardly raises an eyebrow.

EX–PREMIER LEAGUE PLAYER ADMITS
DRINK-DRIVING IN ISLINGTON

"SICKENING" ATTACK ON ENFIELD PENSIONER, 84

I wince at the photo of eighty-four-year-old Margaret Price, who headed out to collect her pension and never made it home. I search for Tania Beckett. One of the newspaper articles mentions a Facebook tribute site, and I click through to it. Tania Beckett RIP, it reads, and the page is filled with emotional messages from friends and family. In some of the messages Tania's name is highlighted, and I realize it's because people have tagged her Facebook page. Without thinking, I click on her name and take an involuntary breath when her page appears, full of status updates.

135 days to go! her last update reads, posted the morning she died.

One hundred thirty-five days till what?

The answer is a few updates down, in a post captioned: How about this one, girls? The photo is a screenshot from a mobile phone—I can see the battery life marked out at the top—a photo of a bridesmaid dress grabbed in a hurry from the Internet. There are three female names tagged.

Tania Beckett died 135 days before her wedding day.

I look at Tania's Friends list; thumbnails of identical girls, all blonde hair and white teeth. My attention is caught by an older woman with the same surname.

Alison Beckett's page is as open as Tania's, and I know straight-away that the photograph I'm looking at is of Tania's mother. Her last Facebook post was two days ago.

Heaven has gained another angel. RIP my beautiful girl. Sleep soundly.

I shut down Facebook, feeling like an intruder. I think about Alison and Tania Beckett. I imagine them planning the wedding together; shopping for dresses; making invitations. I see Alison at home, on that dark red sofa she's sitting on in her profile picture, picking up the phone, listening to the police officer talk but not taking it in. Not her daughter; not Tania. There's a pain in my chest and now I'm crying, only I don't know if I'm crying over a girl I never met, or because it's too easy to replace her name with my own daughter's.

My eyes fall on the card tucked into the clip on the edge of my bulletin board.

PC KELLY SWIFT, BRITISH TRANSPORT POLICE

At least she listened.

I blow my nose. Take a deep breath. Pick up the phone.

"PC Swift."

I hear the sound of traffic in the background, the fading siren of an ambulance. "This is Zoe Walker. The *London Gazette* adverts?"

"Yes, I remember. I haven't found out much more, I'm afraid, but—"

"I have," I cut in. "A woman from the adverts has been murdered. And no one seems to care about who might be next."

There's a pause, and then, "I do," PC Swift says firmly. "I care. Tell me everything you know."

CHAPTER ELEVEN

t was midday before Kelly was able to get back to the station and find a number for DI Nick Rampello, the detective inspector listed as senior investigating officer. She was directed first to the incident number, an all-purpose helpline set up for members of the public who had information to give about Tania Beckett's murder.

"If I can take some details, I'll make sure it's passed on to the investigating team," said a woman, whose disinterested tone suggested Kelly's was one of very many calls she had taken that day.

"I'd really like to speak to DI Rampello, if that's possible. I'm a police officer with British Transport Police and I think one of my cases might be connected with his investigation." Kelly crossed her fingers. It wasn't exactly a lie. Zoe Walker had come to her, and it was still Kelly's name on Cathy Tanning's crime report. Her name, her job.

"I'll put you through to the incident room."

The phone rang and rang. Kelly was about to give up when a woman picked up, slightly out of breath, as though she'd run up the stairs.

"North West MIT."

"Can I speak to DI Rampello, please?"

"I'll see if he's in the office. Who shall I say is calling?" The woman spoke like a BBC newsreader, and Kelly tried to guess what her role was. She had had little experience with Murder Investigation Teams; although BTP had its own, it was far less busy than the Met's, and Kelly had never worked there. She gave her name and shoulder number and waited on hold for the second time.

"Rampello speaking."

No BBC accent there. Nick Rampello's voice was pure London, and he spoke fast: businesslike to the point of abruptness. Kelly found herself stumbling over words in an effort to match his rapid delivery, aware she sounded at best unprofessional, at worst, incompetent.

"Where did you say you worked?" DI Rampello said, cutting into Kelly's explanation.

"BTP, sir. I'm currently based on Central line. I picked up a bag dip the week before last that I believe is linked to Tania Beckett's murder, and I hoped I could come and talk to you about it."

"With respect, PC . . ." An upward inflection turned her rank into a question.

"Swift. Kelly Swift."

"With respect, PC Swift, this is a murder investigation, not a bag snatch. Tania Beckett was nowhere near the Central line on the night she died, and everything points to this being an isolated incident."

"I believe they're connected, sir," Kelly said, far more confidently than she felt. She braced herself for Rampello's response and was relieved when he didn't pull her up for challenging him.

"Have you got a copy of the file there?"

"Yes, I—"

"Send it through to the incident room and we'll take a look." He was humoring her.

"Sir, I believe your victim appeared in an advert in the classifieds of the *London Gazette*. Is that correct?"

There was a pause.

"That information hasn't been released to the public. Where did you hear that?"

"From a witness who contacted me. The same witness who saw a photograph of my bag-dip victim in a different edition of the *Gazette*. The same witness who believes her own photo also appeared in the paper."

This time the silence was even longer.

"You'd better come in."

North West Murder Investigation Team was on Balfour Street, discreetly located between a recruitment agency and a block of apartments with a *For Sale* sign fixed to the third floor. Kelly pressed the buzzer, which simply read *MIT*, and turned slightly to her left so she could look directly at the camera. She lifted her chin a fraction, hoping she didn't look as nervous as she felt. DI Rampello had said he would see Kelly at six, which had just given her time to go home and get changed. What was it they said? Dress for the job you want. Kelly wanted DI Rampello to see her as a serious officer, someone with important information to give about his murder investigation, not as a uniformed beat cop. She pressed the buzzer again, regretting it when a voice instantly replied, an impatient tone suggesting they hadn't needed the prompt.

"Yes?"

"It's PC Kelly Swift, from British Transport Police. I'm here to see DI Rampello."

A loud click released the catch on the heavy door in front of her, and Kelly pushed her way inside, throwing a quick smile of thanks toward the camera, in case they were still watching. Lift doors lay immediately in front of her, but she took the stairs, unsure which floor MIT were on. The double doors at the top of the first flight gave no hint of what lay behind them, and Kelly hovered for a moment, debating whether to knock or simply to go on in.

"Are you looking for the incident room?"

Kelly recognized the BBC tones of whoever she had spoken to on the phone earlier that day, and she turned around to see a woman with long, straight blonde hair, pushed out of her eyes with a black velvet hairband. She wore tapered trousers and ballet flats, and she thrust her hand toward Kelly.

"Lucinda. I'm one of the analysts. You're Kelly, right?"

Kelly nodded gratefully. "I'm here to see the DI."

Lucinda pushed the door open. "The meeting's through here. Come on, I'll show you."

"Meeting?" Kelly followed Lucinda through the double doors, into a large open-plan office filled with around a dozen desks. On one side of the space was a separate office.

"That's the DCI's office. Not that he ever uses it. He's only five months off retirement and he's got so many rest days in lieu to use up he's practically part-time nowadays. He's all right, though, Diggers— when he's here."

Kelly's ears pricked up at the familiar nickname. "That's not Alan Digby, by any chance?"

Lucinda looked surprised. "The very same! How do you know him?"

"He was my DI in BTP. He transferred to the Met not long after, and I heard he'd been promoted. He was a good guv'nor."

Lucinda led the way through the open-plan office, and Kelly looked around, taking everything in. Even empty, the atmosphere had the buzzy feeling she knew so well from her own time working on serious crime investigations. Each desk had two computer screens, and at least three phones were ringing, the sound moving around the room as the calls transferred automatically, in search of a response. Somehow, even the phones here rang more insistently, as though they held the key to unlocking whatever mystery MIT was working on that week. This was what Kelly had joined the job to do, and a familiar surge of energy ran through her.

"They'll go to the answering service," Lucinda said, catching Kelly looking at the flashing phone nearest to them, "and someone will call them back."

"Where is everyone?"

"In briefing. The DI likes everyone to attend. He calls it the NASA theory."

Kelly looked blankly at her, and Lucinda grinned.

"So President Kennedy visits NASA and gets chatting to one of the cleaners. He asks him what his job is, and without missing a beat, the cleaner tells him, 'I'm helping to put a man on the moon, Mr. President.' Nick's theory is that if the whole Murder Investigation Team comes to briefings, including the cleaners, we can't miss anything."

"That's such a great approach. Is he nice to work for?" She followed Lucinda across the room, toward an open doorway.

"He's a good detective," Lucinda said. Kelly got the distinct impression the analyst had chosen her words carefully, but there was no time to push her for more information. They had reached the briefing room and Lucinda ushered her through the open door. "Boss, this is Kelly Swift, from BTP."

"Come on in; we're about to make a start."

Kelly felt her stomach rumble and wasn't sure if it was nerves or hunger. She stood at the back of the room with Lucinda and glanced around her, trying not to make it obvious she was doing so. DI Rampello hadn't said anything about a briefing; she had expected to speak to him in his office, perhaps with one of the inquiry team.

"Welcome, everyone. This is a briefing for Operation FURNISS. I know you've all had a long day, and some of you are far from finished, so I'll keep this as short as I can." The DI spoke as fast as he had done on the phone. It was a large room, and he wasn't making any discernible effort to raise his voice; Kelly had to listen intently to catch every word. She wondered why he didn't speak up, then she looked at the rest of the team, concentrating hard so as not to miss anything, and realized it was a deliberate—and clever—strategy.

"For the benefit of those of you new to the team, Tania Beckett's body was found in Cranley Gardens, Muswell Hill, four days ago; at eleven P.M. on Monday, 16 November by Geoffrey Skinner, a dog walker." Kelly wondered how old DI Rampello was. He looked to be in his early thirties; young to be an inspector. He was square and stocky, with a Mediterranean coloring to match his name, if not his estuary vowels. Five-o'clock shadow covered the lower half of his face, and Kelly could make out the shadow of a tattoo on his forearm, just visible through the fabric of his shirtsleeve.

As the DI spoke he paced from one side of the room to the other, one hand waving the notes to which he hadn't yet needed to refer. "Tania was a teaching assistant at St. Christopher's primary school, on Holloway. She was due home at four thirty P.M., and when she wasn't home by ten, her fiancé, David Parker, reported her missing. Uniform took a MISPER report and graded her as low risk." Kelly wasn't sure if she was imagining the trace of reproach in his voice, and hoped the shift officers who attended the original call weren't blaming themselves for what happened to Tania. From the little Kelly knew about the case it was unlikely her murder could have been prevented.

"Tania's body was found in a wooded section of the park, in an area known to be frequented for casual sex. Crime Scene Investigators found a number of used condoms with deterioration that suggests they predate the murder by several weeks. Tania was fully clothed except for her knickers, which weren't found at the scene and haven't yet been recovered. The strap of her bag had been used to strangle her, and the postmortem confirmed the cause of death as asphyxiation."

He looked around the room, his gaze resting on an older man who was leaning back in his chair, his hands interlocked behind his head. "Bob, can you fill everyone in on the fiancé?"

Bob unlaced his fingers and sat up. "Tania Beckett was engaged to a twenty-seven-year-old tire-fitter called David Parker, who was obviously our first port of call. Mr. Parker has a rock-solid alibi: he spent the evening in the Mason's Arms on the corner of his road, as confirmed by the pub's CCTV and at least a dozen regulars."

"His fiancée goes missing, and he goes to the pub?" someone said.

"Parker claims he wasn't worried until later that night, when he reported her missing. He assumed she'd gone to a friend's house and had forgotten to tell him."

"We're in the process of retracing the victim's route home from work," DI Rampello said. "BTP have been surprisingly helpful with the CCTV footage"—he glanced at Kelly and she felt herself blush; she'd thought he might have forgotten she was there—"so we have her taking the Northern line to Highgate. There's a bit of a gap in the footage, then we have her again, waiting for the bus. Unfortunately the bus driver can't confirm whether she got off at Cranley Gardens, or whether she was alone. We're in the process of tracing other passengers on the bus."

Nick Rampello's eyes rested momentarily on Kelly again. "On Tuesday, 17 November we received a call from a Mrs. Zoe Walker, reporting a close similarity between Tania Beckett and a photograph that appeared in a classifieds advert in the *London Gazette*." He picked up an A3 sheet of paper that had been lying facedown on the table in front of him, and held it up. Kelly saw the familiar advert; the image made fuzzy by the enlargement. "The boxed listing appears among several other adverts for a mixture of"—the DI paused—"personal services"—he allowed the ripple of laughter to subside before continuing—"including chatlines and escorting. This advert is ostensibly for similar services, although nothing is actually specified; the phone number listed is invalid, and the website apparently blank." He put the A3 sheet on the whiteboard behind him, plastic magnets at each corner to hold it up. "The inquiry team has begun looking into Tania Beckett's past for any involvement in the sex industry, even though her parents and fiancé insist it would be wildly out of character for her. We're also analyzing her computer for any indication she was registered on dating sites or was communicating with men she'd met online. So far, they've drawn a blank. This afternoon we received a further development." He looked at Kelly again. "Perhaps you'd like to introduce yourself?"

Kelly nodded and hoped she looked more confident than she felt. "Hello, everyone. Thanks for letting me join your briefing. My name is Kelly Swift and I'm a BTP officer on the Central Line Neighborhood Policing Team." Too late, she remembered she had given Nick Rampello the impression she was a detective on the Dip Squad. She caught the surprise on his face and looked away, focusing on the whiteboard on the other side of the room. "I spoke this morning to Zoe Walker, the witness DI Rampello has just mentioned, who first called me on Monday. She'd seen one of these adverts and recognized the woman; a victim from an ongoing BTP investigation."

"Another murder?" The question came from a slightly built, gray-haired man sitting by the window. Kelly shook her head.

"A theft. Cathy Tanning fell asleep on the Central line and had her house keys stolen from her handbag, which was on her lap."

"Just her keys?"

"It was thought at the time the offender might have been going for something else—a phone, or a wallet. The victim had to get a locksmith to break into her house, which meant she had to change the lock on the front door, but she didn't change the back-door lock. Her address wasn't on the keys and there was no reason to suppose the offender knew where she lived." Kelly paused, her heart racing. Even DI Rampello didn't know this latest piece of intelligence. "I spoke to Cathy Tanning on Monday and she's convinced someone has been in her house."

There was a shift in atmosphere in the room.

"A burglary?" asked the gray-haired man.

"Nothing of value has been taken, but Cathy's adamant the keys have been used, and that her dirty laundry's been disturbed. She's changed the locks and I've passed the job to SOCO in case they can get some forensics. Zoe Walker also believes her own photo appeared in a similar advert, exactly a week ago today."

"And is Zoe Walker a victim of crime?" Lucinda asked.

"Not yet."

"Thank you." The DI showed no sign that Kelly's additional news was of interest, and he moved swiftly on, taking back the focus of the room. Kelly felt suddenly flat. "We'll meet again at eight tomorrow morning, but let's go around the room. Anything to raise?" He looked to his left, moving swiftly around the room collecting updates and questions. As Lucinda had suggested, not a single person was left out. When everyone had been given the opportunity to speak, he gave a curt nod and picked up his notes. The briefing was over.

"I hope you haven't got plans tonight, Lucinda," he said, as he strode past the analyst. She laughed and shot Kelly a conspiratorial look.

"Good thing I'm married to the job, isn't it?" She followed the DI.

Kelly, not knowing whether she was expected to stay or go, went with Lucinda. She had assumed the DI would have his own office, but Nick Rampello's desk space was open-plan, like the rest of MIT. Only the DCI's office appeared to be separate, the door closed and no lights showing through the slatted blinds.

Nick gestured to Kelly to take a seat. "I need links between these two jobs," he said to Lucinda, who was already scribbling in a notebook. "Do they know each other? Are they chatline operatives? Escorts? What does Walker do for a living? Check out where Tanning works—is she a teacher like Beckett? Do her children go to Beckett's school?" Kelly listened, sensing that, even though she had the answers to some of the questions the DI was firing out, an interruption from her wouldn't be welcome.

She would speak to Lucinda afterward and give her as much information as she knew.

Nick continued. "See if any of them used dating sites. I had a call from Zoe Walker's partner; it's possible he found out she was using the site and now she's claiming she knows nothing about it."

"Sir, she wasn't using a dating site," Kelly said. "Zoe Walker was very agitated when she made contact with me."

"As she might be if, say, an aggressive partner discovered she was seeing other people," Nick countered. He turned to Lucinda.

"Get Bob to pull the original file from BTP and go over it; make sure everything was done properly, and do it again if it wasn't." Kelly narrowed her eyes. It was hardly a surprise to find a Met officer dismissing work done by another force, but he could at least have the decency not to do it in front of her.

"CCTV was secured immediately," she said, deliberately looking at Lucinda, and not the DI. "I can get you copies tomorrow, as well as stills of the offender. Given the original offense, I didn't consider it proportionate to request DNA at the time, but I'm assuming budget won't be a problem now. The bag has been correctly exhibited and retained by BTP, and I can arrange for your team to have access. Cathy Tanning has no children, she isn't a teacher, and she has never worked as an escort. Nor, just as pertinently, has Zoe Walker, whose photograph also appears in the *London Gazette*, and who is understandably rather concerned for her safety." Kelly took a breath.

"Have you finished?" Nick Rampello said. He didn't wait for an answer, turning instead to Lucinda. "Come back to me in an hour and let me know how you've got on."

Lucinda nodded, standing up and smiling to Kelly. "Nice to meet you."

The DI waited until Lucinda had returned to her desk before folding his arms and staring at Kelly. "Do you make a habit of undermining your senior officers?"

"No, sir." *Do you make a habit of rubbishing another officer's work?* she wanted to add.

The DI looked as though he was about to continue, but, perhaps remembering that Kelly wasn't his officer to reprimand, unfolded his arms and stood up. "Thanks for letting us know about the link between the jobs. I'll give your boss a call later and take ownership of the bag dip. May as well bring it under one roof, even if it isn't technically a series."

"Sir?" Kelly steeled herself. She knew the answer even without asking the question, but she couldn't leave MIT without trying.

"Yes?" Rampello was impatient, his mind already on the next thing on his list.

"I'd like to carry on working the Cathy Tanning job."

"Sorry, but that doesn't make sense." Perhaps seeing the disappointment in Kelly's face, he sighed. "Look, you identified the link between the two jobs. You were quite right to get in touch, and I really appreciate you coming to the briefing. You're off-duty, right?" Kelly nodded. "But the job needs to come to us. Any series will always be dealt with by the team dealing with the lead crime; in this case, that's

Tania Beckett's murder, which puts the series under MetPol's jurisdiction, not British Transport Police's. As I've already made clear, I'm reserving judgment on whether this is a series, but if it is, your bag-dip victim may have narrowly escaped being a murder victim. That's a job for MIT, not your Dip Squad."

It was unarguable.

"Could I work with you?" The words were out before she'd had a chance to sense-check them. "A temporary transfer, I mean. I investigated the Cathy Tanning job when it came in, and I can help with the Underground inquiries on your murder case—I know every inch of the Tube and you'll need hours of CCTV footage, right?"

Nick Rampello was polite but to the point. "We've got enough resources." He gave her a smile, which softened what came next. "Besides, I have a feeling working with you might be rather exhausting."

"I'm not inexperienced, sir. I spent four years on the Sexual Offenses Unit in BTP. I'm a good investigator."

"As a DC?" Kelly nodded. "Why are you back in uniform?" For a second Kelly thought about bending the truth. Claiming she'd wanted more operational experience, or she was working toward her sergeant's exam. But something told her Nick Rampello would see through her in a heartbeat.

"It's complicated."

Nick surveyed her for a moment and she held her breath, wondering if he was about to change his mind. But he dropped his gaze and opened his daybook, the action dismissing her even before he spoke.

"I'm afraid I don't do complicated."

CHAPTER
TWELVE

pull the gray blanket around my shoulders. It's wool, and looks nice draped across the sofa, but now it scratches my neck and makes me itch. The light makes a buzzing noise you can hear upstairs—yet another thing that needs fixing—and even though I know Simon and the kids are fast asleep I've left it switched off, the light from my iPad making the rest of the living room seem even darker than it really is. The wind is howling and somewhere a gate is banging. I tried to sleep, but every sound made me jump, and eventually I gave up and came downstairs.

Someone took my photo and put it in the classifieds.

That's the only solid fact I have, and it runs through my head on a loop.

Someone took my photo.

PC Swift believes it's my picture, too. She said she's looking into it, that she knows that sounds like a brush-off, but that she really is working on it. I wish I could trust her, but I don't share Simon's romanticized views of the boys and girls in blue. Life was tough when I was growing up, and around our way a police car was something to run away from, even if none of us really knew why we were running.

I tap on the screen in front of me. Tania Beckett's Facebook page has a link to a blog: a diary written by both Tania and her mother in the run-up to the wedding. Tania's posts are frequent and practical: Should we have miniature gin bottles for wedding favors, or personalized Love Hearts? White roses or yellow? There are only a handful of posts from Alison, each one laid out as a letter.

To my darling daughter,

Ten months till the big day! I can hardly believe it. I went into the loft today, to find my veil. I don't expect you to wear it—fashions change so much—but I thought you might like a tiny piece of it sewn into your hem. Something borrowed. I found the box with all your schoolbooks, birthday cards, artwork. You used to laugh at me for keeping everything, but you'll understand when you have children of your own. You, too, will stash away their first pair of shoes, so that one day you can climb into the loft in search of your wedding veil, and marvel at how your grown-up daughter ever had such tiny feet.

My vision blurs and I blink to clear the tears. It feels wrong to read on. I can't get Tania and her mum out of my head. I crept into Katie's room on my way downstairs, to reassure myself she was still there; still alive. There was no rehearsal last night—she did her Saturday-evening shift at the restaurant as usual—yet Isaac brought her home regardless. They walked past the living room window, then paused for the length of a kiss before I heard her key in the lock.

"You really like him, don't you?" I asked her. I expected her to brazen it out, but she looked at me with her eyes shining.

"I really do."

I paused, not wanting to spoil the moment, yet unable to keep quiet. "He's quite a bit older than you." Instantly her face hardened. The swiftness of her response made me realize she'd predicted my concern.

"He's thirty-one; that's a twelve-year age gap. Simon's fifty-four; that makes him fourteen years older than you."

"That's different."

"Why? Because you're an adult?" I felt momentary relief that she understood before I saw the flash of anger in her eyes, and the saccha-rine tone she'd just used was replaced with harshness.

"So am I, Mum."

She's had boyfriends before, but this feels different. I can already feel her slipping away from me. One day Isaac—or some other man—will be the first person she turns to; the one she leans on when life gets too much. Did Alison Beckett feel like that?

People keep reminding me that I'm not losing a daughter, she wrote in her last diary entry.

But she did.

I take a deep breath. I won't lose my daughter, and I won't let her lose me. I can't sit by and hope the police are taking this seriously; I have to do something.

Next to me on the sofa are the adverts. I've cut them out from the back pages of the *London Gazette*, carefully marking the date on each one. I have twenty-eight, spread out on the sofa cushion like an art instal-lation.

Photographic Quilt, by Zoe Walker. It's the sort of thing Simon would go to see at the Tate Modern.

I collected the most recent issues myself, picking up a paper every day, but the back issues I got from the *London Gazette* offices on Fri-day. You'd think you could walk in and ask for old copies, but of course it's not that simple. They screw you for £6.99 for each issue. I should have photocopied the copies I found in Graham's office at work, but by the time it occurred to me it was too late; they'd gone. Graham must already have put them out for recycling.

I hear a creak upstairs and freeze, but there's nothing else and I re-sume my search. *Women murdered in London* brings up mercifully few results, and none with photos that match the adverts beside me. I realize quickly that headlines are little help; Google Images are much more useful, and far faster. I spend an hour scrolling through photographs of police officers, crime scenes, sobbing parents, and shots of unsuspecting women, their lives cut short. None of them are mine.

Mine.

They've all become "mine," these women beside me. I wonder if any of them have seen their own photo; if they—like me—are frightened, thinking someone is watching them, following them.

A blonde woman catches my eye. She's sporting a mortarboard and gown, smiling at the camera, and I feel a glimmer of recognition. I look down at the adverts. They're all familiar to me now, and I know exactly which one I'm trying to find.

There.

Is it the same woman? I tap my screen and the image becomes a news page—from the *London Gazette*'s own website, ironically.

POLICE PROBE MURDER OF WOMAN FOUND
DEAD IN TURNHAM GREEN

West London. *District line*, I think, trying to picture the stops. The other side of London from where Tania Beckett was killed. Could they be connected? The woman's name is Laura Keen and there are three photos of her at the bottom of the article. Another in her graduation gown, standing between a couple who must be her parents. The second is less posed; she's laughing and raising a glass to the camera. *A student flat*, I think, noting the empty wine bottles in the background, and the patterned throw used as a makeshift curtain. Finally there's what looks like a work photo; she's wearing a collared shirt and jacket, and her hair is neatly tied back. I make the photo larger, then pick up the advert and hold it next to the screen.

It's her.

I don't let myself dwell on what this means. I bookmark the page and send the link by e-mail to myself at work so I can print out the article. I change my search term to *sexual assaults on women in London*, then realize it's a fruitless quest. The images that fill my screen are of men, not women, and when I tap to access the articles the victims are nameless; faceless. I find myself frustrated by the very anonymity that is there to protect them.

My attention is caught by a headline above a CCTV image:

POLICE HUNT FOR PERVERT WHO SEXUALLY ASSAULTED WOMAN ON EARLY-MORNING LONDON UNDERGROUND TRAIN

There is scant detail.

> *A 26-year-old woman was traveling on the District line from Fulham Broadway when a man inappropriately touched her. British Transport Police has released a CCTV image of a man they want to trace in connection with the incident.*

I look at the adverts. "Did this happen to one of you?" I say aloud. The CCTV still is absurdly bad: so blurry, and so fleeting it's impossible even to say what color hair the man has. His own mother would be hard-pushed to recognize him.

I bookmark the article, just in case, then stare at my screen. This is pointless. Like a game of Snap with half the cards missing. I turn off the iPad as I hear the unmistakable sound of footsteps on the stairs. I start to gather up the photos, but the action causes several to float onto the floor, and when Simon comes into the living room, rubbing his eyes, I'm still picking them up.

"I woke up and you weren't there. What are you doing?"

"I couldn't sleep."

Simon looks at the adverts in my hand.

"From the *London Gazette*." I start to lay them out again on the cushion beside me. "There's one every day."

"But what are you doing with them?"

"Trying to find out what's happened to the women in the adverts." I don't tell him the real reason I've bought so many back issues of the *Gazette*, because to say it out loud would be to acknowledge that it could actually happen. That one day I'll open a copy of the *Gazette*, and find Katie's face staring out at me.

"But you've been to the police—I thought they were looking into it? They've got intelligence systems; crime reports. If there's a series, they'll find the link."

"We know the link," I say. "It's these adverts." My tone is stubborn, but deep down I know Simon is right. My Nancy Drew approach is pathetic and pointless, costing me a night's sleep and gaining me little.

Except for Laura Keen, I remember.

I find her advert. "This girl," I say, handing it to Simon. "She's been murdered." I open the bookmarked link and pass the iPad to him. "It's her, isn't it?"

He's silent for a while, his face twisting into peculiar shapes as he weighs up his thoughts. "Do you think so? I suppose it could be. She's got that 'look,' though, hasn't she? The one they all have at the moment."

I know what he means. Laura's hair is long and blonde, strategically backcombed and teased into a tousled mane. Her brows are dark and carefully defined, and her skin looks flawless. She could be any one of a thousand girls in London. She could be Tania Beckett. She could be Katie. But I'm sure she's mine. I'm sure she's the one in the ad. Simon passes me the iPad.

"If you're worried, go to the police again," he says. "But right now, come to bed. It's three in the morning and you need rest. You're still getting over the flu." Reluctantly, I put the iPad in its case and gather up the adverts again, sliding them into the case as well. I'm tired, but my mind is racing.

It's getting light before I drop off, and when I wake around ten my head feels full and sluggish. My ears ring as though I've been somewhere noisy, lack of sleep making me stumble in the shower.

Our monthly Sunday roasts with Melissa and Neil have been a tradition ever since Katie, Justin, and I moved in, when Melissa invited us around for Sunday lunch. Our house was crammed with boxes—some from the house I'd rented after leaving Matt, others from storage, unseen for two years—and Melissa's clean, white house seemed enormous in comparison.

Ever since then we've alternated between Melissa and Neil's long glossy table, and my mahogany diner, bought at Bermondsey Market for next to nothing because one of the legs was wobbly. I used to sit the kids there to do homework, and at one end you can still see the marks Justin carved with a pen in protest.

Today it's my turn to host Sunday lunch, and I send Simon out for wine while I make a start on the veg. Katie nicks a piece of raw carrot and I slap her hand away. "Will you clear the table?"

"It's Justin's turn."

"Oh, you two, you're as bad as each other. You can both do it." I yell for Justin and hear a muffled reply I can't understand, shouted from his bedroom. "Lay the table," I shout. He comes downstairs, still in his pajama bottoms, his chest bare. "It's gone midday, Justin, don't tell me you've been asleep all morning?"

"Give me a break, Mum, I've been working all week."

I soften. Melissa's got him working long hours at the café, but he seems to be thriving on it. That's what a bit of responsibility does for you; although I suspect the cash backhanders might have sweetened the deal a bit.

My dining room isn't really a room at all, but an area separated from the living room by an archway. Lots of our neighbors have knocked through from the kitchen, or added an extension like Melissa and Neil, but we still have to carry food from the kitchen into the hall and through the living room; a fact to which the carpet bears testimony. The big Sunday lunch every other month is the only time it's worth it, and nowadays the only time the table gets cleared.

"Be careful with those files," I tell Justin, as I walk through with a bundle of cutlery and see him dump a stack of paperwork on the sideboard. Although the dining table looks a mess, I'm careful to keep everything in separate piles. There are Melissa's two sets of accounts, each with a stack of receipts and invoices; and the books for Hallow & Reed, with Graham's endless receipts for lunches and taxi fares. "You'll need the extra chair from Simon's room," I remind him.

He stops what he's doing and looks at me. "It's 'Simon's room' now, is it?"

Before Simon moved in we'd talked about Justin having the attic room as a sitting room. Somewhere he could have his PlayStation; maybe a sofa bed. He was getting too old to have his friends sitting on his single bed when they came around; he needed a more grown-up space.

"From the attic, then. You know what I mean."

I hadn't meant to give Simon the attic. Justin hadn't said much when I'd told the kids I wanted Simon to live with us, and naively I'd taken his silence as acceptance. It was only after Simon moved in that the arguments started. He didn't bring much furniture with him, but what he did have was good quality, and it seemed unfair to tell him there wasn't space for it. We stashed it in the attic while we worked out what to do with it. It occurred to me that giving Simon a space of his own would be a good thing; it would put some distance between him and Justin, and enable me and the kids to watch telly on our own from time to time.

"Just get the extra chair," I tell him.

Last night, after I'd staggered home from the shops with enough food to feed an army, Katie informed me that she wouldn't be here for lunch.

"But it's roast day!"

She'd never missed one. Neither had Justin, not even when the PlayStation and his mates held more appeal than family.

"I'm seeing Isaac."

It's happening, I thought. *She's leaving us.* "So invite him here."

"For a family meal?" Katie snorted. "No thanks, Mum."

"It won't be like that. Not with Melissa and Neil here. It'll be nice." She didn't look convinced. "I won't interrogate him, I promise."

"Fine," she said, picking up her mobile. "Although he won't want to come."

"Delicious beef, Mrs. Walker."

"Call me Zoe, please," I say, for the third time. *You're closer to my age than my daughter's*, I want to point out. Isaac is sitting between Katie and Melissa.

"A thorn between two roses," he said, when they sat down, and I wanted to stick two fingers in my throat and make gagging noises, like a fourteen-year-old. Surely Katie isn't taken in by this smarm? But she's gazing at him like he's just stepped off a catwalk.

"How are rehearsals going?" Melissa asks. I shoot her a grateful look. The presence of someone new has made the atmosphere stilted and artificial, and there are only so many times I can ask if everyone likes the gravy.

"Really well. I'm amazed at how well Katie's fit in, and how quickly she's got up to speed, given how late she joined us. We've got a dress rehearsal next Saturday. You should all come." He waves a fork around the table. "It's really useful to have a real audience."

"We'd love that," Simon says.

"Dad, too?" Katie asks Isaac. I sense, rather than see, Simon stiffen beside me.

"The more the merrier. Although you have to all promise not to heckle." He grins and everyone laughs politely. I'm dying for the meal to be over, and for Katie and Isaac to leave, so I can ask Melissa what she thinks of him. She's looking at him with a glint of amusement in her eyes, but I can't read her expression.

"How's the sleuthing going, Zoe?" Neil is fascinated by the photographs in the *Gazette*. Every time I see him he asks if there's any news; if the police have found anything out about the adverts.

"Sleuthing?"

I don't want to tell Isaac, but before I can change the subject, Katie is telling him everything. About the adverts, and my photograph, and Tania Beckett's murder. I'm unsettled by how animated she becomes, as though she's telling him about a film release or a new book, instead of real life. My life.

"And she's found another one, too. What's the new one called, Mum?"

"Laura Keen," I say quietly. I picture Laura's graduation photo and wonder where the original is. Whether it's on the desk of whichever journalist wrote the article, or whether it's back on the mantelpiece in her parents' house. Perhaps they've placed it glass-side down, for now, unable to handle seeing it every time they pass.

"Where do you think they got your picture?" Isaac asks, not picking up on my lack of enthusiasm to discuss it. I'm surprised at Katie for encouraging him and put it down to a desire to impress. Neil and Simon are eating in silence; Melissa shooting me sidelong glances every now and then, to check I'm okay.

"Who knows?" I'm trying to make light of it, but my fingers feel clumsy and my knife clatters against my plate. Simon pushes his empty plate away and leans back, reaching one arm out to rest on my chair. To anyone else he is just relaxing, replete after a big meal, but I can feel his thumb circling reassuringly on my shoulder.

"Facebook," Neil says, with a confidence that surprises me. "It's always Facebook. Most of the ID frauds nowadays use names and photos lifted from social media."

"The scourge of modern society," Simon says. "What was that firm you worked for a few months ago? The stockbrokers?"

Neil looks blank, then gives a short bark of laughter.

"Heatherton Alliance." He looks at Isaac, the only one who hasn't heard this story. "They brought me in to gather evidence relating to insider trading, but while I was there they had one of those initiation ceremonies for a new female banker. Real *Wolf of Wall Street* stuff. They had a Facebook group going—a private forum so they could decide what to do to her next."

"How awful," Isaac says, although his eyes don't match his tone. They're bright, interested. He catches me looking at him and reads my mind. "You think I'm being ghoulish. I'm sorry. It's the curse of the director, I'm afraid. Always imagining how a scene might play out, and that one—well, that would be truly extraordinary."

The conversation has sapped my appetite. I put down my knife and fork. "I hardly use Facebook. I only joined to stay in touch with family." My sister, Sarah, lives in New Zealand, with a tanned, athletic husband and two perfect children I've met only once. One's a lawyer and the other works with disabled children. It doesn't surprise me that Sarah's kids have turned out so well; she was always the golden girl when we were growing up. My parents never said it, but it was always in their eyes: why can't you be more like your sister?

Sarah was studious; helpful around the house. She didn't play her music loud or sleep till noon on the weekends. Sarah stayed on at school, left with good grades and a place at secretarial college. She didn't drop out, pregnant. Sometimes I wonder what would have happened if she had; if our parents would have been as hard on her as they were on me.

Pack your bags, my dad said, when he found out. Mum started crying, but whether it was because of the baby or because I was leaving, I couldn't tell.

"You'd be surprised what you can get from Facebook," Isaac says. He pulls his phone—a sleek iPhone 6s—from his pocket and swipes deftly across the screen. Everyone watches him, as though he's about to perform a magic trick. He flashes the screen toward me and I see the blue-and-white branding of Facebook. My name is written in the search field, and beneath it is row upon row of Zoe Walkers, each with a thumbnail photo. "Which one is you?" he says, scrolling through them. He taps through to the second page.

"There." I put my hand out to point. "That one, third from the bottom. The one with the cat." It's a picture of Biscuit sunning himself on the gravel at the front of the house. "You see," I say triumphantly, "I don't even use my own photo for my profile. I'm quite a private person, really." *Not like my kids*, I think, who let their whole lives play out on Instagram, or Snapchat, or whatever's the flavor of the month right now. Katie's forever taking selfies, pouting this way and that, then swiping through endless filters to find the most flattering.

Isaac opens my page. I don't know what I expected to see, but it wasn't my entire Facebook profile.

£50k a year and they think they've got the right to strike? I'd swap jobs with a train driver any day!

Stuck on a train . . . AGAIN. Thank heavens for wifi!

6??! Come on Len that was worth at least an 8!!

"*Strictly*," I explain, embarrassed to see my life reduced to one-liners about TV shows and hellish commutes. I'm alarmed by the ease with which he appears to have accessed my account. "How have you been able to log on as me?"

Isaac laughs. "I haven't. This is what anyone can see if they click on your profile." He catches sight of my horrified face. "Your privacy settings are wide open." To prove it, he clicks on the About Me tab, where my e-mail address is there for anyone to see. Studied at Peckham Comprehensive, it reads, as though that were something to be proud of. Worked at Tesco. I half expect it to say, Knocked up at seventeen.

"Oh God! I had no idea." I vaguely remember filling out these details: the jobs I've had, the films I like, and the books I've read, but I'd thought it was just for me; a sort of online diary.

"The point I'm trying to make," Isaac says, clicking once more, on a tab marked Photos of Zoe, "is if someone wanted to use a picture of you, there are plenty to choose from." He scrolls through dozens of images, most of which I've never seen before.

"But I haven't uploaded these!" I say. I see a photo of me from behind, taken at a barbecue at Melissa and Neil's last summer, and consider whether my bum is really that big, or if it's simply an unflattering angle.

"Your friends have. All these photos"—there must be dozens of them—"are ones other people have uploaded and tagged you in. You can untag yourself if you want, but what you really need to do is sort out your privacy settings. I can help you, if you want?"

"It's fine. I'll sort it out." Embarrassment is making me abrupt, and I make myself say thank you. "Has everyone finished? Katie, love, will you give me a hand clearing the table?" Everyone starts stacking plates and carrying dishes out to the kitchen, and Simon squeezes my hand before very obviously changing the subject.

When everyone has gone I sit in the kitchen with a cup of tea. Simon and Katie are watching some black-and-white movie, and Justin has gone out to see a mate. The house is quiet and I bring up Facebook on my phone, feeling as though I'm doing something wrong. I look at the photos, recognizing the album Isaac showed me on his own phone. I scroll through them slowly. Some of the photos aren't even of me, and eventually I understand I've been tagged in pictures of Katie, or old school photos from back in the day. Melissa's tagged me and a bunch of other people in a photo of her own legs, taken by the pool on a holiday last year.

Jealous, girls???!! reads the caption.

It takes me a while, but finally I find it. The photo from the advert. I let out a breath. I knew I wasn't going mad—I knew it was me. Facebook tells me the photo was posted by Matt, and when I check the date

I see it was three years ago. I follow the link and find twenty or thirty photos, uploaded en masse after my cousin's wedding. That's why I wasn't wearing my glasses.

This photo is really of Katie. She's sitting next to me at the table, smiling at the camera with her head tilted to one side. I'm watching her, rather than the camera. The picture in the advert has been carefully cropped, taking out most of the dress I'd have instantly recognized as one of my few party outfits.

I imagine someone—a stranger—scrolling through my photos, looking at me in my posh frock, at my daughter, my family. I shiver. The privacy settings Isaac mentioned aren't easy to locate, but eventually I find them. I systematically lock down every area of my account: photos, posts, tags. Just as I finish, a red notification blinks at the top of my screen. I tap on it.

> Isaac Gunn would like to be friends. You have one mutual friend.

I stare at it for a second, then press delete.

I know what you're thinking.

You're wondering how I can live with myself. How I can look at myself in the mirror, knowing what's happening to these women.

But do you blame Tinder when a date goes sour? Do you go to the wine bar where you picked up a guy, and have a go at the owner because things didn't go to plan? Do you shout at your best friend because the man she introduced you to turned out to like it rough?

Of course you don't.

Then how can you blame me? I'm just the matchmaker. My job is to give coincidence a head start.

You think you met by accident. You think he held that door open for you by chance; that he picked up your scarf in error; that he had no idea you were walking that way . . .

Maybe he did, maybe he didn't.

Now that you know people like me exist, you'll never know for sure.

CHAPTER
THIRTEEN

The adverts are consuming me; filling my head and making me paranoid. Last night I dreamed it was Katie's face in the classifieds. Katie's face in the *Times* a few days later; assaulted, raped, left for dead. I woke up drenched in sweat, unable to bear even Simon's arms around me until I'd crossed the landing and seen her with my own eyes, sleeping soundly.

I throw my usual ten-pence coin into Megan's guitar case.

"Have a great Monday!" she calls. I make myself smile back. The wind whips around the corner, and I'm amazed she's able to play with fingers that are blue with cold. I wonder what Simon would say if I brought her home for tea one day; whether Melissa might put aside a portion of soup for her from time to time. I hold a conversation in my head as I go through the ticket barriers, practicing the offer of a hot meal without making it sound like charity, worrying I might offend Megan.

I'm so caught up in my thoughts I don't instantly notice the man in the overcoat; I can't even be sure he was watching me before I saw him. But he's watching me now. I walk down the platform as the train arrives, but when I step onto the train and sit down I see him again. He's tall and broad, with thick gray hair and a beard to match. It's neatly trimmed, but there's a speckle of blood on his neck where he's cut himself shaving.

He's still looking at me, and I pretend to study the Tube map above his head, feeling his eyes travel down my body. It makes me uncomfortable, and I look down at my lap, feeling self-conscious and not knowing what to do with my hands. I guess him to be in his fifties; in a well-cut suit and an overcoat to beat the weather, which is threatening the first flurry of snow. His smile is too familiar—proprietary.

The schools must be out today: the trains are far less crowded than usual. At Canada Water enough people get off to leave three seats free opposite me. The man in the suit takes one of them. People do look at you on the Tube—I do it myself—but when you catch their eye, they look away, embarrassed. This man isn't looking away. When I look at his face—and I won't do so again—he holds my gaze challengingly, as though I should be flattered by the attention. I wonder, fleetingly, if I am, but the fluttering sensation in my stomach is anxiety, not excitement.

Transport for London have been running a video campaign. It's called *Report It to Stop It* and it's about sexual harassment on the Underground. *You can report anything that makes you uncomfortable*, it says. I imagine calling a police officer right now. What would I say? *He keeps looking at me . . .*

Looking at someone isn't a crime. At the back of my mind is the group of kids at Whitechapel—the lad in the trainers I was so convinced was running after me. Imagine if I'd have called the police then; if I'd have shouted for help. Despite the logic of this argument I can't shake the unsettled feeling.

It's not just him—this arrogant man taking possession of me with his eyes. It takes more than a man to make me anxious. It's everything. It's the thought of Cathy Tanning, asleep on the Tube while someone ransacks her bag. It's Tania Beckett, lying strangled in a park. It's Isaac Gunn, and the confident way he's pushed his way into Katie's life; into my house. I looked at his Facebook profile last night, after everyone left, and was disappointed to find it locked down so securely that all I could see was his profile picture. I stared at it, at the confident smile—showing even, white teeth—and the wavy black hair flopping nonchalantly over one eye. Film-star looks, undoubtedly, but making me shiver, not swoon; as though he'd already been cast in the role of the villain.

The man in the suit stands up to let a pregnant woman sit down. He's tall, and his hand slips easily through the strap hanging from the ceiling, the loop encircling his wrist as he grips it higher up, where it meets the ceiling of the carriage. He's not looking at me anymore, but he's barely six inches away from me and I pick up my bag from between my feet and hug it to me, thinking again of Cathy Tanning and her pickpocket. The man glances at his watch, then away, gazing without interest at something farther down the carriage. Someone else moves, and the man shifts slightly. His leg touches mine, firmly, and I jump as though I've been scalded. I move away, twisting awkwardly in my seat.

"Sorry," he says, looking straight at me.

"No problem," I hear myself say. But my heart is racing; blood humming in my ears as though I've been sprinting.

I stand up at Whitechapel. It's obvious I'm getting off, but the man doesn't move and I have to squeeze past him. For a second I'm pressed against him and I feel a touch on my thigh so light I can't be certain it was there at all. There are people all around me, I tell myself. Nothing can happen. But I almost trip in my haste to leave the train. I look behind me as the doors close, more confident with some distance between me and the man who was watching me.

He isn't on the train.

Perhaps he's sitting down, I think, gifted a seat by a passenger disembarking. But there's no one in the carriage with a beard. No one in a dark gray overcoat.

The platform is clearing; commuters rushing to get their next train, tourists looking for the exit, bumping into one another as they pay more attention to maps than their surroundings. I stand, rooted to the spot, as they jostle their way past.

And then I see him.

Standing as still as I am, on the platform about ten yards farther down, between me and the exit. Not watching me; looking at his phone. I fight to keep my breathing under control. I need to make a decision. If I walk past him and carry on with my journey, he might follow me. But if I hang back and let him go ahead, he might stay. The platform is practically empty; in a moment it will be just the two of us. I have to decide now.

I walk. Eyes forward. Walking quickly, not running. *Don't run. Don't let him see you're scared of him.* He's standing in the center of the platform, a bench behind him, which means I have to pass in front. As I grow near I sense his eyes on me.

Three feet away. Two.

One.

I can't help myself; I break into a run. I head for the exit, my handbag banging against my side, not caring what I look like. I half expect him to follow me, but when I reach the section of tunnel that will take me to the District line, I turn and see him still standing on the platform, watching me.

I try to concentrate on work, but my head won't comply. I find myself staring blankly at my screen, trying to remember the admin log-in for our accounts package. A man comes in to ask for details for office premises for lease and I end up giving him a sheaf of details for properties for sale instead. When he comes back to complain I burst into tears. He is politely sympathetic.

"It's not the end of the world," he says, when he finally has what he wants. He looks vaguely around for some tissues, relieved when I tell him I'm absolutely fine and would really rather be on my own.

I jump as the door opens and the bell above the frame jangles. Graham looks at me strangely.

"Are you all right?"

"Fine. Where have you been? There's nothing in the schedule."

"There's nothing in the *office* schedule," he corrects, taking off his coat and hanging it on the stand in the corner. "There's always something in *my* schedule." He smoothes his suit jacket over his belly. Today's waistcoat and jacket are green tweed, teamed with red trousers; the ensemble makes him look like a *Country Living* model gone to seed. "A coffee would be nice, Zoe. Have you seen the paper?"

I grit my teeth and head for the kitchen. On my return I find him in his office with his feet on the desk, reading the *Telegraph*. I don't know if it's the adrenaline from this morning, or my annoyance at being the only one at Hallow & Reed who seems to do any work, but I start speaking before I have a chance to filter my words.

"The *London Gazette*. You had a huge pile of them—twenty at least—in your office. What were they for?"

Graham ignores me, his raised eyebrows the only indication he's heard me.

"Where are they now?" I demand.

He swings his feet off the desk and sits upright, with a sigh that suggests my outburst is tedious, rather than offensive. "Pulped, I would imagine. Isn't that where the rest of the newspapers go? Destined for the loo-roll shelves at some budget supermarket."

"What were you doing with them, though?" It's been nagging at me; that small voice in my head reminding me of what I saw, of those newspapers stacked up on his desk. I remember the moment I saw Cathy Tanning's photo; the moment of recognition as I put a name to the face.

Graham sighs. "We're a property firm, Zoe. We sell and rent properties. Offices, shopping malls, industrial units. How do you think people hear about our properties?"

I assume it's a rhetorical question, but he waits expectantly. Not content with patronizing me, he's going to make a fool of me, too.

"In the newspaper," I say, and the words come out staccato, silent full stops between each one.

"In which newspaper?"

I clench my fists by my sides. "In the *Gazette*."

"And where do you think our competitors advertise?"

"Okay, you've made your point."

"Have I, Zoe? I'm a little concerned that you don't seem to know how this business works. Because if you're finding it hard to understand, I'm sure I could find another office manager with bookkeeping skills."

Checkmate.

"I do understand it, Graham."

His lips stretch into a smile. I can't afford to lose my job, and he knows it.

I buy a magazine on my way home from work, determined not to even pick up a copy of the *Gazette*. The station is rammed; winter coats making everyone seem twice their size. I push my way along the platform to my usual spot, the extra effort worth it for the time I will gain when I change for the Overground. Beneath my feet I feel the bumpy surface installed to help blind people; my shoes protrude just beyond the yellow line and I shuffle back as far as the swell of commuters will allow. I look at the cover of my magazine, filled with increasingly impossible headlines.

**MEET THE GRANDMOTHER WHO CHEATED
DEATH—THREE TIMES!**

I MARRIED MY SON'S WIFE!

MY TEN-MONTH-OLD BABY TRIED TO KILL ME!

I feel the rush of warm air on my face that tells me the train is seconds away. A deep rumble builds from within the tunnel and my hair blows across my face. I put up a hand to brush it aside, apologizing as my arm makes contact with the woman next to me. Another raft of commuters push their way onto the platform; the bodies around me move more tightly together. I take a single step forward, less by choice than by necessity.

The front of the train fills the tunnel and I roll up my magazine into my hand. I'm trying to slot it into my handbag when I lose my balance; falling fast toward the edge of the platform. I register a solid shape between my shoulder blades: an elbow, a briefcase, a hand. I feel the bumps beneath my feet as I trip forward; see the movement of dirt from beneath the tracks caused by the draft from the oncoming train. I feel a sensation of weightlessness, as my center of gravity tips forward, my feet no longer anchored firmly on the ground. I see, coming into sharp focus, the train driver, and I register the horror on his face. We're surely both thinking the same thing.

There's no way he can stop in time.

Someone screams. A man shouts. I squeeze my eyes tightly shut. There's a screech of metal on metal and a roaring in my ears. I feel a sharp pain as my shoulder is wrenched back and my body twists around.

"Are you okay?"

I open my eyes. There's a cluster of concern around me, but the train doors are open and commuters are in a hurry. They melt away, and the train completes its exchange of passengers and begins to move.

Again, more urgent this time. "Are you okay?"

The man in front of me has thick gray hair and a neatly trimmed beard. He is tall enough for me to see the speck of congealed blood to the left of his Adam's apple. I take an involuntarily step backward and he grabs hold of my arm.

"Steady—I'm not sure I can handle two rescues in one day."

"Rescue?" I'm trying to process what just happened.

"You're right, *rescue*'s probably an exaggeration." He gives a self-deprecating grin.

"It's you," I say stupidly. He looks at me blankly. "From the District line this morning."

"Oh." He smiles politely. "Right. I'm sorry, I don't . . ."

I'm caught off guard. I'd been so sure he was following me this morning. But he wasn't watching me. He doesn't even remember me.

"No, well, why would you?" Now I feel stupid. "I've made you miss the train. I'm sorry."

"There'll be another along in a minute." Since we've been talking the platform has filled up again with people jostling to be at the front of the queue, clusters forming at regular intervals down the line, behind commuters with inside knowledge of where the doors will open.

"As long as you're all right." He hesitates. "If you need support there are people who listen . . . The Samaritans, maybe."

I'm confused, then I realize what he's saying. "I wasn't trying to kill myself."

He isn't convinced. "Okay. Well, they're there to help. You know, if you need them."

Another burst of warm air; the rumble of an approaching train.

"I'd better . . ." He gestures vaguely toward the tracks.

"Of course. I'm sorry to have kept you. And thank you again. I'm going to walk, I think. Get some fresh air."

"It was a pleasure to meet you . . . ?" He closes with a question.

"Zoe. Zoe Walker."

"Luke Friedland." He offers a hand. I hesitate, then shake it. He steps onto the train; smiles politely as the doors close and the train pulls away. I see a flash of a smile before the carriage disappears into the tunnel.

I don't walk. I wait for the next train, taking care to stand well away from the edge of the platform. The thought that has been lurking at the corner of my mind finally takes shape.

Did I trip?

Or was I pushed?

CHAPTER FOURTEEN

DCI Digby hadn't changed much in the four years since Kelly had last seen him. A little grayer around the temples, perhaps, but still youthful for his age, with the sharp, perceptive eyes Kelly remembered so well. He wore a well-fitting suit with a pale gray pin-stripe, and shoes that shone to military standards too ingrained to ever be forgotten.

"Golf," he said, in response to Kelly's compliment. "Always swore I'd never spend my retirement on the golf course, but Barbara said it was that or a part-time job—she didn't want me under her feet all day. Turns out I rather enjoy it."

"How long have you got left?"

"I retire in April next year. I thought about staying on, but the way we've been shafted lately, I'm glad to be going, to be honest." He took off his glasses and rested his forearms on the table between them. "But you didn't call me out of the blue to find out my retirement plans. What's going on?"

"I'd like a temporary transfer to Operation FURNISS," Kelly said. The DCI didn't speak. He looked appraisingly at Kelly, who didn't flinch. Diggers had mentored Kelly when she had first joined the job, taking her on as a DC on the Sexual Offenses Unit, where he was the detective inspector.

Outstanding candidate, her board feedback read. *A tenacious and perceptive investigator, with high levels of victim care and clear potential for the next rank.*

"Sir, I know I messed up," she began.

"You assaulted a prisoner, Kelly. That's more than messing up. That's six months inside, on D wing with the narcs and the perverts."

Her stomach knotted: the ball of shame and anxiety that had followed her around for the past four years.

"I've changed, sir." She'd had counseling; six months of anger management classes that had served only to make her more angry. She'd passed with flying colors, of course; it was easy to give the right answers when you knew the game to play. The real answers would have been less palatable to the police-payroll therapist, who claimed not to judge but had visibly blanched when Kelly had answered the question *How did it feel to hit him?* with *It felt good.*

She'd kept the truth to herself from that point. Do you regret your actions? *Not in the slightest.* Could you have taken any other course of action? *None that would have given me such satisfaction.* Would you do it again?

Would she?

The jury was still out.

"I've been back for over three years now, boss," she told Diggers. She tried a small smile. "I've served my time." Diggers either didn't notice or didn't appreciate the joke. "I've recently finished a three-month attachment to the Dip Squad, and I'd like to get some experience of a Murder Investigation Team."

"What's wrong with doing that in your own force?"

"I think I'd learn a lot from working in a Met environment," Kelly said, the grounds for her request prepared in advance slipping easily off the tongue, "and I know you've got one of the strongest teams."

The corners of Diggers's mouth twitched, and Kelly knew she wasn't fooling him. She held up her hands.

"I've already asked the Murder Investigation Team at British Transport Police," she said quietly. "They won't touch me." She forced herself to maintain eye contact; not to show him how ashamed she was, how hard she found it that her own colleagues didn't trust her.

"I see." There was a pause. "It's not personal, you know."

Kelly nodded. It *felt* personal. Other uniformed officers were sec-onded to CID and MIT when extra resources were needed. Kelly never was.

"They're worried about no smoke without fire. They're worried about their own jobs, their own reputations." He paused, as though he was debating whether to say something. "And maybe they're just feel-ing guilty by association." He leaned forward, lowering his voice until Kelly could barely hear him. "Because there isn't a man or woman in this job who hasn't at least once wanted to do what you did."

Seconds passed before Diggers broke away, shifting position and bringing his voice back to a normal level. "Why this case? Why Tania Beckett?"

Here, Kelly was on firmer ground. "The case is linked to a theft on the Underground I picked up while I was working with the Dip Squad. I've got a relationship with the victim already; I'd like to see the job through. If it hadn't been for my input, the series wouldn't even have been identified yet."

"What do you mean by that?"

Kelly hesitated. She didn't know what the DCI's relationship was with Nick Rampello. She hadn't taken to the guy, but she wasn't about to rat out a colleague.

Diggers picked up his coffee, took a large and noisy swallow, then set his mug down on the table. "Kelly, if you've got something to say, spit it out. If this was entirely aboveboard you'd be speaking to me in my office, not ringing my mobile for the first time in four years and suggesting we have coffee in this"—he looked around the café, taking in the shabby counter and the peeling posters on the wall—"glamorous establishment." A tiny lift at the corner of his lips mitigated the harsh-ness of his words, and Kelly took a deep breath.

"A woman called Zoe Walker contacted me to say a photo of Cathy Tanning appeared in the classifieds of the *Gazette*, and that her own photo had appeared a few days previously."

"This I know. What's your point, Kelly?"

"It wasn't the first time she'd told the police about the two photos. Zoe Walker alerted MIT the day Tania Beckett's murder was reported." Kelly carefully avoided naming DI Rampello.

"The team responded to the information by investigating Tania for connections to the sex industry but failed to draw any inference from the fact Mrs. Walker's own photo had been used in a similar advert without her permission, with no link whatsoever to chatlines or dating agencies. They didn't accept we had a potential series; not until I insisted."

Diggers didn't speak, and Kelly hoped she hadn't overstepped the mark.

"They?" he said eventually.

"I don't know who Zoe Walker spoke to," she said, taking a sip of her own coffee so she didn't have to meet his eyes.

Diggers thought for a moment. "How long would you want?"

Kelly tried not to let her excitement show. "As long as it took."

"That could be months, Kelly. Years, even. Be realistic."

"Three months, then. I could add value, boss. I wouldn't be a deadweight. I can handle the BTP liaison, all the Underground work . . ."

"Will BTP release you for that long?"

Kelly could imagine how Sergeant Powell would react to such a request. "I don't know. I haven't asked. I hoped that with the right approach, at a senior level . . ." She trailed off, meeting Diggers's gaze.

"You're expecting me not only to authorize a placement for you, but to smooth the way with your own superintendent? Christ, Kelly, you don't do things by halves, do you?"

"I really want this, boss."

The DCI fixed his gaze on her so intently she had to drop her own. "Will you be able to handle it?"

"I know I can."

"I've got a good team up at Balfour Street. They're a close-knit bunch, but they're experienced detectives; they can all work on their own; they can all withstand the pressure of an intense investigation."

"I'm a good copper, boss."

"They can all handle emotionally difficult cases," he went on, and this time there was no ignoring the emphasis.

"It's not going to happen again. I give you my word."

Diggers drained his coffee. "Look, I can't promise anything, but I'll make some calls now and if BTP will release you, I'll take you on a three-month transfer."

"Thank you. I won't let you down, boss, I'll—"

"On two conditions."

"Anything."

"One: that you do not work alone." Kelly opened her mouth to argue that she didn't need a babysitter, but Diggers cut in again. "It's non-negotiable, Kelly. Yes, you're an experienced officer and a good detective, but if you join my team, you're on probation. Do you understand?"

She nodded. "What's the other condition?"

"The second you feel you're losing control—the second it happens—I want you out of there. I saved your neck once, Kelly. I won't do it again."

CHAPTER
FIFTEEN

"What do you make of Isaac?"

It's Tuesday lunchtime, and I'm meeting Melissa for a sandwich midway between Cannon Street and her new café in Clerkenwell, which is undergoing a refit in preparation for opening day. She's wearing skinny black cords and a black fitted shirt, and even with a faint coating of dust on her shoulders she manages to look stylish. Her hair has been swept out of the way with a large tortoiseshell clip.

"I liked him. I'm guessing you're not keen?"

I screw up my face. "There's something about him that puts me on edge." I pick at my BLT.

"You'd say that no matter who Katie was dating." She opens her baguette and peers at the contents. "How they can charge £3.50 for this, I don't know. There can't be more than a dozen prawns in it."

"I wouldn't." Would I? Maybe. I try to think back to the last boyfriend Katie brought home, but there's been no one serious; only a handful of awkward teens with clammy handshakes. "It's not just him, it's the whole setup. The idea of Katie—and the rest of the cast—working for nothing for weeks on end on the vague promise of some sort of profit-share once the ticket money comes in. It's exploitation, if you ask me."

"Or a brilliant business strategy."

"Whose side are you on?"

"No one's. I'm simply saying that, from his point of view—from

Isaac's—it's a good strategy. Limited outlay, minimal risk . . . If I went to my bank manager with that sort of strategy he'd be delighted." She grins, but there's an edge to it that's almost a grimace, and I think I know why.

"I take it your bank manager isn't a fan of your expansion plans?"

"I've got no idea."

"What do you mean? You haven't taken out a business loan?"

She shakes her head and takes another bite of her baguette. When she speaks it's as though I'm dragging the words out of her. "I've re-mortgaged the house."

"I bet that went down well with Neil." Melissa's husband is so averse to the idea of debt that he won't even open a tab for an evening's drinks. Melissa doesn't say anything.

"You have told him, haven't you?"

There's a pause, and Melissa's face changes. The confident, amused look disappears, and for a moment she is anxious and unguarded. The insight is oddly flattering, as though I've been allowed into a secret society. In the years we've known each other it's been rare that the tables are reversed; that I'm the one able to comfort her. I wonder how she was able to take out a loan against the house without Neil knowing—I'm assuming they have a joint mortgage—then decide the less I know, the better. There's no one savvier than Melissa, and if she's borrowing money to finance a new business, she's doing it because she knows it's a sure thing.

"Things aren't great between us at the moment," she says. "Neil lost a major contract earlier this year, and he's worried about money. The new café will make up for the lost business, but it'll take six months or so before it pays off."

"He'd understand that, surely?"

"It's impossible to talk to him at the moment. He's distant. Bad-tempered."

"He seemed on form at lunch on Sunday."

Melissa gives a humorless laugh. "Maybe it's just me, then."

"Don't be ridiculous—Neil adores you!"

She raises her eyebrows. "Not in the way Simon adores you." I blush. "It's true. Rubbing your feet, cooking you supper, escorting you to work . . . That man dotes on you."

I grin. I can't help myself.

"You're lucky."

"We both are," I say, then realize how bigheaded that sounds. "To have a second chance at happiness, I mean. Matt and I were together for so long we hardly noticed each other anymore." I'm thinking out loud; putting into words what I've never really worked through before. "He slept with that girl because he was so used to having me around, it seemed unimaginable that anything could ever change it."

"It was brave of you to leave. With the kids so young, I mean."

I shake my head. "Stupid. A knee-jerk reaction, fueled by anger. Matt didn't love the girl he slept with; I doubt he even liked her that much. It was a mistake. A symptom of a marriage we'd both taken for granted."

"You think you should have stayed?" Melissa asks for the bill, and waves away my attempts to get out my wallet. "My treat."

I'm careful with my response, not wanting to give her the wrong idea. "I don't think that now; I love Simon, and he loves me. I count my blessings every single day. But I threw away a good thing the day I left Matt, and I know the kids think the same."

"Katie and Simon get on well, though. They were thick as thieves over Sunday lunch, talking about *Twelfth Night*."

"Katie, yes, but as for Justin—" I stop, realizing I'm monopolizing the conversation. "I'm sorry, I've made this all about me. Have you tried talking to Neil about how you feel?" But the vulnerability I saw on Melissa's face has vanished.

"Oh, it's nothing. He'll get over it. Midlife crisis, probably." She grins. "Don't worry about Justin. It's completely natural; I loathed my stepfather for no other reason than he wasn't my dad."

"I guess so."

"And don't worry about Katie, either, with this Isaac chap. She's got her head screwed on, your daughter. Brains *and* beauty, that one."

"Brains, yes. So why can't she see that it would make sense to get a proper job? It's not as though I'm telling her to give up on her dream; I just want her to have some insurance."

"Because she's nineteen, Zoe."

I acknowledge her point with a wry smile. "I suggested to Simon he might be able to get her some work experience at his newspaper, doing theater reviews, but he wouldn't even entertain the idea. Apparently they only take graduates."

That had stung; that Katie's clutch of hard-won GCSEs wasn't enough even to work for free. "Can't you pull some strings?" I'd asked Simon, but he'd been immovable.

"She's an adult, Zoe," Melissa says. "Let her make her own decisions—she'll soon learn which ones were right." She holds open the door for me and we walk toward the Tube. "I might not have brought up a teenager, but I've employed enough of them to know that if you want to make them do something, you have to make them think it's their idea. They're a bit like men, in that respect."

I laugh. "Speaking of which, how's Justin getting on?"

"Best manager I've ever had." She sees the doubt in my face and loops her arm through mine. "And I'm not just saying that because you're my friend. He turns up on time, hasn't got his fingers in the till, and the customers seem to like him. That's good enough for me."

She gives me a hug before heading off on the Metropolitan line back to the café, and I feel so buoyed up by our lunch that the afternoon passes in no time at all, and even Graham Hallow's pomposity doesn't take the edge off my feelings of positivity.

"Hello again."

It's twenty to six, the Underground packed with people who would rather be anywhere but here. I can smell sweat, garlic, rain.

And I know that voice.

I recognize the confidence in it; the rich tones of someone used to being the center of attention.

Luke Friedland.

The man who saved me from falling onto the tracks.

Falling. Did I fall?

I have a fleeting, half-formed memory; the sensation of pressure between my shoulder blades. It all seems like a blur, and longer—far longer—than twenty-four hours ago.

Luke Friedland.

Yesterday I practically accused him of stalking me; today I'm the one stepping onto a train in which he's already standing. *You see?* I tell myself. *He can't have been following you.*

Despite my embarrassment, the back of my neck is prickling so badly I feel as though everyone must be able to see the hairs standing up. I run a hand across the nape of my neck.

"Bad day?" he says, perhaps mistaking my gesture for stress.

"No, good day, actually."

"That's great! I'm glad you're feeling better." He has the over-cheery tone of someone who works with children, or in a hospital, and I remember his suggestion yesterday that I might want to speak to the Samaritans. He thinks I'm suicidal. He thinks I tipped myself toward that train on purpose, as a cry for help, perhaps, or a genuine attempt to end my life.

"I didn't jump," I say. I'm speaking quietly—I don't want the whole carriage to hear—so he maneuvers his way past the woman in front, to stand next to me. My heart rate quickens. He puts his hand up to hold the rail above our heads and I feel the faint brush of tiny hairs, like an electric charge between us.

"It's okay," he says, and the disbelief in his voice makes me doubt my own story. What if I *did* jump? What if my subconscious propelled me toward the track, even as my brain sent messages saying the opposite to my body? I shiver.

"Well, this is my stop."

"Oh." We're at Crystal Palace. "Me, too." There's no shaving cut today, and the blue striped tie has been replaced by one in pale pink, standing out against the gray shirt and suit.

"You're not following me, are you?" he says, then apologizes when he sees my horrified face. "It was just a joke." We fall into step together, heading toward the escalators. It's hard to move away from someone walking in the same direction as you. At the ticket barrier he stands aside to let me tap my Oyster first. I thank him, then say good-bye, but we both turn the same way out of the station. He laughs.

"It's like at the supermarket," he says, "when you say hello to someone in the veg section then end up saying hello to them again in every single aisle."

"Do you live around here, then?" I've never seen him, although that's ridiculous; there are dozens of people on my street alone who I've never seen. I throw ten pence in Megan's guitar case and smile a hello as we pass.

"Just visiting a friend." He stops walking, and automatically I do the same. "I'm making you feel uncomfortable, aren't I? You go ahead."

"No, no, really, you're not," I say, although my chest feels as though someone's squeezing it.

"I'll cross the road, then you won't feel obliged to talk to me." He grins. He has a nice face; warm and open. I don't know why I feel so uneasy.

"There's no need, honestly."

"I need some cigarettes anyway." We stand still as people weave their way around us.

"Well, good-bye, then."

"'Bye." He opens his mouth to say something, then stops. I turn to walk away. "Um, would it be terribly forward of me to ask you to have dinner with me one evening?" The question is delivered in one breath, rushed as though he feels embarrassed asking, although his face still wears the same confident expression. It crosses my mind that the delivery is deliberate. Practiced, even.

"I can't, I'm sorry." I don't know why I'm apologizing.

"Or a drink? I mean, I don't want to play the 'I saved your life' card, but . . ." He holds up his hands in mock surrender, then lets them fall and assumes a more serious expression. "It's an odd way to meet, I know, but I'd really like to see you again."

"I'm seeing someone," I blurt out, like a sixteen-year-old. "We live together."

"Oh!" Confusion crosses his face, before he composes himself. "Of course you're with someone. Foolish of me; I should have expected that." He takes a step away from me.

"I'm sorry," I say again.

We say good-bye and when I glance back he is crossing the road toward the newsagents. To buy his cigarettes, I suppose.

I call Simon's mobile, not wanting to walk along Anerley Road without company, even if it's at the end of a phone. It rings but goes to voice mail. This morning he reminded me he was having dinner at his sister's tonight. I'd planned to watch a film; perhaps persuade Justin and Katie to join me. Just the three of us; like old times. But my encounter with Luke Friedland has left me unsettled, and I wonder if Simon would postpone his trip to see his sister; if he'd come home instead.

If I call now I might catch him before he leaves work. I used to have a direct line for him, but the paper moved to hot-desking a few months ago and now he never knows where he's going to be from one day to the next.

I Google the switchboard number. "Could you put me through to Simon Thornton, please?"

"I'll just put you on hold."

I listen to classical music until the line connects again. I look at the Christmas lights on the lampposts lining Anerley Road and see they're already coated with grime. The music stops. I expect to hear Simon's voice, but it's the girl from the switchboard.

"Could you give me the name again, please?"

"Simon Thornton. He's an editor. Mostly features, but sometimes he's on the news desk." I repeat the words I've heard Simon use, without knowing whether these two roles are in the same place or miles apart. Without knowing if they're in the same building, even.

"I'm sorry, I've got no one here of that name. Is he freelance? I wouldn't have him listed if he was freelance."

"No, he's on the payroll. He's been there for years. Could you check again? Simon Thornton."

"He's not on my system," she repeats. "There's no Simon Thornton working here."

CHAPTER
SIXTEEN

Kelly took out her chewing gum and dropped it into a trash can. Despite having left home early, she was in danger of being late if she loitered anymore, and that was hardly going to endear her to Nick Rampello. She took a deep breath, pushed up her chin, and walked briskly to the door she'd stood in front of on Friday, her umbrella doing little to protect her from the drizzle that seemed to be coming at her horizontally.

Wanting to make a good impression on her first day, Kelly had instinctively reached for her suit that morning, before feeling the coldness of an unwelcome memory. She had worn it for her disciplinary hearing; she could still feel the woolen cuffs scratching her wrists as she stood outside the chief's office, waiting to be called in.

The reminder had made her nauseous. She had taken the suit off the hanger and bundled it into a garbage bag to go to the charity shop, wearing instead her striped shirt with a pair of wide gray trousers that were now dark with rainwater where they met her shoes. Even without the sartorial prompt of the suit, Kelly was assaulted by memories, appearing in reverse order, like a film on rewind. Her return to shift; slinking into that first briefing with her cheeks ablaze, the echo of gossip reverberating in the air. Her months away from work; days on end in her room, unwashed and uncaring, waiting for a disciplinary hearing that could have ended her career. The sound of the alarm, signifying a crisis in custody; an urgent need for support. Running feet; not coming to back her up but to pull her off.

There were no images of the assault flashing in her head. There never had been. During her anger management classes Kelly had been encouraged to talk about the incident; to walk her counselor through what had happened, what had triggered it.

"I don't remember," she'd explained. One minute she'd been interviewing the prisoner; the next . . . the custody alarm. She didn't know what had caused her to lose control so horrifically; she had no memory of it.

"That's good, though, isn't it?" Lexi had said, when she'd come to visit Kelly after a particularly difficult anger management session. "It'll make it easier to move on from it. Forget it even happened."

Kelly had buried her face in her pillow. It wasn't easier to move on. It was harder. Because if she didn't know what had caused her to lose control, how could she be certain it wouldn't happen again?

She pressed the buzzer for MIT and waited, huddled inside the shallow doorway, out of the rain. A disembodied voice rang out onto the street.

"Hello?"

"It's Kelly Swift. I'm here on temporary transfer to Op FURNISS."

"Come on up, Kelly!"

Kelly recognized Lucinda's voice and her nerves abated a little. This was a clean slate, she reminded herself; a chance to start again, to prove herself without being judged on her past. She took the lift, walking into MIT without any of the hesitation of her previous visit. A nod of recognition from one of the team—Bob, she remembered, just too late to greet him by name—buoyed her mood, and when Lucinda bobbed up from behind her desk, Kelly was reassured further.

"Welcome to the madhouse."

"Thanks—I think. Is the DI around?"

"He went out for a run."

"In this weather?"

"That's the DI for you. He's expecting you, though; Diggers sent an e-mail around yesterday, letting us know."

Kelly tried to read Lucinda's expression. "How did it go down?"

"With Nick?" She laughed. "Oh, you know Nick. Well, I guess you don't. Look, the DI's great, but he's not good with authority. If it had been his idea to have a BTP officer on temporary assignment, he'd be all smiles. As it is, Diggers and he don't exactly see eye to eye, so . . ." Lucinda stopped. "It'll be fine. Now, let me show you where you'll be working."

At that moment the door opened and DI Rampello came in. He wore shorts and a Gore-Tex T-shirt; a lightweight fluorescent jacket zipped partway up his chest. He pulled his earphones out and balled them up, rolling them into a pair of Lycra gloves. Water dripped onto the floor.

"What's it like out?" Lucinda said casually.

"Lovely," Nick said. "Almost tropical." He headed for the locker rooms without acknowledging Kelly, who envied Lucinda her easy relationship with the DI.

She had switched on her computer and was looking for the piece of paper with the temporary log-in Lucinda had given her when Nick returned, a white shirt sticking to his still-damp back, and a rolled-up tie in one hand. He slung his jacket over the chair next to Kelly.

"I'm not sure whether to be pissed off that you went to the DCI after I'd already said no to this attachment, or to admire your negotiation skills. In the interest of working relationships, I'll go for the latter." He grinned and stuck out his free hand toward her. "Welcome on board."

"Thank you." Kelly felt herself relax.

"So you're an old friend of the DCI's, I hear?"

"Not a friend, no. He was my DI on the Sexual Offenses Unit."

"He thinks very highly of you. I understand you got a commendation."

Nick Rampello had done his homework. The chief constable's commendation had followed several months of painstaking work tracking down a man indecently exposing himself to schoolchildren. Kelly had taken scores of witness statements, working closely with the Intelligence unit to eliminate known sex offenders and other undesirables on the police radar. Eventually, Kelly had successfully bid to use decoys—a team of undercover surveillance officers deployed to high-risk areas to pose as potential victims—and caught the offender red-handed. She was flattered that Diggers had remembered, and touched that he had smoothed the waters with Nick by singing her praises. The feeling was short-lived.

"The DCI wants you working with someone else at all times." Nothing about his delivery suggested that Nick knew the reason behind Diggers's condition of Kelly's transfer, but she wasn't naive enough to think the two men hadn't discussed it. She felt her cheeks grow hot and hoped it wasn't obvious to Nick, and to Lucinda, who was listening with interest. "So you can work with me."

"With you?" Kelly had assumed she'd be paired with a DC. Was it Diggers who had decided the DI would need to keep an eye on her, or Nick himself? Was she really that much of a liability?

"You might as well learn from the best." Nick winked at her.

"Cocky bastard," Lucinda said. Nick shrugged in an "I can't help it if I'm brilliant" way, and Kelly couldn't help but smile. Lucinda was right; he was cocky, but at least he could laugh at himself.

"Have you sponsored me, Luce?" Nick said, and Kelly realized—not without some relief—that their conversation was over.

"I gave it to you weeks ago!"

"That was for the Great North Run. This is for the Great South Run." He looked at Lucinda, whose arms were crossed tightly across her chest. "Think of the children, Lucinda. Those little orphaned children . . ."

"Oh fine! Put me down for a fiver."

"Per mile?" Nick grinned. Lucinda gave him a stern look.

"Cheers. Right, I need an update. On the face of it there's nothing to link Tania Beckett and Cathy Tanning apart from the adverts, but I want to know if we're missing something."

"Put the kettle on and break open that secret stash of Hobnobs, and I'll fill you in at briefing."

"What secret stash?" Nick began, but Lucinda gave him a withering stare.

"I'm an analyst, Inspector." She raised an eyebrow as she stressed his rank. "You can't hide anything from me."

She returned to her desk, and Kelly risked a smile. "If you point me in the direction of the kitchen, I'll make the tea."

Nick Rampello looked at her appraisingly. "You'll go far. Out in the lobby, second door on the right."

By the end of Kelly's first day she was intimately acquainted with the kettle. Between rounds of tea-and-coffee making she had read through the case papers and at five P.M. she headed to the incident room with Nick and Lucinda, and a smattering of people to whom she had been introduced and whose names she had instantly forgotten. Several free chairs littered the briefing room, but most people were standing, their restlessness a not particularly subtle message that they had more important things to be getting on with. Nick Rampello was having none of it.

"Grab a pew and settle in," he instructed. "I won't keep you long, but we're dealing with a complex investigation and I want us all on the same page." He looked around the room, waiting until all eyes were on him, before continuing. "It's Tuesday, 24 November and this is a briefing for Operation FURNISS, an investigation into the murder of Tania Beckett, and into related crimes committed against women, namely theft of keys and a suspected burglary of a woman called Cathy Tanning. The link between these crimes relates to adverts placed in the *London Gazette* featuring the women's photographs." Nick looked for Lucinda. "Over to you."

Lucinda moved to the front of the room. "I was tasked with looking at murders from the last four weeks, but I've also done some work around sexual assaults, harassments, and burglaries where the victims were lone females. For the purposes of this exercise I discounted domestics, but even so, there are quite a few." As she was speaking, she inserted a USB drive into the laptop at the front of the room, the connected projector ready and waiting. The first slide showed thumbnail images Kelly recognized as the women from the *London Gazette* adverts, the results taken from the file Tamir Barron had reluctantly given to Kelly on her visit to their offices. Lucinda clicked through the next four slides, another dizzying mosaic of thumbnails.

"These women have all been victims of relevant crime during the last month. You'll see I grouped them according to physical characteristics. Skin color, then hair color, then subcategories according to their approximate age. Obviously it's not an exact science, but it made the next bit slightly easier."

"Pairing them up with the adverts?" The guess came from somewhere behind Kelly.

"Precisely. I've identified four matches, digging deeper into the case files to cross-reference the advert image against other victim photos." Lucinda moved the PowerPoint on, briskly summarizing each slide in turn. "Charlotte Harris. A twenty-six-year-old legal secretary from Luton who works in Moorgate. Attempted sexual assault by an unidentified Asian man." To the left of the slide was a photo labeled with the victim's name; to the right, the corresponding *London Gazette* advert.

"Snap," Nick said grimly.

"Emma Davies. Thirty-four-year-old female, sexually assaulted in West Kensington."

Kelly let out a slow breath.

"Laura Keen. Twenty-one. Murdered in Turnham Green last week."

"That one's already on our radar," Nick interrupted. "West MIT flagged it as a possible link to Tania Beckett because of her age."

"Not just possible," Lucinda said. "I'd pin it as a dead cert, if you'll excuse the pun. Right, last one." She flicked to the next slide, which showed a dark-haired woman in her forties. As with the other women, her photo had been laid out next to a copy of her advert in the *Gazette*. "This is an odd one. Ongoing complaints from a Mrs. Alexandra Chatham near Hampstead Heath that someone is breaking into her house when she's asleep and moving things around. It's sitting with the Safer Neighborhood Team at the moment, but there's been a bit of a question mark over it from the start. Apparently the attending officer wasn't convinced anything had ever happened, even though Mrs. Chatham is adamant someone is coming into her house."

Lucinda surveyed her board. "Then, of course, we have Cathy Tanning—another victim of a possible midnight prowler—and Tania Beckett, our murder victim. Six. So far. I'm still working on it."

There was silence in the briefing room, as Nick allowed the significance of Lucinda's update to sink in, then he pointed to Lucinda's closing slide, on which the six confirmed cases were listed next to their relevant advert. "In total, fifty-five adverts have run so far, which means there are forty-nine women yet to identify, who may or may not have been victims of crime. Copies of these adverts are here"—Nick indicated a second whiteboard—"as well as in your briefing pack."

There was a shuffling of paper as everyone immediately began looking through the stapled document they'd been handed on arrival, while Lucinda continued to talk. "I'm still working on matching the adverts that have run with crimes against women carried out in our force area, and I'm also in touch with Surrey, Thames Valley, Herts, Essex, and Kent, in case there's anything cross-border that might fit. I've found a couple of possibles, but I'd like to wait till I'm certain before muddying the waters with those, if that's all right, boss?"

"That's fine."

"You asked me to do some work on the similarities between the victims, and between the crimes committed. I haven't got a lot for you, I'm afraid. At first glance the crimes are very different, but when you strip out the obvious—the offense itself, the primary MO—the common thread is public transport: all these women were on their way to, or from, work."

Nick nodded. "I want all their journeys mapped. Let's see if there's any crossover."

"Already on it, boss."

"What do we know about the offender?"

"*Offenders*," Lucinda said, stressing the plural. "Charlotte Harris describes a tall Asian man with a distinctive aftershave. She didn't see his face, but he was smartly dressed, in a pinstripe suit and gray overcoat. Emma Davies, who was sexually assaulted in West Ken, described her assailant as white and significantly overweight. We've got very little on the Turnham Green job, but one of the CCTV images shows a tall white man in the vicinity immediately prior to Laura Keen's murder."

"Cathy Tanning's keys weren't taken by a Caucasian man," Kelly said. "The CCTV doesn't show his face, but the skin on his hands is clearly visible."

"Six crimes," Nick said, "and potentially six different offenders. It doesn't take a genius to work out that the adverts are a key part of this investigation; our focus will therefore be on identifying who is placing them." He moved to stand at the front of the room, and Lucinda clicked onto the next slide, which showed an enlarged version of Zoe Walker's advert.

"The adverts have been running since the beginning of October. They appear in the classifieds, on the second-to-last page, and all in the bottom right-hand corner. None of the photos have been professionally taken."

"Zoe Walker rang me yesterday," Kelly said. "Turns out her photo was taken from Facebook—she sent me the uncropped version. It's a picture of her and her daughter, Katie, taken at a wedding a few years ago."

"I'll check out Tanning's and Beckett's Facebook pages again,"

Lucinda said, preempting Nick. "There are similarities between all of the photos, in that none of the women are looking directly at the camera." *As though they didn't know they were being photographed*, Kelly thought.

Nick carried on: "Every advert carries this web address." He pointed to the top of the screen, where *www.FindTheOne.com* was written.

"A dating agency?" The woman next to Kelly had been taking copious notes in a spiral-bound notebook. She looked at Nick, her pen poised. A detective on the other side of the room was looking at his phone, glancing up at the screen to double-check the URL.

"Possibly. None of the victims recognize the name. Cathy Tanning was a member of Elite for a while, and we're in touch with them to see if their systems have been compromised. Tania Beckett's fiancé unsurprisingly insists she's never been near a dating site, and Zoe Walker says the same. As some of you have no doubt already discovered, the web address takes you to an empty page, black except for a box asking for a password. Cyber Crime have taken on this aspect of the investigation and I'll keep you updated on their findings. Okay, I'm conscious of time. Let's move on."

"The phone number," Lucinda said. She turned to the whiteboard behind her and underlined a number, written in large red letters: **0809 4 733 968**. "No trace on our intel systems, and an invalid number, which makes its inclusion on the advert—unless it's an error—rather pointless."

Nothing was pointless. That number was there for a reason. Kelly stared at the enlarged *London Gazette* advert on the screen behind Lucinda. There was a line of text beneath the photo.

> Visit the website for more information. Subject to availability. Conditions apply.

The website, yes, but then what? What was the password? Nick had moved to stand next to Lucinda, issuing actions and impressing upon the team the importance of keeping him updated. Kelly stared at the adverts, wondering what they were missing.

"At this stage of the investigation we've got lots of information coming in, with no clear understanding of how it's linked," Nick was saying. "Whoever put these adverts in the *Gazette* is either announcing their intention to commit a crime, or facilitating the commission of crimes by other offenders."

Kelly was only half listening, her mind twisting itself into knots. What was the point of an advert without a call to action? Why send potential customers to a website without giving them the means of accessing the site?

0809 4 733 968

She sat up, jolted by a sudden thought. What if the phone number wasn't a phone number at all, but a password?

She made sure her phone was switched to "silent," opened Safari, and typed in the domain name.

FindTheOne.com

The cursor blinked at her. She typed 0809 4 733 968 into the white box and pressed enter.

Your password has not been recognized.

Kelly suppressed a sigh. She'd been so certain the phone number was the key. Just as she closed down Safari a text message flashed onto the screen.

Looking 4wrd 2 cing u 2nite. Call + let me no if u will b L8.xx

The abbreviated words and the combinations of letters with numbers would have told her the text was from Lexi, even without her seeing her sister's name. Kelly didn't know anyone else who still wrote texts as though it were the nineties. She imagined her sister frowning over the tiny screen, patiently holding down each key on her ancient Nokia to cycle through the letters.

0809 4 733 968

A thought began to take shape, and she brought up the keypad on her phone. She looked at the number four; at the letters beneath it.

G. H. I.

Reaching one-handed for her notebook, she flipped it open randomly, flicking the lid off her pen and writing down the letters without taking her eyes off her phone.

There were four letters beneath number seven: P, Q, R, S. Kelly wrote them all down.

Up next, two number threes: the letters D, E, and F.

Kelly scribbled furiously, the briefing forgotten as she worked her way through to the last number. She picked up her notebook and scoured the numbers, looking for a pattern, a word.

I.

A space.

S. E. E . . .

I SEE YOU.

Kelly took a sharp intake of breath. She glanced up to see DI Rampello looking at her, his arms folded.

"Do you have an update on the investigation you'd like to share with us?"

"Yes, sir," Kelly said. "I think I do."

The first match I witnessed was hardly a matter for the police.

There was a girl on the Bakerloo line. Every Friday she'd get off at Piccadilly Circus and buy a lottery ticket for the EuroMillions.

"These are the winning numbers," she said to the man behind the counter, as she handed him the money.

He laughed. "You said that last week."

"This time I'm sure of it."

"You said that, too."

They both laughed, then, and I knew this was a conversation they had every Friday, at exactly this time.

The following Friday I watched her get off the train at Piccadilly Circus and make her way to the newsagent.

He was waiting for her.

Standing five meters or so from the kiosk, pumping his fists by his sides like he was psyching himself up for a job interview. Expensive suit; nice shoes. A man with more money than time. He stopped when he saw her; wiped his damp palms against his trouser leg. I expected him to speak to her, but instead he fell into step with her, walking toward the kiosk and reaching it a fraction before her. He's lost his nerve, I thought.

"A lucky dip for tonight's EuroMillions, please," he said. He paid for it and took the ticket. "These are the winning numbers, you know." The girl behind him smiled to herself.

He made a show of putting his wallet away, waiting to one side so he could interrupt as the girl asked for a lucky dip of her own. "I think I jumped ahead of you in the queue. I'm so sorry."

"It's fine, really."

"But what if you were meant to have this ticket?" He handed it to her. "Take it. I insist."

She protested, but not for long. They smiled at each other.

"You can buy me dinner if you win," he joked.

"What if I don't win?"

"Then I'll buy you dinner."

You can't deny you'd have enjoyed that encounter. You might have blushed at his approach; perhaps even found it a little forward. But you'd have been flattered; grateful for the attention from a good-looking man. Someone rich. Successful. Someone you might not otherwise have met.

Now that you know what I do, you're intrigued, aren't you? You're wondering what information I've collected about you; what's listed on my ever-growing website. You're wondering if you'll be stopped, like this girl, by an attractive stranger. You're wondering if he'll ask you out for dinner.

Maybe he will, maybe he won't. Maybe he's already found you; already been watching you. Maybe he's been following you for weeks.

Life's a lottery.

He might have something entirely different in mind for you.

CHAPTER SEVENTEEN

Listed: Friday, 13 November

White.

Late thirties.

Blonde hair, usually tied up.

Glasses (may wear contact lenses).

Flat shoes, black trousers with fitted top. Red three-quarter-length waterproof coat.

Size 12–14

0810: Enters Crystal Palace Tube station. Speaks briefly to street musician, and throws coin in guitar case. Takes the Overground northbound to Whitechapel. Changes to District line (westbound), boarding carriage 5, to arrive opposite exit at Cannon Street. Turns right out of station and walks on road to avoid crowded section of pavement. Carries phone in right hand, and handbag across chest. Works at Hallow & Reed estate agent, Walbrook Street.

Availability: Monday to Friday

Duration: 50 minutes

Difficulty level: Moderate

"We have to tell her." Kelly looked in horror at the screen, on which was listed in precise detail what could only be Zoe Walker's commute to work.

"Is it definitely her?" Lucinda asked. Kelly and Nick were leaning over the DI's desk, his laptop open in front of them. The lights were off elsewhere in the large, open-plan space, and the yellow strip light above Nick's desk was flickering slightly, as though the bulb were about to go. Lucinda was working at a neighboring desk, painstakingly checking each image on the website against the *London Gazette* adverts.

"The description matches, the date of the listing fits, and Hallow and Reed is where she works," Kelly said. "There's no doubt it's her. Should we tell her over the phone, or go and see her?"

"Wait." Nick hadn't said much when Kelly had explained how she'd worked out the password. He'd taken one look at her phone; the small screen showing a change to the text above the white box.

Log in or create an account.

He had dispatched the rest of the team home, with strict instructions to return at eight A.M. the following day for another briefing. "Tomorrow's going to be a long day," he'd said grimly.

It had taken them just seconds to fire up Nick's computer and access the website. Far longer to try to get through to Finance; a process that, out of hours, was so frustrating that Nick eventually slammed down the phone and took out his own credit card from his wallet.

"We can't let the media get hold of this," he said now. "It would cause a riot. That means keeping it from Zoe Walker for the time being."

Kelly took a second to compose a more appropriate response than the one that threatened to burst from her lips. "Sir, she's in danger. Surely we have a duty of care to warn her?"

"At the moment the situation is contained. The person—or persons—responsible for this website doesn't know the police are involved, which means we have a chance of identifying them. If we show this to Zoe Walker she'll tell her family, her friends."

"So we ask her not to."

"It's human nature, Kelly. She'll want to make sure other women she knows are safe. Before we know it, the papers will pick up on it and there'll be widespread panic. Our offender'll go underground and we'll never find him."

Kelly didn't trust herself to speak. Zoe Walker wasn't cannon fodder.

"We'll see her tomorrow and suggest she changes her route to work," Nick said. "We can give her the standard advice for anyone concerned about their personal safety: mix it up a little, don't be predictable. She doesn't need to know any more than that." He closed the laptop, sending a clear message to Kelly that the conversation was over. "You two can head off now, if you like. I'll see you bright and early tomorrow morning." Just as he finished talking, the bell for the outside door sounded. Kelly went to answer it.

"It'll be the Cyber Crime guy," Nick said. "Buzz him up."

Andrew Robinson had black-rimmed glasses and a goatee trimmed to next to nothing. He wore a gray T-shirt and jeans beneath a khaki parka he took off and dropped on the floor next to his chair.

"I appreciate you coming by," Nick said.

"It's no bother. We're snowed under at the moment, so I wasn't planning on going home anytime soon. I've had a look at your website. Whoever owns the domain name has paid to opt out of the WHOIS directory—that's like a telephone book for websites—so I've submitted a data protection waiver to obtain their name and address. In the meantime I'm working on identifying the site administrator via their IP address, although my guess is they'll be using a proxy, so that's not going to be straightforward."

Despite understanding little of what Andrew was saying, Kelly would have liked to have stayed to listen, but Lucinda was already putting on her coat. Reluctantly, Kelly did the same. She wondered how late Nick would stay working on the case, and if he had anyone waiting for him at home.

They took the stairs down to the ground floor. Lucinda's hair was as sleek and shiny as it had been first thing that morning, and Kelly felt suddenly conscious of the unkempt crop that stood on end every time she ran her fingers through her hair. Perhaps she should dig out some makeup. Lucinda didn't seem to be wearing much, but a slick of lip gloss and defined brows gave her a groomed, professional look that Kelly definitely lacked.

"Where are you heading?" Lucinda asked, as they walked toward the Tube station. She was taller than Kelly by a good couple of inches, with long strides that made Kelly move rather more briskly than usual.

"Elephant and Castle. I share a flat with two other BTP coppers and an A-and-E nurse. You?"

"Kilburn."

"Very nice."

"My parents' place. Mortifying, at twenty-eight, I know, but it's the only way I'll ever be able to save enough for a deposit on a flat. Nick takes the piss out of me something rotten." She slipped behind Kelly as a woman in lurid leggings ran toward them, a knit hat pulled low over her ears, and raised her voice to continue their conversation. "How did you find your first day?"

"My head's spinning. I loved it, though. It's been a while since I was in an incident room; I'd forgotten what a buzz it is."

"What's the deal with that, then? You were on the Sexual Offenses Unit, right?"

Even though she had been anticipating the question, it still made Kelly catch her breath. Was Lucinda genuinely interested, or did she already know full well what had happened? Was she fishing for gossip? Kelly glanced sideways but the other woman's face gave nothing away.

"I was suspended," she said, the truth catching her by surprise. *I left*, she usually said, in advance of some cock-and-bull story about wanting more frontline experience. Or *I was ill*, which wasn't far from the truth. She kept her eyes on the pavement in front. "I assaulted someone."

"A colleague?" Lucinda sounded curious, rather than judgmental. Kelly took a deep breath.

"A prisoner."

Call him by his name, her therapist had reminded her on more than one occasion. *Important that you see him as a person, Kelly, as human as you or I.* Kelly had complied, but the syllables had tainted her tongue every time.

"He raped a schoolgirl."

"Shit."

"That doesn't excuse what I did," Kelly said quickly. She hadn't needed therapy to understand that.

"No," Lucinda said. She paused, choosing her words carefully. "But perhaps it explains it." They walked in silence for a while and Kelly wondered if Lucinda was thinking about what she'd just said; if she was judging her. She braced herself for further questions, but none came. "You did a great job on that password," Lucinda said, as they neared the station. "Nick was very impressed."

"Was he? He didn't show it." Kelly had tried not to care about the DI's understated response to her discovery. She hadn't expected a round of applause, but something more than a muttered *good job* would have been nice.

"You'll get used to him. I like his approach, personally. He doesn't dish out praise readily, so when he does, you know you've done well."

Kelly suspected she might be waiting a long time.

At the entrance to the Tube station a bearded man was playing a guitar, a hat on the ground in front of him, empty but for a few coins. His dog slept on a carefully folded sleeping bag, in front of a bundle of belongings. Kelly thought of Zoe Walker and her Crystal Palace musician.

"If you were Zoe Walker," she said to Lucinda, "wouldn't you want to know?"

They walked past the street musician and into the station, both reaching automatically for their Oyster cards.

"Yes."

"So . . ."

"There are lots of things I'd like to know," Lucinda said firmly. "State secrets, Bill Gates's PIN, George Clooney's mobile number . . . That doesn't mean it would be right for me to know them."

"Even if it's the difference between staying alive and being murdered? Or raped?"

Lexi's attacker had been following her movements for weeks, the police had concluded. Since the beginning of term, possibly. He was almost certainly responsible for the flowers left outside her bedroom, and the notes tucked into her pigeonhole. Friends had brushed it off; laughed about her secret admirer. When the police asked if she'd noticed anyone following her, she told them about those Thursday evenings, walking home from her four P.M. lecture. The same boy leaning against the library wall, listening to music; the feeling of being watched as she walked away; the crack of a twig behind her as she took a shortcut through the woods. She wasn't the only one who had felt like that, the police admitted. They'd had several reports of suspicious circumstances. Nothing concrete, they'd said.

Lucinda stopped walking and looked at Kelly. "You heard what Nick said; restricting this information is our best chance of finding whoever set up the website. Once we've caught him, the rest will be easy."

Kelly was disappointed. She had hoped Lucinda might side with her; that she would use the influence she clearly had with Nick to persuade him to change his mind.

Lucinda saw the look on her face. "You might not agree with his decision, but he's the boss. If you want to stay in his good books, you'll play by his rules." They took the Northern line together and the conversation moved on to safer territory, but by the time they separated at Euston, Kelly had already made her decision.

Rules were made to be broken.

CHAPTER
EIGHTEEN

'm still on my way back from the station when Simon phones from his sister's. He must have been on the Tube when I called his mobile, he tells me. He's just picked up my voice mail.

"I won't be late back. Ange has got an early start in the morning, so I'll head off after supper."

"Did you have a good day at work?" The words are the same ones I use every evening, but there's an edge to my voice that makes him pause, and I wonder if it's enough to prompt whatever truths he's been hiding from me.

It isn't.

"Not bad."

I listen to Simon lie to me; to the detail he gives me about the guy at the desk next to him, who eats with his mouth open and spends half the day on the phone to his girlfriend. I want to confront him but I can't find the words; and more than that, I still can't believe it's true.

Of course Simon works at the *Telegraph*. I've seen his desk. At least, I've seen pictures of it. Soon after we started dating he'd texted me.

I miss you. What are you doing now? I want to picture it.

I'm in Sainsbury's, I replied. I sent him a photo of the frozen food aisle, laughing out loud in the supermarket.

It became a game, abbreviated to *WAYDN?* and responded to with a photo of whatever was in front of us at that precise moment. A packed

Tube train, a sandwich at lunch, the underside of my umbrella as I walked to work in the rain. It was a window into our lives; into the days and nights between our evenings together.

I've seen his desk, I repeat to myself. I've seen the vast open-plan space with its computer screens and ever-present *Sky News* feed. I've seen the piles of newspapers.

You've seen a desk, a voice says in my head. *It could have been anyone's.*

I shake it off. What am I suggesting; that Simon sent me photos of somewhere he didn't even work? That he took pictures of a newsroom from the Internet? It's ridiculous. There'll be an innocent explanation. A missed entry in the switchboard directory; an incompetent receptionist; a practical joke. Simon wouldn't lie to me.

Would he?

I cross the road so I can stop by Melissa's café. I know that Justin's shift finishes shortly, and I see them sitting at a table poring over paperwork, Melissa leaning forward until her head is almost touching Justin's. They move apart as I come through the door, Melissa jumping up to give me a kiss.

"Just the person! We were just arguing about the Christmas menu. Turkey baguettes with cranberry, or with sage and onion? Stick those menus away, Justin, we'll finish off tomorrow."

"Cranberry *and* sage and onion. Hi, love."

Justin picks up the papers and shuffles them into a pile. "I said both, too."

"That's because it's not your profits you're giving away," Melissa says. "Sage and onion *or* cranberry sauce. Not both."

"I thought we could walk home together," I say to Justin, "but you're busy."

"You go on," Melissa says. "I'll lock up." I watch my son take off his apron and hang it behind the counter, ready for tomorrow.

I loop my hand through Justin's arm as we walk home. My stomach feels hollow as I remember the certainty with which the *Telegraph*'s switchboard operator had delivered her news.

There's no Simon Thornton working here.

"Has Simon ever talked to you about his job?" I try to speak casually, but Justin looks at me as if I've suggested he might have chatted with Biscuit. The antagonism between Simon and Justin is the elephant in the room; ignored in the hope it will one day leave of its own accord.

"Only to make the point that I'd never get a job like his without qualifications. Which was nice."

"I'm sure he was just trying to motivate you."

"Well, he can stick his motivation up his—"

"Justin!"

"He's got no right to lecture me. He's not my dad."

"He's not trying to be." I put the key in the lock. "Can't you just try to get on? For my sake?"

He stares at me, his expression registering a flicker of remorse beneath the bitterness. "No. You think you know him, Mum, but you don't. You really don't."

I'm peeling potatoes when my mobile rings. I'm about to leave it, when I catch sight of the name on the screen. *PC Kelly Swift.* I wipe my hands on a tea towel and snatch up the phone before it can go to voice mail. "Hello?"

"Have you got a minute?" PC Swift sounds hesitant. "There's something I need to tell you. Off the record."

I'm still standing in the middle of the kitchen, holding my phone, long after she's ended the call. Katie wanders into the kitchen, opens the fridge, and shuts it again, all the while looking at her own phone, her right thumb scrolling continuously. She's always been addicted to her mobile, but since meeting Isaac she's hardly put it down, her eyes lighting up when a text comes through.

I hear the creak of the stairs as Justin heads downstairs, and I make up my mind. This is something I need to see for myself, without my family peering over my shoulder. Without Katie panicking, and Justin threatening to punch whoever's responsible.

"We're out of milk," I say suddenly, grabbing my bag and shrugging on my coat. "I'll go and get some."

"There's some in the fridge," Katie calls, but I'm already slamming the front door behind me.

I walk fast, hugging my coat across my chest. There's a café down here; not Melissa's, but a small, slightly grubby place I've never felt compelled to visit. But I know it's open late and I need to be somewhere no one knows me, somewhere anonymous.

I order a coffee. It's bitter and I add a lump of sugar, letting it dissolve on the spoon until it disappears. I put my iPad on the table in front of me and take a deep breath, steeling myself for . . . for what?

The password—I SEE YOU—makes me shiver. Hidden in plain sight just like the adverts themselves; boldly displayed among the job ads and the items for sale. The page seems to take forever to load, and when it does little changes. The background is still blank, but the white box asking for the access code has been replaced.

Log in or create an account.

"Don't set up an account," PC Swift said, after she'd told me what they'd uncovered. "I'm only telling you because I think you have a right to know." She paused. "Because if this was happening to me, or to someone in my family, I'd want to know. Please: trust us."

I tap on Create an account and type in my own name before coming to my senses and pressing backspace until it disappears. I glance up and catch sight of the café owner, his fat belly straining under a dirty white apron with the word Lenny embroidered on the left breast.

Lenny Smith, I type. I create a password.

Select a membership package.

Bronze membership, £250: Viewing access. Profile downloads from £100.

Silver membership, £500: Viewing access. One free download per month.

Gold membership, £1,000: Viewing access. Unlimited free downloads.

Bile rises in my throat. I take a swig of tepid coffee and swallow it down. Is that what I'm worth? Is that what Tania Beckett was worth? Laura Keen? Cathy Tanning? I stare at the screen. My credit card is maxed out and this close to the end of the month I can't spare enough even for a bronze membership. A few days ago I might have asked Simon for help, but right now he's the last person I want to put my trust in. How can I, when he's been lying to me about where he works?

There's only one person I can think of to turn to. I pick up the phone.

"Can I borrow some money?" I say, as soon as Matt answers.

"City boy finally bled you dry, has he? Newspapers not paying much nowadays?"

If only he knew. I close my eyes. "Matt, please. I wouldn't ask if it wasn't important."

"How much?"

"A grand."

He gives a low whistle. "Zo, I haven't got that sort of cash lying around. What do you need it for?"

"Could I borrow your credit card? I'll pay it off, Matt, every penny. The interest, too."

"Are you in some sort of trouble?"

"Please, Matt."

"I'll text you the details."

"Thank you." I'm so relieved it's almost a sob.

"No worries." He pauses. "You know I'd do anything for you, Zo." I'm about to thank him again when I realize he's hung up. His text comes through a minute later. I enter his credit card details against the fake membership profile I've created for Lenny Smith.

And it's done. Matt's credit card is a thousand pounds in the red, and I'm now a member of FindTheOne.com, the *Dating Site with a Difference*.

Even though PC Swift has prepared me for it, it's hard to take in what I'm looking at. Rows and rows of photographs, all women, and each with a word or two listed beneath.

Central line
Piccadilly
Jubilee / Bakerloo

I feel a chill creep across my neck.

I scan the photos, looking for my own. I tap on More Photos to load a second page, then a third. And there I am. The same photo from the *Gazette*; the photo from my Facebook page, from my cousin's wedding.

Click to download.

I don't hesitate.

Listed: Friday 13 November
White.
Late thirties.
Blonde hair, usually tied up.

I read it twice: the precise listing of each train I catch; the coat I'm wearing right now; the casual summary of my appearance. I register the absurdity of being annoyed that my dress size is listed as twelve to fourteen, when really, it's only my jeans that are size fourteen.

Around me, Lenny is wiping tables, noisily stacking chairs to let me know I've overstayed my welcome. I try to stand up, but my legs won't work. Bumping into Luke Friedland today was no accident, I realize, just like it was no accident that he was standing next to me when I fell toward the tracks.

Luke Friedland downloaded my commute in order to follow me.

Who else has done the same?

Simon comes home just as I'm getting into bed. He's so pleased to see me I feel a stab of confusion. How can a man who loves me this much have been lying to me?

"How was Ange?" It occurs to me suddenly that maybe he didn't even go and see his sister. If he's been lying to me about where he works, what else has he been lying about? Justin's words ring in my ears, and I look at Simon with a new watchfulness.

"Great. She sends her love."

"Good day at work?" I say. He pulls off his trousers and leaves them in a puddle on the floor with his shirt before sliding into bed. *Tell me*, I think. *Tell me now, and it'll all be okay. Tell me you've never worked at the* Telegraph; *that you're a junior reporter at some local rag, or that you're not a journalist at all; that you made it up to impress me, and you actually work the deep-fat fryer at McDonald's. Just tell me the truth.*

But he doesn't. He strokes my stomach; circles his thumbs against my hip bones. "Pretty good. That story about MP expenses broke first thing, so it was a busy one."

I feel wrong-footed. I saw the story at lunchtime, when I nipped out to get Graham's sandwich. My head starts to throb. I need to know the truth.

"I called the *Telegraph*."

The color drains from Simon's face.

"You weren't answering your mobile. Something happened on my way home from work; I was upset, I wanted to talk to you."

"What happened? Are you okay?"

I ignore his concern. "The switchboard operator had never heard of you." I push his hands off my waist. There's a pause, and I can hear the click of the central heating switching off.

"I was going to tell you."

"Tell me what? That you'd lied to me? Made up a job you thought would impress me?"

"No! I didn't make it up. God, Zoe, what do you think of me?"

"Do you really want me to answer that?" No wonder he was so negative when I suggested putting Katie forward for work experience, I think; why he snapped when I asked him to pitch a story about the adverts.

"I did work at the *Telegraph*. Then they . . ." He breaks off, rolling away from me and staring up at the ceiling. "They let me go." I can't decide if the shame I can hear in his voice is because he lost his job or because he's been lying to us.

"Why? You've been there for—what?—more than twenty years."

Simon gives a hollow laugh. "Exactly. Out with the old and in with the new. A younger workforce. Cheaper. Kids who don't know what the subjunctive is but who can blog and tweet and upload content to the website in the blink of an eye." His voice is bitter, but there's no real fight in his words, as though the battle is long since lost.

"When did this happen?"

"At the start of August."

For a second I'm struggling for words. "You were let go four months ago, and you said nothing? What the hell have you been doing all this time?" I get out of bed and walk toward the door, then stop and turn around, not wanting to stay but needing to hear more.

"Walking around, sitting in cafés, writing, reading." The bitterness creeps into his voice again. "Looking for jobs; having interviews; being told I'm too old; worrying about how to tell you." He won't look at me, his eyes trained resolutely on the ceiling. Deep grooves form across his forehead. He is broken.

I stand watching him, and gradually my anger begins to disappear. "What about money?"

"They gave me a severance package. I hoped I'd find something fairly quickly; I thought I'd tell you when I'd sorted it all out. But it went on and on, and when the money ran out I had to use credit cards." When he finally looks at me I'm shocked to see his eyes are bright with the beginnings of tears. "I'm so sorry, Zoe, I never meant to lie to you. I hoped I'd have it sorted in no time, and I'd be able to surprise you with a new job; carry on looking after you the way you deserve to be looked after."

I move to sit next to him. "Shhh, it's okay," I say, like he's one of my children. "It'll all be okay."

Simon makes me promise not to tell the kids.

"Justin already thinks I don't pay my way. He doesn't need any more reason to hate me."

"We've been through this," I say. "It's me he's angry with, not you. He blames me for the divorce; having to move from Peckham, leave his friends."

"So tell him the truth. Why should you take the blame for something that wasn't your fault? It's been ten years, Zoe, why are you still protecting Matt?"

"I'm not protecting Matt, I'm protecting the kids. They love their father; they don't need to know Matt cheated on me."

"It isn't fair on you."

"It's what we agreed." It was a deal that made us both liars. I agreed never to tell the kids Matt had cheated, and he agreed to pretend he didn't love me anymore; that the decision to separate was mutual. I sometimes wonder which of us found the bargain harder to keep.

Simon leaves it. It's a battle he knows he won't win. "I want to get back on my feet before we tell them. Please."

We agree to tell Justin and Katie that Simon has arranged to work from home full-time so he doesn't have to leave the house each day; staying out till after five, drinking cups of coffee he doesn't want in cafés he can no longer afford. When he tells me he's been living off credit cards I feel sick.

"Why did you keep buying me presents? Taking me out to dinner? I'd never have let you do that if I'd known you couldn't afford it."

"If I'd stopped you'd have wondered what had happened; you'd have guessed. Thought less of me."

"I could have paid my way, if we'd have gone out at all."

"How do you think that would have made me feel? What kind of man lets a woman pay for dinner?"

"Oh, don't be ridiculous! It's not the fifties." I laugh, then realize how serious he is. "It'll be okay, I promise."

I just hope I'm right.

CHAPTER NINETEEN

"Are you sure you did the right thing?" Lexi said. She hoisted Fergus out of the bath and wrapped him in a towel before passing him to Kelly ("Make sure you dry between his toes") and doing the same with Alfie.

"Yes," Kelly said firmly. "Zoe Walker had a right to know." She sat her nephew on her lap and rubbed his hair vigorously with the towel, making him laugh.

"Won't you get into trouble?"

Kelly didn't say anything. She'd been thinking about it ever since she picked up the phone to Zoe Walker. Unable to get it out of her head, she'd come to Lexi's in search of distraction and ended up telling her the whole story. "There we go, all clean and dry." She bent her head close to Fergus's and inhaled the sweet smell of warm skin and talcum powder. Zoe had been grateful to Kelly for keeping her in the loop, and Kelly had told herself that in itself justified her actions.

"Do you want to stay tonight? I can make up the sofa bed." Kelly loved Lexi's house. It was an unexciting redbrick semidetached on an estate filled with cars and garbage cans, but inside it was warm and cozy; a stark contrast to the bedroom waiting for her in Elephant and Castle. Kelly was sorely tempted.

"I can't. I've got to meet Zoe Walker in Covent Garden in the morning. I'll need to catch the last train." She had hoped Nick would allow her to meet Zoe on her own, thereby avoiding the risk of the DI finding out about Kelly's call, but he was insisting on accompanying her. Kelly was relying on Zoe to be discreet.

"Isn't it—I don't know—disobeying a lawful order or something?" Lexi said, refusing to let the subject drop.

"Technically, I suppose."

"Technically? Kelly!"

Alfie twisted his head around, surprised by his mother's sharp tone, and Lexi gave him a reassuring kiss. Dropping her voice a notch, she looked at Kelly and said, "Have you got some sort of death wish? Anyone would think you were actively trying to get the sack."

"I was doing the right thing."

"No, you were doing what you *thought* was the right thing. It isn't always the same, Kelly."

Zoe had arranged to meet Kelly and Nick in a café called Melissa's Too on a side street near Covent Garden. Despite the early hour the café was already busy, the smell of bacon sandwiches making Kelly's stomach rumble. A young girl behind the counter was making take-away coffees with impressive efficiency, and Zoe was sitting at a table in the window. She looked tired; unwashed hair pulled into a hasty ponytail that contrasted sharply with the sleek French plait of the woman sitting next to her.

"I'm sure something will come up," the woman was saying, as Kelly and Nick arrived. She stood to free up the chair. "Try not to worry about it."

"We were talking about my partner," Zoe said, although neither Kelly nor Nick had asked. "He's been laid off."

"I'm sorry," Kelly said. Perhaps that explained the tiredness.

"This is my friend Melissa. It's her café."

Kelly stuck out her hand. "PC Kelly Swift."

"DI Nick Rampello."

A flicker of recognition passed across Melissa's face. "Rampello? Where have I seen that name recently?"

Nick smiled politely. "I'm not sure. My parents run the family Italian restaurant in Clerkenwell—perhaps you saw it there."

"That's where your new café is, isn't it?" Zoe said.

"That must be it. Now, what can I get you all to drink?" Melissa tugged a small notepad from the breast pocket of her navy blazer and took their order, insisting on serving them all personally, despite the queue that stretched from the counter to the door.

"Something happened," Zoe said, when Melissa had delivered their coffees.

"What do you mean?" Nick sipped his espresso, wincing when it burned his tongue.

"I was followed. On Monday morning on my way to work. I thought I was being paranoid, but I saw him again that evening—I tripped and he grabbed me before I fell in front of a train." Kelly and Nick exchanged a glance. "I put it down to coincidence, but then the next day he was there again."

"Did he speak to you?" Kelly said.

Zoe nodded. "He asked me out for a drink. I said no, of course. I still thought it might have been coincidence, but it wasn't, was it? He knew exactly which way I was going; he was waiting for me. He must have gotten my details from the website." She glanced at Kelly and flushed, and Kelly willed her not to say anymore. She sneaked a sidelong look at Nick, but there was nothing about his demeanor that suggested he suspected anything.

"Did this man give you a name?" Kelly said.

"Luke Friedland. I could describe him for you, if that would help."

Kelly reached for her briefcase and found the paperwork she needed. "I'd like to take a statement, if that's okay? I want everything you can remember about this man, including the route you were traveling, and any times you can be certain of."

"I'm going to organize a personal attack alarm," Nick said. "You'll have it with you at all times, and if anything happens you can press it. It'll be monitored 24/7 by our control room and they'll be able to pinpoint your location."

"Do you think I'm in danger?"

Kelly looked at Nick, who didn't hesitate.

"I think you could be."

"You told her."

It wasn't a question.

They were heading toward Old Gloucester Road, to the address provided for them by the *London Gazette*; the address of the person responsible for placing the adverts in the classifieds. Nick was driving, spinning the steering wheel to switch lanes with the dexterity that came from years of practice. Kelly could imagine him in uniform, racing down Oxford Street.

"Yes."

She jumped as Nick slammed the heel of his palm against the horn as a cyclist cut across in front of him, bowling through a set of red lights.

"I specifically said you were not to inform Zoe Walker about the developments in this case. Which bit of that was so hard to understand?"

"I wasn't comfortable with that decision."

"To hell with whether you're *comfortable*, Kelly. It wasn't your call to make." They turned right onto Shaftesbury Avenue, an ambulance screaming past in the opposite direction. "We're dealing with a complex and wide-ranging investigation, with multiple offenders, multiple victims, and God knows how many witnesses. There are more important matters than the way Zoe Walker feels."

"Not to her," Kelly said quietly.

They drove in silence. Gradually Nick stopped gripping the wheel as though it were about to fly off, and the pulse Kelly had seen throbbing in the side of his temple began to subside. She wondered if she'd made her point in such a way that Nick was actually reconsidering his decision to keep Zoe in the dark, or whether he was mulling over how best to take her off the investigation and send her back to BTP.

Instead, he simply changed the subject.

"How come you joined BTP and not the Met?" he said when they were on the A40.

"They weren't recruiting, and I wanted to stay in London. I've got family close by."

"A sister, right?"

"Yes. My twin."

"There are two of you? Heaven help us." Nick glanced at her and Kelly grinned, less at the joke itself than at the olive branch it represented.

"How about you? Are you a Londoner?"

"Born and bred. Although I'm second-generation Italian. Mum and Dad are Sicilian; they came over when Mum was pregnant with my older brother, and opened a restaurant in Clerkenwell."

"Rampello's," Kelly said, remembering the conversation with Melissa.

"De preciso."

"Do you speak Italian?"

"No more than your average tourist, much to Mum's eternal shame." Held at green lights while the driver in front worked out which way to turn, Nick gave two short beeps on the horn.

"My brothers and I had to work in the restaurant at weekends and after school, and she used to yell instructions at us in Italian. I refused point-blank to answer."

"Why?"

"Stubborn, I guess. Plus I knew even then that one of us would have to take over the restaurant when Mum and Dad retired, and I didn't want to encourage them. Joining the police was all I ever wanted to do."

"Your parents weren't keen?"

"They cried at my passing-out parade. And not with happiness."

They turned onto Old Gloucester Road, and Kelly brought up Google Maps on her phone to see on which end of the road they would find number twenty-seven. "There's not much residential housing down here—it must be converted flats."

"Or it's a wild-goose chase," Nick said grimly, pulling up on double-yellow lines outside a Chinese restaurant. Number twenty-seven was sandwiched between a laundrette and a boarded-up bookies.

"I think our chances of finding Mr. James Stanford here are slim."

Nick took the car's logbook from the glove box and left it prominently on the dashboard, the police crest on the cover usually sufficient to deter traffic wardens.

The door to number twenty-seven was grimy with exhaust fumes. It opened into an empty lobby, its tiled floor cracked and dirty. There was no reception desk and no internal door or lift, only rows of locked mailboxes covering three of the walls.

"Are you sure we've got the right place?" Kelly asked.

"It's the right place, all right," Nick said grimly. "We're just not going to find James Stanford here." He pointed to a poster on the door, its edges peeling away from the grubby paintwork.

Sick of picking up your mail? Upgrade your account and we'll forward it to your door!

"It's a mail center. A posh PO box number—nothing more." He pulled out his phone and took a photograph of the poster, then scanned the rows of mailboxes, which seemed to be in no discernible order.

"Here it is." Kelly had started at the opposite side of the lobby. "James Stanford." She tugged the handle hopefully. "Locked."

"The credit card used to pay for the adverts is registered to this address, too," Nick said. "Get a data protection waiver to them as soon as we get back, and find out who put the mail forwarding in place. We're being given the runaround, and I don't like it."

The company behind the Old Gloucester Road postal address was surprisingly helpful. Keen to avoid any accusation of wrongdoing and— Kelly suspected—aware they had been less than robust with their own checks, they handed over everything they had on James Stanford without waiting for a data protection waiver.

Stanford had provided copies of a credit card bill and a utility statement, as well as his driving license, showing him to be a white male born in 1959. All three documents gave an address in Amersham, a town in Buckinghamshire at the end of the Metropolitan line.

"Bet house prices are steep around here," Nick commented as they drove past a series of huge detached houses, each set behind imposing metal gates.

"Do you want me to let local CID know?" Kelly said, picking up her phone to find the number.

Nick shook his head. "We'll be in and out before they know it. Let's check out the house and make a few discreet inquiries with the neighbors if no one's home."

Tudor House, Candlin Street, was not Tudor at all, despite the black-painted beams crisscrossing the exterior. A large, modern build, the house was set on what Kelly estimated to be an acre or so of garden. Nick pulled up in front of the gates and looked for a buzzer, but they swung open automatically.

"What's the point of those, then?" Kelly said.

"Just for show, aren't they?" Nick said. "More money than sense."

The gravel drive crunched beneath the wheels of their car, and Nick looked at the house for signs someone was at home.

They parked parallel to a gleaming gray Range Rover, and Nick whistled. "Very nice."

The doorbell had an old-fashioned pull mechanism, at odds with the age of the house but presumably meant to add to the "ye olde" feel Kelly supposed had been intended by the mock-Tudor facade. *Keeping up with the Joneses*, she thought. Long before the jangling of the bell had begun to die away, they heard footsteps behind the large front door. Nick and Kelly both stepped away, putting distance between themselves and whoever they were about to meet. It never did to make assumptions about the way people might behave, even in a house like this.

The door swung open, and an attractive woman in her early fifties smiled at them expectantly. She wore a black velvet tracksuit with a pair of slippers. Kelly held out her warrant card and the smile disappeared from the woman's face.

"Is someone hurt?" The woman's hands flew to her throat, an instinctive reaction Kelly had seen a hundred times. There were some people for whom the mere sight of a uniform prompted fear of discovery, or arrest. This woman wasn't one of them. For her the police meant an accident, or worse.

"There's nothing to worry about," Kelly said. "We're just making some inquiries. We're looking for a Mr. James Stanford."

"That's my husband. He's at work. Is there a problem?"

"Could we come in?" Kelly said. The woman hesitated, then stood aside to allow them inside a bright, spacious hall. A neat stack of post lay on a narrow hall table, and Kelly glanced at the top envelope as Mrs. Stanford led them into the kitchen.

Mr. J. T. Stanford.

Nick's face was impassive, showing none of the excitement Kelly felt certain must show on her own. Was Stanford running the website from this house?

"James is a management consultant with Kettering Kline," Mrs. Stanford said. "He's in London today meeting a new client. He won't be home till late, I'm afraid. Can I help at all? What's this about?"

"We're investigating a crime series," Nick said. Kelly watched the woman's expression carefully. If James Stanford was their man, did his wife know anything about it? Did she have any idea about the adverts or the website? Kelly noted the photographs displayed on the dresser, all featuring what appeared to be the same young man, at various ages.

"Our son," Mrs. Stanford said, catching Kelly looking. "What sort of crimes? You surely don't think James is involved?"

"We need to eliminate him from our inquiries. It would be a great help if you could answer some questions."

Mrs. Stanford paused, unsure of what to do. Eventually manners won. "You'd better sit down. Would you like a cup of tea?"

"No, thank you. This won't take long."

They installed themselves at a large oak table. "Mrs. Stanford," Nick began, "you said your husband is a management consultant. Does he have any other businesses?"

"He's a director of a couple of charities, but no other businesses, no."

"Has he ever been involved in running a dating agency?"

Mrs. Stanford looked confused. "What do you mean?"

"Premium-rate numbers," Kelly explained. "This sort of thing." She slid a piece of paper across the table and showed Mrs. Stanford a single advert from the *London Gazette*.

Again, the hand at her throat. "No! I mean . . . God, no. Why would he? I mean, what makes you think he'd . . ." She looked wildly between Nick and Kelly. Either she was a superb actress, or she knew nothing about what her husband had been up to. Was that why Stanford had used a mailbox address? Not to hide from the police but from his wife?

Kelly handed Mrs. Stanford the rest of the file she was holding.

"These documents were used to open a mailbox on Old Gloucester Road three months ago, paid for by your husband's credit card. The same documents, and the same credit card, paid for the insertion of a number of adverts in a London newspaper."

"Adverts," Nick said, looking intently at Mrs. Stanford, "we believe are at the heart of a series of crimes against women."

Mrs. Stanford looked at a document, anxiety written across her face, her hand tugging at her necklace. Nick watched her eyes flick from left to right, the confusion and fear gradually giving way to relief.

"This is nothing to do with my husband," she said, the release of tension making her laugh.

"James Stanford is your husband, though?" Kelly said.

"Oh yes," Mrs. Stanford said. "But this photo"—she pointed at the photocopied driving license—"that's not my husband."

CHAPTER
TWENTY

When the police have gone, Melissa silently brings me another pot of tea. She picks up the ten-pound note DI Rampello left on the table. "Are you okay?"

"Yes. No." I comb my fingers through my hair, loosening it from the band, which suddenly feels too tight. "They think I'm in danger." This shouldn't have been news to me. I felt the danger when I downloaded my commute details yesterday; I felt it when Luke Friedland grabbed my arm to save me from falling; I've felt it ever since I saw my photo in the *Gazette*—a photo I allowed my family to convince me wasn't even of me. But when I asked DI Rampello if I was at risk I was looking for a different answer. I wanted reassurance. I wanted to be told I was overreacting; paranoid; delusional. I wanted false promises and glasses half-full. A few days ago I worried the police weren't taking me seriously; now I'm worried because they are.

Melissa sits down in the chair previously occupied by DI Rampello, ignoring the dirty cups at the next table and the never-decreasing queue at the counter. "What are they going to do about it?"

"They're getting me an alarm. It'll be linked straight to their control room—in case I'm attacked."

"Fat lot of good that'll do." She sees my panic and screws up her face, leaning forward to pull me into a hug. "Sorry. But when this place was broken into it was fifteen minutes before the Old Bill rocked up; the burglars were long gone. They're a joke."

"So what do I do?" There's a note of hysteria in my voice and I take a deep breath. Try again. "What do I do, Melissa?"

"Have they said what they're doing to catch the people behind the website? That's what'll keep you safe, not some crappy alarm."

"They just said they're working on it."

"They're 'working on it'? Jesus. And you're supposed to be reassured by that, are you? A woman's been murdered—"

"Two women. At least."

"—and you're supposed to just sit by and let them 'work on it'? You need to find out exactly what they're doing. Who they're talking to, how they're trying to trace this website."

"They won't tell me, Melissa. I wasn't even supposed to know how to get into the website. PC Swift implied she'd get into trouble if anyone found out she'd told me."

"You have a right to know how close they are to solving this. You pay their wages, don't forget."

"I guess so." I imagine marching into the police station and demanding to see the investigation paperwork.

"I could come with you to speak to them, if you want."

I put my elbows on the table and press my face into my cupped hands for a second. "I'm out of my depth," I say when I surface. I can feel the anxiety rising inside me, making my heart race. "I don't know what to do, Melissa."

"You demand to know what the police are doing. Every lead they have. Every breakthrough."

I don't know if I'd find that reassuring or terrifying.

"I feel as though everything's out of my control. The adverts, Katie, even our finances. I used to be so on top of everything, and now . . ."

"How much does Simon owe?"

"He won't tell me. But he's been using credit cards every time he's done the food shop, or paid a utility bill. Meals out, presents . . . It must be thousands, Melissa. He says he got us into this mess, and he'll get us out of it."

"Well, if he won't let you help it sounds as though you're just going to have to trust him." She picks up DI Rampello's empty espresso cup. I don't tell her that right now I'm finding it hard to trust anyone at all.

It's already nine A.M. when I leave the café, but I decide to walk along the Embankment to work. The thought of taking the Underground—even a route that bears no relation to my commute on the website—makes my heart beat so fast I feel light-headed. I cross the Strand and head for Savoy Place, then I drop down to walk beside the river. I'm watching everyone. That man walking toward me, with his hands in his pockets: Does he know about the website? Is he a member? The businessman talking on the phone, a scarf around his neck to keep out the cold: Does he follow women? Rape them? Kill them?

My breath is fast and shallow, and I stand for a moment and stare at the river, trying to keep it under control. A dozen figures in wet suits are taking paddleboard instruction from a lithe blonde wearing a bright pink all-in-one. They're laughing, despite the cold. Beyond them, in the middle of the river, a pleasure cruise cuts a foamy channel through the gray Thames; a handful of early-bird tourists shivering on the deck.

Someone touches my arm.

"You all right, there?"

I flinch as though I've been burned. The man is young, around Justin's age, but in a suit and tie, and with the confidence that comes with a good education or a good job. Or both.

"You looked like you were about to keel over."

My heart is pounding so hard it hurts my rib cage, and I can't find the words to tell him I'm fine. Not to touch me. Instead, I step away from him. Shake my head. He holds up both his hands and exaggerates the wide berth he gives me before walking away.

"Fucking loony."

When he's ten or more paces away he turns around and taps the side of his head twice with his index finger. *Mad*, he mouths, and I feel as though I am.

It's almost ten before I reach the office. The walk has done me good, and although my feet ache I feel stronger; invigorated. Graham is talking to a woman wearing red high heels with a black trouser suit. She's holding a sheaf of property particulars and Graham is telling her about the office on Eastern Avenue with the customer toilets and the newly refurbished kitchen area, perfect for staff breaks. I tune out the well-practiced blurb as I slide behind my desk, knowing from the way Graham is bristling that he's furious with me.

He starts the second the woman leaves, her reluctance to fix an immediate viewing serving to add to his outrage. "Good of you to drop in, Zoe."

"I'm sorry. It won't happen again."

"But it is happening again, isn't it? You've been late every morning lately."

"I've had to change the way I come to work—it's hard to predict how long it will take."

Graham doesn't ask why. He's not interested. "Then leave home earlier. You can't just saunter in at nigh on ten o'clock without so much as an apology—"

I did apologize, but I'm not going to repeat it. "I was with the police." I half expect Graham to carry on as though I haven't said anything, but he stops short.

"Why? What's happened?"

I hesitate, not sure how much I want this man to know. I think of the website, with its menu of women, and it occurs to me Graham Hallow is exactly the sort of man who would be drawn to the idea of an exclusive membership site. I'm in no doubt that if I tell him, he won't be able to resist looking, and I feel protective of these women. I don't want people looking at their photos; buying their commutes like they were nothing more than objects. And then . . . what? I'm finding it hard to reconcile what I know is happening: that women are being attacked—murdered—because their commutes have been sold. It's grotesque; the stuff of science fiction.

"I'm being followed," I say instead. It isn't so far from the truth. I think I see concern in my boss's face, but it's so unfamiliar I'm not sure. "The police are going to give me a personal alarm."

"Do they know who's doing it?" The question is accusatory, barked in the manner of someone who doesn't know how else to be.

"No." And then, because I've been holding it in for days, I start to cry. *Of all the people to cry in front of*, I think, as Graham stands there, rooted to the spot. I hunt for a tissue in my pockets, eventually finding one tucked up my sleeve, and blow my nose hard, but I can't stop the tears from coming. The release is making my chest heave, and I take gulps of air that come out in juddering cries. "I—I'm sorry," I manage to say, after several false starts. "It—it's all a bit overwhelming."

Graham is still standing by my desk, staring at me. Suddenly he strides to the door and I think for a second he's going to walk out and leave me here sobbing at my desk. But he flicks the catch that locks the door and flips over the sign that reads *Closed*, then he walks across to where we keep the tea things and switches on the kettle. I'm so surprised by this show of compassion that I stop crying, my sobs morphing into occasional hiccups. I blow my nose again.

"I'm really sorry."

"You're clearly under a lot of strain. How long has this been going on?"

I tell him as much as I can without mentioning the name of the website, or the way that it works. I tell him I've been followed for a while, and that the police are now linking my case with the murder of two women, and to attacks on several others.

"What are the police doing about it?"

"They're sorting out the alarm for me. I had to give a statement this morning—that's why I was late."

Graham shakes his head, making the soft folds of flesh beneath his chin wobble. "It's fine. Don't trouble yourself about that. Do they know who's behind the attacks?"

I'm touched—and surprised—by how interested Graham is.

"I don't think so. They haven't arrested anyone for Tania Beckett's murder, yet, and the website is apparently untraceable."

Graham is thinking. "I'm out at meetings all day. I was planning to go home straight from my five P.M., but if you don't mind staying slightly later than usual I'll swing by and give you a lift home." Graham comes in from Essex every day. He mostly takes the train, but occasionally he drives, leaving his car in a ludicrously expensive car park around the corner from the office.

"It's miles out of your way! Really, I'm fine. I'm going to go home a different way, and I can get Justin to meet me at Crystal Palace—"

"I'm taking you home," Graham says firmly. "I can go on to Seven-oaks to see my brother and his wife. To be frank, I'm surprised that bloke of yours isn't coming to get you."

"I don't want to worry him."

Graham looks at me curiously. "You haven't told him?"

"He knows about the website, but not . . . I haven't told him I'm in danger. Things are a bit difficult at the moment." I see Graham's face and explain before he gets the wrong end of the stick. "Simon's lost his job. Laid off. So it's not a great time. I don't want to give him any more reason to worry."

"Right, well, I'm taking you home tonight, and that's the end of it." Graham looks satisfied. If he were a caveman he'd be beating his chest.

"Okay," I say. "Thank you."

Half an hour later Graham goes to his meeting. "Keep the door locked," he tells me, "until you've seen who they are."

The office door is glass, as is the entire front of the shop, but I don't know how I'm supposed to assess whether a man standing outside is here to rape and kill me, or to inquire about the mobile phone shop that's closing down on Lombard Street.

"The whole place is covered by CCTV anyway," he says. I'm so surprised by this parting shot I don't point out that having my attack on film will be of little comfort to me when I'm dead.

"Since when have we had CCTV?" I look around the office. Graham looks mildly uncomfortable. He looks at his watch.

"A couple of years. They're in the automatic sprinklers. It's an insurance thing. Anyway, the point is you've got nothing to worry about while you're here. I'll see you before six." The bell above the door jangles as he opens the door, and again when he closes it. I turn the lock but leave the sign to *Open*, then sit down at my desk. I had no idea Graham had installed cameras. Don't employers have some sort of obligation to inform their employees—and customers, come to that—they're under surveillance? I look up at the ceiling.

A couple of years.

A couple of years when I've thought I was on my own in the office; Graham's door shut. Eating a sandwich, making a call, adjusting an uncomfortable bra strap. Does he watch me? The thought is unsettling, and when the office phone rings it makes me jump.

At half past five I turn around the *Closed* sign. It hasn't been busy: a new tenant, in to sign a lease, and a handful of inquiries about the new office block. No one suspicious; no one predatory, and I was starting to feel I'd been overreacting. But now that it's dark outside and the lights are on in the office, putting me on display to anyone passing, I begin to feel anxious again.

I'm grateful when Graham returns, waving his car keys and asking for my postcode so he can program the GPS. I'm relieved I don't have to get on the Tube tonight; I don't have to worry about who's behind me, or risk ending up dead in a park, like poor Tania Beckett.

For tonight, at least, I'll be safe.

I'll always be grateful to that first dead girl.

She changed everything.

She helped me see that FindTheOne.com could be so much more than just a new kind of dating site; opened up a world of possibilities to me.

Sure, there'll always be the clients who don't want to play dirty, who want to use the site the way it was first intended; to chat you up and ask you for dinner.

But Tania Beckett showed me there were other men; men who would pay to play cat and mouse through the Underground, to hover by the park at the exact moment you walk by, with something bigger on their mind than dinner.

Such potential.

Higher prices. A more specialist market.

I could be more than just a matchmaker. I'd be a facilitator for desires hidden so deep inside they're barely acknowledged. Who among us can truly say they haven't imagined what it would feel like to hurt someone? To go further than society deems acceptable; to experience the rush of forcing someone's hand?

Who among us wouldn't take that chance, if it were handed to us?

The chance to kill someone.

"Boss, we've got a problem."

Nick looked up from his desk as Kelly approached. The morning meeting had only just finished, but Nick had already loosened his tie and undone the top button of his shirt. Kelly knew that by lunchtime the tie would be off altogether, tucked into the breast pocket of his jacket, in case the top brass dropped by.

"The account you opened with the website has been revoked. I just tried to sign in to see what new profiles had been added and it threw me out." Kelly couldn't stop herself from logging on to the site every hour or so, even reaching for her phone when she woke up in the early hours of that morning. She did so with a growing feeling of dread in the pit of her stomach, knowing the *New Profiles Added!* banner that flashed onto the screen meant more women in danger; more potential victims. The website was moving faster than the investigation could keep up with, and the previous day's wild-goose chase to Amersham hadn't helped. James Stanford's credit card had been cloned a year previously; he'd lost his wallet—or had it stolen—and suffered various incidents of identity theft as a result. The mail-forwarding center on Old Gloucester Road was simply the latest in a string of crimes involving credit card details that had no doubt been sold numerous times, and MIT were no closer to finding out who was responsible for targeting London's female commuters.

The incident room walls were covered with rows of their photos—some identified, most nameless—with more added to the website since

they'd first gained access. Kelly had logged on automatically this morning after the briefing, her fingers finding the keys of their own accord.

Log-in not recognized.

Kelly had blinked at the screen. Tried again, assuming operator
error.

Log-in not recognized.

She had checked and double-checked the details for the account
Nick had created, using his own credit card and a Gmail address, but
the mistake wasn't hers. The account had disappeared.

"Do you think we've been rumbled?"

Nick tapped his pen against the side of his laptop. "Maybe. How
many profiles did we download?"

"All of them. Maybe it looked suspicious."

"Or the whole thing's a scam just to get your money. Who's going
to call the Old Bill and complain they were promised unlimited
stalking opportunities?"

"Finance have organized a prepaid credit card," Kelly said. She'd
seen the e-mail come in while she was trying to log in to Nick's account.

"Great. Get a new account set up and let's see how long before
that one's taken down, too. I want you to look for any profiles based
in Kent."

"They've all been London-based so far, boss."

"There was an abduction in Maidstone yesterday. A witness reported seeing a man drag a woman into a black Lexus and drive off.
An hour later Kent police received a call from a distressed female who
had been abducted and sexually assaulted before being pushed out of
the car in an industrial estate on the outskirts of the town." He handed

several printed sheets to Kelly, who glanced at the details written at the top of the statement.

Kathryn Whitworth, 36.

"Commuter?"

"She travels from Pimlico every day to a recruitment firm in Maidstone."

"Did she get the plate number of the Lexus?"

"No, but the car triggered a speed camera a few miles from the incident. Local officers are bringing in the driver now."

It didn't take Kelly long to set up a new account, and to find Kathryn Whitworth, promoted as *Newly Listed* on the first page of the website. She checked the details given in Kathryn's victim statement against the profile on the screen in front of her.

White. Blonde.

Mid thirties.

Flat shoes, dresses with fitted jackets. Woolen checked wrap. Black umbrella with tortoiseshell handle. Gray Mulberry laptop bag.

Size 8–10.

0715: Enters Pimlico Tube. Takes escalator and turns left to northbound platform. Stands by large advert to the left of Tube map. One stop to Victoria. Exits platform, turns right and up escalator. Turns left toward platforms 1–8.

Goes to Starbucks adjacent to platform 2, where barista prepares venti skinny decaf latte without instruction. Takes Ashford International train from platform 3. Opens laptop and works for duration of journey. Gets off at Maidstone East. Walks

up Week Street, turns left into Union Street. Works at Maidstone
Recruitment.

    Availability: Monday to Friday

    Duration: 80 minutes

    Difficulty level: Moderate

There was no doubt it was the same woman. On impulse Kelly
looked up Maidstone Recruitment. A professional headshot accompanied the short bio beneath Kathryn's name and job title: *Senior Recruitment Consultant*. In the photograph on FindTheOne.com Kathryn
had her hair tucked behind her ears; she looked—if not stressed,
exactly—as though her mind was elsewhere. In her work shot she sat
left shoulder forward against a white background, shiny blonde hair
resting on her shoulders in a neat bob. She met the camera with a
gleaming smile; professional, trustworthy, confident.

What did Kathryn Whitworth look like now? Kelly wondered.
What did she look like when she gave this ten-page statement to a
Maidstone detective; when she sat in the rape suite in a borrowed robe,
waiting for the Force Medical Examiner to violate her all over again?

The images came all too easily.

She took the profile off the printer and leaned over her desk to pass
them to Lucinda.

"It's a match."

Kelly's mobile rang, *Number withheld* flashing on the screen. She
picked up.

"Hi, is that DC Thompson?"

Kelly was on the verge of telling the caller he had the wrong number, when she remembered. "Yes, that's me." She glanced at Lucinda,
but she had turned back to her computer.

"It's DC Angus Green, from Durham CID. I've dug out the rape
file you were after."

"Hang on a sec, I need to take this outside."

Kelly hoped it wasn't obvious to anyone else in the office that her heart was racing. She forced herself to walk casually away from her desk, as though the call were of little importance.

"Thanks for returning my call," she said, when she was in the corridor. She stood at the top of the stairwell, where she could see who was coming up the stairs and keep an eye on the door to MIT at the same time.

"No problem. Have you got someone in custody?"

"No, we're just doing some work on similar jobs around the country, and this one came up. I was calling to see if there had been any developments in the last few years?" Kelly's heart was banging so hard now it was hurting her chest. She pressed the flat of her palm squarely over her sternum. If anyone ever found out about this she'd lose her job for sure; there'd be no second chances this time.

"Nothing, I'm afraid. We've got DNA on file, so if he's ever nicked for something else we'll get a match, although our chances of a prosecution are slim, even then."

"Why's that?" An arrest was what Kelly had hoped for, ever since she joined the job, when she realized how many historic crimes were solved not by dogged investigation work but by sheer chance. An elimination swab submitted after a burglary at work; an evidential sample taken after a positive roadside breath test. That sharp intake of breath, when a simple job turns into so much more, and a crime committed twenty years previously is finally solved. It had happened to Kelly a couple of times, and it was what she wanted now more than anything. Kelly had never seen the man who raped Lexi, but she could almost visualize the arrogance on his face morphing into fear; a relatively innocuous charge paling into insignificance beside the positive DNA match that would prove unequivocally he had stalked her sister; watched her; attacked her.

"There's a letter from the victim on file," DC Green was saying. "A Miss Alexis Swift. The letter says that although the evidence given in her written statement still stands, she does not support a prosecution, and does not wish to be informed of any developments in the case."

"But that's impossible!" It was out before Kelly could stop it, her voice echoing in the empty corridor. She could hear DC Green's confusion in the silence that followed. "I mean, why would a victim retract her support? It doesn't make sense."

"There's no explanation, just the signed declaration. Maybe it wasn't quite as cut-and-dried as she'd put forward in her initial statement? Perhaps it was someone she knew, after all; maybe she consented then changed her mind."

Kelly fought for control. An image of Lexi flashed into her mind; curled up in an armchair in the police rape suite, too broken even to stand up when Kelly arrived, every speed limit from Brighton to Durham ignored. Lexi dressed in borrowed clothes that didn't fit, her own in paper bags, neatly labeled and forensically sealed. Lexi on the medical examiner's bed, tears escaping from beneath closed lids; her hand squeezing Kelly's so tightly it left a mark. There was nothing consensual about what happened to Lexi.

"Yeah, maybe," she said lightly. "Well, thanks for calling back. I don't think it's part of our series, but you never know." She ended the call and turned around, pressing her forehead against the cool plaster of the wall.

"If you want to meditate, Kelly, perhaps you could do it on your own time."

She wheeled around to see Nick in his running gear, his trainers quiet on the stairs behind her. Dark patches circled his armpits and dotted the front of his T-shirt.

"Sorry, boss, I was just taking five." Kelly's mind was racing. What had Lexi done? And why?

"You've had them. I'm going for a shower. I'll see you in the briefing room in ten minutes."

Kelly forced herself to focus on the job in hand. "You were right about the Maidstone rape; I've given the details to Lucinda."

"Okay. Let Kent police know they're off the hook. We'll take over from here. First things first, though: I've asked Cyber Crime to come and enlighten us as to what the fuck they've been doing for the last two days. You can't move without leaving a digital footprint nowadays; just how hard can it be to ID the person behind this website?"

"Very hard," Andrew Robinson said. "He's covered his tracks too well. The details for the site are registered in the Cayman Islands."

"The Cayman Islands? Is that where he's running the website from?" Kelly said.

Nick looked at her. "Don't get excited—you're not going off on some Caribbean jolly."

"It doesn't mean the offender's there," Andrew said, "only that his contact details are held there. It won't surprise you to know there's no love lost between the British police and the Cayman Islands—the chances of us getting the information we need from them are zero. However, what it did give us was the IP address of where the website is answering from." Andrew took in Kelly's and Nick's blank faces and started again. "Basically, when I look up a domain it sends a signal out to that website. If the website doesn't exist, we don't get a response, but if it does—as in this case—the reply tells us not only where the domain details are held but which device is being used to join that particular network. So, for example"—he indicated Nick's phone, which was on the table in front of them—"if you were to log on to, say, Internet banking now, that website would record the IP address of your phone, enabling us to track you."

"Got it," Nick said. "So where is the administrator logging on from?"

Andrew laced his thin fingers together and cracked his knuckles; first one hand, then the other. "It's not that simple, sadly." He opened his notebook and showed Nick and Kelly a number: 5.43.159.255.

"This is the IP address—it's like a postcode for computers. It's a static IP but it's hosted on a Russian server, and unfortunately the Russians—"

"Let me guess," Nick cut in. "The Russians don't cooperate with British police. For Christ's sake!"

Andrew raised both hands. "Don't shoot the messenger."

"Is there any way at all to trace the website?" Kelly said.

"Honestly? No. At least, not within the time frame you need, given the threat level. It's a virtually undetectable website."

"Does this mean we're looking for someone particularly savvy?" Kelly asked. "Someone with a background in IT, perhaps?"

"Not necessarily. All this stuff is available online for anyone who wants to find it. Even the DI could do it."

Kelly hid a smile. Nick let it go. "So what do you suggest?"

"It's that old adage: you've got to follow the money."

"What do you mean?" Kelly said.

"Have you never seen *All the President's Men*?" Andrew said. "You've missed out. The offender is taking payment from people registering on his dating site, right? That's the money we need to follow. Each transaction can be traced from the customer's credit or debit card to the PayPal account associated with the site, and finally to the offender's bank account. When you know how the money's being withdrawn, and by whom, then you're onto something."

Kelly felt a glimmer of optimism. "What details do you need?"

"You used your own credit card, right?"

Nick nodded.

"The date of transaction, the amount, and the credit card you used to pay. Get me those, and I'll get you our man."

CHAPTER TWENTY-TWO

We sit in near-stationary traffic on Norwood Road for half an hour, inching forward in Graham's car. He's an impatient driver, jerking the car into any available space he sees and leaning on his horn if the car in front dares wait more than a split second before moving forward at the lights. It's the second day running that Graham has driven me home, and we've run out of conversation, exhausting our usual topics about whether the old video shop will go for the asking price, and how there are never enough split-level offices to keep up with demand, and so we sit in silence.

Every now and then I say sorry again for taking Graham so far out of his way, and he dismisses my apology.

"Can't have you wandering around London with some pervert after you," he says.

Fleetingly it occurs to me that I've never been specific about the nature of the attacks on other women in London, then I realize it's a natural assumption to make about a man who stalks women.

I know I could ask Matt to pick me up, and that he would insist on driving me between work and home for as long as I needed him to. I don't ask because Simon would hate it, and Matt would like it too much.

The fact that Matt still loves me is the unspoken truth that circles between us all. Between me and Matt, when we see each other to talk about the children, and he holds my gaze for a fraction longer than he needs to. Between me and Simon, when I mention Matt's name, and see the hard flash of jealousy in Simon's eyes.

Simon can't take me. He sold his car a few weeks ago. At the time I thought he was mad; he might not have used it much during the week, but our weekends were full of supermarket shops and trips to IKEA, or heading out of town to see friends and family.

"We can take the train," he told me, when I suggested we'd miss having a car. It never once crossed my mind he couldn't afford to keep one.

I wish I had a driving license. There never seemed to be a need for it, living in London, but now I wish I could drive myself to work. Ever since I found out about the adverts I've been on high alert; every nerve ending tingling, waiting for the time I will need to run. Or fight. I look everywhere; watch everyone.

It feels safe here, in Graham's car, where I know no one is following me, and I can lean into the soft leather and shut my eyes without worrying I'm being watched.

The traffic begins to move freely again once we're over the river. The heating is on and I feel warm and relaxed for the first time in days. Graham puts the radio on and I listen to Capital FM's Greg Burns interview Art Garfunkel. The strains of "Mrs. Robinson" play over their closing remarks, and I think how funny it is that I still remember all the words, but before I can shape them in my mind, I'm falling asleep.

I slide in and out of consciousness as we drive. The traffic noise changes constantly and I'm pulled awake, only to drift off again moments later. I hear the start of a new song on the radio; shut my eyes for what seems like a split second, then wake to the closing refrain of a different track entirely.

My subconscious confuses the sounds that push their way into my sleep; the busses, the music, the radio adverts. The car's engine becomes the dull rumble of an Underground train; the presenter's voice an announcer telling me to *Mind the gap*. I'm standing on the Tube, commuters packed in beside me; the smell of aftershave and sweat in the air. The aftershave is familiar and I try to place it, but it eludes me.

Listed: Friday, 13 November
White.
Late thirties.

Eyes, everywhere. Watching me. Following me. Knowing every step of my journey. The train stops and I try to get off, but someone's pushing against me, forcing me against the wall of the carriage.

Difficulty level: Moderate

It's Luke Friedland. He's pressing hard against my chest. *I rescued you*, he's saying, and I try to shake my head; try to move. The smell of aftershave is overpowering; it fills my nostrils and chokes me.

My eyes are closed.

Why are my eyes closed?

I open them, but the man pressed against me isn't Luke Friedland.

I'm not on a train; not surrounded by commuters. I'm in Graham Hallow's car.

It's Graham with his face next to mine, his arm across me, pressing me into my seat. It's Graham I can smell; that woody, cinnamon fragrance mixed with body odor and the musty scent of his tweed jacket.

"Where are we? Get off me!"

The pressure on my chest disappears but I'm still fighting for breath; panic filling my throat as surely as though there were two hands around it. Darkness surrounds the car and seeps in through the windows, and I fumble for the door handle.

The light makes me blink.

"I was undoing your seat belt," Graham says. He sounds angry; defensive.

Because I accused him?

Or because I stopped him?

"You fell asleep."

I look down and see my seat belt has been unclipped, the strap hanging over my left arm. I realize we are parked in my street: I can see the front door of our house.

Color floods my face. "I—I'm sorry." Sleep has left me confused. "I thought . . ." I try to form the words. "I thought you were . . ." I can't say it, but I don't need to. Graham turns the ignition key, the roar of the engine putting a full stop to our conversation. I get out of the car and shiver; the temperature is fifteen degrees lower than inside. "Thank you for the lift. And I'm sorry I thought—"

He drives off, leaving me standing on the pavement.

With FindTheOne.com there are no blind-date nerves, there's no stilted conversation over dinner. I'd argue it's more honest than most online dating sites, with their airbrushed photos and their profiles full of lies. Salary range, hobbies, favorite foods . . . all irrelevant. Who builds a relationship on a mutual love of tapas? A match might be perfect on paper yet lack the spark needed to set it alight.

FindTheOne.com cuts through all that rubbish; the pretense that anyone cares if you like opera or walks in the park. It means men can take their time. They can follow you for a while, engage you in conversation; see if you're interesting enough to take for dinner, instead of wasting their time on a garrulous airhead. It means men can get up close and personal. Smell your perfume; your breath; your skin. Feel a spark. Act on it.

Are you wondering who my clients are? Who would use a website like this? Are you thinking the market can't possibly be big enough?

I can assure you it is.

My customers come from all walks of life. They're men with no time to form relationships. Men with enough money not to care. Men who haven't found that "special someone"; men who get their kicks from being in control. Everyone has their own reason for joining FindTheOne.com; it isn't my job to care what it is.

So who are these men?

They're your friends. They're your father, your brother, your best friend, your neighbor, your boss. They're the people you see every day; the people you travel to and from work with.

You're shocked. You think you know them better than that.

You're wrong.

CHAPTER
TWENTY-THREE

"Is this your vehicle?" Kelly pushed a photograph of a black Lexus across the table. Gordon Tillman nodded. "For the benefit of the tape, the suspect is nodding his head." Kelly looked at Tillman, less confident now that his flashy suit had been exchanged for a gray custody-issue tracksuit but still arrogant enough to try to outstare his interviewers. His date of birth put him at forty-seven, but he looked ten years older, his skin mottled by years of excess. Drugs? Or drink? Drink and women. Late nights spent flashing the cash to attract girls who wouldn't otherwise give him a second glance. Kelly tried to keep the look of disgust off her face.

"Were you driving it at approximately quarter to nine yesterday morning?"

"You know I was." Tillman was relaxed, his arms folded across his chest as he answered Kelly's questions. He hadn't asked for a solicitor, and Kelly hadn't yet worked out how the interview was going to go. Full admission? It was looking that way, and yet . . . there was something in Tillman's eyes that suggested it wasn't going to be quite that easy. She had a sudden memory of another interview room—a different suspect; the same crime—and she clenched her fists tightly beneath the table. It had been a one-off. He'd pressed her buttons, but she was younger then, less experienced. It wouldn't happen again.

But sweat trickled down her spine nevertheless, and she had to fight to keep focus. It had never come back to her; the words whispered in her ear. The words that had tipped her over the edge and caused the red mist to descend so completely that she lost control.

"Could you tell me, in your own words, what happened between half past eight and ten o'clock yesterday?"

"I was returning from a conference I'd been to the night before. There was a dinner afterward and I stayed the night in Maidstone so I was about to head back to Oxfordshire. I was going to work from home for the rest of the day."

"Where do you work?"

Tillman looked at her, letting his eyes flick briefly, but very deliberately, down to her chest before he answered. Kelly felt, rather than saw, Nick lean forward in his chair. She willed him not to speak. She didn't want to give Tillman the satisfaction of knowing she'd even noticed where his gaze fell.

"In the city. I'm a wealth manager for NCJ Investors."

Kelly hadn't been surprised when the DI had told her he'd be sitting in on the interview. She had begged him to let her interview Tillman, reminding him of how hard she'd worked on the case, and how badly she wanted to be there, at the finish. He had taken forever to reply.

"Okay. But I'll be there, too." Kelly had nodded. "You're too inexperienced to lead this alone, and there'll be a few noses out of joint in the office as it is."

The other reason lay unspoken between them. He didn't trust Kelly not to lose it. How could she blame him? She didn't trust herself.

She had been suspended instantly, the threat of criminal proceedings running alongside the internal disciplinary hearing.

"What the hell were you thinking?" Diggers had said, when Kelly had been hauled out of custody, her shirt ripped and a bruise forming on the side of her face where the suspect had fought back. She was shaking violently, the adrenaline leaving her body as quickly as it had arrived.

"I didn't think at all." That wasn't true. She'd been thinking about

Lexi. It was inevitable; she'd known that as soon as the case came in. A girl, raped by a stranger on her way home from school. "I'll take it," she'd told her DS instantly. She'd treated the victim with the compassion she had wished her sister had experienced, feeling like she was making a difference.

A few days later they brought in the offender; a DNA hit on a known sex offender. He declined a brief; sat smirking in the interview room in a paper suit. *No comment. No comment. No comment.* Then he yawned, as if the whole situation was boring him, and Kelly had felt the rage building inside her like a kettle about to boil.

"So you were driving home . . ." Nick prompted, when Kelly didn't say anything. She forced herself to focus on Tillman.

"I was coming past the station and I realized I was probably still over the limit from the night before." The corner of Tillman's mouth curled into a smile, and Kelly realized he knew full well the admission could never result in legal proceedings. She would have bet her pension on Gordon Tillman being a regular drink driver: he was just the sort of arrogant wanker who would claim to drive better after a few pints. "I thought I'd better stop for a coffee, so I pulled over and asked a woman if there was somewhere nearby."

"Can you describe this woman?"

"Mid thirties, blonde hair. Tidy figure." Tillman smiled again. "She recommended a café relatively close, and I asked if she wanted to come with me."

"You asked a complete stranger out for coffee?" Kelly said, not bothering to disguise her disbelief.

"You know what they say," Tillman said, the smirk still playing across his face. "A stranger's simply a friend you haven't met yet. She was giving me the eye as soon as I pulled up."

"Do you make a habit of asking women you haven't met out for coffee?" Kelly persisted.

Tillman took his time; looking Kelly up and down again, and shaking his head very slightly before answering. "Don't worry, love, I only ask the pretty ones," he said.

"If you could continue," Nick interrupted, "with your *version* of events." Tillman registered the emphasis but carried on.

"She got in, and we headed toward the café, but then she made me an offer I couldn't refuse." The grin on Tillman's face made bile rise in Kelly's throat. "She said she'd never done anything like this in her life, but she'd always had this fantasy about having sex with a stranger, and what did I think? Well"—he laughed—"what would you think? She said she wasn't going to tell me her name, and she didn't want to know mine, and then she directed me to an industrial estate on the outskirts of Maidstone."

"And what happened there?"

"You want all the details?" Tillman leaned forward, looking at Kelly challengingly. "There's a name for your sort, you know."

Kelly didn't miss a beat. "And there's a name for your sort." There was a knot of rage in her stomach, and she concentrated on keeping it there.

There was a pause. Tillman smirked. "She gave me a blow job, then I fucked her. I offered her a lift back but she said she wanted me to leave her there. Part of the fantasy, I guess." He held Kelly's gaze, as if he could sense there was a battle raging inside her; that this entire situation was unlocking something she'd so successfully suppressed. "She liked it rough, but then, a lot of women do, don't they?" He smirked again. "Judging by the noise this one made, she loved it."

She loved it.

The suspect hadn't taken his eyes off Kelly for the entire interview. She'd been with a male colleague, and the offender hadn't said anything provocative; hadn't made any move to intimidate Kelly. It was when the tapes were off, and Kelly was leading him back to his cell alone, that he leaned in toward her. She felt the warmth of his breath on her neck, and smelled the stale tang of body odor and cigarettes.

"She loved it," he whispered.

It had been like an out-of-body experience, Kelly had thought afterward. As though it were someone else who had spun around with her fist raised, hitting him squarely on the nose, clawing at his face. Someone else losing control. Kelly's colleague had dragged her off, but it was too late.

Kelly wondered when Lexi had written that letter to Durham Constabulary; whether even by that point Lexi cared less about the outcome than Kelly did; whether Kelly had almost lost her job for no reason.

"That's it, is it?" Kelly said, pushing the image away. "That's your story?"

"That's what happened." Tillman folded his arms again and leaned against his chair, making the plastic creak. "But let me guess: she's had an attack of the guilts, or her boyfriend's found out, and now she's crying rape. Right?"

Kelly had learned a lot over the past few years. There were better ways to deal with criminals than by getting angry. She leaned back, mirroring Tillman; the palms of both hands raised as though she were accepting defeat. Waiting for the smug smile she knew was coming.

And then, "Tell me about FindTheOne.com." The change was immediate.

Panic flashed in Tillman's eyes and his whole body tensed.

"What do you mean?"

"How long have you been a member?"

"I don't know what you're talking about."

Now it was Kelly's turn to smile. "Oh really? So when we search your house—which we'll be doing while you're in custody—and we look at your computer, we won't find any record of your visits to the website?"

A sweat broke out on Tillman's forehead.

"We won't find details of the victim's commute? Paid for? Down-loaded?"

Tillman wiped his palm across his face, then rubbed the fabric of his tracksuit bottoms, leaving a dark patch of sweat on his right thigh.

"What membership level did you go for? Gold, right? A man like you wouldn't settle for anything but the best."

"Stop the interview," Tillman said. "I've changed my mind. I want a solicitor."

It didn't surprise Kelly that Gordon Tillman wanted his own solicitor summoned, rather than the duty brief, and it was no skin off Kelly's nose that he had to wait three hours for the privilege. In the meantime police in Oxfordshire seized Tillman's laptop, along with the under-pants he'd been wearing at the time of the alleged assault, which were lying half in, half out of the laundry basket in his bathroom. Met offi-cers visited Tillman's office to seize his work computer and the con-tents of his desk drawers, and Kelly took comfort from the fact that, whether a court found Tillman guilty or not, his career was over.

"How fast can you process the laptop?" Nick asked Andrew. He and Kelly were back at MIT while Tillman consulted with his solicitor.

"Three to five days on urgent. Twenty-four hours if you can find the budget."

"I'll find it. I want his search history for the last six months, with every visit to the website documented. I want to know which profiles he's viewed, what he's downloaded, and if he's Google Earthed their locations. And trawl the hard drive for porn—he's bound to have some, and if any of it is within an inch of being illegal, we'll have him for it. Arrogant arsehole."

"You didn't take to Tillman, then?" Kelly said, after Andrew had disappeared off to his cubbyhole. "But he was so charming." She gri-maced. "How much do you think he knows?"

"Hard to tell. Enough to clam up when he realized we knew about the website, certainly, but whether he knows who's behind it, I'm not sure. If his brief's got any sense he'll advise him to go no comment, so it'll come down to forensics. Have we had the report from the medical examiner?"

"I spoke to Kent's sexual offenses team before we went into the interview, and they've faxed through the full report. There's clear evidence of sexual intercourse, but of course that's not in dispute."

She handed the fax to Nick, who scanned its contents.

"No defensive injuries, and no obvious signs of force?"

"That doesn't mean anything."

Lexi hadn't been injured. She'd frozen, she told Kelly; it was what she blamed herself for more than anything else. Not fighting.

"No, but it makes it a damn sight harder for us to prove a lack of consent. It's critical we prove a link between Gordon Tillman and the victim's profile on the website. If we can do that, his story about randomly meeting her on the street comes instantly undone."

"And if we can't?" Kelly said.

"We will. Where's Lucinda?"

"In a tasking meeting."

"I want her to identify the outstanding victims on the website. We don't have their names but we have their photos and we know exactly where they'll be between home and work. I want them identified, brought in, and warned."

"Consider it done."

Nick paused. "That was a tough interview. You did a good job. I'm impressed."

"Thank you."

"Let's get him back in. I can't imagine it will take long."

The DI's prediction was correct. On the advice of his solicitor, a thin, anxious-looking man with wire-rimmed glasses, Gordon Tillman answered "No comment" to every question asked of him.

"I trust you'll be bailing my client," the solicitor said when Tillman had been taken down to his cell.

"That's not what we had in mind, I'm afraid," Kelly said. "This is a serious investigation and we have extensive forensic inquiries to carry out. Your client will need to make himself comfortable for quite a while." Nick's positive feedback had given her confidence, and she had felt more like her old self during the second half of the interview. The DC she used to be, before she messed up.

They could hold Tillman for up to twenty-four hours, but Nick had been in touch with the duty superintendent for an extension. Given the time frame from Andrew, even the additional twelve hours the superintendent could authorize were unlikely to be enough; they would need a magistrate's authority to keep Tillman behind bars for any longer.

Kelly flicked through the case papers while she waited to update the custody sergeant. The victim statement made for grim reading. The black Lexus had pulled up alongside her; the man inside asking for directions, pushing open the passenger door because "the window doesn't open."

"I thought it was odd," Kathryn's statement read, "given how new the car looked, but it didn't occur to me to be suspicious." She had leaned into the car to give directions—the driver said he was looking for the M20—and described a man who seemed friendly and unthreatening.

"He apologized for taking up my time," she said, "and thanked me for being so helpful."

Kathryn had been going over the directions a second time ("He said his memory was terrible") when Gordon Tillman's true intention had become clear.

"He suddenly reached out and grabbed me. He took a huge handful of the gray wrap I was wearing, gripping it somewhere behind my right shoulder, and hauled me into the car. It happened so fast I don't think I even managed to scream. He drove off, my feet still out of the car, and my face pushed into his lap. I could feel the steering wheel on the back of my head, and he used his free hand to push my head against his crotch."

At some point the car had stopped long enough for Tillman to reach across the victim and slam the passenger door shut, but he kept her head pressed into his groin; the car in a low gear he didn't once change.

"I tried to turn my head but he wouldn't let me," she had told the Kent detective taking her statement. "My face was pressed against his penis and I felt it getting harder and harder. That's when I knew he was going to rape me."

A note from the attending officer told Kelly the victim had two children, the youngest just eighteen months old. She worked full-time as a recruitment consultant and had been married for eleven years.

I fully support police proceedings and am willing to attend court, if required.

Of course she did. Why wouldn't she? Why didn't Lexi?

"I need some fresh air," she told Nick, who barely looked up from his desk. Kelly left MIT, running down the stairs and making her way to the gated area at the rear of the station. She realized her fists were clenched into tight balls, and she made herself unfurl her fingers and take a deep breath.

Lexi picked up the phone just as Kelly thought it was going to go to voice mail.

"Why did you tell Durham police you wouldn't go to court?" Kelly heard a sharp intake of breath.

"Hold on."

There was a muffled conversation; voices Kelly recognized as Lexi's husband and one of the children. Fergus, she thought. A door closed.

When Lexi spoke again she was quiet but firm. "How do you know that?"

"Why did you tell them you wouldn't support a prosecution, Lexi?"

"Because I wouldn't."

"I don't understand. How could you walk away from the biggest thing that's ever happened to you?"

"It isn't the biggest thing that's ever happened to me, that's how! My husband is the biggest thing that's ever happened to me. Fergus and Alfie are the biggest things. You, Mum, Dad . . . all more important than what happened in Durham a lifetime ago."

"What about other people? How would you feel if he raped someone else, because he hadn't been found guilty of attacking you?"

Lexi sighed. "I do feel guilty about that, I really do. But it's self-preservation, Kelly. I would have cracked up otherwise, and then where would I have been? What use would I have been to the boys?"

"I don't understand why you've made it so black-and-white. It might be years before he's caught—if ever. You might feel completely differently then."

"But don't you see, that's exactly what made it so hard?" Kelly heard the break in her sister's voice and felt a lump in her own throat. "I never knew when it might happen. I didn't know if I'd suddenly get a call to say they had someone in custody, or that someone had come forward with information. What if it was the day before a job interview? What if it was one of the kids' birthdays? I'm happy, Kelly. I've got a good life, with a family I love, and what happened in Durham was a million years ago. I don't want it all dragged up again."

Kelly said nothing.

"You must be able to understand that. You must see why I did it?"

"No. I don't understand it at all. And I don't understand why you never told me that's what you did."

"Because of this, Kelly! Because you've never let me move on, even when I wanted to. You're a police officer; you spend your life digging up the past, looking for answers. But sometimes there aren't any answers. Sometimes shit just happens, and you have to deal with it in the best way you can."

"Denial isn't the best way to—"

"You live your life, Kelly. Let me live mine."

The line went dead, and Kelly stood in the freezing yard, half-hidden in the shadows.

CHAPTER
TWENTY-FOUR

"Are you nervous, love?"

"A bit."

It's one o'clock on Saturday and we're in the kitchen, clearing away the remains of the soup I made. I wanted Katie to have something hot inside her before her rehearsal, but she picked at a bread roll and barely touched her soup.

"I'm nervous, too," I tell her. I smile, intending to show solidarity, but Katie's face falls.

"Don't you think I can do it?"

"Oh, love, that's not what I meant." I kick myself for yet again saying the wrong thing. "I'm not nervous *for* you; I'm excited. Butterflies, you know." I give her a hug, but the doorbell rings and she pulls away.

"That'll be Isaac."

I follow her out to the hall, wiping my hands on a tea towel. They've got a technical rehearsal first, then we're all joining them for the dress rehearsal. I so want to like it. For Katie's sake. I paste on a smile as Katie disentangles herself from Isaac and he says hello.

"Thank you for picking her up." I mean it. Isaac Gunn isn't who I'd choose for my daughter to go out with—he's too smarmy, too old for her—but I can't deny he's looking after her. She hasn't once taken the Tube home alone after a rehearsal, and he's even driving her home after her restaurant shifts.

PC Swift promised to call me the moment they traced Luke Friedland, and the absence of a call has made me jittery. I've twice logged on to the website today and looked at the other women listed; downloaded those showing as "available on weekends," and wondered if they're being followed right now.

Justin comes downstairs. He nods to Isaac. "All right, mate? Mum, I'm heading out. I might stop out tonight."

"No, you're not. We're going to see Katie's play."

"I'm not." He turns to Katie and Isaac. "No offense, guys, but it's really not my sort of thing."

Katie laughs. "It's fine."

"No, it isn't," I say firmly. "We are going as a family to watch Katie perform in her first professional play. End of discussion."

"Look, there's really no need to cause an argument," Isaac says. "If Justin doesn't want to come, we're cool with that, aren't we, Kate?" He slides a hand around her waist as he speaks, and she looks up at him and nods.

Kate?

I'm standing just a few feet away from my daughter, yet it feels as though there's a great chasm between us. A few weeks ago it would have been Katie and me against the world; now it's Katie and Isaac. *Kate* and Isaac.

"It's only a dress rehearsal," she says.

"All the more reason why we should be cheering you on, so you're ready for opening night."

Even Justin knows when I won't be moved.

"Fine."

Isaac coughs. "We'd better—"

"We'll see you there, Mum. You know how to find the theater?"

"Yes, yes. Break a leg!" My smile is making my cheeks ache. I stand at the open door and watch them walk away, waving when Katie turns around. I close the door, the hallway cold from the outside air.

"She doesn't care if I'm there or not, you know."

"I care."

Justin leans against the banister. He eyes me thoughtfully.

"Do you? Or do you just want Katie to think you're taking her acting seriously?"

I flush. "I *am* taking it seriously."

Justin puts a foot on the bottom step, bored with the conversation. "And the rest of us have to sit through some Shakespeare shite just so you can prove it. Cheers, Mum."

I've arranged for Matt to pick us all up at three. He rings the bell but when I open the door he's next door, ringing Melissa's doorbell.

"I'll wait in the cab," he says.

By the time I've chivvied Justin and Simon, and put on my coat, Melissa and Neil are already in the cab. Neil's sitting in the front, and Melissa's in the backseat. I slide in next to her, leaving room for Justin. Simon sits on the folding seat behind Matt.

"Well, isn't this nice?" Melissa says. "I don't know when I last went to the theater."

"Lovely." I give her a grateful smile. Simon is staring out of the window. I move my foot so it's nudging his, but he ignores it, shifting his legs away from me.

He didn't want Matt to pick us up.

"We can take the Tube," he said, when I told him Matt had offered.

"Don't be absurd. It's really kind of him. You've got to get over this, Simon."

"How would you like it, if the situation were reversed? My ex, driving us around . . ."

"I wouldn't give two hoots."

"You can go in the cab, then. I'll meet you there."

"So that everyone else can see how ridiculous you're being? And know we've had a row?"

If there's one thing Simon hates, it's people talking about him.

Matt calls over his shoulder to me. "Rupert Street, isn't it?"

"That's right. Apparently it's next to a pub."

Simon twists around in his seat, the screen on his mobile phone lighting up his face. "Waterloo Bridge, past Somerset House and left onto Drury Lane," he says.

Matt laughs. "On a Saturday? No chance, mate. Vauxhall Bridge, Millbank all the way to Whitehall, and we can take a gamble on the finish when we get to Charing Cross."

"It's ten minutes quicker via Waterloo, according to the GPS."

"I don't need a GPS, mate. It's all up here." He taps the side of his head. Simon's shoulders tense. When Matt was doing the taxi licensing course he used to ride around the city on a bike, learning every backstreet, every one-way system. There isn't a GPS on the market that could get you across the capital more reliably than my ex-husband.

But that isn't the issue right now. I glance at Simon, who is looking out of the window; the only sign of his irritation his fingers, drumming on his thigh. "I do think Waterloo might be quicker, Matt," I say. He looks at me in the rearview mirror and I hold his gaze, silently asking him to just do this one thing for me; knowing that however much he'd like to score points over Simon, he'd never do anything to upset me.

"Waterloo it is, then. Then Drury Lane, you say?"

Simon checks his phone again. "That's right. Shout if you need directions." His face shows no triumph, or relief, but his fingers cease their drumming, and I see him relax into his seat.

Matt looks at me again and I move my lips in the tiniest of silent thank-yous. He shakes his head, and I don't know if he's dismissing my thanks or despairing that I felt it necessary. Simon turns to face the rear seat and I feel something against my foot; when I look down, Simon's is pressed against mine.

Nobody speaks when, fifteen minutes later, we're in barely moving traffic at Waterloo. I try to think of something to say, but Melissa gets there before me.

"Have the police got any answers for you yet?"

"Nothing new." I speak quietly, hoping to gloss over it, but Simon leans forward.

"Answers? About the photographs in the *Gazette*, you mean?"

I glance at Melissa, who shrugs awkwardly. "I thought you'd have told him."

The inside of the windows has steamed up. I pull my sleeve over my hand and use the cuff to wipe it clear. Outside, the traffic is nose to tail, their lights blurring into streaks of red and white through the rain.

"Told me what?"

Matt edges forward. He looks at me through the mirror. Even Neil has turned around and is waiting for me to speak.

"Oh, for heaven's sake. It's nothing."

"It's not nothing, Zoe," Melissa says.

I sigh. "Okay, it's not nothing. The adverts in the *Gazette* showcase a website called FindTheOne.com. It's a sort of dating site."

"And you're on it?" Matt says, with a horrified laugh.

I keep talking, as much for my own benefit as anyone else's. Every time I talk about what's happening, I feel stronger. It's secrecy that's dangerous. If everyone knew they were being watched—if everyone knew they were being followed—surely no one would get hurt? "The site sells details of women's commutes to work; which Tube line they take, which carriage they sit in, that sort of thing. The police have linked the site to at least two murders, and to a number of other crimes against women." I don't tell them about Luke Friedland; I don't want Simon to worry about me any more than he already does.

"Why didn't you tell me?"

"Christ, Zoe!"

"Mum, are you okay?"

"Do the police know who's behind the website?"

I hold my hands up in front of my face, fending off the questions. "I'm fine. No, they don't know." I look at Simon. "I didn't tell you because I thought you had enough going on." I don't mention the job loss—not in front of everyone—but he nods to show me he understands.

"You should have told me," he says quietly.

"What are the police doing?" Melissa says.

"Apparently the website is practically untraceable. Something about a proxy something or other . . ."

"A proxy server," Neil says. "Makes sense. He's logging on via someone else's server, to avoid detection. I'd be surprised if the police have any joy there. Sorry, that's probably not the answer you want."

It isn't, but it's the answer I'm starting to get used to. I look through the window as we cross Waterloo Bridge, and let the others talk about the website as though I'm not there. They ask the questions I've already asked the police; go around the same circles I've already traveled. My fears are unpacked and examined; analyzed for entertainment like an *EastEnders* plotline.

"How do you think they get the details of people's commutes in the first place?"

"Follow them, I suppose."

"They can't follow everyone, though, can they?"

"Can we change the subject now?" I say, and everyone falls silent. Simon looks at me, making sure I'm okay, and I give a little nod. Justin is staring straight ahead, but his fists are clenched on his knees and I kick myself for talking about the website in such a flippant way. I should have sat the kids down privately and explained what was going on; given them a chance to tell me how they felt. I reach out a hand toward Justin, but he stiffens and angles his shoulders away from me. I'll have to find a quiet moment to talk to him later, after the play. Outside there are people walking in pairs and on their own, holding umbrellas and tugging hoods over windswept hair. No one is looking behind them; no one is checking to see who's watching them, so I do it for them.

How many of you are being followed? Would you even know?

The Rupert Street theater doesn't look like a theater from the outside. The neighboring pub is noisy and full of young people, and the theater itself has no windows to the street. The brickwork is painted black and a single poster on the door gives the dates of *Twelfth Night*.

"Katherine Walker!" Melissa squeals, pointing at the tiny writing toward the bottom of the poster.

"Our Katie, a proper actress." Matt grins. I think for a second he's about to put his arm around me, and I take a step to the side. Instead he gives me an awkward punch to my shoulder, like he's greeting another cabbie.

"She's done all right, hasn't she?" I say. Because although she isn't being paid, and although the Rupert Street theater is really just an old warehouse with block staging and rows of plastic seats, Katie is doing exactly what she always dreamed of. I envy her. Not for her youth, or her looks—the way people assume mothers envy their daughters—but for her passion. I try to think what I might have done; what grand passion I might have followed.

"Did I have a passion when I was her age?" I say to Matt, quietly enough for no one else to hear.

"What?" We're trooping downstairs, but I need to know. I feel my identity slipping away from me, reduced to a commute on a website for someone to buy. I pull Matt's arm, making him fall behind the others, and we stand in the shadowed curve of the staircase while I try to explain.

"Something like Katie's acting. She's so *alive* when she talks about it; so driven. Was there something like that for me?"

He shrugs, not sure what I mean; why it's suddenly so important.

"You liked going to the cinema. We saw so many films when you were pregnant with Jus."

"I don't mean like that—that's barely even a hobby." I'm convinced I've simply forgotten; that somewhere, buried inside me, is a passion that defines me. "Remember how you were mad for motocross? You'd spend all weekend at the track, or fixing up bikes. You loved it so much. Didn't I have something like that; something I loved more than anything else?"

Matt comes closer, the smell of cigarettes and extra-strong mints reassuringly familiar. "Me," he says quietly. "You loved me."

"Are you two coming?" Melissa runs up the stairs, then stops, one hand on the railing. She eyes us curiously.

"Sorry," Matt says. "We were just taking a trip down memory lane. It won't surprise you to know that our Katie has always loved the limelight." They walk on down the stairs, Matt recounting how five-year-old Katie once took to the stage on our Haven holiday, to sing "Somewhere Over the Rainbow." I follow behind them, letting my heart rate slowly return to normal.

Downstairs, Isaac makes a big fuss of showing us to our seats. We're surrounded by seventeen-year-olds clutching well-thumbed copies of the play, colored Post-it notes protruding from the pages.

"We always send out invitations to the local schools when we need an audience for a dress rehearsal," Isaac says, seeing me looking around. "It helps the actors to have a proper audience, and *Twelfth Night*'s always on the syllabus somewhere."

"What kept you?" Simon says, when I slide into my seat beside him.

"I was looking for the loo."

Simon points to the door to the side of the auditorium, clearly marked *Toilet*.

"I'll go later. They're about to start." I'm aware of Matt sitting down next to me, radiating warmth I can feel even without touching him. I lean toward Simon, my hand in his. "What if I don't understand it?" I whisper. "I didn't do Shakespeare in school—all that stuff you and Katie were talking about, I don't have the first clue about it."

He squeezes my hand. "Just enjoy it. Katie's not going to ask you about themes; she just wants to know you thought she was brilliant."

That's easy. I know she will be. I'm about to say as much to Simon, when the lights dip and there's a hush across the audience. The curtain opens.

If music be the food of love, play on.

There's only one man on stage. I had imagined Elizabethan ruffs and frilly cuffs, but he's dressed in skinny black jeans and a gray T-shirt, his feet in red-and-white Converse. I let his words fall around me like music; not understanding every line but enjoying the sound they make. When Katie comes on, accompanied by two sailors, I almost call out in excitement. She looks sensational, her hair twisted into an elaborate plait that hangs over one shoulder, and wearing a tight silver top. Her skirt is ripped, a consequence of the shipwreck conveyed to us a moment ago through flashing lights and crashing sound effects.

My brother he is in Elysium. Perchance he is not drowned: what think you, sailors?

I have to remind myself it's Katie up there. She doesn't miss a beat, her presence filling the auditorium even when she isn't speaking. I mean to watch her, and her alone, but I'm swept away by the story; by the other actors, who throw words at one another as though they're sparring—the winner the one who has the final say. I surprise myself by laughing, then being moved to tears.

Make me a willow cabin at your gate.

Her voice carries across the silent audience and I realize I'm holding my breath. I've seen Katie in school plays, practicing audition pieces, singing in holiday camp talent competitions. But this is different. She is breathtaking.

> *Oh, you should not rest,*
> *Between the elements of air and earth,*
> *But you should pity me.*

I squeeze Simon's hand, and look to my left, where Matt is grinning fit to burst. I wonder if he sees her as I do. *Practically an adult*, I often say, when I'm telling people about Katie, but now I realize there's no *practically* about it. She's a grown woman. Whether she makes the right decisions in life or the wrong ones, they're her choices to make.

We clap wildly when Isaac takes to the stage to tell us "This is where the interval will be," laugh in all the right places, and sit in sympathetic silence when the lighting guy messes up his cues and plunges Olivia and Sebastian into darkness. By the final curtain call I'm dying to jump out of my seat and find Katie. I wonder whether Isaac will take us backstage, but Katie runs onto the stage and hops down into the audience with us. We crowd around her, and even Justin tells her it was "all right."

"You were amazing . . ." I realize I have tears in my eyes, and I blink them away, laughing and crying at the same time. I hold both her hands. "You were amazing!" I say again. She hugs me and I smell greasepaint and powder.

"No secretarial course?" she says. She's playing with me, but I drop her hands and instead cup my palms around her chin. Her eyes are glittering and she's never looked so beautiful. I rub a smudge of makeup away with one thumb.

"Not if it isn't what you want to do."

I register the surprise on her face, but now isn't the time to talk. I step aside and give the others a chance to tell her how brilliant she was, basking in her reflected glory. From the corner of my eye I see Isaac watching her. He catches my eye and walks over.

"Wasn't she brilliant?" I say.

Isaac nods slowly, and as if she can feel his eyes on her, Katie looks up and smiles.

"The star of the show," he says.

CHAPTER
TWENTY-FIVE

The London Underground CCTV hub still had the smell of new carpets and fresh paint. Twenty wall-mounted monitors faced the row of desks, behind which three operators switched deftly between cameras using joysticks and computer keyboards. In one corner a door led to the editing suite, where footage could be captured, enhanced, and circulated to investigating officers. Kelly signed in and made her way to Craig's station on the far side, one eye on a follow at King's Cross being monitored by one of the other operators.

"He's passing Boots now . . . something dumped in the bin below the clock. Green hoodie, black Adidas tracksuit bottoms, white trainers."

A uniformed officer ran across the screen, gaining on the tracksuited figure, who was now level with Claire's Accessories. All around them stood people with suitcases, briefcases, shopping bags. They looked up at the huge screens above their heads; waiting for platform information, train times, delays. Oblivious to the crimes that went on around them every day.

"Hi, Kelly, how's Met life treating you?"

Kelly liked Craig. He was in his early twenties and desperate to join the job. He soaked up everything officers said and had better instincts than half the coppers Kelly had worked with, but the fitness test was proving a bit of a challenge.

"It's great, I'm loving it. How's the training going?"

Craig looked proud. He patted his not-inconsiderable stomach.

"Four pounds down this week. Slimming World."

"Good for you. Can you help me find someone?"

Locating Luke Friedland on CCTV was easy; Zoe Walker's timings were spot-on. The platform at Whitechapel was too crowded for Kelly to clearly see Zoe, but after the train had pulled away, taking the crowd of people with it, the camera footage showed her standing opposite a tall man.

Luke Friedland.

Assuming that really was his name.

If she hadn't been aware of the context, Kelly would have taken them for a couple. They seemed at ease together, Friedland touching Zoe lightly on the arm as they said good-bye.

"Play that clip again for me?" she asked Craig.

A swell in the crowd, like a muted stadium wave, indicated some sort of commotion as the train approached, but it was swiftly replaced by the surge of commuters getting onto the train. The camera was too far away to see exactly what had happened to make Zoe trip.

Kelly's phone vibrated against the desk. She looked down to see an incoming call from Lexi and flipped the phone onto its front so she could ignore it. Let Lexi leave another voice mail—Kelly didn't want to speak to her.

U dont undrstnd, Lexi's last text had said.

Kelly didn't. What was the point in the job she and her colleagues did? In the CPS files, the court system, the prison service? What was the point in fighting for justice if victims—people like Lexi—couldn't be bothered to support proceedings?

She gave Craig the second date and time. Tuesday, 24 November; around 1830 hours. Zoe's next encounter with Friedland; when he had accompanied Zoe from the train at Crystal Palace to the exit, then asked her out for a drink. Had he downloaded other women's profiles from the website? Tried the same approach with them? Andrew

Robinson had seemed confident his Cyber Crime team would identify the man behind the website, but how long would it take? In the meantime Kelly was treating the case in the same way she'd tackle a drug ring: from the bottom up. Gordon Tillman had refused to answer her questions, but perhaps Luke Friedland would be more talkative.

"This him?" Craig pressed pause and Kelly nodded.

They were walking toward the barriers; Kelly recognized Zoe's red waterproof jacket, and the more formal overcoat she'd seen Friedland wearing in the previous clip. Exactly as Zoe had said in her statement, as they approached the ticket barriers, Friedland waited, letting Zoe go first.

Kelly smiled as she saw Friedland tap his Oyster on the barrier. "Gotcha," she muttered, noting down the precise time on the screen. Picking up the phone, she dialed from memory.

"Hey, Brian, what's new?"

"Same shit, different day; you know how it is," Brian said cheerfully. "How's the transfer going?"

"Loving it."

"What can I do you for?"

"Tuesday, 24 November, Crystal Palace, second barrier from the left, 1837. If it helps, the system should show a Mrs. Zoe Walker immediately preceding it."

"Give me a second."

Kelly heard the tapping of Brian's keyboard. He was singing under his breath, and Kelly recognized the same tuneless refrain he'd been humming ever since she had known him. Brian had done his thirty years in the job, kick-started his pension, then returned the next day to a new job with London Underground.

"I'd be bored at home," he'd told Kelly, when she'd questioned why he wasn't off enjoying his retirement. After thirty years working in London there was nothing Brian didn't know about the city; when he finally retired he'd be hard to replace.

"Any idea who you're after, Kelly?"

"Definitely a man," she said, "possibly a Luke Friedland."

Another pause, then Brian chuckled; a throaty, phlegmy sound fueled by coffee and Benson & Hedges. "Not very imaginative, your chap. His Oyster's registered to a Luke Harris. Want to have a stab at what street he lives on?"

"Friedland Street?"

"Got it in one."

They were waiting for him when he got home from work, stepping out of the car as he paused to enter his door code.

"Could we have a quick word?" Kelly said, showing her warrant card and watching Harris intently. Was she imagining it, or was there a flash of panic in his eyes?

"What about?"

"Shall we go up?"

"It's not terribly convenient; I've got a lot of work to do tonight. Perhaps you could leave a number . . ."

"We can take you down to the station, if you'd prefer?" Nick said, moving from behind Kelly to stand next to her. Harris looked from one to the other.

"You'd better come in."

Luke Harris lived in a penthouse apartment in W1, the highest of six floors housing more modest flats. They stepped out of the lift into a vast open-plan space, the gleaming white surfaces of a rarely used kitchen to their left.

"Very nice," Nick said, walking across the living room and looking out at the city. To the right the BT Tower loomed over its neighbors, and Kelly could see The Shard and Heron Tower in the distance. In the center of the room two overstuffed sofas sat facing each other, separated by a huge glass coffee table, its surface piled with glossy travel books. "Read all these, have you?"

Harris was nervous, tugging at his tie and looking first at Kelly, then at Nick. "What's all this about?"

"Does the name Zoe Walker mean anything to you?"

"I'm afraid not."

"You asked her out for a drink last week, outside Crystal Palace station."

"Ah! Yes, of course. Zoe. She said no." Kelly detected a note of indignation that didn't match the careless shrug Harris had given.

"Unusual for a woman to resist your charms?" Kelly said, her voice thick with sarcasm. Harris had the grace to blush slightly.

"Not at all. It's only that we'd got on rather well, I thought, in the short time we'd spent together. And although she was attractive she must have been pushing forty, so . . ." He trailed off under Kelly's withering stare.

"And you thought she might be a bit more grateful?"

Harris said nothing.

"How did you meet Zoe Walker?" Nick turned away from the floor-to-ceiling windows and walked to the middle of the room. Harris hadn't invited her to take a seat, and had remained standing himself, so Kelly had done the same. The DI had no such reservations. He sat heavily on one of the sofas, the cushion billowing out on either side of him. Kelly followed his lead. Reluctantly, as though he had up to that point hoped they wouldn't be staying long, Harris sat down opposite them.

"We got chatting on the Underground on Monday. Then we bumped into each other again and seemed to hit it off." He shrugged again, but there was something forced about it. "It's not a crime to ask someone out, is it?"

"You met on the Tube?" Kelly said.

"Yes."

"Completely by chance?"

Harris paused. "Yes. Look, this is all quite absurd. I've got work to do, so if you don't mind—" He began to stand up.

"You didn't buy her commute details on a website called FindTheOne?"

Kelly kept her tone casual, enjoying the look on Harris's face, which oscillated between shock and fear. He sat down, and Kelly waited for him to speak.

The pause seemed to go on forever.

"Are you arresting me?"

"Should I be?"

Kelly let the silence answer for her. Had he committed an offense? It wasn't a crime to ask Zoe Walker out for a drink, but if he'd been following her . . .

Gordon Tillman had been charged with rape, remanded, and put before a Saturday-morning magistrates court. On his solicitor's advice Tillman had gone no comment to all the questions put to him, despite Kelly's suggestion that he was only making the situation worse.

"Who's behind the website, Gordon?" Kelly had asked again. "The courts will look far more favorably on you if you help us out."

Tillman had looked at his solicitor, who was quick to answer on his behalf.

"That's a bold promise, PC Swift, and one you are not at liberty to make. I have advised my client to make no further comment."

There had been a halfhearted attempt at a bail application at court, based on Tillman's previous good character, his standing in the community, and the impact his absence would have on his career, but the speed with which the magistrate refused the request suggested he had made up his mind some time earlier.

They hadn't managed to get any information out of Tillman, but perhaps Luke Harris would prove more forthcoming. The stakes were lower; no allegation of rape, no custody-issue tracksuit, no time in a cell. Softly, softly.

"The website," Kelly prompted now.

Harris leaned his elbows on his knees and rested his head between splayed-out fingers. "I joined a few weeks ago," he muttered to the thick pile of the rug beneath the coffee table. "Someone at work put me on to it. Zoe's was the first profile I'd downloaded."

Highly unlikely, Kelly thought, but she decided to let it go. For now. "So why not tell us that when we first asked?"

Harris looked up. "It's run on the QT, as I understand it. Members are encouraged to be discreet."

"By whom?" Nick said. "Who runs the site, Luke?"

"I don't know." His eyes widened. "I don't! That's like asking me who owns Wikipedia, or Google Earth. It's just a site I use—I've got no idea who runs it."

"How did you find out about it?"

"I told you, someone at work."

"Who?"

"I don't remember." Harris became more agitated with each question Nick fired at him.

"Try."

He rubbed his forehead. "A load of us were talking in the pub after work. It was a bit hardcore. Some of the guys had been to a strip club over the weekend—there was a lot of banter about it. You know what it's like when lads get together." This was directed at Nick, who remained expressionless. "Someone mentioned the website. They said I'd need a password to open an account—that it was hidden in the phone number on an advert in the back of the *London Gazette*. A sort of secret code, just for people in the know. I wasn't going to look but I was curious and . . ." He trailed off, looking between Nick and Kelly. "I wasn't doing anything wrong."

"I think you should leave us to decide that," Nick said. "So you downloaded Zoe Walker's details, then you followed her."

"I didn't follow her! I'm not a stalker. I just engineered it so I'd bump into her, nothing else. Look, all this"—he waved an arm around, encompassing the penthouse—"is great, but I work bloody hard for it. I'm in the office seven days a week, on conference calls to the States every night . . . It doesn't leave much time to meet women. The website gives me a leg-up, that's all."

A leg-over, Kelly thought, catching Nick's eye. "Tell me what happened on the platform at Whitechapel, the first time you spoke to Zoe Walker."

That shifty look again from Harris; his eyes flicking up to the left.

"What do you mean?"

"We've got a statement from Zoe," Kelly said, chancing her arm. "She's told us everything."

Harris closed his eyes briefly. When he opened them, he avoided eye contact, staring instead at an illustrated guide to Italy in front of him on the coffee table. "I'd tried to get chatting to her that morning. I found her on the Overground, right where her profile said she'd be. I tried to speak to her, but she ignored me. I decided if I helped her with something it would break the ice: I thought I could give up my seat for her, or carry her shopping or something. But nothing like that came up. Then I was behind her at Whitechapel, and she was standing really close to the edge of the platform, and . . ." He stopped talking, his eyes still fixed on the book in front of him.

"Go on."

"I pushed her."

Kelly took an involuntary breath. Next to her she felt Nick sit up. So much for the softly, softly approach.

"I pulled her to safety instantly. She was never in any danger. Women like being rescued, don't they?"

Kelly bit back her instinctive response. She glanced at Nick, who nodded. Kelly stood up. "Luke Harris, I'm arresting you on suspicion of the attempted murder of Zoe Walker. You do not have to say anything, but it may harm your defense if you do not mention, when questioned, something you later rely on in court."

CHAPTER
TWENTY-SIX

PC Swift rings me on Monday evening.

"We've arrested the man you spoke to at Whitechapel."

"Luke Friedland?"

"His real name's Luke Harris." She pauses just long enough for me to wonder why he lied to me. The answer comes in the next breath. "He's admitted to pushing you; we've arrested him for attempted murder."

I'm glad I'm already sitting down, because the blood rushes from my head. I reach for the remote and mute the television. Justin turns to look at me, the half-formed reproach on his lips freezing when he sees my face. He looks at Simon and nods toward me.

"Attempted murder?" I manage. Justin's eyes widen. Simon reaches out a hand and touches the only part of me he can reach: my feet, curled up between us on the sofa. On the telly, a nine-year-old boy with a fractured femur is rushed down a corridor on *24 Hours in A&E*.

"I don't think it will stick," PC Swift says. "To charge him we'd need to prove an intent to kill"—my breath catches in my throat and she rushes to finish—"and he claims that wasn't why he did it."

"Do you believe him?" Attempted murder. *Attempted murder.* The term rattles around my head. If I'd said yes to a drink, would he have killed me?

"I do, Zoe. It isn't the first time he's used this technique to approach a woman. He . . . er . . . he thought you'd be more receptive to being asked out, if you believed he'd saved your life."

I can't find the words to express how revolted I am that someone would think that way. I pull my feet under myself, sliding Simon's hand off my ankle. I don't want to be touched right now. Not by anyone. "What will happen to him?"

PC Swift sighed. "I hate to say it, but possibly nothing. We'll pass the file to the CPS to look at, and he'll be released on police bail with conditions not to make contact with you, but my guess is, he'll be refused charge." She pauses. "I shouldn't be telling you this, but we brought him in to shake him up a bit. To see if we could get any information out of him that would help us identify the ringleader."

"And did you?"

I know the answer before it comes.

"No. I'm sorry."

After she ends the call I keep the phone pressed to my ear, wanting to delay the point at which I explain to my partner and son that there is a man in custody in North London under arrest for pushing me in front of a train.

When I do, it's Justin who reacts instantly, while Simon seems stupefied, unable to process what I'm telling him.

"He thought you'd go out with him if he pushed you?"

"White Knight Syndrome, PC Swift called it," I mumble. I feel numb, as though it's happening to someone else.

"They'll harass kids on the street for hanging out, but they won't charge someone who's actually admitted to trying to kill someone? Pigs."

"Justin, please. Their hands are tied."

"They fucking should be. To a pipe at the bottom of the Thames."

He leaves the room and I hear his heavy tread on the stairs. Simon is still looking lost.

"But you didn't go out with him. Did you?"

"No!" I take his hand. "He's obviously nuts."

"What if he tries to do it again?"

"He won't. The police won't let him." I say it more firmly than I believe. Because how can they stop him? And even if they stop Luke Friedland—*Harris*, I remind myself—how many other men have downloaded my commute? How many other men might be waiting for me on an Underground platform?

"I'll come to work with you tomorrow."

"You've got to be in Olympia at half nine." Simon has an interview with a trade magazine. He's absurdly overqualified for what even I can see is an entry-level journalism job, but it's a job, nevertheless.

"I'll cancel."

"You can't cancel! I'll be fine. I'll ring you at Whitechapel before I take the Underground, and again as soon as I'm out. Please, don't cancel."

He doesn't look convinced, and although I hate myself for doing it, I twist the knife a little. "You need this job. We need the money."

The following morning we walk to the station together. I throw a coin in Megan's guitar case then slip my hand into Simon's. He insists on putting me on the Overground before taking his train to Clapham, and I watch him looking around us on the platform.

"What are you looking for?"

"Them," he says grimly. "Men." There are men in dark suits all around us, like badly lined-up dominoes. None of them are looking at me, and I wonder if it's because Simon's here. Sure enough, once Simon has left me and I'm sitting on the Tube alone, I notice one of the suits sitting opposite me. He's watching me. I catch his eye and he looks away, but seconds later he's looking at me again.

"Can I help you?" I say loudly. The woman next to me shifts in her seat, gathering her skirt so it isn't touching me anymore. The man flushes red and looks down at his feet. Two girls at the end of the carriage giggle to each other. I've become one of those madwomen on the

Tube; the sort you go out of your way to avoid. The man gets off at the next stop and doesn't look at me again.

At work it's increasingly hard to concentrate. I start updating the Hallow & Reed website but find myself listing the same property three times. At ten thirty Graham comes out of his office. He sits in the chair on the opposite side of my desk, where clients sit if they're waiting for property details. Silently he hands me a printout of some particulars I typed out this morning.

> These superior serviced offices offer meeting rooms, super-fast Internet and a professionally staffed reception.

I stare at it but don't see the problem.

"At £900 per calendar month?"

"Bugger, I missed off a zero. Sorry." I start to log on, to correct my mistake, but Graham stops me.

"It's not the only mistake you've made today, Zoe. And yesterday was just as bad."

"It's been a difficult month, I—"

"As for the other evening, in the car—I'm sure I don't have to tell you that I found your reaction extremely irrational, not to mention insulting."

I blush. "I misunderstood, that's all. I woke up and it was dark and—"

"Let's not go there again." Graham looks almost as embarrassed as I feel. "Look, I'm sorry, but I can't have you here when your mind's not on the job."

I look at him in dismay. He can't fire me. Not now. Not with Simon out of work.

Graham doesn't look me in the eye. "I think you should take some time off."

"I'm fine, honestly, I just—"

"I'll put it down as stress," he says. I wonder if I've misheard.

"You're not firing me?"

Graham stands up. "Should I?"

"No, it's just—thank you. I really appreciate it." He colors slightly but gives no other acknowledgment of my gratitude. It's a side of Graham Hallow I've never seen before, and I suspect it's as strange for him as it is for me. Sure enough, moments later business trumps sympathy and he retrieves a pile of receipts and invoices from his office, stuffing them into a carrier bag.

"You can do this from home. The VAT needs listing separately; give me a call if it doesn't make sense."

I thank him again and get my things, putting on my coat and slinging my handbag over my chest before walking to the station. I feel lighter, knowing I have one thing, at least, less to worry about.

I'm turning left from Walbrook Street onto Cannon Street when I get the feeling.

A tingle down my spine; the feeling of being watched.

I turn around but the pavement is busy; there are people all around me. No one stands out. I wait at the crossing and resist the temptation to look behind me, even though the back of my neck burns under the gaze of imaginary eyes. We cross the road like sheep, tightly packed together, and as we reach the other side I can't help but scan the group for a wolf.

No one is paying me any attention.

I'm imagining the feeling, just like this morning, with the man on the Overground. Just like I assumed the boy in the trainers was running after me, when the truth was, he probably didn't even notice me. The website is pushing me over the edge.

I need to get a grip.

I walk briskly up the first flight of steps, my hand touching lightly on the metal handrail, keeping pace with the suits. Around me, people are finishing calls.

I'm just going into the station. I might lose you in a minute.

I'll call you when I'm ten minutes away.

Up the second flight of steps and into the bowels of the station. Here, the sound of feet changes, bouncing between concrete surfaces. My senses feel acutely tuned; I can hear individual shoes as they walk behind me. A pair of heels, clicking ever louder as they overtake me. The soft pad of ballet flats. The old-fashioned ring of steel on concrete; a set of shoe protectors fitted to a man's shoes. *He'll be older than me*, I think, distracting myself by imagining what he looks like. A hand-tailored suit; shoes made from a bespoke last. Gray hair. Expensive cuff links. Not following me, just heading home, to his wife and their dog and their Cotswolds cottage.

The prickle on my neck is insistent. I take out my Oyster, but at the barriers I step to one side, standing against the wall by the Underground map. The barriers funnel the crowds of commuters to a walk, their feet marching virtually on the spot, as if they can't bear to be standing still. Every now and then the flow is broken by someone who doesn't know the rules; who doesn't have their ticket in hand, and is rifling through their pockets or fishing in a bag. There are audible tuts from the waiting commuters, until the ticket is produced and the line can continue moving. No one pays me any attention. *It's in your head*, I tell myself, repeating it in the hope that my body will believe what my head is telling it.

"Sorry, could I just . . . ?"

I move to let a woman with a small child look at the Underground map behind me. I have to get home. I tap my Oyster and push through the barrier, walking on autopilot toward the District line platform. I start walking toward the end of the platform, to where the doors to carriage one will open, then I think of PC Swift's advice: *Change where you sit. Don't do what you always do.* I turn sharply on my heels and walk back the way I came. As I do so, something moves rapidly on the edges of my vision. Not something: someone. Someone hiding? Someone who doesn't want to be seen? I scour the faces of the people around me. I don't recognize anyone, but something I've seen feels familiar. Could it be Luke Friedland? *Luke Harris*, I remember. Let out on bail but ignoring the order to stay away from me.

My breath is quickening and I exhale through rounded lips to slow it down. Even if it is Luke Harris, what can he do on a crowded platform? But nevertheless I take a step away from the edge of the platform as the train approaches.

There's a free seat on carriage five but I decline an invitation to take it. I maneuver myself to the rear, where I can see down the full length of the carriage. There are several seats dotted about, but a dozen or so people standing, like me. There's a man facing the opposite way. He's wearing an overcoat and a hat, but my view is blocked and I can't see him properly. The same sensation creeps over me; a sense of the familiar, yet with a prickle of unease. I take my house keys out of my bag. The fob is a wooden "Z" that Justin made at school. I grasp it firmly in my fist and work the Yale key until it pokes between my fingers, before putting my hand—with its makeshift knuckle-duster—in my pocket.

At Whitechapel I don't hang around. I wait by the door as the train slows to a halt, impatiently jabbing the release button long before it has lit up. I run as though I might miss my connection, weaving between people who couldn't care less as long as I don't make them late, too. I listen for the sound of running feet, but there are only mine, hitting the ground in time with each jagged breath.

I make the platform just as my Overground train pulls in, and I jump on with seconds to spare. My breathing slows. Only a handful of people are on this carriage, and nothing about them makes me feel uncomfortable. Two girls with armfuls of shopping; a man lugging a television in an old IKEA bag; a woman in her twenties, plugged into her iPhone. By the time we reach Crystal Palace I release my grip on the key in my pocket, and the tense feeling in my chest begins to dissipate.

It reappears as my foot hits the platform, and this time there's no mistaking it. Someone is watching me. Following me. As I walk toward the exit, I know—I just *know*—that someone has stepped off the carriage next to mine and is walking behind me. I don't turn around. I can't. I find the key in my pocket and twist it between my fingers. I walk faster, and then I abandon all pretense at nonchalance and I run as though my life depended on it. Because right now, I think that it might. My breath is shallow, each inhalation prompting a sharp pain in my chest. I hear footsteps behind me; they're running, too. Leather on concrete. Hard and fast.

I push between a couple about to say good-bye, leaving outraged cries in my wake. I can see the way out now; a darkening sky framed by the square of the Tube exit. I run faster and I wonder why no one is shouting—no one is doing anything—and I realize they don't even know anything is wrong.

In front of me, I see Megan. She looks at me and her smile freezes on her face. I keep running, my head down and my arms pumping by my sides. She stops playing. Says something to me, but I don't hear it. I don't stop. I just keep running, and as I do I tear open the flap of my handbag, shoving in my hand and stirring the contents in search of my police alarm. I curse myself for not keeping it in my pocket, or clipped to my clothing, as Kelly Swift suggested. I find it and press the two indentations on either side. If it's worked, the alarm has already communicated with my phone, which is even now dialing 999.

There's shouting behind me. A bang and a cry, and a commotion that makes me turn around, still poised to run if I have to. More confident, now that I know—I hope—police operators are listening; that the GPS on the device means a patrol car is already on its way.

What I see stops me dead in my tracks.

Megan is standing above a man in an overcoat and a hat. Her guitar case, normally beside her by the railings, is beneath him, its coins spewed out onto the tarmac.

"You tripped me up deliberately!" the man is saying, and I start to walk back toward the station.

"Are you okay?" Megan calls to me, but I can't take my eyes off the man on the ground, who is now sitting up and dusting off his knees.

"You," I say. "What on earth are you doing down there?"

There's a certain demand for the older woman, it seems. They have just as many page views as the younger ones; their profiles are downloaded just as often. Like in any business, it's important to respond to trends; to ensure I'm offering the right products for my customers.

I quickly became obsessed with analytics; staring at figures on a screen to understand how many people have looked at the website, how many have clicked on a link, how many have gone on to download a profile. I consider the popularity of each woman on the site and am ruthless about deleting any who attract no interest. Each one carries a cost, after all; it takes time to keep their profiles updated, to make sure their descriptions are accurate, that their route hasn't changed. Time is money, they say, and my girls need to earn their place online.

Most do. There's no accounting for tastes, and it is—after all—a seller's market. They won't find this particular brand of entertainment anywhere else, which means they can't afford to be picky.

Good news for you, don't you think? No need to feel left out. Young or old; fat or thin; blonde or brunette . . . there'll be someone who wants you.

Who knows? There could be someone downloading your profile right now.

CHAPTER TWENTY-SEVEN

"Right, chaps, listen in. This is a briefing for Operation FUR-NISS, on Tuesday, 1 December."

It was like *Groundhog Day*, Kelly thought. Every morning and every evening, the same group of people gathered in the same room. A lot of the team were looking tired, but Nick's energy never wavered. It had been precisely two weeks since Tania Beckett's body was found, and in that time he had been the first one in the office each morning; the last one to leave at night. Two weeks in which Operation FURNISS had gathered three murders, six sexual assaults, and more than a dozen reports of stalkings, attempted assaults, and suspicious incidents, all relating to FindTheOne.com.

"Those of you who worked on the Maidstone rape—well done. Tillman's a nasty piece of work and your efforts have taken him off the streets." Nick looked for Kelly. "What's the latest on his computer activity?"

"Cyber Crime say he made no attempt to cover his tracks," Kelly said, looking at the notes she'd made from her earlier conversation with Andrew Robinson. "He downloaded the victim's details and e-mailed them to himself; presumably so he could have them on his phone, which is where we found them."

"Has he bought any others?"

"No. But he's browsed a fair number. Cached files suggest he's looked at the profiles of around fifteen women but never purchased one before Kathryn Whitworth's."

"Too expensive?"

"I don't think that's an issue for him. He joined in October as a Silver member, paying with—get this—a company credit card."

"Nice."

"We found a welcome letter in his deleted files—exactly like the one we received when we set up a pseudonymous account, but with a different password. It seems the security settings for the website are changed periodically; like Harris told us, the phone number on the adverts is the code for the latest password."

"Which you were clever enough to figure out," Nick said.

"Tillman's lazy," Kelly said, thinking out loud. "He drives to work—he'd have to go out of his way to find most of the women listed on the site. I think he's been lurking on the site; maybe even getting some sort of sexual kick out of it. When he saw Kathryn Whitworth's profile was Maidstone-based, and he knew he was heading that way for a conference, he went for it."

"Put his plate number through automatic number plate recognition. See if his car has been anywhere near Maidstone in the days leading up to the rape."

Kelly wrote *ANPR* on her pad and underlined it while Nick continued to brief the room.

"During the analysis of Tillman's computer, Cyber Crime found an encrypted section of his hard drive that contains one hundred and sixty-seven indecent images, the vast majority of which fall under Section 63 of the Possession of Extreme Pornographic Images Act. He's not going anywhere in a hurry." Kelly had wanted to call Kathryn Whitworth herself to tell her they had charged Tillman with rape, and that he would be charged with the possession of indecent images. It was Lucinda who had stopped her.

"Leave it to Kent's Sexual Offenses Investigation Team; they're the ones who have a relationship with her."

"They don't know anything about the case," Kelly had argued. "This way I can answer her questions. Reassure her."

Lucinda had remained firm. "Kelly, stop trying to do everyone's job. Kent SOIT will update the victim; you've got work to do here."

Although the MIT detectives frequently made jokes at the expense of civvy staff, Lucinda's skill and experience meant she was universally respected by the detectives who worked with her. Kelly was no exception. She had to trust that whoever updated Kathryn did so with compassion and understanding; there was a lengthy court process ahead of her and it wasn't going to be an easy ride.

Nick was still briefing the others. "You may already be aware that yesterday Kelly and I brought in Luke Harris, another user of the website. Harris initially claimed Zoe Walker's was the only profile he had downloaded, but he changed his tune in custody." Appalled to find himself arrested for attempted murder, Luke Harris had rolled over completely; handing over passwords for all his accounts, and admitting to having downloaded four other women listed on FindTheOne.com. In each case he'd employed the "white knight" routine as an icebreaker, jostling each woman from the safety of a crowd, then stepping forward to make sure she was all right. The technique had brought him limited success; a grateful coffee and subsequent dinner date from one woman had swiftly petered out.

"Harris maintained he had done nothing wrong," Nick told the team. "He claimed he never intended any harm to any of the women he followed, and that his aim throughout was simply to instigate a relationship."

"What's wrong with using uniform.com, like the rest of us?" someone yelled. Nick waited for the laughter to die down.

"Apparently dating sites 'reek of desperation,'" Nick said, repeating the words Harris had used. "Luke Harris prefers what he calls 'the thrill of the chase.' I suspect he'll find this option rather less thrilling from now on."

Kelly's phone rang. She looked at the screen, expecting to see Lexi's name flash up, but it was Cathy Tanning. "A witness," she said to Nick, holding her phone up in explanation. "Excuse me." She accepted the call, walking out of the incident room toward her own desk.

"Hi, Cathy, are you okay?"

"I'm fine, thank you. I was calling to let you know I'm not in Epping anymore."

"You've moved? That was sudden."

"Not really. I've been toying with the idea of getting out of London for ages. Then this place came up, and it's Romford, so not a million miles away. I couldn't relax in the house, even after I changed the locks."

"When do you move?"

"I've already gone. I was supposed to give a month's notice, but the landlord wants to redecorate and put the place on the market, so he let me go early. It's all worked out really well."

"I'm glad."

"Actually, that's not the only reason I'm calling," Cathy said. She hesitated. "I want to withdraw my statement."

"Has someone been giving you grief? Did the *Metro* article cause problems for you? Because if you've been threatened—"

"No, it's nothing like that. I just want to put it behind me." She sighed. "I feel bad—I know you've been trying so hard to find out who took my keys, and you were great when I told you I thought someone had been in the house."

"We're close to finding the person behind the website," Kelly interrupted. "When we charge them we'll need your evidence."

"You've got other witnesses, though, haven't you? Other crimes? Those poor girls who were killed—those are the crimes that matter, not mine."

"They're all important, Cathy. We wouldn't investigate them if we didn't believe that."

"Thank you. And if I thought my evidence would make all the difference, I'd give it, I promise. But it won't, will it?"

Kelly didn't answer.

"I have a friend who gave evidence in a case last year," Cathy said. "She got hassled for months by the offender's family. I don't need that sort of aggravation. I've got a chance to make a fresh start, in a brand-new house no one else has the keys for. It was a scary thing to happen but I wasn't hurt—I just want to forget about it."

"Can I at least let you know when we charge someone? In case you change your mind?"

There was a lengthy pause.

"I guess so. But I won't change my mind, Kelly. I know putting someone behind bars is important, but surely how I feel must count for something, too?"

It was always about the victims, Kelly thought, annoyed by the suggestion that it wasn't. She had thought Cathy one of the more reliable witnesses in this case, and she was disappointed to be proved wrong. She opened her mouth to warn Cathy her refusal to give evidence could well result in her being treated as a hostile witness; held in contempt of court for failing to cooperate.

Then she stopped. Did the pursuit of justice ever justify treating a victim as though they were in the dock? Thoughts of Lexi arrived unbidden in her head. She took a deep breath before speaking.

"The way victims feel is the only thing that matters. Thanks for letting me know, Cathy." Kelly ended the call, leaning against the wall and shutting her eyes, walking back to the incident room only when she was confident she had her emotions under control. The briefing had finished and the MIT office was once again buzzing with activity. She walked over to where Andrew Robinson was sitting next to Nick and moved a chair from a nearby desk so she could join them.

"Still following the money?" Kelly asked, remembering the phrase the Cyber Crime DC had used.

"We certainly are. I've tracked the credit card payments from the DI, from Gordon Tillman, and from Luke Harris, all of which have been paid into a PayPal account—like this." Andrew took a blank sheet from the printer and wrote three names—*RAMPELLO, TILLMAN, HARRIS*. "The money goes from these three sources"—he drew arrows from each of the names—"to here"—Andrew sketched a box around the word *PayPal*—"then continues to here." An arrow, and another box, this time around the words *Bank Account*.

"And this account belongs to our offender. Right?" Nick said.

"Spot on."

"Can we get the details?"

"Already got them." Andrew caught Kelly's hopeful expression. "It's a student account in the name of Mai Suo Li. I've got copies of the identification documents used to open it, and they're all kosher; passport control confirms Mai Suo Li left the UK for China on 10 July this year and hasn't returned."

"Could he be operating the site from China?"

"It's possible, but I can tell you now we won't get anywhere with the Chinese authorities."

It was making Kelly's head hurt.

"In the meantime I can tell you your offender uses a Samsung device to transfer funds from PayPal to the bank account. I can't say whether it's a phone, a tablet, or a laptop, but it's a safe bet it's something portable."

"How do you know?" Kelly said.

"Every time your phone is turned on it sends signals out as it searches for Wi-Fi or Bluetooth. If it was a home computer you'd expect a fixed location, but the results suggest a degree of thought into avoiding detection." Andrew handed a piece of paper to Nick, who moved his chair a fraction so Kelly could see it, too. "If the Wi-Fi was switched on all the time I'd expect hundreds more locations, but as you can see, they're few and far between. This suggests the device is being turned on only for specific purposes; almost certainly to transfer money from PayPal to the account. My guess is this is a dirty phone, not his regular one."

Typed onto the sheet of paper was a list of locations. The top one was underlined.

Espress Oh!

"What's that?"

"A coffee shop near Leicester Square, and our man's preferred location for activity on his dirty phone. On three occasions in the last month he's used their Wi-Fi to transfer money from PayPal to his bank account. You'll find the dates and times below."

"Nice work," Nick said.

"Now it's down to old-fashioned policing methods, I'm afraid." Andrew looked pleased with himself, and rightly so. Kelly and the DI were on firmer ground now. A coffee shop in a busy place like Leicester Square would have CCTV, maybe even conscientious members of the staff who would remember a particular customer on a particular day. If they could pull some decent stills from the footage they could get national coverage for a case as serious as this one.

"Sir!" The call came from the other side of the room. "Response are on their way to Crystal Palace. We've had an activation on Zoe Walker's alarm."

Nick was already grabbing his jacket. He looked at Kelly.

"Let's go."

CHAPTER
TWENTY-EIGHT

"You tripped me up!" Isaac says, looking up at Megan. He puts a hand on the road to push himself up. The small crowd of people that had gathered to watch the excitement begins to separate.

"Yes," she says. She stoops and begins picking up the scattered coins littering the road. I help her, if only to stop myself from staring at Isaac, who appears both mildly affronted and amused by what's happened. "You were chasing her," Megan adds, with a shrug that suggests it was really the only course of action available to her.

"I was catching up with her," Isaac says. "There's a difference." He stands up.

"Megan, this is my daughter's . . ." I trail off, not knowing what to call him. "We know each other," I finish.

"Right."

Megan doesn't seem embarrassed. Perhaps, in her world, the fact that Isaac and I know each other means nothing. He could still have been chasing me.

He could still have been chasing me.

I brush off the thought as ridiculous before it can take hold. Of course he wasn't chasing me.

I turn to him. "Why are you here?"

"Last time I checked," he says, "it was a free country." He's smiling as he says it, but nevertheless irritation seeps through me. I assume it registers on my face, because he decides to be serious. "I'm on my way to see Katie."

"Why were you running?" I'm emboldened by the presence of Megan, who has stepped away but is watching my interrogation with interest, her guitar held loosely at her side.

"Because *you* were running," he says. It's so logical that I'm no longer sure how I feel. I hear the sound of police sirens in the distance. "I knew you were on edge about the adverts in the *Gazette*, and then Katie told me about the website. When I saw you running I thought someone had frightened you."

"Yes, you!" My heart is still racing, and I feel the heady buzz of an adrenaline spike. The sirens grow louder. Isaac holds his hands skyward in an "I can't win" gesture, annoying me further. Who is this man? The sirens are deafening; I look up Anerley Road and see a police car coming toward us, its lights flashing. The car pulls up ten meters in front of us; the siren is extinguished, mid-wail.

Will Isaac run? I wonder, and I realize I'm hoping he does. I want this to be it; the end of the adverts, the website, the fear. But he puts his hands in his pockets and looks at me, shaking his head as though I've done something utterly incomprehensible. He walks toward the officers.

"This lady's had a bit of a scare," he explains, and I'm so filled with rage I can't speak. How dare he act as though he's in charge? Dismiss what just happened as a *bit of a scare*?

"Your name, sir?" The policeman gets out a notebook, while his colleague—a woman—walks toward me.

"He was chasing me," I tell her, and just saying it makes me think that it's true. I start telling her about the adverts, but she already knows. "He began following me at Cannon Street, and when we got to Crystal Palace he started running after me." Had he run first, or had I? Does it matter? The policewoman takes notes but seems uninterested in the detail.

A car pulls up behind the police car, and I recognize DI Rampello behind the wheel. PC Swift is with him, and I feel a surge of relief, knowing I won't have to convince her about what just happened. DI Rampello speaks to the policewoman, who puts away her notebook and joins her colleague.

"Are you okay?" Kelly asks.

"I'm fine. Except for Isaac scaring me witless."

"You know him?"

"His name's Isaac Gunn—he's my daughter's boyfriend. She's in a play at the moment and he's the director. He must have downloaded my commute from the website." I catch an exchange of glances between them and know exactly what they're going to say.

"The website provides users with a means of following strangers," PC Swift says. "Why would someone you know need to use it?"

DI Rampello looks at his watch. "It's not even midday. Would you usually leave work so early?"

"My boss sent me home. That's not a crime, is it?"

He is more patient than my tone deserves. "Of course not. But if Isaac Gunn had downloaded your commute and was using it to follow you, he wouldn't have been successful today, would he? You've not stuck to the script."

I'm silent. I think about the footsteps I heard at Cannon Street; the glimpse of an overcoat on the District line. Was it Isaac I saw then? Or someone else? Could I have imagined the feeling of being followed?

"You should at least question him. Find out why he was following me; why he didn't try to get my attention when he first saw me."

"Look," DI Rampello says gently. "We'll bring Gunn in for a voluntary interview. Find out if there's any connection with the website."

"And you'll let me know?"

"As soon as we can."

Across the road I see Isaac getting into the police car.

"Can we give you a lift home?" PC Swift says.

"I'll walk, thank you."

Megan reappears at my side as DI Rampello and PC Swift drive away, and it's only then I realize she had melted away the second the police arrived. "So you're all right, then?"

"I'm fine. Thanks for looking out for me today."

"Thanks for looking out for me every day," she counters, smiling.

I throw a coin into her guitar case as she starts strumming the chords for a Bob Marley song.

The day is crisp and cold. They've been forecasting snow for days and I think it's on its way tonight. Thick white clouds hang above me, and the road sparkles with early frost. I replay the journey home from work in my head, trying to pinpoint the exact moment I knew someone was following me; the exact moment I broke into a run. The act of remembering is a distraction from what is really troubling me: What the hell am I going to say to Katie? That her boyfriend was stalking me? The closer I get to home, the more I doubt myself.

When I open the door I hear the radio playing in the kitchen, Simon's tuneless accompaniment fading in and out in proportion to his familiarity with the lyrics. I haven't heard him singing for a long time.

The front door bangs behind me; the singing stops.

"I'm in here!" Simon calls, unnecessarily. When I join him I see he's set the kitchen table for lunch. "I thought you might like something hot," he says. There's a pan bubbling on the hob; prawn risotto with asparagus and lemon. It smells delicious.

"How did you know I'd be home early?"

"I phoned you at work and your boss told me he'd sent you home."

I think how much I'd like to live without someone monitoring my every move, then instantly feel ungrateful. The police, Graham, Simon: they're trying to keep me safe, that's all.

"I thought he was going to sack me."

"Let him try. We'll have him in an unfair dismissal tribunal before you can say 'to let.'" He grins at his own joke.

"You're very chipper. Can I assume the job interview went well?"

"I had a call even before I'd reached the Tube station. They've invited me in tomorrow for a second interview."

"That's fantastic! Did you like them? Does the job sound good?" I sit down and Simon places two steaming bowls of risotto on the table. I have the sudden hunger that follows a period of high adrenaline, but the first mouthful turns to acid in my stomach. I have to tell Katie. She'll be waiting, wondering where Isaac is. Worrying, maybe.

"Everyone's about twelve years old," Simon is saying, "the circulation's only eight thousand, and I could do the job blindfolded." I open my mouth to ask about Katie, but he misreads my intention and cuts me off. "But, like you said yesterday, it's a job, and the hours would be better than at the *Telegraph*. No weekend working, no late shifts covering the news desk. It would give me a chance to work on my book."

"It's great news. I knew something would come up." We eat in silence for a while. "Where's Katie?" I say, as though it's only just occurred to me.

"In her room, I think." He looks at me. "Is something wrong?" And at that moment I decide I'm not going to tell him.

Let him focus on tomorrow's interview without worrying that he should be staying home to look after me; without worrying that Katie is involved with a potential stalker. I ignore the insistent voice in my head; the voice that says I don't want to tell him because I'm not even certain I'm right.

I hear footsteps on the stairs and the unmistakable sound of Katie's shoes heading toward the kitchen. She walks in, staring at her phone. "Hey, Mum. You're home early."

I look between her and Simon; a rabbit in the path of an oncoming car, wondering which side of the road to run to. Katie flicks on the kettle; frowns at her phone.

"Everything okay, love?"

Simon looks at me curiously but doesn't say anything. If he can hear the note of anxiety in my voice I know he'll put it down to what's been going on. The "stress" with which Graham has signed me off work.

"Isaac was supposed to be coming over, but he texted to say something's come up," Katie says. She seems surprised rather than upset, and I know it's because she isn't used to being let down. I hate myself for being the one to do it to her.

I assumed the police would have taken Isaac's phone straightaway. I imagine the conversation in the police car, or in custody.

I need to get a message to my girlfriend.

One text. Then hand over the phone.

Maybe it was nothing like that. Maybe they all got along famously: Isaac charming the female officer; getting chummy with her male colleague.

I really need to let my girlfriend know what's happened—she'll be worried. You've seen her mother, she's not stable . . .

"Did he say what had come up?" I ask Katie.

"Nope. It'll be something to do with the show. He's always working—I suppose you have to be, when you're self-employed. I hope everything's all right, though—it's curtain up in seven hours!" She takes a Pot Noodle upstairs and I rest my fork on the edge of my bowl. It's the opening night tonight. How could I have forgotten? What if Isaac is still with the police?

"Not hungry?" Simon says.

"Sorry."

I've dug myself into a mess I don't know how to get out of, and for the rest of the day I prowl the house, offering Katie cups of tea she doesn't want, braced for the moment she tells me she knows I had Isaac hauled off in a cop car.

A voluntary interview, I remind myself. He wasn't arrested. But I know the distinction will mean little to Isaac. Or to Katie. At five Matt picks up her to take her to the theater.

"She's just getting her stuff," I say. Matt stands on the step, and I feel the cold slide in through the open door. "I'd ask you in, but it's . . . you know, it's awkward."

"I'll wait in the cab."

Katie runs down the stairs, pulling on her coat. She kisses me.

"Break a leg, love. Isn't that what they say?"

"Thanks, Mum."

As Matt drives off, my mobile rings; PC Swift's number flashing on the screen. I take my phone upstairs, pushing past Justin on the stairs with a hurried "Excuse me." I go up to Simon's office and close the door behind me.

Kelly Swift doesn't bother with niceties. "We've let him go."

"What did he say?"

"What he said to you. That he saw you on the Tube and thought you looked anxious. He said you kept looking around you; that you seemed jumpy."

"Did he admit to following me?"

"He said he was going to see your daughter, so naturally he walked the same way. When you broke into a run he was concerned, so he ran to catch you up."

"Why didn't he come and speak to me?" I demand. "When he saw me on the Tube? He could have approached me then."

PC Swift hesitates. "He seems to think you don't like him." There's a Post-it note peeling away from Simon's computer screen, and I press the corners down with my thumb. "We've got his phone and his laptop, Zoe—he was quite happy to let us have access—and at first glance there's nothing linking him to FindTheOne.com. Cyber Crime will investigate more thoroughly over the next few hours, and of course I'll let you know if they turn anything up." She pauses again, and when she speaks her voice is softer. "Zoe, I don't think he's got anything to do with the website."

"Oh God, what have I done?" I shut my eyes, as if that will help me block out the mess I'm making of everything. "My daughter's never going to forgive me for this."

"Isaac was very understanding about the mix-up," PC Swift says. "He knows you've been under a lot of stress. I got the impression he was happy to keep things between you and him."

"He's not going to tell Katie? Why would he do that?"

She exhales, and I think I detect a note of exasperation in her voice. "Maybe he's just one of the good guys, Zoe."

The following day the house is quiet when I get up. It's strangely bright in our bedroom and when I open the curtains I see that the promised snow has come. The roads are already clear—grit and traffic making short work of the overnight fall—but the pavements and gardens, the roofs and stationary cars, are covered in two inches of soft white snow. Fresh flakes drift past the window to cover the footprints on the path outside.

I kiss Simon on the lips. "It's snowing!" I whisper, like a child wanting to go out and play. He smiles without opening his eyes and pulls me back into bed.

When I get up again the snow has stopped. Justin has another long shift at the café, and Katie is sleeping off her opening night. She's left a note for me propped against the kettle.

We had a full house! Best audience ever, Isaac reckons! x

He didn't tell her. I let out a slow breath.

I'll need to speak to him. Apologize. But not today.

"What time's your interview?" I ask Simon.

"Not till two o'clock, but I thought I'd go in this morning and pick up a few back issues so I can mug up a bit over lunch. You don't mind, do you? You'll be all right here?"

"I'll be fine. Katie's home. I'm going to have a tidy-up, I think."

The house is a mess; the dining table we sat around only two weeks ago has reverted to its usual cluttered state. Last night I tipped out the receipts and invoices Graham gave me, but I can't make a start on his books until I've cleared up.

Simon kisses me good-bye and I wish him luck. I hear him whistling as he unlocks the front door, and I smile to myself.

Katie emerges around eleven. Despite the bags under her eyes, and the line of kohl she hasn't completely removed, she looks radiant.

"It was amazing, Mum." She takes the tea I hand her and follows me into the dining room, where she pulls out a chair and sits down, hugging her knees to her chest. Her feet are encased in huge fluffy boots. "I didn't need a single prompt, and at the end, someone actually stood up! I think it was someone Isaac knew, but even so."

"So there's some money coming in, then?"

"There will be. We have to pay the theater hire, and box office costs, and that sort of thing first." I say nothing. I wonder if Isaac's already taken his cut. Katie suddenly looks at me.

"Why aren't you at work?"

"I'm off sick."

"Mum, why didn't you say? You shouldn't be doing that. Here, let me." She leaps up and takes a pile of files from me, looking around and eventually dumping them back on the table where they were. A receipt wafts off the table and onto the floor.

"I'm not that sort of sick. Graham's signed me off for a bit. Just while the police sort out this website nonsense." It feels good, dismissing it as nonsense. Empowering, Melissa would call it. I bend down to pick up the receipt, which has floated under the table.

Diet Coke £2.95.

I don't know if it's come from one of the piles of accounts, or whether it's just another of the receipts we all crumple up and dump on the table.

The receipt is for a place called Espress Oh! A terrible name for a café, I think. It's trying too hard; the labored pun making you cringe, like those Curl Up and Dye hairdressers, or that salad bar in E16 called Lettuce Eat. I turn the receipt over and see the numbers *0364* written in a hand I don't recognize. A PIN, perhaps?

I put the receipt to one side. "Leave all this, love," I tell Katie, who is still moving papers around with helpful enthusiasm but little efficiency. "It's easier if I do it. That way nothing gets mixed up." I let her tell me about the opening night—about the four-star review from *Time Out*, and the rush she got when they came on stage for a second curtain call—while I tidy and sort and rearrange the papers on the dining table. The process makes me feel calmer, as though simply by tidying the house I can get some control over my life.

I'd never have asked Graham for time off, and I'm grateful to him for forcing my hand. At least now I can stay at home while the police do whatever they're doing to solve this case. I'm through with detective work. Let them take the risks; I'm staying here, where it's safe.

CHAPTER
TWENTY-NINE

Espress Oh! had an uninviting exterior, which made the sign in the window claiming the ownership of *The Best Coffee in London* seem a little unlikely. The door stuck slightly, eventually giving in and propelling Kelly inside with such force she almost fell over.

"CCTV," she said to Nick triumphantly, pointing to the sticker on the wall that read *Smile, you're on camera!* Inside, the café was much bigger than first appearances had suggested. Signs informed customers there was more seating upstairs, and a spiral staircase led down to what Kelly presumed were the toilets, judging from the steady stream of people going up and down it. The noise levels were high; conversations competing with the hiss of the vast silver coffee machine behind the counter.

"We'd like to speak to the manager, please."

"You'll be lucky?" The girl on the till was Australian, her accent turning everything she said into a question. "If you need to make a complaint, we've got a form for it, yeah?"

"Who's in charge today?" Kelly said, flipping open her warrant card so the badge was showing.

The girl didn't seem fazed. She looked slowly and deliberately around the café. There were two other baristas, one wiping tables and the other piling coffee cups into an industrial dishwasher with such speed and ferocity Kelly was amazed they didn't shatter. "I guess that would be me? I'm Dana." She wiped her hands on her apron. "Jase, take the till for a bit? We can go upstairs."

The second floor of Espress Oh! was filled with leather sofas that looked as though they should be comfortable but were actually too hard and too shiny to want to settle into for long. Dana looked between Nick and Kelly expectantly. "What can we do for you?"

"Do you have Wi-Fi here?" Nick asked.

"Sure. Do you want the code?"

"Not right now, thank you. Is it free for customers to use?"

Dana nodded. "We're supposed to change the code every now and then, but it's been the same for as long as I've been here, and the regulars like it that way. It's a pain for them to keep asking for the code, and it makes more work for the staff, you know?"

"We need to trace someone who's logged on to your network here several times," Kelly said. "They're wanted in connection with a very serious crime."

Dana's eyes widened. "Should we be worried?"

"I don't think you're in any danger here, but it's vital we track them down as soon as we can. I noticed on our way in you have CCTV—could we have a look at it?"

"Sure thing. It's in the manager's office, through here." They followed her to a door on the other side of the room, where she rapidly pressed numbers on the keypad fixed to the frame. She welcomed them into a room a little bigger than a broom cupboard, which housed a desk with a computer, a dusty printer, and an in-tray filled with invoices and delivery slips. On a shelf above the computer was a black-and-white screen showing a flickering CCTV image. Kelly recognized the counter they had seen downstairs, and the gleaming coffee machine.

"How many cameras do you have?" Kelly said. "Can we take a look at the other angles?"

"It's just that one, you know?" Dana said.

As they watched, Kelly could see Jase, the lad Dana had handed over to, put a steaming latte on a black tray. It was just about possible to see a side view of his customer before they turned away. "The only camera is pointing at the till?" Kelly clarified.

Dana looked abashed. "The owner thinks we're all on the take. It's the same for the whole chain. We had a problem with antisocial behavior last year and moved the camera to point at the front door. The boss went apeshit. Now we leave it be. Sleeping dogs, yeah?"

Nick and Kelly exchanged grim glances.

"I'm going to have to seize whatever footage you've got from the last month," Kelly said. She turned to the DI. "Surveillance?" He nodded.

"We're investigating a very serious offense," Nick told Dana, "and it may be we need to put in additional cameras for a few weeks. If that happens, it's imperative your customers don't know about it, which means"—he gave Dana a serious look—"the fewer staff who know, the better."

Dana looked terrified. "I won't tell anyone."

"Thank you—you've been really helpful," Kelly said, although her heart was sinking. Every time she thought they had a strong lead on the offender behind the website, it collapsed into nothing. They could look at the CCTV footage at the times the offender used the Wi-Fi connection to transfer his customers' money, but with 90 percent of the camera screen taken up with the staff and the till, their chances of getting a positive ID were tiny.

As they left the café, Kelly's mobile beeped. "It's from Zoe Walker," she said, reading the text. "She's working from home for the foreseeable; just wanted to let me know she wouldn't be on her office number."

Nick shot her a warning look. "If she asks, there are no significant developments, okay?"

Kelly took a deep breath and tried to answer calmly. "I told Zoe how to access the website because I thought she had a right to see her own commute listed."

Nick strode off toward the car, delivering his parting shot over his shoulder. "You think too much, PC Swift."

Back on Balfour Street Kelly took the disk with Espress Oh!'s CCTV footage to the exhibits officer. Tony Broadstairs had more than twenty-five years as a detective on CID and MIT and was fond of giving Kelly advice she neither wanted nor needed. Today he took it upon himself to outline the importance of the chain of evidence.

"So you have to sign to say you're passing this exhibit to me," he said, his pen drawing a circle in the air above the relevant section on the exhibit tag, "and I sign to say I've received it from you."

"Got it," Kelly, who had been seizing and signing for exhibits for the past nine years, said with a nod. "Thanks."

"Because if one of those signatures is missing, you can kiss goodbye to your case at court. You can have the guiltiest man in the land, but once the defense get wind of a procedural cock-up, it'll collapse faster than a soufflé taken out of the oven too early."

"Kelly."

Turning around, Kelly saw DCI Digby walking toward them, still wearing his overcoat.

"I didn't realize you were in, sir," Tony said. "I thought you were still using up all that leave you've accrued. Didn't fancy golf today, then?"

"Trust me, Tony, I'm not here out of choice." He looked at Kelly, unsmiling. "My office, now." He called across to the DI. "Nick, you, too."

The relief Kelly felt at no longer having to listen to Tony's lesson in exhibit-handling was swiftly tempered by the look on the DCI's face. She scurried after him across the open-plan space to his office, where he threw open the door and told her to sit down. Kelly did so, a feeling of dread creeping over her. She tried to think of some other reason why the DCI would have hauled her so unceremoniously into his office—and indeed come in on his rest day to do so—but kept returning to the same thing.

Durham.

She'd really fucked up this time.

"I went out on a limb for you, Kelly." Diggers had stayed standing, and now he strode from one side of the tiny room to the other, leaving Kelly unsure whether she should keep her eyes on him, or stay facing forward, like a defendant in the dock. "I agreed to this transfer because I had faith in you, and because you convinced me I could trust you. I fought your bloody corner, Kelly!"

Kelly's stomach clenched with fear and with shame; how could she have been so stupid? She'd hung on to her job by the skin of her teeth last time; the suspect she'd flown at had decided against pressing criminal charges, after a visit from Diggers persuaded him he didn't want to be in the spotlight any more than was necessary. Even the disciplinary hearing had gone in her favor, thanks to Diggers having another quiet chat with the superintendent. *Mitigating circumstances due to family history*, the report had read, but she'd been left in no doubt it was a card she couldn't play twice.

"I got a phone call last night." The DCI finally sat down, leaning forward across the expanse of dark oak desk. "A DS from Durham Constabulary, alerted to the fact that we'd been inquiring about historical rapes. Wondered if they could help any further."

Kelly couldn't meet his eyes. To her left she could feel Nick looking at her.

"Of course, this came as rather a surprise to me. I might be counting down to retirement, Kelly, but I like to think I still know what jobs the office is dealing with. And none of them"—he slowed his speech, pausing between each word for added emphasis—"relates to Durham University. Would you care to explain what the hell you've been doing?"

Slowly, Kelly looked up. The blind rage that had consumed Diggers seemed to have blown itself out, and he looked less terrifying than when he had first started. Even so, Kelly's voice shook, and she swallowed hard in an attempt to get herself under control.

"I wanted to find out if there had been any developments on my sister's case."

Diggers shook his head. "I'm sure I don't need to tell you that what you've done represents a serious disciplinary offense. Quite apart from the criminal implications of breaching the Data Protection Act in this way, abusing your position as a police officer for personal gain is a sackable offense."

"I know that, sir."

"Then why on earth . . . ?" Diggers spread his hands wide, his face registering total incomprehension. When he spoke again, it was softer. "*Have* there been any developments in your sister's case?"

"Sort of. Only not the kind I expected, sir." Kelly swallowed again, wishing the hard lump in her throat would go away. "My sister . . . she's withdrawn support for the prosecution. She's left explicit instructions that she doesn't want to be kept informed of any developments and has no wish to know if the offender is ever arrested."

"I take it this was news to you?"

Kelly nodded.

There was a long pause before Diggers spoke again. "I think I know the answer to this already, but I have to ask: is there any professional reason for you making such a request to another force?"

"I asked her to," Nick said. Kelly turned to look at him, trying to conceal her shock.

"You asked Kelly to contact Durham about a historical rape involving her sister?"

"Yes."

Diggers stared at Nick. Kelly thought she saw amusement in his eyes, but his mouth was set hard and she decided she was imagining it. "Would you care to explain why?"

"Operation FURNISS has proved to be more wide-ranging than first anticipated, sir. The Maidstone rape indicated that offenses aren't confined to within the M25, and although the adverts only started in October the full extent of the crimes aren't yet clear. We've so far struggled for leads on the principal offender and I thought it would be a good idea to take a broader look at rapes with a history of stalking. I thought it possible the pattern might have been repeated in other cities."

"Over a decade ago?"

"Yes, sir."

Diggers took off his glasses. He eyed Nick thoughtfully, then looked at Kelly. "Why didn't you tell me this in the first place?"

"I—I'm not sure, sir."

"I take it you haven't found a link between Operation FURNISS and Durham?" The question was directed at Kelly, but it was Nick who answered.

"I've ruled it out," he said, without any of Kelly's hesitation.

"I thought as much." Diggers looked from Kelly to Nick and back again. Kelly held her breath. "Might I suggest we consider the background research into similar crimes complete?"

"Yes, sir."

"Get back to work, the pair of you."

They were in the doorway when Diggers called to Kelly. "One more thing . . ."

"Sir?"

"Offenders, coppers, witnesses, victims . . . there's one common thread running through them all, Kelly, and it's that no two people are the same. Every victim deals differently with what's happened to them; some are hell-bent on revenge, others want justice, some are looking for closure, and some"—he looked her straight in the eye—"some just want to move on."

Kelly thought of Lexi, and of Cathy Tanning's desire to start over, in a house to which no one but her had the keys. "Yes, sir."

"Don't get hung up on the victims who want a different outcome to the one we want. It doesn't make them wrong. Focus that drive of yours—your not inconsiderable talent—on the case as a whole. Somewhere out there is a serial offender responsible for the rapes, murders, and stalking of dozens of women. Find him."

People get caught when they get careless.

You won't find my name in the digital trail leading to FindTheOne .com—I've only ever used other people's names, borrowed from wallets and coat pockets.

James Stanford, who had no idea he had a mailbox on Old Gloucester Road, or a credit card with which he was paying for adverts placed in the London Gazette. *Mai Suo Li, the Chinese student who was happy to hand over his British bank account in exchange for enough cash for his flight home.*

Other people's names. Never mine.

The receipt, though. That was careless.

A door code, scribbled thoughtlessly on the nearest scrap of paper, never a consideration given to the fact that it could mean the end of everything. When I think of it now—when I think of the carelessness—it fills me with rage. So stupid. Without that receipt everything was perfect. Untraceable.

It isn't over, though. When you're cornered, there's only one thing to do.

Go down fighting.

CHAPTER
THIRTY

By lunchtime the dining table is clear again and the house has regained some semblance of order. I sit at the table and work my way through Graham's accounts, finding the methodical process of logging taxi fares and lunches strangely relaxing. My phone beeps with a message from PC Swift, returning the text I sent her earlier.

> Sorry haven't been in touch. Quick update—I'll try to call later. We believe offender has administered the website from a café called Espress Oh! near Leicester Square—inquiries ongoing. Luke Harris still on bail—I'll let you know what the CPS say. Sounds like working from home is a good move. Take care of yourself.

I read the message twice. Then I pick up the file of miscellaneous paperwork from the table and retrieve the receipt for Espress Oh! I look at the number scribbled on the back, then search for the date. The ink at the bottom is smudged and I can't make it out. How long has it been here? It's not cold in the house, but I'm shaking and the receipt flutters in my hand. I walk into the kitchen.

"Katie?"

"Mmm?"

She's buttering bread on the counter without using a plate. She brushes the crumbs into her hand and shakes them into the sink.

"Sorry." She sees my face. "It's only a few crumbs, Mum."

I hand her the receipt. "Have you ever been to this place?" I feel light-headed, as though I've come up for air too fast. I can feel my pulse ticking, and I count each beat in an effort to slow it down.

Katie screws up her nose. "Don't think so. Where is it?"

"Near Leicester Square." When you face danger your body is supposed to go into one of two modes: fight or flight. But mine isn't doing either. It's frozen, wanting to run but unable to move.

"Oh, I know it! At least, I think so. I've not been there, but I've walked past it. Why do you want to know?"

I don't want to panic Katie. I tell her about PC Swift's text, but calmly, as though it's nothing of great importance. The buzzing in my ears grows louder. It's not a coincidence. I know it.

"It's just a receipt. It doesn't have to belong to the person behind the website. Does it?" Her eyes flicker across my face, trying to read me; trying to gauge how worried I am.

Yes.

"No, of course not."

"It could have come from anyone; a coat pocket, an old plastic bag, anything." We're both pretending it's something innocuous. A lone sock. A stray cat. Anything but a receipt that somehow links a maniac to our house. "I leave receipts in bags all the time."

I want her to be right. I think of all the times I've grabbed a carrier bag from the dozens stuffed into the cupboard under the sink, and found abandoned receipts from previous shopping trips.

I want her to be right, but I know from the prickle of fear across my neck that she isn't. That the only reason that receipt is in our house is because someone brought it in.

"Bit of a coincidence, though, don't you think?" I try to smile but it falls apart, morphing into something quite different.

Fear.

There's a voice in my head I won't listen to; a creeping sense of dread telling me the answer is staring me in the face.

"We need to think rationally about it," Katie is saying. "Who's been in the house recently?"

"You, me, Justin, and Simon," I say, "obviously. And Melissa and Neil. The pile of paperwork I put on the table last night—the receipts and the invoices—that belongs to Graham Hallow."

"Could it be his?"

"Maybe." I think of the pile of *Gazette*s on Graham's desk and remember his perfectly plausible explanation for them. "But he's been really supportive lately—he's given me time off work. I can't see him doing something like this." A thought enters my head. The police might not have found any evidence against Isaac, but that doesn't mean there isn't any to find. "We cleared the table before Sunday lunch last month. Isaac was here."

Katie's mouth opens. "What are you suggesting?"

I shrug, but it's unconvincing, even to me. "I'm not suggesting anything. I'm simply listing the people who have been in the house recently."

"You can't think Isaac has anything to do with this? Mum, I hadn't even met him when this all started—you said yourself the ads have been running since October."

"He took a picture of you, Katie. Without you knowing. Don't you think that's creepy?"

"To send to another cast member! Not to use on a website." She's yelling at me, defensive and angry.

"How do you know?" I shout back.

There's a silence between us as we both take stock of ourselves.

"It could be anyone's," Katie says stubbornly.

"Then we should search the house," I say.

She nods. "Justin's room first."

"Justin? You can't think . . ." I see her face. "Fine."

Even as a toddler Justin loved computers above books. I used to worry I'd done something wrong—let him watch too much television—but when Katie came along and became such a bookworm, I realized they were just two different children. We didn't even have a computer at home when they were young, but ICT was about the only subject Justin would turn up for at school. He begged Matt and me for his own computer, and when we couldn't afford it he saved his pocket money and bought the parts, each one arriving in a Jiffy bag to the house, to be stored under his bed with his Meccano sets and Lego figures. He built that first computer himself, with instructions he'd printed at the library, and as time went on he added more memory, a bigger hard disk, a better graphics card. At twelve, Justin knew more about computers and the Internet than I did at thirty.

I remember making him sit down after school one day, before he ran upstairs to join whatever gaming network he was into, impressing upon him the dangers of giving too much away online; that the teens he spent so long chatting to might not be teens at all, but fifty-year-old perverts, salivating over their keyboards.

"I'm too clever for the pedos," he said, laughing. "They could never catch me."

I was impressed, I suppose. Proud my son was so savvy, so much more clued up about technology than I was.

In all those years of worrying that Justin might fall prey to an online attacker, it never once crossed my mind he might be one himself. *He can't be*, I think, in the very next beat. I'd know it.

Justin's bedroom smells of stale smoke and socks. On the bed is a pile of clean laundry I put there yesterday, the neatly folded stack now fallen to one side, where Justin has slept in his bed without bothering to move them or put them away. I open the curtains to let in some light and find half a dozen mugs, three used as ashtrays. A neatly rolled joint lies next to a lighter.

"Check his drawers," I tell Katie, who is standing in the doorway. She doesn't move. "Now! We don't know how long we've got." I sit on the bed and open Justin's laptop.

"Mum, this feels wrong."

"And running a website selling women's commutes to men who want to rape or kill them isn't?"

"He wouldn't do that!"

"I don't think so, either. But we need to be sure. Search his room."

"I don't even know what I'm looking for," Katie says, but she pulls open his wardrobe doors and starts rifling through his shelves.

"More receipts from Espress Oh!," I say, trying to think of something incriminating. "Photos of women, information about their commutes . . ." Justin's laptop is password protected. I stare at the screen, and his username, Game8oy_94, looks back at me, beside the tiny avatar of Justin's palm thrust toward the camera.

"Money?" Katie says.

"Definitely. Anything out of the ordinary. What could Justin's password be?" I try his date of birth and ACCESS DENIED: TWO AT-TEMPTS REMAINING appears on the screen.

"Money," Katie says again, and I realize it isn't a question. I look up. She's holding an envelope, exactly like the one Justin handed me with my rent money. It's stuffed so full of twenty- and ten-pound notes the flap won't stay shut. "His wages from the café, do you think?"

Katie doesn't know about Melissa's cash-in-hand tax dodge, and although I doubt she'd care I don't plan on telling her. The more people who know, the more likelihood there is that HMRC will find out, and that's trouble neither Melissa nor I need.

"I guess so," I say vaguely. "Put it back."

I take another stab at Justin's password, this time entering a mash-up of our address and the name of his first pet; a gerbil called Gerald who escaped and lived under the floorboards in our bathroom for several months.

ACCESS DENIED: ONE ATTEMPT REMAINING

I daren't risk another try. "Is there anything else in the wardrobe?"

"Not that I can find." Katie moves on to the tallboy, pulling out each drawer and running a hand expertly beneath each one, checking to see if anything has been taped there. She feels among his clothes and I close the laptop and leave it on the bed in what I hope is the same position I found it. "How about the laptop?"

"I can't get in."

"Mum . . ." Katie doesn't look at me as she speaks. "You know the receipt could be Simon's."

My answer is immediate. "It isn't Simon's."

"You don't know that."

"I do." I've never been more sure of anything in my life. "Simon loves me. He would never hurt me."

Katie slams a drawer shut, making me jump. "You'll point the finger at Isaac, but you won't even entertain the idea of Simon being involved?"

"You've known Isaac five minutes."

"It's only fair, Mum. If we're going through Justin's stuff, and accusing Isaac, then we have to consider Simon, too. We need to search his room."

"I'm not searching Simon's room, Katie! How could I ever expect him to trust me again?"

"Look, I'm not saying he's involved, or even that the Espress Oh! receipt is his. But it could be." I shake my head and she throws up her hands. "Mum, it could be! At least consider it."

"We'll wait until he gets home, and then we can all go up together."

Katie is unflinching. "No, Mum. Now."

The staircase leading to the attic is narrow, and the door on the second-floor landing gives the impression there is nothing but a cupboard be-hind; perhaps a bathroom or a small bedroom. Before Simon moved in I used to use it as a sort of escape: it wasn't properly furnished, but I piled cushions up here and would shut the door and lie down for half an hour, stealing time for myself from the maelstrom of single parenting. I used to love how hidden it felt. Now it feels dangerous, each step up taking me away from the openness of the rest of the house, away from safety.

"What if Simon comes home?" I say. Simon and I have nothing to hide from each other, but we're both adults; we've always agreed it's important to have our own space. Our own lives. I can't imagine what he'd say if he could see Katie and me now, snooping around his office.

"We're not doing anything wrong. He doesn't know we've found the receipt. We have to stay cool."

Cool is the last thing I feel.

"We're getting the Christmas decorations down," I say suddenly.

"What?"

"If he comes home and asks what we're doing. We're up here to get the decorations out of the eaves."

"Right, okay." Katie isn't interested, but I feel better, knowing I have an excuse ready.

The door at the bottom of the stairs swings shut with a bang that makes me jump. It's the only door that does; the only one with a fire-regulation-compliant closer. Simon wanted to take it off: he said he liked having the door open, so he could hear the hustle and bustle of life below him. I insisted it stay, worrying about fire, worrying about anything that might threaten my family.

All that time, is it possible the real threat has been right there in front of us?

Living in our house?

I feel nauseated, and I force the bile down, trying to capture an ounce of the strength my nineteen-year-old daughter is now showing. Katie stands in the middle of the room and takes a slow, careful look around. There's nothing on the walls, which slope from ceiling to floor at an angle that leaves only a narrow strip of full head height along the center of the room. The single skylight lets in a paltry amount of winter sun, and I turn on the main light.

"There." Katie points to the filing cabinet, on which Simon's Samsung tablet is resting. She hands it to me. She's decisive, almost snappy. I wish I knew what she was thinking.

"Katie," I say, "do you really think Simon's capable of . . ." I don't finish.

"I don't know, Mum. Look at the search history."

I open the case and enter Simon's password, then open the browser. "How do I see what he was looking at?"

Katie looks over my shoulder. "Tap there." She points. "It should bring up a list of sites visited, as well as what he's been searching for."

I breathe a sigh of relief. There's nothing obvious. News sites, and a couple of holiday brokers. A Valentine's weekend break. I wonder how Simon can even think about booking a holiday when he's so much in debt. Window-shopping, I suppose, thinking of the evenings I spend looking online at million-pound properties I could never hope to afford.

Katie is looking again in the filing cabinet drawer. She pulls out a piece of paper. "Mum," she says slowly, "he hasn't been telling the truth."

The nausea returns to the pit of my stomach.

"'Dear Mr. Thornton,'" she reads. "'Further to your recent meeting with Human Resources please accept this letter as formal notification of your dismissal.'" She looks at me. "It's dated first of August."

The relief is instant.

"I know about the layoff. I'm sorry I didn't tell you. I only found out myself a week ago."

"You knew? Is that why he started working from home?" I nod. "And before that? Since August, I mean. He's been wearing a suit, going out every day . . ."

I feel too loyal to Simon to admit that he spent those weeks pretending to be at work, lying to us all, but I don't need to; I can tell from Katie's face she's already worked it out.

"You don't know for sure, though, do you?" she says. "You don't know what he was doing—not what he was *really* doing. You only know what he told you. For all you know, he spent that time following women on the Underground. Taking their photographs. Posting their details on the Internet."

"I trust Simon." My words sound hollow, even to me.

She starts searching through the filing cabinet, throwing files on the floor. The top drawer is filled with Simon's paperwork: work contracts, life insurance . . . I don't know what's there. In the middle drawer I keep all the documentation relating to the house: buildings and contents insurance, my mortgage statements, the building regs certificate for the loft conversion we're in right now. In another folder are the children's birth certificates and my divorce certificate, along with all our passports. In a third, old bank statements, kept for no other reason than I don't know what else to do with them.

"Check the desk," she says, just as I ordered her to search Justin's room. Frustrated by the time it's taking to look at each document, she pulls out the filing cabinet drawer and tips the contents onto the floor, swirling them around with one hand until everything is uncovered. "There'll be something, I know it."

My daughter is strong. Feisty.

She gets that from you, Matt always used to say, when Katie stubbornly refused the laden spoon I was waving in front of her, or insisted on walking to the shops when her little legs were barely stable. The memory hurts, and I mentally shake myself. I'm the grown-up. I'm the strong one. This is my fault. I'm the one who was taken in by Simon; flattered by the attention, by his generosity.

I need answers, and I need them now.

I open the first desk drawer and pull out the contents, dumping files on the floor and shaking them in case anything of interest lies beneath the pages of otherwise dull documentation. I meet Katie's eye and she gives me a grim nod of approval.

"This drawer's locked." I rattle the handle. "I don't know where the key is."

"Can you force it?"

"I'm trying." I hold the top of the desk with one hand and yank hard on the handle of the drawer with the other. It doesn't budge. I look around the chaotic desk to see where Simon might keep the key, tipping up a pen pot but finding only a collection of paperclips and pencil shavings. Remembering how Katie searched Justin's tallboy I run my hand under the desk in case the key is taped there and look at the underside of all the open drawers for the same reason.

Nothing.

"We'll have to pick the lock." I say this with more confidence than I feel, having never picked a lock in my life. I take a pair of sharp scissors from the floor, where they have been tipped out from a drawer, and jam them into the lock. With no real method, I wiggle the blades violently from side to side and then up and down, at the same time pulling on the handle. There is a small crunching noise, and to my amazement the drawer opens. I drop the scissors onto the floor.

I wanted the drawer to be empty. I wanted it to contain nothing more than a dusty paperclip and a broken pencil. I wanted it to prove to Katie—to me—that Simon has nothing to do with the website.

It isn't empty.

Scraps of paper, torn from a spiral pad, lie innocently on one side of the drawer. *Grace Southeard*, the first is headed, above a series of bullet points.

36
Married? London Bridge.

I pick up the sheaf of papers and look at the second.

Alex Grant
52
Gray hair, bobbed. Slim. Looks good in jeans.

I feel like I'm going to be sick. I remember how reassuring Simon was, that night we went out for dinner, when I was so worried about the adverts.

Identity theft, that's all it is.

"What have you found, Mum?" Katie walks toward me. I turn the papers over but it's too late, she's already seen them.

"Oh my God . . ."

There's something else in the drawer. It's the Moleskine notebook I gave Simon for our first Christmas together. I pick it up; feel the soft leather beneath my fingertips.

The first few pages make little sense. Half-written sentences; words underlined; arrows drawn from one boxed name to another. I flick through the notebook and it falls open at a diagram. In the center, the word *How?* surrounded by a hand-drawn cloud. Around it, more words, each in their own clouds.

> *Stabbing*
> *Rape*
> *Asphyxiation*

The book falls from my hands, landing in the open drawer with a dull thud. I hear Katie's strangled cry and I turn to comfort her, but before I have a chance to say anything there's a noise I instantly recognize. I freeze and look at Katie, and I know from her face she's recognized it, too.

It's the bang of the door at the bottom of the stairs.

CHAPTER
THIRTY-ONE

"Coffee?"

"No, thank you." Kelly hadn't eaten all day but she didn't think she could stomach anything. Diggers had hung around for half an hour after dismissing her, before disappearing to do whatever a nearly retired DCI did with an accumulation of rest days in lieu. He hadn't spoken to Kelly again; only paused by Nick's desk on his way out, for a muttered conversation Kelly had been certain was about her.

"It wasn't a suggestion," Nick said. "Get your coat, we're going across the road."

The Starbucks on Balfour Street was more of a takeaway than a café, but it boasted two high stools in the window, which Kelly commandeered while Nick got the drinks. Kelly ordered a hot chocolate, suddenly craving its sweet comfort. It arrived topped with whipped cream and sprinkled with chocolate, looking embarrassingly gauche next to Nick's flat white.

"Thank you," Kelly said, when it became clear Nick wasn't going to do the talking.

"You can get the next ones," he said.

"For bailing me out, I mean."

"I know what you meant." He fixed her with an unsmiling gaze. "For future reference, if you fuck up, or you do something stupid, or for some other reason you're likely to need bailing out, for God's sake tell me. Don't wait until we're sitting in the DCI's office."

"I really am sorry."

"I'm sure."

"And very grateful. I didn't expect you to do that."

Nick took a sip of his coffee. He grinned. "To be honest, I didn't expect me to, either. But I couldn't sit by and see one of the best detectives I've worked with"—Kelly looked down at her hot chocolate to hide how pleased she was—"get the boot for doing something so monumentally stupid as to use her position for some sort of personal campaign. What exactly were you doing?"

The pleasurable flush Kelly had felt at Nick's compliment disappeared.

"I think an explanation is the least you owe me."

Kelly spooned some of the warm cream into her mouth, feeling it dissolve on her tongue. She tested the words out in her head before she spoke. "My sister was raped in her first year at Durham University."

"That much I gathered. And the offender was never caught?"

"Never. There had been several suspicious incidents prior to the rape; Lexi found cards in her pigeonhole asking her to wear certain clothes—outfits she had in her wardrobe—and once someone left a dead goldfinch outside her door."

"Did she report it?"

Kelly nodded. "The police weren't interested. Even when she told them she was being followed they just said they'd make a note of it. She had a late lecture on a Thursday evening and no one else walked back the same way as her, so she was on her own. The night it happened she was on the phone with me. She called because she was feeling nervous—she said she could hear footsteps behind her again."

"What did you do?"

Kelly felt her eyes burn with the threat of tears. She swallowed hard. "I told her she was imagining it." She could hear Lexi's voice, even now; breathless as she walked to her building.

There's someone behind me, Kelly, I swear. Just like last week.

Lex, there are seventeen thousand students at Durham—there's always someone behind you.

This is different. They're trying not to be seen. Lexi spoke in an urgent whisper, Kelly straining to hear every word. *When I turned around just now there was no one walking, but they're there, I know it.*

You're getting yourself in a state. Give me a call when you get home, yeah?

Kelly had been getting ready to go out, she remembered. She'd cranked the music up as she did her hair; threw another rejected dress on the pile at the end of the bed. It never crossed her mind that Lexi hadn't called until her mobile had rung with a number she hadn't recognized.

Kelly Swift? This is DC Barrow-Grint from Durham police. I've got your sister with me.

"It wasn't your fault," Nick said gently.

Kelly shook her head. "He wouldn't have attacked her if I'd stayed on the phone."

"You don't know that."

"If he had, I'd have heard—I'd have been able to call the police straightaway. It was two hours before Lexi was found—she'd been beaten up so badly she could hardly see—and by that time the offender was long gone."

Nick didn't contradict her. He turned his coffee cup around in its saucer until the handle was facing him, cupping both hands around it. "Does Lexi blame you for what happened?"

"I don't know. She must."

"You haven't asked her?"

"She won't talk about it. Hates it when I do. I thought she'd be affected for months—forever, even—but it was as though she just drew a line under the whole thing. When she met her husband she sat him down and said, 'There's something you need to know,' and she told him the whole story then made him promise never to mention it again."

"She's a strong woman."

"You think so? I don't think it's healthy. Pretending something didn't happen isn't the way to deal with a traumatic event."

"You mean, it's not the way *you* deal with traumatic events," Nick said.

Kelly looked at him sharply. "This isn't about me."

Nick drained his coffee and set the cup carefully on the saucer before looking Kelly in the eye. "Exactly."

Kelly's mobile rang as they returned to work. She hung back at the top of the stairs, avoiding the noise of the busy MIT office. It was Craig, from the CCTV hub.

"Kelly, have you seen BTP's internal briefing today?"

She hadn't. It was hard enough to keep up with the volume of e-mails relating to this job, without reading her own force's daily missives.

"The CCTV room here has been compromised. Given what you told me the other day about your Met job, I thought I should give you a ring."

"A break-in?"

"Worse. A hacking."

"I thought that was impossible?"

"Nothing's impossible, Kelly, you should know that. The system's been sluggish for a few weeks; we called an engineer and when he came to take a look he identified some malware. We've got a firewall in place that makes it nigh on impossible to be hacked over the web, but doesn't stop someone physically introducing viruses to the system."

"An inside job, then?"

"All the staff were interviewed in turn this morning by the superintendent, and one of the cleaners broke down. Said she'd been bribed to carry a USB stick in and put it in the main computer. Of course she claims to have had no idea what she was doing."

"Bribed by whom?"

"She doesn't know his name, and conveniently doesn't remember what he looks like. She says she was approached on the way to work one day and offered more than a month's salary for a few minutes' work."

"What's the extent of the hacking?"

"The malware introduces a program that talks to the hacker's computer and replicates the entire system. They can't control the camera direction, but the bottom line is whatever our control room sees, the hacker can see."

"Oh my God."

"Does it fit with what you're dealing with?"

"It's certainly possible." Despite her good working relationship with Craig, Kelly was mindful of what Diggers might say if she were to release any more information than necessary. The last thing she needed was another telling-off, although there was no doubt in her mind the two jobs were related.

"Our offender's been using London Underground's own cameras to stalk women," Kelly announced, walking into the office and interrupting a conversation Nick was having with Lucinda. She filled them in on the call from Craig. "BTP's Cyber Crime unit are there now, but although they've identified the malware, it's less straightforward to eradicate it."

"Couldn't they switch off the whole system?" Lucinda asked.

"They could, but then the entire city would potentially be at risk, instead of—"

"Instead of a small number of women definitely at risk," Nick finished. "We're between a rock and a hard place." He stood up, his whole body energized, and Kelly realized how much he thrived on the adrenaline of a fast-moving investigation. "Right, we need a statement from your CCTV contact, and I want that cleaner nicked for unauthorized access to computer systems with intent to commit crime." He looked around for the HOLMES loggist, who was already entering the actions into the laptop in front of him. "And get Andrew Robinson here. I want to know where that CCTV feed is being copied to, and I want to know it now."

CHAPTER
THIRTY-TWO

There's no time to do anything but stand there and wait for Simon to come up the stairs.

I reach for Katie's hand, only to find it already sliding into mine. I squeeze it tightly and she squeezes it back. It's something we used to do when she was little, walking to school. I'd squeeze once, and she'd do the same: she'd squeeze twice and I'd mirror it. Morse code for mother and child.

"Three means 'I love you,'" she told me once.

I do it now, not knowing if she'll remember, listening to the sound of footsteps on the wooden stairs. Instantly Katie returns the message, and I feel the hot stab of tears.

There are thirteen steps from the landing.

I count the footsteps as they grow closer. Eleven, ten, nine. My hand is clammy in Katie's, my heart beating so fast I can't distinguish between its beats. She squeezes my fingers so tightly it hurts, but I don't care—I'm squeezing hers just as hard.

Five, four, three . . .

"I used my key; I hope you don't mind."

"Melissa!"

"Oh my God, you almost gave us a heart attack." Relief makes Katie and me laugh hysterically.

Melissa looks at us strangely. "What are you two up to? I called you at work and your boss said you were off sick—I just popped around to see if you were okay, and I was worried when you didn't answer the door."

"We didn't hear it. We were—" Katie breaks off and looks at me, unsure how much to share.

"We were looking for evidence," I tell Melissa. Suddenly sober, I sink onto the chair by Simon's desk. "It sounds crazy, but it looks like it was Simon who put all those women's commutes online—who put *my* commute online."

"Simon?" I see in Melissa's face the disbelief and confusion I know still registers on my own. "Are you sure?"

I explain about the Espress Oh! receipt; the e-mail from PC Kelly Swift. "Simon lost his job in August—right before the adverts started. He lied to me about it."

"What the hell are you still doing here? Where's Simon now?"

"He's got an interview at Olympia. I'm not sure what time—early afternoon, I think he said."

Melissa looks at her watch. "He could be here any moment. Come to mine; we can call the police from there. Did you have any idea? I mean—God, Simon!" I feel my heart rate soar again, my rib cage thudding and my pulse singing in my ears. I'm suddenly convinced we won't make it out; that Simon will come home while we're all in the attic. What will he do, once he knows he's been found out? I think of Tania Beckett and Laura Keen, unhappy casualties of his sick online empire. What difference would another three make to him?

I stand up and grip Katie's arm. "Melissa's right, we need to get out of here. Where's Justin?" Fear grips me and I want my family together; I need to know that both my children are safe. Once Simon discovers we know what he's done, there's no way of knowing what he'll do.

"Relax, he's at the café," Melissa says. "I've just come from there."

My relief is momentary. "He can't stay—Simon will know to find him there. Someone will have to take over."

Melissa has snapped into business mode. She reminds me of a paramedic at a major disaster, issuing practical help and soothing words. "I'll call him and tell him to shut up shop."

"Are you sure? He might—"

Melissa cups my face between her hands. She puts her face close to mine, forcing me to focus on what she's saying. "We need to get out of here, Zoe, do you understand? We don't know how much time we've got."

The three of us clatter down the stairs onto the carpeted second-floor landing and continue down to the first floor without stopping. In the hall Katie and I take our coats from where they've been slung over the banister. I look around for my bag but Melissa stops me.

"There's no time. I'll come for it once you and Katie are safe next door."

We slam the front door and run down the path without bothering to lock it behind us, turning immediately in through Melissa's garden gate. She unlocks the door and ushers us through to the kitchen.

"We should lock ourselves in," Katie says. She looks between Melissa and me, fear written across her face. Her bottom lip trembles.

"Simon's not going to try to get in here, love, he doesn't even know we're here."

"Once he sees we're not at home he's bound to try here. Lock the door, please!" She's close to tears.

"I think she's right," Melissa says. She double-locks the front door, and despite what I said to Katie, I'm reassured by the sound of the barrel shooting home.

"What about the back door?" Katie says. She's shaking, and I'm filled with rage. How dare Simon do this to my daughter?

"It's always locked. Neil's paranoid about burglars—he won't even keep the key where it can be seen from the garden." Melissa puts an arm around Katie. "I promise you, sweetheart, you're safe now. Neil's working away this week, so you can stay here as long as you want. Why don't you put the kettle on, and I'll call this PC Swift and tell her about the receipt you found. Have you got her number?"

I take my phone out of my pocket and unlock it, scrolling through until I find Kelly Swift's number. I hand Melissa the phone. She peers at it.

"I'll get more reception upstairs. Give me two seconds. Do me a favor and make me a coffee, will you? The capsules are next to the machine."

I switch on the coffee machine; a newfangled chrome thing that froths milk and mixes cappuccinos and goodness knows what else. Katie crosses the kitchen. She looks through the bifold doors to the garden, and rattles the handle.

"Locked?"

"Locked. I'm scared, Mum."

I try to keep my voice calm, belying the turmoil I feel instead. "He won't get us here, love. PC Swift will come and talk to us, and they'll get officers to arrest Simon. He can't hurt us."

I stand in front of the coffee machine and place my hands flat on the worktop; the granite cold and smooth beneath my palms. Now that we're safely out of the house my fear is turning to anger, and I'm struggling to keep it hidden from Katie, who is already teetering on the edge of hysteria. I think of the lies Simon told me during the months when I thought he was still working; his insistence, when I brought home the *Gazette* all those weeks ago, that it wasn't me in the photo. How could I have been so stupid?

I think of the debt Simon claimed to have run up. The website must be bringing in far more than he ever earned at the *Telegraph*. No wonder he didn't get another job—why would he bother? The role he's been called back for today—I doubt it even exists. I picture Simon sitting in a café, not preparing for his interview but scrolling through photos of women on his phone, copying details of their commutes from his notebook to upload to the website.

Katie's restless, pacing between the window and Melissa's long, white table, picking up artfully arranged objects from the floating shelves. "Be careful with that," I tell her, "it probably cost a fortune."

From upstairs I hear the strains of Melissa's voice as she talks to PC

Swift. I hear her ask, "Are they in danger?" and I cough loudly, not wanting Katie to dwell on it any more than she already is. She's replaced the vase and picked up a glass paperweight; she runs her thumb over the smooth surface.

"Please, love, you're making me nervous."

She puts it down and wanders across the kitchen to the opposite side, where Melissa's desk is.

The green light on the coffee machine blinks, to tell me the water is hot. I press start, watching the dark liquid spew into the waiting cup. The smell is strong, almost overpowering. I don't usually drink coffee but today I think I need one. I take out a second capsule. "Do you want one?" I ask Katie. She doesn't answer. I turn to see her looking at something on the desk. "Love, please stop fiddling with Melissa's stuff." I'm wondering how long the police will take to arrive and whether they'll go out and look for Simon, or wait for him to return home.

"Mum, you need to see this."

"What is it?" I hear the creak of Melissa's footsteps on the landing, and I put her coffee on the island behind me. I stir a sugar into mine and take a sip, scalding my tongue.

"Mum!" Katie is insistent. I walk across to the desk to see what's got her in a state. It's a London Underground map—the one I saw when I picked up Melissa's accounts. Katie has unfolded it, and now it spreads across the entire surface of the desk. The familiar colors and routes of the Underground have been annotated with a spider's web of arrows, lines, and scribbled notes.

I stare at it. Katie is crying but I make no move to comfort her. I'm searching for a route I know by heart; Tania Beckett's commute to work.

The Northern line to Highgate, then the 43 bus to Cranley Gardens.

The route has been marked out with a yellow highlighter, and at the end is a handwritten note.

No longer active.

You hear a lot of things in coffee shops.

I imagine working in a busy café is much like being a bartender, or a hairdresser. We see the highs and lows of everyday life in our customers' faces; hear the tail end of conversations between friends. We benefit from your bonuses—a lunch paid for with crisp twenty-pound notes; a pound coin thrown carelessly on the table—and we suffer the consequences of a bad month, when you count out your change for a smaller-than-usual coffee and pretend not to see the tips jar on the counter.

A café provides the perfect financial detergent when you need to move large amounts of cash around. Who cares what the footfall's like? Invisible customers can still pay the bills. Money comes in dirty; it goes out clean.

Over time, regulars become loose-lipped. We know your secrets, your ambitions, your bank details. Casual customers share confidences; the Formica counter acting as a therapist's couch. You talk; we listen.

It's the perfect environment to source more girls, and—just occasionally—more customers. A card, slipped into the jacket pocket of a man who fits the brief. A man who's already proved his mettle with his smutty comment to the girl on the till; whose pinstripe suit and suspenders mark him out as someone with money. A man who will, later, look at the invitation in his pocket, and be flattered enough to take a look.

An exclusive members' club. The finest girls.

Access to a service he won't find anywhere else in the city. Access to you.

CHAPTER
THIRTY-THREE

Melissa stands in the doorway between the hall and the kitchen. She registers the horrified look on Katie's face, the unfolded Underground map in my hand, and slowly the smile disappears from her face. I realize I'm hoping she'll deny it; that she'll produce some plausible explanation for the evidence I'm holding.

She doesn't even try. Instead she gives a deep sigh, as though our actions are tedious in the extreme.

"It's very bad manners to rifle through someone's personal belongings," she says, and I have to swallow the automatic apology it prompts. She walks across the kitchen, her heels clicking against the tiled floor, and takes the Underground map from my hand. I realize I'm holding my breath, but when I let it out there isn't anything there; my chest feels tight, as though someone is pushing against it. I watch her refold the map, tutting when a crease bends the wrong way, but not hurried, not panicked in the slightest. Her coolness disorients me, and I have to remind myself that the evidence is incontrovertible. Melissa is behind the website; behind the *London Gazette* adverts. It's Melissa who has been hunting women across London; selling their commutes so that men can hunt them, too.

"Why?" I ask her. She doesn't answer.

"You'd better sit down," she says instead, gesturing to the long white table.

"No."

Melissa gives an exasperated sigh. "Zoe, don't make this any more difficult than it's going to be. Sit down."

"You can't keep us here."

She laughs then; a humorless bark that says she can do exactly what she wants. She walks the few steps toward the kitchen counter, an expanse of black granite broken only by the coffee machine and a knife block next to the stove. Her hand hovers over the block for a second, her index finger playing a silent game of Eenie, Meenie, Miney, Mo before she pulls out a black-handled knife around six inches long.

"Can't I?" she says.

I sink slowly into the chair nearest to me. I tug at Katie's arm, and after a moment she does the same.

"You won't get away with this, Melissa," I tell her. "The police will be here any minute now."

"I very much doubt that. Judging from the updates you've so helpfully shared with me over the last few weeks, the police have proved themselves to be largely incompetent."

"But you told PC Swift where we were. She'll—" I stop even before I see the pitying look on Melissa's face. How stupid of me. Of course Melissa didn't really call Kelly Swift. The realization is like a punch to the stomach and I fold forward in my chair, suddenly spent. There are no police coming. My panic alarm is in my bag at home. No one knows we're here.

"You're sick," Katie spits, "or mad. Or both." There's more than just anger in her voice. I think of all the time Katie has spent in this kitchen over the years; baking cakes, doing her homework, talking to Melissa in a way that sometimes isn't possible between a mother and a daughter, no matter how close they are. I try to imagine how she must feel, then I realize I'm already there. Lied to. Taken advantage of. Betrayed.

"Neither. I saw a business opportunity and I took it." Melissa walks toward us, the knife held casually in one hand, as though she has been interrupted in the middle of preparing dinner.

"This isn't a business!" I say, so outraged I stumble over the words.

"It most certainly is a business, and a very successful one. I had fifty clients within a fortnight of setting up the website, with more joining every day." She sounds like an advert for a franchise opportunity; like she's bragging about adding to her chain of coffee shops.

She sits opposite us. "They're so stupid. Commuters. You see them, every day, oblivious to the world around them. Plugged into their iPods, staring at their phones, reading their papers. Taking the same route every day, sitting in the same seat, standing on the same spot on the platform."

"They're just going to work," I say.

"You see the same ones every day. I was watching this woman once, doing her makeup on the Central line. I'd seen her a few times, and she always had the same routine. She'd wait till Holland Park, then she'd get out her makeup bag and start plastering her face. Powder first, then eye shadow, mascara, lipstick. As the train slowed down at Marble Arch she'd be putting her makeup bag away. I watched her this one time, and as I looked away I caught a man watching her, too, with a look in his eyes that suggested he was thinking about more than her face. That's when I first had the idea."

"Why me?" And as I say it I can't believe it has only now occurred to me to ask. "Why put me on the website?"

"I needed a few older women." She shrugs. "There's no accounting for people's tastes."

"But I'm your friend!" Even as I say it I hate myself for how pathetic it sounds, like a schoolyard catfight over who plays with whom.

Melissa's lips tighten. She stands up abruptly, striding toward the bifold doors and gazing into the garden. It's several seconds before she speaks.

"I've never known anyone to moan about their life as much as you do." I'd been expecting something different; some indiscretion, committed years ago. Not this. "*I had my kids too young,*" she mimics.

"I've never said that." I look at Katie. "I've never regretted having you. Either of you."

"You walk out on a textbook husband—solvent, funny, hands-on with the kids—and replace him with someone equally textbook."

"You have no idea what my marriage to Matt was like. Or what my relationship with Simon is like, come to that." At the thought of Simon, guilt overwhelms me. How could I have thought he was responsible for the website? I think of the names, and the scribbled threats I found in Simon's desk drawer, and for a second I doubt myself, then I realize what they are: research notes. He's used the Moleskine for exactly the purpose it was intended: to plan his novel. Relief makes me smile, and Melissa looks at me with venom in her eyes.

"It's all so *easy* for you, isn't it, Zoe? Yet you never stop complaining."

"Easy?" I'd laugh, were it not for the knife in her hand, which catches the light from the skylight and throws rainbows around the room.

"And from the second you move in next door it's the 'poor me' routine. Single mum, struggling to pay the bills, bursting into tears every five minutes."

"It was a difficult time," I say, in my defense, speaking more to Katie than to Melissa. Katie reaches for my hand; gives me the silent support I need.

"Whatever you asked for, I gave you. Money, a job, help looking after the kids." She spins around; I hear her heels scrape on the tiles then she bends over me, her hair falling over mine, and hisses in my ear. "What have you ever given me?"

"I—" My mind is blank. Surely I must have done something? But there's nothing. Melissa and Neil have no children, no pets to look after, no houseplants to water when they're away on holiday. There's more to friendship than that, though, isn't there?

Do the scales of friendship have to balance so absolutely? "You're jealous," I say, and it seems such an insignificant word to justify something of this magnitude; of this horror.

Melissa looks at me as though she's stepped in something unpleasant. "Jealous? Of you?"

But the idea takes root. Grows into something that feels right.

"You think you'd have been a better mother than me."

"I'd have been a more grateful one, that's for sure," she bites back.

"I love my children." I can't believe she's even questioning it.

"You hardly saw them! They were an inconvenience, parceled off to mine whenever you were sick of them. Who was it who taught Katie how to cook? Who got Justin away from the thieving kids at school? He'd have ended up in prison if it hadn't been for me!"

"You said you were happy to have them."

"Because they needed me! What else did they have? A mother who was constantly working, constantly moaning, constantly crying."

"That's not fair, Melissa."

"It's the truth, whether you like it or not."

Next to me, Katie is silent. I look at her and see she is shaking, her face completely devoid of color. Melissa straightens. She moves to sit at the swivel chair by her desk, and switches on the computer.

"Let us go, Melissa."

She laughs. "Oh, come on, Zoe, you're not that stupid. You know about the website now; you know what I've done. I can't just let you go."

"So leave us here!" I cry, suddenly realizing there's another way. "You go, now. Lock us in. We won't know where you've gone, and we won't tell the police anything you've told us. You could delete everything from your computer!" I'm aware I'm sounding hysterical. I stand up, unsure even as I do so exactly what I'm planning to do.

"Sit down."

I can't feel my legs, yet they move toward Melissa on autopilot.

"Sit down!"

"Mum!"

It happens so fast I don't have time to react. Melissa gets out of her chair and slams into me, knocking us both to the ground and landing on top of me, pinning me to the floor. Her left fist is clutching my hair, forcing my chin up, and her right hand is holding the knife to my throat.

"I'm getting tired of this, Zoe."

"Get off her!" Katie screams, pulling at Melissa's jacket and placing a well-aimed kick to her stomach. Melissa scarcely registers it and I feel the blade of her knife pressing against my skin.

"Katie." My voice is barely a whisper. "Stop." She hesitates, then backs away, shaking so hard I can hear her teeth chattering. There's a stinging sensation at my throat.

"Mum, you're bleeding!"

I feel the wetness trickle down the side of my neck.

"Are you going to do as you're told?"

I nod my head, the tiny movement causing another trickle of blood to escape from the cut on my throat.

"Excellent." Melissa gets up. She brushes her knees, then pulls a tissue from her pocket and wipes the blade of the knife carefully. "Now, sit down."

I do as I'm told. Melissa returns to her desk. She taps the keyboard and I see the familiar background to the FindTheOne website. Melissa enters a username and password, but the site looks different; and I realize she has logged in as an administrator. She minimizes the window then opens a new one, making several swift keystrokes. I see an Underground platform. It's not busy; there are about a dozen people standing up, and a woman with a wheeled shopper sitting on a bench. I think at first we're looking at a photograph, then the woman with the wheeled shopper stands up and begins walking along the platform.

"Is that CCTV?"

"Yes. I can't take the credit for the cameras, just the redirection of the footage. I contemplated installing my own cameras but it would have meant restricting myself to just a couple of Underground lines. This way we can see the whole network. This is the Jubilee line." Another flurry of keystrokes, and the image changes to a different platform, a handful of people waiting for a train. "I can't get the whole network, and annoyingly there's no opportunity to control the direction of the cameras—I can only see what the operators can see. But it's made the whole operation far easier, not to mention more interesting."

"What do you mean?" Katie says.

"Before I had the network I never knew what happened to the women. I had to take them off the website once their profiles were sold, as well as check they hadn't changed jobs, or altered their route to work. Sometimes it would be days before I'd realize a woman was wearing a new coat. That's not good for business. CCTV means I can watch them whenever I want. It means I get to see what happens to them."

She continues tapping at the keyboard, before pressing enter with an exaggerated flourish. A slow smile spreads across her face as she turns to us.

"Now, how about we play a little game?"

CHAPTER
THIRTY-FOUR

Kelly looked at the phone on her desk and steeled herself to dial. She had tried several times, always canceling the call before it started ringing, and once hanging up just as it was answered. Before she could change her mind again, she picked up the phone and dialed. Cradling the receiver between her shoulder and her ear she listened to the ringtone, half wanting it to go to voice mail, half wanting to get it over and done with. Nick wanted everyone in the briefing room in ten minutes, and she'd be unlikely to get another chance to make a personal call till much later.

"Hello."

At the sound of Lexi's voice, Kelly was suddenly mute. Around her everyone was getting ready to go into briefing; picking up notebooks and bending down over their desks to read last-minute e-mails. Kelly contemplated hanging up.

"Hello?" Then again, annoyed now. "Hello?"

"It's me."

"Oh. Why didn't you say anything?"

"Sorry, there was something wrong with the line, I think. How are you?" An e-mail pinged into her inbox and she moved her mouse to open it. It was from the DI.

Is that the kettle I can hear boiling?

Through the open door to the briefing room Kelly could see Nick on his BlackBerry. He looked up and grinned, making a drinking action with his free hand.

"Fine. You?"

"Fine." She nodded to the DI and held up her forefinger, intended to indicate she'd only be a minute, but the DI had already looked away.

The stilted conversation continued until Kelly could bear it no longer.

"Actually, I rang to say I hope you have a good time tonight."

There was a pause. "Tonight?"

"Isn't it your reunion? At Durham?" Did she sound enthusiastic? Kelly hoped so. However much she hated the idea of Lexi back on that campus, however much she would balk at doing it herself, she had to accept what Lexi had been telling her for years. It wasn't her life.

"Yes." Suspicion lingered in Lexi's voice. Kelly could hardly blame her.

"Well, I hope you have fun. I bet some people won't have changed at all. Who was that girl you lived with in your second year—the one who only ever ate sausages?" She was speaking too fast, the words falling over themselves in her effort to be as lighthearted and as supportive as she knew she should have been when Lexi first mentioned returning to Durham.

"Gemma, I think."

"That was it. Weird as they come!"

"Sis, what's going on? Why did you really call?"

"To say sorry. For interfering in your life; for judging the choices you made." She took a deep breath. "But mainly, for not staying on the phone that night."

Lexi made a small sound; a stifled cry from the back of her throat. "Don't, Kelly, please. I don't want to—"

She sounded so distraught Kelly almost stopped, hating the fact she was hurting Lexi. But she had already waited too long to say it. "Just

hear me out, and then I promise you I won't ever mention it again."
She took Lexi's silence as acceptance. "I'm sorry I hung up on you. You
were frightened and I wasn't there for you, and there isn't a day goes by
that I don't feel guilty about it."

The line was so quiet Kelly thought Lexi had put down the phone,
but finally she spoke.

"It wasn't your fault, Kelly."

"But if I'd only—"

"It wasn't your fault for hanging up, and it wasn't my fault for
walking by the woods on my own. I don't blame you, and I don't blame
the police."

"They should have taken your earlier reports more seriously."

"Kelly, the only reason I was raped that night is because one man decided that's what he was going to do. I don't know if he'd ever done it
before, or if he's done it since, and rightly or wrongly I don't care. It was
one night—one hour—of my life, and I've had thousands more that
have been filled with light and happiness and joy." On cue, Kelly heard
her nephews laughing in the background; infectious, uncontrollable
giggles that made her heart lift. "It was no one else's fault, Kelly."

"Okay." Kelly couldn't say more, for fear of bursting into tears. She
wished now she'd called Lexi from her mobile, instead of being teth-
ered to her desk where everyone could see her. She closed her eyes and
put her hand to her forehead. In the background, Fergus and Alfie
continued to play, the giggles now interspersed with indignant shouts
over the ownership of some toy or other. In her head, Kelly could see
Lexi standing in the kitchen, the boys still full of energy despite a full
day at school and nursery, scattering Lego bricks around her feet.
Nothing about Lexi's life was defined by her past; she lived in the
moment. It was time for Kelly to do the same. She pulled herself
together, and they both spoke at the same time.

"What do you think I should wear?"

"What are you going to wear to the reunion?"

Kelly smiled, remembering the times they would finish each oth-

er's sentences at school. Lexi used to claim they had special twin pow-
ers, but really it was simply that they spent so much time together. The
very best of friends.

"I have to go, actually," Kelly said, catching sight of Nick repeating
his earlier coffee-drinking mime. "I've got to go into a meeting. Let me
know how it goes. And whether Gemma eats something other than
sausages nowadays."

Lexi laughed. "Thank you for calling. I do love you, you know."

"I love you, too."

Kelly walked backward into the briefing room, pushing the door open
with her bottom and trying not to drop the tray, which was bent and
wobbled ominously with every step she took. "We're low on tea bags,
Lucinda, so I've done one of your herbal things, is that all right?"
There was no reaction from the analyst; in fact, no one looked up at all.
"Something's happened, hasn't it?" Kelly said.

"Cyber Crime have just received notification of a new profile," Nick
said. He shifted his chair to make space for her, and Andrew Robinson
gestured toward the laptop in front of him.

Andrew said, "Fifteen minutes ago I received this through our
pseudonymous account."

The e-mail was brief; a line of text at the top, beside a thumbnail
photograph of a blonde woman.

Brand-new download: FREE today only.

"Have any of the others been free?" Kelly asked.

"Only to Gold members. None of the profiles have ever been priced
at less than £200, and this is the first time we've been notified of a new
listing. As far as we knew, the only notification came from the adverts
in the *Gazette*."

Kelly read the profile.

White.

19 years old. Long blonde hair, blue eyes.

Blue jeans, gray ankle boots, black V-neck T-shirt with oversized belted gray cardigan. White knee-length puffa coat, also belted. Black handbag with gilt chain.

Size 8–10.

1530: Enters Crystal Palace Tube station. Takes Overground train to Canada Water, choosing the first carriage and sitting by the doors. Changes to the Jubilee line, walking down the platform to stand next to the Tube map, where the doors to carriage #6 will open. Sits and reads a magazine. Changes at Waterloo, turning right and going down the steps to Platform 1; northbound Northern line. Walks down the platform to stand in the middle, near a worn section of the yellow line. The central carriage opens directly opposite this. Stands by the doors until Leicester Square. Takes the escalators, then leaves via exit three on to Charing Cross Road.

Availability: TODAY ONLY.

Duration: 45 minutes

Difficulty level: Extremely challenging

"It's gone out to all members," Andrew said, moving his cursor to the address box, where the *To* box said exactly that. There was a pause, as everyone considered the significance of FindTheOne's entire membership list—however large that might be—clicking on this woman's profile and downloading her commute. How many men would already be sitting in front of their computers, or looking at their phones, reading exactly what Kelly had just read? And on reading it, knowing she would be making her way through London, unaware she was being watched, how many would take that a step further?

"Can you make that photo any bigger?" Kelly asked. Andrew obliged, filling the screen with an enlarged version of the thumbnail they had just seen. The photo was a selfie, the teenager pouting at the camera; masses of streaked blonde hair half over her eyes. The soft-focus filter suggested it had been taken from Instagram, or been doctored for some other social media site.

The photo was new to Kelly, but the girl wasn't. A different photo, given to Kelly as the example from which a smaller image had been cropped. Kelly had read every inch of the Operation FURNISS file. She knew she'd seen this girl before. The same blonde hair, the same pouty expression.

She turned to look at Nick. "I recognize her. This is Zoe Walker's daughter."

CHAPTER THIRTY-FIVE

"What sort of game?" I say. Melissa smiles. She is still sitting at her desk, spinning the chair so she can face us. She looks at the computer screen.

"More than a hundred hits already." She looks at Katie. "You're a popular girl."

My stomach lurches. "You're not putting her on that website."

"She's already on there." Melissa clicks again, and I see Katie's photo on the screen, pouting at us with a careless confidence in stark contrast to our current situation. Katie cries out and I put my arm around her, pulling her toward me so fiercely her chair scrapes across the floor.

"So here's how it will work." Melissa is using her business voice; the one she adopts when she's on the phone to suppliers, or cajoling the bank manager into yet another loan. I've never heard her use it with me before, and it makes my blood run cold. "I've made Katie's profile free to download for a limited period, and I've sent the link to all members."

There's another ping from the computer; a notification box appears, then another and another.

Downloaded.
Downloaded.
Downloaded.

"As you can tell, they're quick off the mark. Hardly surprising, when you think they're usually paying up to five hundred quid for someone far less . . ." She takes time choosing the right word, finally settling on one that makes me sick to my stomach. "Enticing."

"She's not going anywhere."

"Oh, come on, now. Where's your sense of adventure? Not all my clients have nefarious aims, you know. Some of them are really rather romantic."

"She's not going."

"Then I'm afraid it's going to end very badly for both of you."

"What do you mean?"

She ignores my question. "Here are the rules. Katie follows her normal commute, and if she gets to the restaurant without any . . . shall we say, interruptions . . . then you win and I let you go. If she doesn't . . . well, you both lose."

"That's sick," Katie says.

Melissa looks at her, a sneer on her face. "Oh, come on, Katie, it's not like you to pass up the opportunity to be in the limelight."

"What's that supposed to mean?"

"This is your chance to be the star of the show. We all know you're not happy unless you're the center of attention. Never mind that Justin might have wanted a chance, or one of your friends. It always has to be about you, doesn't it? Like mother, like daughter."

I'm stunned by the hatred in her voice. Katie is crying, as shocked as I am.

"So," Melissa says, "that's the game. Ready to play? Or would you rather skip straight to the part where you both lose?" She tests the blade of the knife on her thumbnail, where it's too sharp to slide smoothly across the red lacquer Melissa always wears.

"You're not using my daughter as bait for a bunch of sick men. I'd rather die."

Melissa shrugs. "Your call." She stands up and walks toward me, the knife held out in front of her.

"No!" Katie screams. She clings to me, tears streaming down her face. "I'll do it, I'll go—I won't let her hurt you."

"Katie, I'm not letting you do it. You'll get hurt."

"And if I don't, we both will! Don't you understand? She's mad!"

I glance at Melissa but she seems entirely unperturbed by Katie's accusation. There's no sign of agitation, or of anger, which makes her actions even more terrifying. She would push that knife into me, I realize, and not even break into a sweat. I'm struggling to accept that the woman I thought was my friend—the woman I thought I knew—is someone else entirely. Someone who hates me. Who resents me so deeply for being a mother that she's prepared to hurt me; to hurt my daughter.

Katie squeezes my shoulder. "I can do this, Mum. The Tube will be busy—there'll be people everywhere—no one's going to hurt me."

"But, Katie, they *have* been hurt! Women have been murdered. Raped! You can't go." Even as I say it, I'm thinking of the alternative. If Katie stays here, what will happen to her? I'm in no doubt now that Melissa is going to kill me, but I won't let her kill Katie, too.

"The other women didn't know they were being watched. I do. I'll have the advantage. And I know that route, Mum. I'll know if someone's following me."

"No, Katie."

"I can do this. I want to do it." She's not crying anymore; her face is set with a determination I know so well I catch my breath. She thinks she's saving me. She really thinks she can play this game—that she can cross London without being caught—and that winning the game means Melissa will spare me.

She's wrong—Melissa won't let me go—but in trying to save me, I can save Katie. Out there, she has a fighting chance. In here, we're already dead.

"Okay," I tell her. It feels like a betrayal.

She stands up and looks at Melissa. Her chin juts out defiantly, and for a second I'm reminded of her character in the play, hiding her identity behind boys' clothing and clever words. If Katie's scared, she isn't showing it.

"What do I have to do?"

"You just have to go to work. Nothing simpler. You'll leave in"—
she checks the computer screen—"five minutes, and you'll follow your
usual route to the restaurant. You'll give me your phone, you won't
stop, or change your routine, and you won't do anything stupid like call
for help or try to contact the police." Katie hands over her mobile. Melissa walks to her desk and presses a series of keys. The computer
screen switches to a color CCTV image I recognize; it's looking out of
Crystal Palace Tube station. I can see the taxi stand to the left, and the
graffiti on the wall that's been there for as long as I can remember. As
we watch, a woman hurries into the station, checking her watch.

"Step out of line," Melissa continues, "and I'll know. And it doesn't
take a genius to work out what will happen to your mother."

Katie bites her lip.

"You don't have to do this," I say softly.

She tosses her hair. "It's fine. I'm not going to let anything happen
to me, Mum. Or you." She has a look of grim determination in her
eyes, but I know her too well to believe she feels as confident as she
looks. She's playing a part, but this isn't a play. It isn't a game, whatever
Melissa calls it. Whatever happens, someone's going to get hurt.

"Time to go," Melissa says.

I hug Katie so tightly it forces the air from my lungs. "Be careful."
I must have said the same thing thousands of times since becoming a
mother, each time a shortcut for something more.

"Be careful," when she was ten months old and cruising the furniture. *Don't break anything*, I really meant. *Watch that vase*.

"Be careful," when she learned to ride her bike. *Watch out for cars*, I
could have said.

"Be careful," the first time she got serious about a boyfriend.
Don't get hurt, I meant. *Don't get pregnant*.

"Be careful," I say now. *Don't let them catch you. Keep your eyes
open. Be quicker than them. Run fast.*

"I will be. I love you, Mum."

Pretend it's a normal day, I tell myself, as tears well in my eyes. *Pretend she's just going to work, and that she'll be home later and we'll put* Desperate Housewives *on Netflix and eat pizza. Pretend this isn't the last time you'll ever see her.* I'm crying openly now, and so is Katie, her temporary bravado too fragile to survive such an onslaught of emotion. I want to tell her to look out for Justin when I'm gone, to make sure Matt doesn't let him go off the rails, but doing so would acknowledge what I don't want in her head: that I won't be here when she gets back. *If* she gets back.

"I love you, too."

I take in every last detail of her: the way her hair smells; the smudge of lip gloss in the crease of her mouth. I fix her so firmly in my mind that whatever happens in the next hour I know it will be her face I see in my head when I die.

My baby girl.

"Enough, now." Melissa opens the kitchen door and Katie walks along the narrow hall toward the front of the house. *This is my chance,* I think. I consider charging after Katie as the front door opens, pushing us both outside and running; running to safety. But although the knife hangs by Melissa's side, she is gripping it so tightly her knuckles have whitened. She would use it in a heartbeat.

Knives.

I should have thought of it instantly. The knife block, now missing one resident, still contains a carving knife and three vegetable knives, in descending sizes. I hear the sound of a key in the lock and then, all too quickly, the door slams again and I'm assaulted by an image of Katie, walking toward the Tube station. Walking toward danger. *Run away,* I beg her silently. *Go the opposite way. Find a phone box. Tell the police.*

I know she won't. She thinks Melissa will kill me if she doesn't appear on that CCTV camera in precisely eight minutes.

I know she'll kill me even if she does.

When Melissa returns I'm halfway between the table and the kitchen counter. She's carrying something she must have picked up in the hall. A roll of duct tape.

"Where are you going? Get over there." She gestures with the tip of the knife, and I need no further persuasion. Melissa moves my chair so it is facing her computer. I sit.

"Put your hands behind your back."

I comply, and hear the distinctive ripping sound of duct tape, torn off into strips. Melissa wraps a strip around my wrists, then pushes the tape around the wooden struts of the chair so I can't move my arms. She tears off two more strips and secures my ankles to the legs of the chair.

I watch the clock in the right-hand corner of the screen. Six minutes to go.

I'm comforted by the thought that Katie's journey to work is on busy routes, and that it's still light. There are no dark alleyways in which she could be trapped, and so surely if she keeps her wits about her, she will be okay. The women who have become victims—Tania Beckett, Laura Keen, Cathy Tanning—they didn't know they were being targeted. Katie knows. Katie has the upper hand.

"Ready for the show?" Melissa says.

"I'm not watching." But I find I can't help myself. I have a sudden memory of taking Katie to the hospital when she was a baby and forcing myself to look while they put an IV into her tiny hand, rehydrating her after a bad sickness bug. I wanted so badly to take it all away from her, but if I couldn't do that, then the least I could do was carry the pain of seeing her suffer; live through it with her.

The score across the front of my neck has already started to scab over, and the tightness pulls at my skin and makes it itch. I stretch my neck in an attempt to relieve the feeling, releasing fresh blood that drips onto my lap.

Four minutes.

We watch the screen in silence. There's so much I want to know, but I don't want to hear Melissa's voice. I indulge myself with a fantasy in which even now the police are speeding toward Anerley Road. Any moment now I'll hear a crash as police officers break open the front door. It's so real I strain to hear the police sirens. There is nothing there.

Two minutes.

It seems an eternity until we see Katie appear on the CCTV image. She doesn't pause, but she looks up at the camera as she approaches, staring straight at us until she passes underneath the camera and out of view. *I see you*, I mouth. *I'm with you*. I can't stop my tears falling.

"We can't follow her through the ticket barrier, unfortunately." Melissa's tone is companionable—chatty, almost—as though we're working on a project together. It's unnerving, more so than if she were shouting at me, or threatening me. "But we'll pick her up again once she's on the platform."

She moves her mouse across the screen and I catch sight of a list of what I assume must be cameras: Aldgate East—entrance; Angel—entrance; Angel—southbound platform; Angel—northbound platform; Bakerloo—ticket barriers . . . The list goes on and on.

"Quite a few of the early profiles aren't in the right area for the cameras I can access," Melissa explains, "but we'll be able to get most of Katie's commute. Look—there she is."

Katie is standing on the platform, her hands thrust into her pockets. She's looking around and I hope she's searching for cameras, or working out which of her fellow passengers might be a threat. I see a man in a suit and overcoat approach her. Katie steps back slightly, and I dig my nails into my closed palms until he passes without checking his pace. My heart is pounding.

"Quite the little actress, isn't she?"

I ignore her. The Overground train arrives and Katie steps on, the doors closing and swallowing her up all too quickly. I want Melissa to click onto the next camera, but she doesn't move. She picks a piece of cotton from her jacket and frowns at it, before letting it float from her fingers onto the floor. My fantasy evolves: I imagine Simon returning from his interview; finding the house empty—the door unlocked—and somehow knowing I am next door. Rescuing me. My imaginings grow in detail and absurdity in inverse proportion to my dwindling hope.

No one is coming.

I will die here, in Melissa's house. Will she dispose of my body, I wonder, or leave me here, festering, for Neil to find when he returns from his work trip?

"Where will you go?" I ask her. She turns to look at me. "Once you've killed me. Where will you go?" She starts to say something—to deny that I'm going to die—then she stops. There's a flash of what looks like respect in her eyes, and then it's gone. She shrugs.

"Costa Rica. Japan. The Philippines. There are still plenty of countries without extradition agreements."

I wonder how long it will take them to find me. Whether Melissa could make it to another country by then. "They'll stop you at passport control," I say, more confidently than I feel.

She looks at me scornfully. "Only if I use my own passport."

"How—" I can't find the words. I have stumbled into a parallel universe, in which people wield knives and use fake passports and murder their friends. I suddenly realize something. Melissa is clever, but she's not that clever. "How did you learn all this?"

"All what?" She's distracted, tapping the keyboard. Bored with the conversation.

"The CCTV, a false passport. PC Swift said the adverts were placed by a man; that he had a mailbox set up in his name. The website is untraceable. You had help—you must have."

"That's rather insulting, Zoe. I think you underestimate me." She doesn't look at me, and I know she's lying. She couldn't have done this alone. Is Neil really away with work? Or is he upstairs? Listening. Waiting until reinforcements are needed. I glance nervously toward the ceiling. Did I imagine the creak in the floorboards?

"That's been fifteen minutes," Melissa says abruptly, looking at her watch. "I can't get into the Overground trains, but the next camera will get her changing at Canada Water." She clicks on the next camera and I see another platform; a group of schoolchildren being shepherded away from the edge by three teachers wearing high-visibility vests. A train arrives and I scour the screen for Katie but can't find her. My heart beats faster: Has something happened to her already? On that short journey from Crystal Palace to Canada Water? But then I catch a glimpse of a white puffa coat, and there she is, her hands still pushed into her pockets, her head still turning this way and that, looking at everyone she passes. I let out the breath I've been holding.

Katie goes out of sight, and despite Melissa bringing up two more cameras, we don't see her again until she's waiting on the Jubilee line platform. She's standing close to the platform edge and I want to tell her to step away, that someone could push her in front of the train. Watching her like this, on CCTV, is like watching a film in which you know something terrible is about to happen to the main character, and you scream at them not to be so stupid.

Don't go outside, don't ignore that sound you heard . . . Haven't you read the script? Don't you know what happens next?

I remind myself that Katie *has* read the script. She knows what the danger is, she just doesn't know exactly where it's coming from.

There's a man standing behind Katie, and to her left. He's watching her. I can't see his face—the camera is too far away—but his head is turned toward her and it moves slightly as he looks her up and down. He takes a step closer and I grip the edge of my seat, leaning forward in a vain attempt to see more. There are other people on the platform— why aren't they looking the right way? They won't see if he does something. I used to feel so safe on the Underground. So many cameras, so many people all around. But no one's watching, not really. Everyone's traveling in their own little bubble, oblivious to what's happening to their fellow commuters.

I say her name under my breath and as if she's heard me she turns around. Looks at the man. He steps closer and immediately Katie backs off. I can't read her body language—is she frightened? She walks to the other end of the platform. Melissa shifts in her chair and I look at her. She's gazing intently at the screen, but she isn't sitting forward, tense in her chair, like I am. She's leaning backward, her elbows resting on the arms of her chair, and her fingertips pressed together. A small smile plays across her lips.

"Fascinating," she says. "I always liked the idea that the women didn't know they were being followed, but this adds something quite interesting. Cat and mouse on the Underground. It might work rather well as an extra package for members." Her flippancy revolts me.

The man hasn't followed Katie to the other end of the platform, but as the train arrives, and a surge of tourists and commuters disembark, I see him move through the mêlée toward her. He doesn't get on at the same place as her, and I'm feeling relieved, until I realize he has nevertheless chosen the same carriage.

"Can you get into the camera on that train? I want to see it. I want to see what's happening on the train!"

"Addictive, isn't it? No, I've tried but it's very secure. We've got"— she checks another tab, open on the computer—"seven minutes till she gets to Waterloo." She drums her fingers on the desk.

"The carriage is busy. No one will try anything on a busy train." I say it to myself as much as to Melissa.

If Katie cried out, would someone do something? I've always taught her to make a noise if something happens. "Be loud about it," I told her. "If some perv pushes himself against you, don't tell him, tell everyone. Shout, 'Stop touching me this instant!' Let the whole carriage know. They might not do anything, but he'll stop straightaway, you'll see."

It's only four minutes from Waterloo to Leicester Square. I know because Melissa has told me, and because every second feels like an hour. As soon as we lose Katie into a Northern line train at Waterloo, Melissa brings a new image onto the screen; the camera looking toward the bottom of the escalators leading up to Leicester Square.

We watch in silence until she appears.

"There she is." Melissa points to Katie. Instantly I look for the man I saw approaching her on the platform, and when I find him a couple of yards behind her my chest tightens.

"That man . . ." I say, but I trail off because—what is there to say?

"He's persistent, isn't he?"

"Do you know who he is? Where he comes from? How old he is?" I don't know why any of these things matter.

"The profile's been downloaded almost two hundred times," Melissa says. "It could be any one of them."

The man pushes past a woman with a stroller. Katie steps onto the escalator.

Keep walking, I say in my head, but she stands still, and the man walks up on the left-hand side and then slots in on the right to stand behind her. He puts a hand on her arm and leans in. He's saying something to her. Katie shakes her head, and then they reach the top of the escalator and are out of view.

"The next camera! Get the next camera!"

Melissa responds with deliberate slowness, enjoying my panic. There are lots of people at Leicester Square, and when she finally pulls up another CCTV image I can't immediately see Katie. But then I spot her, walking alongside the man from the train. My heart races: something isn't right. Katie is walking at an odd angle, bent to one side. Her head is bowed and although she doesn't look as though she's fighting him, everything about her body language tells me she can't get away. I look closer and realize he is gripping the top of her left arm with his right hand. With his other hand he is gripping her wrist: it is the pressure on this arm pulling her off balance. He must have a weapon. He must be threatening her. Otherwise why isn't she screaming? Running? Fighting?

I watch Katie walk toward the ticket barriers with this man, her arm pulled awkwardly across the front of his chest. There are two ticket collectors standing by a Tube map, chatting, and I will them to notice something is wrong, but they pay no attention. How can this be happening in broad daylight? Why is no one seeing what I'm seeing?

I can't take my eyes off the screen.

Surely once Katie and the man reach the barriers he'll have to let her go? That will be her chance to get away. I know Katie; she'll be planning it now—working out where to run, which exit to take. I feel a surge of adrenaline. She'll do it—she'll get away from him.

But they don't reach the gates. Instead the man leads her to the left of the concourse, where there is an empty information kiosk and a door marked *No Entry*. He glances behind, as if to see whether they're being observed.

And then my blood runs cold as I see him open the door and take Katie inside.

You think I've gone too far. Risking the lives of women I've never met is bad enough, you think, but this? It's too much. How could I risk the life of someone I'm supposed to care about?

You need to understand something. Katie deserves this.

She's always been the same. Demanding to be the center of attention; clamoring to be heard, to be noticed, to be loved. Not a thought to how that made others feel.

Always talking; never listening. So now she's got her wish. Center stage.

Her most important production yet; her most challenging part. The performance to end all performances.

Her final curtain call.

CHAPTER
THIRTY-SIX

"What phone numbers do we have for Zoe Walker?" Nick demanded.

Lucinda checked her files. "Mobile, work, and home."

"Call them all."

Kelly was already dialing Zoe's mobile number, shaking her head as it went to voice mail. "Zoe, could you please call the Murder Investigation Team as soon as you get this message?"

"What do we know about the daughter?" Nick asked.

"Her name's Katie," Kelly said, desperately trying to recall anything Zoe Walker had mentioned. "She wants to be an actress but at the moment she's doing shifts in a restaurant near Leicester Square—I don't know which one." Kelly tried to remember if Zoe had ever said anything else about her children; she had a son, Kelly knew, and a partner, but they'd never really spoken about anything other than the case.

"Nick, Zoe Walker isn't at work today," Lucinda said, putting the phone down. "Her boss sent her home yesterday; he said she wasn't able to concentrate on anything but—and I quote—this bloody case. I've asked him to tell Zoe to call us if he hears from her first."

"Call her at home."

"There's no reply."

"There are no other numbers for her on the system?" Nick had started pacing, in the way he did when he wanted to think faster.

"Not for Zoe, and nothing for Katie. We've got an old mobile number for her son, Justin—he was ASBO'd in 2006 after a shoplifting, and received a caution for possession of class C in 2008. Nothing since then, although we've got a dozen stop checks for him."

"What did the Telephone Intelligence Unit say?"

"There's no phone registered to Katie Walker at their home address. Either she's on Pay-As-You-Go or she's got an additional handset on Mum's account; I've asked them to look into it."

"Where was the e-mail with Katie Walker's profile sent from?" Nick fired the question at Andrew, who seemed unperturbed by the DI's ferocity.

"Not Espress Oh!, if that's what you're thinking. The IP is different. I'll need to put in a request."

"How long will that take?" Nick glanced at his watch and didn't wait for a response. "Whatever it takes, it'll be too long. British Transport Police are on their way to Leicester Square, but there's no guarantee they'll get to Katie in time, and in the meantime there's every chance Zoe's in real danger."

"She's still not home," Lucinda said, putting down the phone, "and her mobile's been switched off."

"I want a cell-site trace on her mobile. Find out when her phone was last used and where. Kelly, the second Lucinda gets a location I want officers making on immediate."

"On it." Kelly moved to sit next to Lucinda, who was already starting the trace. Nick was pacing again, reeling off instructions without pausing for breath. A thought was forming; something someone had said, just a moment ago. Kelly tried to get hold of it, but it slipped away in the midst of the growing chaos in the briefing room.

"Can we get the daughter's mobile number from Zoe Walker's billing?" Nick was saying.

"Potentially," Lucinda said. "It's a long process, though, and not an exact science; I'll need to look at the most frequently dialed numbers and make assumptions about which ones are likely to be family numbers."

"Do it. Please," he added as an afterthought. It was the first time Kelly had seen the DI rattled. His tie was already loosened, but now he took it off and chucked it on the table, flicking open the top button of his shirt and stretching his neck first one way, then the other.

"Andrew, keep an eye on the website and tell me the second anything changes. Do what you can to find out where that most recent e-mail was from. If it isn't Espress Oh! maybe it's another café. Kelly, if it is, get officers there pronto to view CCTV for customers in there around the time it was sent."

Espress Oh!

That was it. The thought that had been circling Kelly's head finally solidified. Meeting Zoe at the café in Covent Garden. The friend with the chain of coffee shops; the new business in Clerkenwell. The Australian girl at Espress Oh! and the absent owner with the chain of shops. "Not customers," she said, suddenly certain she knew who they were looking for. The person behind the website; the person who, right now, was sending nineteen-year-old Katie into danger, and who was potentially holding Zoe Walker hostage.

Nick looked at her expectantly. Kelly felt a rush of adrenaline.

"We need to do a Companies House check," she said. "It isn't a customer who's been using the Wi-Fi at Espress Oh! to administer the website. It's the owner."

CHAPTER
THIRTY-SEVEN

"Katie!" I scream so loudly my voice cracks, my mouth suddenly devoid of moisture. I pull at the tape, feeling the adhesive tug at the hairs on my wrists. I find a strength I didn't know I had, and I feel the tape give a fraction. Melissa smiles.

"I win." She spins her chair around to face me, folding her arms and looking thoughtfully at me. "But then, I was always going to."

"You bitch. How could you do that?"

"I didn't do anything. You did. You let her walk into danger; danger you knew was out there. How could you do that to your own flesh and blood?"

"You—" I stop. Melissa didn't make me. She's right; I let Katie go. It's my fault.

I can't look at her. There's a pain in my chest that's making it hard to breathe. Katie. My Katie. Who was that man? What is he doing to her?

I try to keep my voice calm. Rational. "You could have had children. You could have adopted; had IVF." I look at the screen again but the door to what I assume is some kind of cupboard or maintenance room remains stubbornly closed. Why did no one notice? There are people everywhere. I see a fluorescent-jacketed Underground worker and I want so much for her to open the door; to hear Katie crying out; to do something—anything—to stop whatever is happening right now to my baby girl.

"Neil refused." Melissa is staring at the screen, and I can't see her eyes. I can't see if there's any emotion in them, or whether they're as dead as her voice. "Said he wanted his own child, not someone else's." She gives a hollow laugh. "Ironic, given the amount of time we spent looking after yours."

On the screen life is continuing as usual; people are getting in one another's way, searching for Oyster cards, rushing to catch trains. But for me, the world has stopped.

"You lose," she says, as easily as if we've been playing cards. "Time to pay up." She picks up the knife and runs a speculative finger across the blade.

I should never have let Katie go, no matter what she said. I thought I was giving her a chance, but I was sending her into danger. Melissa would have tried to kill us, but would she have succeeded, with two of us to fight her off?

And now she's going to kill me anyway. I feel dead inside already, and part of me wants her to finish it; to hasten the darkness that began to descend after Katie left, and which now threatens to overcome me.

Do it, Melissa. Kill me.

I catch sight of the penholder on Melissa's desk—the one Katie made for her in woodwork—and feel a surge of rage. Katie and Justin worshiped Melissa. They saw her as a surrogate mother; someone to trust. How dare she betray us like this?

I mentally shake myself. If Katie dies, who will be there for Justin? I work my wrists again, twisting my hands in opposite directions and finding perverse pleasure in the pain that ensues. It is a distraction. My eyes are still trained on the screen as though I can make the door to that maintenance cupboard fly open through the power of thought alone.

Perhaps Katie isn't dead. Perhaps she's been raped, or beaten up. What will happen to her if I'm not there, at a time when she needs me most? I can't let Melissa kill me.

Suddenly I feel cool air on a tiny patch of newly exposed skin.

I'm loosening the tape. I can get free.

I think quickly, allowing my head to sink down to my chest, in an attempt to make Melissa think I've given up. My thoughts are whirring. The doors are locked, and the only windows in the kitchen extension are the huge skylights, too high above my head to reach. There is only one way to stop Melissa from killing me, and that is to kill her first. The thought is so ridiculous I feel light-headed: How did I get here? How did I become the sort of woman who could kill someone?

But kill Melissa I can. And I will. My legs are too tightly strapped to even think about getting loose, which means I'm not going to be able to move fast. I've managed to loosen the duct tape around my wrists enough to gently pull out one hand, careful not to move my upper arms. I'm convinced my plan—such as it is—is written all over my face, so I glance at the screen, without hope of seeing Katie, but nevertheless desperate for some sign of movement from that shut door.

"That's odd," I say, too fast to consider whether I should have kept my thoughts to myself.

Melissa looks at the screen. "What?"

Both my hands are free now. I keep them clasped behind my back.

"That sign"—I nod toward the upper left-hand corner of the screen—"at the top of the escalator. It wasn't there a minute ago." The sign is a plastic yellow folding one, warning of wet surfaces. There's been a spillage. But when? Not while I was watching.

Melissa shrugs. "So someone's put out a sign."

"They didn't. It just appeared." I know the sign wasn't there when Katie came up the escalator, because it would have been in front of her for a second. As for when it appeared . . . well, I can't be certain, but I haven't taken my eyes off the CCTV image for more than a few seconds since Katie disappeared, and every time I've seen a high-vis jacket I've kept my eyes trained on the wearer, desperately hoping I'll see them walk into the room where Katie is.

There is a shadow of concern in Melissa's eyes. She leans close to the screen. The knife is still in her right hand. Both my hands are now free, and slowly I move one of them; first to the side of the chair, then by tiny degrees down toward my legs. I keep my eyes trained on Melissa. The second she moves, I sit up straight, putting my hands behind my back, but it's too late; she sees the movement in the corner of her eye.

Beads of sweat form on my brow and sting my eyes.

I don't know what makes Melissa glance toward the kitchen counter, but I know instantly she's realized what I've done. Her eyes flick to the knife block. Counting the knives; seeing one missing.

"You're not playing by the rules," she says.

"Neither are you."

I lean down and wrap my fist around the handle of the knife, feeling a sharp pain as the blade cuts my ankle on its way out of my boot.

This is it, I think. This is the only chance I'm going to get.

CHAPTER
THIRTY-EIGHT

The marked car raced along Marylebone Street, narrowly missing an open-top bus that pulled out in front of them as they passed Madame Tussauds. Kelly listened to the response officers in the front discussing that day's game at Old Trafford over the wail of the siren.

"How Rooney could have missed that, I don't know. If I was paying someone three hundred grand a week I'd bloody make sure they could kick straight."

"Can't perform under pressure, that's the problem."

The lights changed to red at Euston Square. The driver pressed his horn, switching the sirens to a high-pitched warble, and the cars in front began to peel apart, allowing them through. They turned right onto Bloomsbury and Kelly turned up her radio, waiting for the update they were all desperate for. It came as they neared the West End. Kelly closed her eyes and let her head fall briefly against her seat.

It was over. For Katie Walker, at least.

Kelly leaned forward between the two front seats. "You may as well slow down now."

The driver had already heard the update and was switching off the sirens, dropping down to a more appropriate speed, now that there was nothing to gain from making on immediate. No one to save.

When they reached Leicester Square he dropped her off outside the Hippodrome and she ran toward the Underground station, flashing her warrant card to a bored-looking woman standing at the ticket barriers. She had come in via a different entrance than she had intended, and she looked around, trying to get her bearings.

There.

The door to the maintenance cupboard was scuffed at the bottom, where people had pushed it open with their feet, and a poster urging passengers to report any suspicious packages curled up at the corners. A sign told members of the public that access was forbidden.

Kelly knocked twice on the door, then went inside. Even though she knew what she'd find inside, her heart was still racing.

The maintenance room was dark and windowless, with a desk and a metal chair on one side, and a pile of signs stacked against the opposite wall. A yellow bucket on wheels stood in one corner, filled with greasy gray water. Beside it, a young girl sat on a plastic crate, cradling a cup of tea. Even without the confident pout evident in the photo on the website, Katie was instantly recognizable. Her mass of highlighted hair fell around the shoulders of her coat; its padded white segments making her look bigger than Kelly knew she was.

White.

19 years old. Long blonde hair, blue eyes.

Blue jeans, gray ankle boots, black V-neck T-shirt with oversized belted gray cardigan. White knee-length puffa coat, also belted. Black handbag with gilt chain.

Size 8–10.

Leaning against a wall behind Katie was a broad-shouldered man with dark hair. He stepped forward and held out his hand to Kelly.

"John Chandler, covert officer with British Transport Police."

"Kelly Swift." She crouched down. "Hi, Katie, I'm Kelly, one of the detectives involved in this case. Are you okay?"

"I think so. I'm worried about Mum."

"Officers are on their way there now." She put out a hand and squeezed Katie's arm. "You did really well." DC Chandler's radio message confirming that Katie was safe had been swiftly followed by confirmation of what Kelly had suspected: Zoe was being held by Melissa West, owner of several cafés in London, including Espress Oh!

"It was horrible." Katie looked up at John. "I didn't know whether to believe you or not. When you whispered in my ear, I wanted to run. I thought, 'What if he isn't an undercover cop at all? What if that's just his cover story?' But I knew I had to trust you. I was scared Melissa would realize what was going on, and hurt Mum."

"You did brilliantly," John said. "An Oscar-winning performance." Katie attempted a smile, but Kelly could see she was still shaking.

"I didn't have to do much acting. Even though you'd told me what was going to happen, the minute you pulled me in here, I decided everything you'd said to me was a lie. I thought that was it. Game over."

"I'm sorry we had to put you through that," Kelly said. "We knew the CCTV had been hacked, but we didn't know to what extent—we didn't know exactly how much could be seen. When we saw your profile on the website we knew we had to get you safely off the Underground and away from anyone who might want to hurt you, without letting Melissa know we were onto her."

"How much longer do we have to wait in here? I want to see Mum."

"I'm sorry, we needed confirmation from the control room they'd switched over the CCTV feed."

Craig had responded swiftly to Kelly's concerns that Melissa might be able to see Katie and DC Chandler leaving the maintenance room, thereby blowing their cover. He had switched the live feed with recorded footage from the same time the previous day, when the footfall at Leicester Square would be roughly the same, and the risk of Melissa noticing the jump would be small. Kelly hoped he had been right. "It's all fine now. We can leave and she won't be able to see us."

As she opened the door, Kelly's radio crackled into life.

"We need an ambulance to Anerley Road," came the disembodied voice. "It's urgent."

Katie's eyes widened.

"Tell them to make on silent, and hold off when they get to the address."

"It's just a precaution," Kelly said quickly, as the younger girl's eyes filled with tears. She turned the volume on her radio down until it was virtually inaudible. "Your mum's fine."

"How do you know?"

Kelly opened her mouth to give more platitudes, then closed it again. The truth was, she didn't even know if Zoe Walker was still alive.

CHAPTER
THIRTY-NINE

The blood is everywhere. It spurts uncontrollably from Melissa's neck, covering her desk and turning her shirt crimson. The fingers on her right hand spring open, and the knife she was holding clatters to the floor.

I start to shake. I look down and realize I, too, am covered in blood. My own knife is still gripped tightly in my right fist, but the adrenaline I felt when I stabbed her has passed, leaving me dizzy and disoriented. If she comes at me now, I think, I won't be able to stop her. I have nothing left. I reach down and with my free hand I pull off the duct tape from around my ankles, kicking over the chair in my haste to move away from Melissa.

I needn't have worried. Both her hands are clamped around her throat, in a futile attempt to stem the stream of blood that pulses between her fingers and coats her hands. She opens her mouth but no sound comes out, beyond a rasping, bubbling noise that causes red foam to coat the inside of her lips. She stands, but her legs won't comply, and she sways unsteadily as though she's drunk.

I cover my face with my hands, realizing too late that they are speckled with blood, which smears across my cheeks. It forms a dull shadow on the edge of my vision and fills my nostrils with a metallic tang that makes my stomach heave.

I don't speak. What would I say? I'm sorry?

I'm not. I'm filled with hatred.

Enough hatred to stab the woman I thought was my friend.

Enough hatred to watch her now, fighting for breath, and not care. Enough hatred to stand by as her lips turn blue and the urgent beat of her blood slows to a quiet, imperceptible rhythm. The fluid that a moment ago was spurting feet away from her now ebbs gently, its urgency spent. Her skin is gray; her eyes the only living thing in a dying husk. I look for remorse, or for anger, but see none. She is already dead.

When she falls it isn't to her knees. She doesn't stagger, or clutch at the desk in front of her like in a film, or reach out to grab me and take me down with her. She falls like a tree, crashing backward onto the floor with a bang to her head that makes me foolishly worry it might have hurt her.

And then she's still; hands splayed out to her sides, and her eyes wide open, bulging slightly out of her ashen face.

I've killed her.

It's only now the regret sets in. Not because of the crime I've committed, or even because of what I've seen—a woman drowning in her own blood. I regret it only because now she'll never have to face her crimes in a court. Even at the end, she's won.

I sink to the floor, feeling as drained as though the blood had left me, too. The key to the door is in Melissa's pocket, but I don't want to touch her body. Even though there are no signs of life left in her—her chest does not rise, there is no death rattle as air leaves her lungs—I don't trust her not to suddenly rise up; to grip my wrists with bloodied hands. She lies between me and the desk and I sit and wait for my body to stop shaking. In a moment I will need to step carefully around her, to dial 999 and tell them what I've done.

Katie. I need to tell them about Katie. They need to go to Leicester Square; I need to know if she's still alive—she needs to know I'm okay, that I haven't given up on her . . . I stand up too fast, my feet skating on the slick of blood that seems to cover the entire floor. A stripe of blood dissects the computer screen on which I can still see the CCTV image, the door to the maintenance cupboard still resolutely closed.

As I find my balance I hear the distant wail of sirens. I wait for them to die away but they grow louder, more insistent, until they hurt my ears. I hear shouting, then a crash that echoes through the house.

"Police!" I hear. "Stay where you are!"

I stay where I am. I couldn't move even if I wanted to. There's a thunderous noise in the hall, and an almighty bang as the kitchen door flies open and hits the wall behind it.

"Hands in the air!" one of them shouts. I'm just thinking how ridiculous it is to expect Melissa to do that, when she is clearly incapacitated, when I realize they mean me. Slowly, I raise my hands. They are covered in blood, which has streaked across my arms, and my clothes are stained dark red.

The officers wear dark boilersuits and helmets with visors down and *POLICE* in white letters on the side. There are two at first, swiftly followed by another pair who arrive in response to the first's clear command.

"Support!"

The first two approach me, stopping several feet in front of me. The other pair move rapidly around the room, shouting instructions to each other. Elsewhere in the house I hear more police moving around. The sound of running feet is interspersed with cries of "Room clear!" which drift down into the room in which we stand.

"Medic!" someone shouts. Two new officers push through and run to where Melissa is lying on the floor. One of them presses their hands against the wound in her neck. I don't understand why they're trying to save her life. Don't they know? Don't they know what she's done? It is a pointless endeavor anyway; the life has long since left her.

"Zoe Walker?" It is one of the two police officers in front of me who says my name, but their helmets mean I can't tell which one is speaking. I look from one to the other. They have positioned themselves two meters or so apart, so that as I look forward one is at ten o'clock, the other at two. In every respect they are mirror images of each other; one foot slightly forward, their hands above their waists and open-palmed; nonthreatening but ready for action. Behind them

I see the medics kneeling beside Melissa. They have laid a clear plastic guard across her face and one of them is pushing measured breaths into her mouth.

"Yes," I say eventually.

"Drop the weapon."

They've got it all wrong. It was Melissa who had the knife; Melissa who held the blade to my throat until the skin split. I take a step forward.

"Drop the weapon!" the police officer says again, louder this time. I follow his gaze, looking up to my right hand, where the silver blade gleams through its coating of blood. My fingers snap open of their own accord, as though they have only just become aware of their contents, and the knife skitters across the floor. One of the officers kicks it farther away from my reach, then pushes up the visor on his helmet. He looks practically as young as my children.

I find my voice. "My daughter's in danger. I need to get to Leicester Square—will you take me?" My teeth are chattering and I bite my tongue. More blood; my own, this time. The officer looks to his colleague, who lifts his own visor. He is much older, a gray beard neatly trimmed beneath kind eyes that crinkle at the corners as he reassures me.

"Katie's fine. She was intercepted by one of our officers." The rest of my body begins to shake.

"There's an ambulance on its way—they'll take you to the hospital and get you sorted out, okay?" He looks at his young colleague.

"Shock," he explains, but it isn't shock I feel, it's relief. I look beyond the officers. A paramedic is kneeling beside Melissa, but he isn't touching her, he's writing something down.

"Is she dead?" I don't want to leave this room until I know for sure. The paramedic looks up.

"Yes."

"Thank God."

CHAPTER
FORTY

"Not much of a celebration," Lucinda said, looking at the packet of peanuts Nick had torn open and put in the middle of the table.

"I'm sorry it's not up to your usual standards, your ladyship," Nick said. "I'm not sure the Dog and Trumpet does caviar and quail's eggs, but I can see what's on the specials board, if you like?"

"Ha-ha. I didn't mean that. I just feel a bit flat, you know?"

"I feel the same," Kelly said. It had been so frantic; the drive on blues and twos to get to Katie Walker, followed immediately by the race to reach Zoe, marked police cars screaming to a halt outside Melissa's house. The ambulance had held off at the end of Anerley Road; the waiting paramedics unable to do their job until it was safe to enter. Kelly doubted her heart rate had dropped below a hundred beats a minute for the past few hours, but now she was crashing.

"It's just an anticlimax, that's all," Nick said. "You'll bounce back tomorrow, when the hard work really starts."

There was a huge amount to do. With access to Melissa's computer, Cyber Crime had been able to swiftly shut down FindTheOne.com and access the full list of members. Tracing them—and establishing what, if any, crimes had been committed—would take somewhat longer.

Companies House checks had revealed that Melissa West was the registered director of four cafés in London; Melissa, Melissa Too, Espress Oh!, and an as-yet-unnamed business in the heart of Clerkenwell, banking impressive profits despite the absence of sink, fridge, or cooking facilities.

"Money laundering," Nick had explained. "Coffee shops are perfect vehicles because so many people pay in cash. On paper she can legitimately take a few hundred quid a day, whilst letting the businesses run at a loss."

"How much do you think her husband knew?"

"I guess we'll find out when we bring him in." Neil West was overseeing the installation of a multimillion-pound IT system at a law firm in Manchester. His schedule, conveniently synched to his wife's, and easily accessible from her computer, told them he'd be flying into London City airport the following day, where police would be waiting to arrest him. On his computer, upstairs in the home office, were files relating to each company Neil had worked with, each including an expansive contact list. The firms employing Gordon Tillman and Luke Harris had both contracted Neil in the past, and there was every expectation that further parallels would be drawn between Neil's contact list and the list of FindTheOne.com customers found on Melissa's computer.

"Do you think she'd have left him to pick up the pieces?" Lucinda said. Zoe had outlined the plans Melissa had shared to leave the country, and Cyber Crime had identified flights to Rio de Janeiro that she had looked at online.

"I think so," Nick said. "I don't think Melissa West cared about anyone but herself."

Kelly thought about what Katie had told her, about the bitterness in Melissa's voice when she talked about looking after Zoe's children; about not having children of her own. "I think she did. I think that was part of the problem. Setting up the website was strictly business, but involving Zoe and Katie? That bit was personal."

"I hate that she got away with it," Lucinda said, reaching for the peanuts.

"She was stabbed in the carotid artery and bled to death," Nick said. "I wouldn't call that getting away with it."

Kelly gave a half smile. "You know what she means. She put Zoe and Katie Walker through hell, not to mention the hundreds of women who had no idea they were even at risk. I'd have liked to have seen her in the dock." Kelly's phone flashed, and she swiped the screen to unlock it, idly scrolling through notifications she didn't have the inclination to respond to.

"What's this? A celebration or a wake?" Diggers appeared at the table, and Kelly sat up, as though standing to attention. It was the first time she'd seen him since the dressing-down in his office, and she avoided making eye contact with him.

"Can I get you a chair, sir?" Lucinda said.

"I'm not stopping. I just dropped in to buy you a drink. You've all done a grand job; I've already had the commissioner on the phone congratulating us on a good result. Well done."

"Thanks, boss," Nick said. "I was just telling them the same."

"And as for you . . ." Diggers looked at Kelly, who could feel herself going red. "I hear we've got a lot to thank you for."

"Everyone was working on it at the same time," Kelly said, reluctantly looking up, relieved to find genuine warmth in Diggers's face. "I just happened to be there when the final piece dropped into place, that's all."

"Well, that's as may be. You've certainly made a valuable contribution to the team. Now, what's everyone having?" The DCI went to the bar, returning with a tray of drinks and another bag of nuts. He hadn't bought one for himself, and Kelly realized she risked missing her opportunity if she didn't ask now.

"Sir? Do I have to go back to BTP?" As she spoke, she realized how much she was dreading it; how much she'd loved being part of a team again, without the gossip and suspicion that plagued her time in her home force.

"Three months, we said, didn't we?"

"Yes, but I thought that, with Melissa dead and the website blocked—" Kelly knew there was work to be done—that Laura Keen's murderer was still on the loose, and Cathy Tanning's prowler remained uncaught—but at the back of her mind was the telling-off she'd had in Diggers's office. Was this the opportunity he needed to bring an end to her transfer?

"Three months," Diggers said briskly. "You can lead on the interview with Neil West, then let's have a proper talk about your career. Maybe it's time for a fresh start in a new force, eh?" He winked at her and shook Nick's hand before leaving them to it.

Sheer relief prompted tears to form in Kelly's eyes. She blinked them away and picked up her phone, swiping through apps in search of distraction. She scrolled through her Facebook feed, filled with photos of decorated Christmas trees and tiny snowmen made from the pathetic smattering of snow they'd had the previous night. A status update from Lexi caught her eye.

A few more wrinkles, she'd posted, but still the same Durham gang!

They'd re-created a photograph from their student days; Lexi posting the two side by side, prompting a stream of amused comments from the friends and family of those tagged. In both pictures Lexi had the biggest grin of anyone in the group, and Kelly couldn't help but smile.

Great photos, she typed. You haven't changed a bit.

CHAPTER
FORTY-ONE

Matt drives carefully, taking every corner slowly and approaching speed bumps as though I've broken a bone. The hospital insisted on checking me over thoroughly, in spite of my insistence that—aside from the cut on my neck, which required no stitches—Melissa hadn't touched me.

I was placed in a bed next to Katie, treated for shock but otherwise unharmed. The ward nurse gave up on keeping us separate, eventually opening the dividing curtain so we could see each other. We'd only been there half an hour when Isaac arrived, racing through the doors without any of his usual assurance.

"Kate! My God, are you okay? I came as quickly as I could." He sits on the side of her bed and takes her hands, his eyes traveling over her face, her body, looking for injuries. "Are you hurt?"

"I'm fine. I'm so sorry about tonight's show."

"Christ, don't worry about that. I can't believe what you've been through."

"But everyone's tickets—"

"I'll give them a refund. Forget about the play, Kate. It's not important. You are." He kisses her on the forehead, and for the first time he doesn't look as though he's putting on a performance. He really does like her, I realize. And she likes him.

He looks up and our eyes meet, and I wish the curtain hadn't been pulled back after all. I can't read his expression, and I don't know if mine says all I want it to.

"You've had quite a time of it," he says.

"Yes."

"I'm glad it's all over for you." He pauses, emphasizing what comes next. "Hopefully you'll be able to forget about it now. Put everything that happened in the past." If Katie is wondering why her boyfriend is taking such care over the way he speaks to her mother, she doesn't comment on it. Isaac holds my gaze, as if wanting to make sure I've understood. I nod.

"I hope so, too. Thank you."

"Nearly there," Matt says now. Simon, sitting next to me in the backseat of the cab, puts his arm around my shoulder, and I rest my head against him.

I told him in the hospital I had thought he was the one behind the website. I had to—the guilt was consuming me.

"I'm so sorry," I say now.

"Don't be. I can't imagine what you've been through. You must have felt as though you couldn't trust anyone."

"That notebook . . ." I remember the scribbled notes I'd seen; the woman's name, her clothing. How convinced I'd been that I was holding evidence of a crime.

"Jottings for my novel," Simon says. "I was creating characters." I'm grateful that Simon has taken it in stride; that he seems not the slightest bit offended to be accused of something so horrific. On the other side of Simon, Katie gazes out of the window as we near Crystal Palace; Justin is in front of her, in the passenger seat next to Matt. Isaac has gone into town to handle the disappointed theatergoers and convince them to come and see the show tomorrow evening, when Katie is adamant she'll be fit to go on stage.

How can everything look as though nothing has happened? On the edge of the road, gray slush dirties the pavements and drips from the tops of buildings. A sorry excuse for a snowman sits in the walled yard outside the primary school, its carrot long since lost. People are heading out for the evening, while others are still coming home from work, checking phones as they walk, oblivious to the world around them.

We drive past Melissa's café, and I can't stop the intake of breath; the tiny cry that escapes me. All the times I've joined her there after work for a cup of tea; given her a hand with the lunchtime prep. There's a light on in the café, casting dark shadows as it falls on the unstacked tables and chairs.

"Should you go and close up properly?" I ask Justin. He turns to look at me.

"I don't want to go in there, Mum."

I can understand that. I don't, either. Even just being on Anerley Road is making my pulse quicken, and I feel a fresh wave of hatred for Melissa for sullying the memories of a place in which I've loved living. I never imagined moving again, but now I wonder if we might. A fresh start for Simon and me. Space for Justin and Katie, of course, but a new chapter for us all.

We pass the Tube station. I'm seized by the image of Katie, walking toward the entrance and looking up at the cameras; terrified, yet determined to succeed. Determined to save me.

I glance at her, wondering what she's thinking, but her profile gives nothing away. She's so much stronger than I gave her credit for.

"What will happen now?" Matt asks. It was all over by the time I called him, and he walked into the hospital to find his ex-wife and his daughter in a bizarre assortment of garments that Simon had hastily gathered from home. The police seized the clothes we'd been wearing at Melissa's house. They'd been gentle about it, explaining that i's had to be dotted, and t's crossed, and that I shouldn't worry. Everything would be fine.

"I've got to give a voluntary interview next week," I reply, "then the

Crown Prosecution Service will look at the file and make a decision over the following few days."

"They won't charge you," PC Swift had reassured me; the furtive glance over her shoulder suggesting she was overstepping the mark with this assertion. "It's very clear you were acting in self-defense." She stopped talking abruptly as DI Rampello appeared in the ward, but he nodded in agreement.

"A formality," he said.

As we near the end of Anerley Road I see a police officer in a fluorescent jacket standing in the road. A line of cones closes off one lane, in which two police cars and a white forensics van are still parked, and the police officer is allowing cars to pass in turn. Matt pulls up as close as he can get to the house. He gets out and opens the rear door, helping Katie out and keeping his arm around her as they walk toward the house. Justin follows, his eyes glued to the blue-and-white police tape that flutters in the breeze outside Melissa's house.

"Hard to believe, isn't it, love?" I say. I pull away from Simon's embrace and slip my hand into Justin's. He looks at me, still trying to process everything that's happened today.

"Melissa," he starts, but words fail him. I know how he feels; I've been struggling to find the words ever since it happened.

"I know, love."

We wait by the gate, until Simon catches us up and unlocks the door. I don't look at Melissa's house, but even without seeing it, I can imagine the white-suited figures in her beautiful kitchen.

Will Neil continue living there? The blood will have dried now, I think, its glossy finish darkening; the edges of each spatter crisping into flakes. Someone will need to clean it, and I imagine them scrubbing and bleaching; the tiles forever hanging on to a shadow of the woman who died there.

My front door swings open. Inside the house is warm and welcoming.

I'm comforted by the familiar pile of coats on the banister, and the disorderly heap of shoes by the doormat. Matt stands to one side, and I follow Katie and Simon indoors.

"I'll leave you to it, then," Matt says. He turns to leave, but Simon stops him.

"Will you join us for a drink?" he says. "I think we could all do with one."

Matt hesitates, but only for a second. "Sure. That would be great."

I wait in the hall, taking off my coat, and adding to the pile of shoes by the door. Justin, Katie, and Matt go through to the living room, and I hear Matt asking when the tree's going up, and if there's anything they want for Christmas this year. Simon comes out of the kitchen carrying a bottle of wine and a fistful of glasses, their stems precariously slotted between the fingers of one hand.

"Are you coming through?" He looks at me anxiously, not sure how to help me. I smile reassuringly and promise that I will.

The door is still ajar, and now I open it a fraction more, and stand with the cold air on my face. I make myself look next door, at Melissa's front garden with its fluttering police tape.

Not to remind myself what's happened, but to remind myself that it's over.

And then I shut the door and go to join my family.

Melissa never could see the potential for expansion. Couldn't, or wouldn't. It wasn't clear. It was the only thing we ever argued about. She was so clever in many respects; so willing to work with me, so ready to believe in me when no one else would. Yet so shortsighted, in other ways.

Things were fine as they were, *she said.* We were making money. Why rock the boat? *But I knew we could do so much more, and it frustrated me that she wouldn't accept that. Some entrepreneur she turned out to be.*

She liked to think of herself as my mentor, but the truth is she needed me more than I needed her. She would never have hidden her tracks as successfully without me.

Melissa was nothing without me.

The game of cat and mouse—hunting Katie across London; that was my idea.

The two of them wouldn't let it lie, and the police were getting closer all the time. A final fling, *I told Melissa.* Do this, and you can disappear to Rio with 80 percent of everything we've made, and no one will ever find you. *It had been a good partnership, but it was time for us both to move on.*

Oh yes, 80 percent.

Ever the hard-nosed businesswoman. Even though it was me who placed the adverts, me who hacked the CCTV system, me who approached the clients—with a little help from Neil's address book. And what did I get for all that? Twenty fucking percent.

Do this, I told Melissa. Play this game, and walk away. Do it for me. Do it because I've helped you, and now it's your turn to help me.

And she did.

I saw Katie's profile go out, and I knew it had started. I felt my blood pulse, and I wondered if Melissa was excited. We'd never done anything like this before, but it felt right. It felt good.

As for Katie . . . I considered this payback. Payback not only for her constant need for attention but for being the favorite. For never being in trouble; never bringing the police to the door or getting thrown out of school.

It was payback for her, too. Zoe.

From your loving son.

Payback for leaving Dad even though he'd sacrificed everything for her. Payback for taking me away from my friends. Payback for fucking a man she'd only just met, then bringing him into our house without caring what I thought.

They think they've won the game, now that Melissa's dead. They think it's all over.

They're wrong.

This is just the beginning.

I don't need Melissa, I don't need adverts in the Gazette, I don't need the website.

I have the concept, I have the technology, and I have a mailing list of customers all interested in the sort of niche service I can provide for them.

And of course, I have you.

Hundreds of thousands of you, doing the same thing every day. I see you, but you don't see me.

Until I want you to.

I
SEE
YOU

CLARE
MACKINTOSH

DISCUSSION QUESTIONS

1. Do you commute to work on a daily basis, and follow the same routine when you do so? How much variation is there in your commute? If you take the train, do you always sit in the same car? How much do you notice about the people around you? Do you ever notice the same people in the same places?

2. When Zoe first realized she was being followed, did you think she was being stalked by someone she knew or someone she didn't know?

3. Once you realized it was someone she knew, did you develop a favorite suspect as you read the book? Or did you suspect different people? Who, and why?

4. Do you think you could ever really know, or trust, another human being? How about your friends? Your own family members?

5. Discuss Kelly's approach to victim support. Do you think she was justified in her way of dealing with Lexi's sexual assault? How do you think her being a twin affected her reaction to her sister's trauma?

6. *I See You* explores themes of parenting. How do you reconcile protecting your children with giving them their independence?

7. The mastermind behind the website in *I See You* used people's predilection for routine against them. Did *I See You* change the way you view the world around you?

8. How do you think the person behind the website rationalized their actions?

9. The ending of *I See You* reveals the true culprit. Did you suspect this person at all? How do you feel about this ending?

TURN THE PAGE FOR A SNEAK PEEK
AT CLARE MACKINTOSH'S
UPCOMING HEART-STOPPING NOVEL
OF PSYCHOLOGICAL SUSPENSE . . .

LET ME LIE

COMING SOON IN HARDCOVER FROM BERKLEY!

CHAPTER ONE

CAROLINE

*D*eath doesn't suit me. I wear it like a borrowed coat; it slips off my shoulders and trails in the dirt. I want to shrug it off, throw it back in the cupboard and take back my well-tailored life. I'm hopeful for my next life—hopeful I can become someone beautiful and vibrant. For now, I am trapped.

Between lives.

In limbo.

They say sudden death is easier. Less painful. They're wrong. Any pain saved from the lingering goodbyes of a drawn-out illness is offset by the horror of a life stolen without notice. A life taken violently. On the day of my death, I walked the tightrope between two worlds, the safety net in tatters beneath me. This way safety; that way danger. Roll up, roll up.

I stepped.

I died.

Tom and I joked about death when we were young enough—still vital enough—for it to be something that happened to other people.

"Who do you think'll go first?" he asked one night when the wine had run dry and we were lying by the electric fire in our rented Balham flat. An idle hand, stroking my thigh, softened his words. I was quick to answer.

"You, of course."

He aimed a cushion at my head.

"Women live longer." I grinned. "It's a well-known fact. Genetic. Survival of the fittest. Men can't cope on their own."

He grew serious, cupped my face in his hand, and made me look at him. His eyes were dark pools in the half-light; the bars of the fire were reflected in his pupils. "It's true." His fingers held me still when I moved to kiss him, putting pressure on my chin as his thumb pushed against bone. "If anything happened to you, I don't know what I'd do."

I felt the briefest chill, despite the fierce heat from the fire. Footsteps on my grave.

"Give over."

"I'd die too," he insisted.

I put a stop to it then and pushed aside his hand to free my chin, keeping my fingers tangled with his so the rejection didn't sting. I kissed him, softly at first, then harder, until he rolled backward and I was lying on top of him, my hair curtaining our faces.

Tom would die for me.

I was flattered by the depth of his feeling, the intensity I'd seen in his eyes. He would die for me. And in that moment, I thought I might die for him too.

I just never thought either of us would have to.

CHAPTER
TWO

ANNA

walk through clouded breath, on ground so frosted it glitters under the yellow of the street lamps. Today is the winter solstice, the shortest day of the year. It's a day of rebirth. Spring. Hope. My hands clench around the handle of the pram, and I stop walking, steadying myself both physically and mentally.

I tuck the fleece blanket more tightly around Ella's chin. Her skin is soft and warm beneath my touch, and I smile in spite of myself. She returns it with a wide, gummy grin that squashes her cheeks until her eyes crease closed. Ella is a miniature version of her father with her dark hair and eyes, and the tiny cleft in her chin—but not her smile. Her smile is mine. When Mark smiles, it's as though he holds back a piece of himself; as though he won't let himself be happy when others around him don't feel the same. His smile is cautious. Reserved.

My daughter smiles the way I've seen my own smile in countless photographs from my childhood: from the tip of her toes to the ends of her fingers. It fills me with joy every time. If I could wish one thing for her, it would be for that smile never to diminish.

Pram walks. Better pacifiers than any dummy. Better, even, than my arms. However fractious Ella—or I—might be feeling, however much she arches her back or kicks out her legs in protest, a turn around the block will soothe us both. Five minutes ago, Ella was screaming blue murder; now, wide yawns punctuate her smiles. Long, dark lashes brush apple cheeks. My chest swells with love.

We turn into Chestnut Avenue, where glossy railings flank double-fronted town houses and bay tree sentries are wrapped in twinkling white lights. One or two of the huge houses on the avenue have been turned into flats, but most are still intact, their wide front doors uncluttered by doorbells and post boxes. Christmas trees positioned in bay windows mean no curtains to block my view, and I catch glimpses of activity in the high-ceilinged rooms. In the first, a teenage boy flops on a sofa; in the second, small children race around the room, heady with festive excitement. At number six, an elderly couple reads from their respective papers.

Ella yawns again. Her lids drop, lift, then drop again. She lets out a breathy sigh of contentment, cherry lips pursing in her sleep as though she's dreaming of milk. I resist the temptation to lean into her pram for a kiss. She needs to sleep. I need her to sleep. If Ella is awake, she will be a distraction, lightening the mood until it feels incongruous to ask.

The door to number eight is open. A woman—late forties, I guess—stands in a French Gray hall, with one hand resting lightly on the door. I nod hello, and although she lifts a hand in greeting, her smile is directed toward a squabbling trio wrestling a Christmas tree from a car.

"Careful, you're going to drop it!"

"Left a bit, watch the door . . . Oops!"

A peal of laughter from the teenage girl; a wry grin from her clumsy brother.

"You'll have to lift it over the railings." Dad, directing proceedings, getting in the way. Proud of his children.

For a second, it hurts so much I can't breathe. I squeeze my eyes shut and push the pram faster along the avenue and out the other side, fresh determination in my stride.

Johnson's car showroom is on the corner of Victoria Road and Main Street, a beacon of light at the point where shops and hairdressers give way to flats and houses. The fluttering bunting I remember from my childhood has long gone, and heaven knows what Granddad would have made of the iPads tucked under the sales reps' arms, or the huge flat screen displaying this week's special deal.

I cross the forecourt, navigating Ella's pram between a sleek Mercedes and a secondhand Volvo. The glass doors slide soundlessly open as we draw near, warm air luring us in. Christmas music plays through expensive speakers. Behind the desk, where Mum used to sit, a striking girl with caramel skin and matching highlights taps acrylic nails on her keyboard. She smiles at me, and I catch the flash of diamanté fixed to one of her teeth. Her style couldn't be more different than Mum's. Perhaps that's why Uncle Billy hired her; it can't be easy coming to work day after day, the same, but different. Like my house. Like my life.

"Annie!"

Always Annie. Never Anna.

"Uncle Billy." I wrap my arms around him and inhale the familiar mix of aftershave and tobacco, along with something indefinable that makes me bury my face in his jumper. He smells like Granddad did. Like Dad. Like all the Johnson men. Only Billy left now.

I was christened Mariana.

"From the Tennyson poem," Mum would say, when people commented on how unusual it was. Sometimes she'd quote a few lines, and they'd nod politely, no doubt wondering why she'd chosen such a bleak poem as her only child's namesake. The christening prompted much mirth from Dad's side of the family, where books were balanced, not read, and the only poetry recited were dirty limericks on the way back from the King's Arms. It was inevitable my name would be shortened, and my memory doesn't extend to a time when I wasn't just Anna. My mother mitigated the compromise by omitting the extra "n" whenever she was in charge of birthday cards, but then even she gave up.

Billy waits until I'm done. Then he puts his arm around my shoulders and steers the pram and me toward the office, stopping to show off his great-niece to a spotty sales executive who makes a decent fist at looking interested. Billy's wearing a navy pinstripe suit, red socks, and braces that lend him a Wall Street air I know is entirely deliberate. Billy does nothing by accident. On anyone else I'd find the bling crass, but Billy wears it well, with a touch of irony that makes him endearing rather than flashy. He's only two years younger than Dad, but his hairline shows no sign of receding, and what gray there might be around his temples is carefully touched up. Billy takes the same care in his appearance as he does in the showroom.

"Long time," he says when we're settled in the leather seats that have been here forever. He's gentle, not chiding, but guilt creeps over me. I look at my feet, remembering how they used to dangle off the edge.

"Sorry."

He nods to Ella. "I expect this one keeps you busy."

I'm grateful for the life belt, but you can't lie to family. "It's hard," I tell him, nodding at the salesmen circling the punters like sharks, "coming here." I hear Dad's voice in my head. *Think like a waiter in a posh restaurant. Unobtrusive, but always there.*

I was fifteen, toying with the idea of joining the family business. That was before it became clear I'd have struggled to sell water in the Sahara.

"You could do admin, like Mum," Dad had suggested, and then Billy gently pointed out I took twenty minutes to type an invoice and twice filed crucial correspondence under the sender's first name instead of their last. I didn't mind. I hadn't inherited my dad's passion for cars, or my mum's ability to charm customers.

"I know," Billy says now, seeing the tremor that flits across my face. "I miss them too."

I have always been quick to cry, and since my parents died, tears have fallen at the slightest invitation. The crack in Billy's voice is enough of a catalyst, and he reaches for my hand, knowing better than to try and make them stop. The glass between Billy's office and the showroom is tinted one-way, and on the other side of it, I see one of the salesmen shaking hands with a customer. He glances toward the office, hoping the big boss is watching. Even in the midst of my distress, Billy has one eye on the business; he nods approvingly, a mental note filed away for the next appraisal. Married to the business, Mum used to say, though she was just as bad.

It was Dad who had the glass installed a few weeks after Granddad retired and Billy and Dad had moved into the office, a desk on either side.

"Keeps them on their toes."

Mum had grinned. "Keeps them from catching you having forty winks, more like."

I take a shuddering breath and squeeze Billy's hand before letting go.

"Thanks, Uncle Billy."

"Cup of tea?"

The cure for all ills. I shake my head. "I should get this one back. Mark'll be wondering where I am." I remember why I came, but I lose my nerve when I open my mouth and close it again without words.

"What is it, Annie?"

"I'd like their things." It rushes out before I've had a chance to sense-check it, and Billy raises both brows. The doubt in his face makes me feel it myself. "You said . . . when I was ready."

"Of course, of course." He pauses. "Perhaps after Christmas?"

I shake my head. "I've been putting it off for too long. I sorted their clothes when Mark moved in, and I should have done their desks at the same time. It's just . . ." I trail off. Mum and Dad lived and breathed Johnson's Cars. At times, the showroom was more a home to them—and to me—than the gated house we slept and ate in. Sorting through their wardrobe felt easy; rifling through their desks seemed intrusive. Instead, I tipped the contents of each drawer and cupboard into stout filing boxes, sealed each one tightly, and left them in the walk-in cupboard in the office. "Until you're ready," Billy had told me.

"I'm ready," I say now.

And because it's late and I need to get home, and because it's a conversation we've had many, many times, I don't tell him the other reason I want the boxes.

I don't tell him I'm looking for answers.

Two and a half years ago, my father took a car—the newest and most expensive—from the forecourt. He drove it to Beachy Head, where he parked, left the door unlocked, and walked toward the cliff top. Along the way, he collected rocks to weigh himself down. Then, when the tide was at its highest, he threw himself off the cliff. Six months later, consumed with grief, my mother followed him, with such devastating accuracy the local paper reported it a "copycat suicide."

I know all these facts because on two separate occasions, I heard the coroner take us through them, step by step. I sat with Uncle Billy as we listened to the gentle but painfully thorough account of two failed coastal rescue missions. I stared at my lap while experts proffered views on tides, survival rates, and death statistics. And I closed my eyes while the coroner recorded the verdicts of suicide. My parents died six months apart, but their inquests were the same week. Finally, they were declared legally dead, and life could begin to move, haltingly, once more.

The inquest told me all this and more. But it didn't tell me the only thing that mattered.

Why they did it.

Photo by Charlie Hopkinson

Clare Mackintosh, the *New York Times* bestselling author of *I Let You Go*, spent twelve years on the police force in England and has written for the *Guardian, Good Housekeeping*, and other publications. A columnist for *Cotswold Life* and *Writing Magazine*, she is the founder of Chipping Norton Literary Festival and lives in North Wales with her family. Visit her online at claremackintosh .com, facebook.com/ClareMackWrites, Twitter @claremackint0sh, and #ISeeYou.

NEW YORK TIMES BESTSELLING AUTHOR

CLARE MACKINTOSH

"Mackintosh scripts a hair-raising ride."
—*Publishers Weekly* (starred review)

For a complete list of titles,
please visit prh.com/claremackintosh